THE ROUTLEDGE INTRODUCTION TO CANADIAN CRIME FICTION

Who are the most important Canadian crime and detective writers? How do they help represent Canada as a nation? How do they distinguish Canada's approach to questions of crime, detection, and social justice from those of other countries? *The Routledge Introduction to Canadian Crime Fiction* provides a much-needed investigation into how crime and detection have been, are, and will be represented within Canada's national literature, with an attention to contemporary popular and literary texts. The book draws together a representative set of established Canadian authors who would appear in most courses on Canadian crime and detective fiction, while also introducing a few authors less established in the field. Ultimately, the book argues that crime fiction is a space of enormously productive hybridity that offers fresh new approaches to considering questions of national identity, gender, race, sexuality, and even genre.

Pamela Bedore is Associate Professor of English at the University of Connecticut, where she teaches courses in American Literature and Popular Culture. She holds BA and BEd degrees from Queen's University, an MA in English from Simon Fraser University, and a PhD in American Literature from the University of Rochester. She has published widely on detective fiction and speculative fiction, including the monograph *Dime Novels and the Roots of American Detective Fiction* (2013) and the lecture series *Great Utopian and Dystopian Works of Literature* (The Great Courses, 2017). Pam was the book review editor for *Clues: A Journal of Detection* for ten years and was recently a visiting scholar at an NEH Summer Institute on Climate Futurism.

THE ROUTLEDGE INTRODUCTION TO CANADIAN CRIME FICTION

Pamela Bedore

Routledge
Taylor & Francis Group

NEW YORK AND LONDON

Designed cover image: Getty

First published 2024
by Routledge
605 Third Avenue, New York, NY 10158

and by Routledge
4 Park Square, Milton Park, Abingdon, Oxon, OX14 4RN

Routledge is an imprint of the Taylor & Francis Group, an informa business

© 2024 Pamela Bedore

The right of Pamela Bedore to be identified as author of this work has been asserted in accordance with sections 77 and 78 of the Copyright, Designs and Patents Act 1988.

All rights reserved. No part of this book may be reprinted or reproduced or utilised in any form or by any electronic, mechanical, or other means, now known or hereafter invented, including photocopying and recording, or in any information storage or retrieval system, without permission in writing from the publishers.

Trademark notice: Product or corporate names may be trademarks or registered trademarks, and are used only for identification and explanation without intent to infringe.

ISBN: 978-0-367-64573-1 (hbk)
ISBN: 978-0-367-64571-7 (pbk)
ISBN: 978-1-003-12524-2 (ebk)

DOI: 10.4324/9781003125242

Typeset in Sabon
by Newgen Publishing UK

*To Izzy and Zoe Phelps,
who give me hope for the future.*

CONTENTS

Preface ix
Acknowledgments xii

1 Negotiations of National Identity in Canadian Crime Fiction 1

PART I
Historical Confrontations 25

2 John McFetridge and the Legacy of French/English Tensions 27

3 Giles Blunt and the Canadian North 42

4 Thomas King and the Liminal Indigenous Detective 58

5 Ausma Zehanat Khan and Multiculturalism in Canada 75

6 Canada and the American Dream: Linwood Barclay's *Promise Falls* Series 91

PART II
Canadian Genre Play 109

7 The Police Procedural: Registering Change with
  Peter Robinson's DCI Banks 111

8 The Amateur Detective: Gail Bowen's Joanne
  Kilbourn as Canadian Revisionist 129

9 The Gay Private Eye: Anthony Bidulka's Hardboiled
  Romantic, Russell Quant 143

10 The Legal Thriller: Trauma and Resilience in Pamela
   Callow's Kate Lange Series 158

11 The Postmodern Detective: Literary Detection in
   Timothy Findley and Carol Shields 175

PART III
Futuristic Explorations 193

12 Louise Penny's Cozy Exploration of Trauma and
   Temporality in the Anthropocene 195

13 Storytelling, Guilt, and Games in Margaret Atwood's
   Post-apocalyptic Crime Fiction 214

14 Interpretive Mysteries and Impossible Crimes in
   Emily St. John Mandel's Speculative Fiction 227

Glossary of People and Terms 245
Further Reading on Crime Fiction 255
Works Cited 260
Index 270

PREFACE

As a youngster growing up in Ontario, I learned that Canada was a "cultural mosaic" or "tossed salad" in which immigrants were encouraged to keep their cultural and linguistic practices alive in their new country, creating a proudly heterogeneous nation. This metaphor was explained and expounded upon for Canadian children in the 1980s through a contrast to the United States, described as a "melting pot" in which all newcomers were presumably incorporated into the soup of a hegemonic state that valued homogeneity. Decades later, having spent almost an equal part of my life in each country, I consider this simplification about national identities to be somewhere between parodic and profound. From my perspective as a Canadian citizen who earned a PhD in American Literature from an American institution and is now in my third decade of residency in the United States, I can confidently assert that the United States is not a melting pot. I live in a racially, economically, and religiously diverse small city in which my children attend a bilingual school and have a far more heterogeneous palette of friends than I ever did in small-town Ontario. At the same time, the metaphor, simplistic as it may be, nonetheless has value in helping us understand the ways Canada defines itself through an imagined cultural, intellectual, and political heterogeneity that is often figured as in contrast to the cultural hegemony of America.

Canada, as any Canadian knows, whether or not they are well-versed in the nation's literary and cultural theory, is a country full of contradictions. A powerful economic force on the world stage, with an advanced economy and a wealth of natural resources, Canada nonetheless is dwarfed by its neighbor to the south, and much of its national literature is concerned with clearly and incisively delineating the differences between Canadian and American culture, literature, and aesthetic sensibility. Canada has often been represented—and sometimes caricatured—as the cold, vast, sparsely populated land above the 49th parallel inhabited by hardy, resilient, unfailingly polite socialists who mostly keep to themselves. In reality, Canadian politics are nuanced and often heated, as are Canadians themselves, who are far from isolationist in their political, economic, and cultural lives and national identity. Canada has a good international reputation as a country committed to multiculturalism and championing human rights, and yet, as the Truth and Reconciliation Commission of 2015 has laid bare, Canada has a shameful history of forced assimilation of Indigenous peoples through the Indian Residential School System that isolated children from their families in order to integrate them into dominant Canadian culture. Canada is thus a capacious physical and imaginative space capable of much complexity.

One of Canada's finest poets, Leonard Cohen, provides us with an evocative image in his acclaimed 1992 song, "Anthem," whose chorus states, "There is a crack in everything. It's how the light gets in." This has always been one of my favorite lines from one of my favorite writers. I have been twice delighted to see the line in much-loved detective texts. It is printed on a pen and discussed at length in a 2010 episode of *Fringe*, a science fiction/crime television show that melds the police procedural with the speculative and that has at least two Canadian connections, as it is filmed largely in Vancouver and features several Canadian actors, including Joshua Jackson. The Cohen line also features centrally in several of Louise Penny's Three Pines novels, including extensive discussion of the metaphor in *A Fatal Grace* as well as placement in the epigraph and title position of *How The Light Gets In*.

Cohen's insights in "Anthem" are applicable to many issues in contemporary life, including democracy, morality, globalization, and revolution. I would like to suggest that these recent deployments of Cohen's lyric by detective writers also invite us to consider the crack in everything as a powerful metaphor for detective fiction, which finds its origins in a rational materialist understanding of the world where shining a light in the right direction, at the right weak spot, is expected to reveal a "real" and graspable truth about the subversive act of committing a crime. "Anthem" suggests that the "crack in everything"—which can be read, in the context of detective fiction, as the corruption and criminality underlying the social contract—is necessary for allowing in the light, producing a visual metaphor quite obviously associated with understanding. And yet, "Anthem" says, "You can add up the parts/You won't have the sum," an idea we see increasingly in twenty-first-century detective fiction, with its simultaneous embrace and suspicion of the genre's classic metanarrative of neat epistemological and ethical orderings. The adoption of Cohen's potent metaphor speaks to the power of crime fiction to reveal—to identify, explore, and interrogate—the many fissures in cultural identity. Throughout the chapters of this book, we will return repeatedly to the ways in which various writers reveal the gaps between Canada's self-definitions and its realities, repeatedly exploring not only the contradictions of Canada's national ethos in an increasingly globalized world, but also the desire of Canada and Canadians to revisit and even revise our understanding of the past as we imagine and seek a better future.

ACKNOWLEDGMENTS

I am grateful to many friends and colleagues for their help in the completion of this book. My first acknowledgment certainly goes to Robert Lecker for inviting me to write this volume, which has allowed me to combine two of my great loves: Canada and crime fiction.

This book has been great fun to write and would not have been possible without years of vigorous discussion and debate with the many wonderful reading and research communities to which I belong. These include the Popular Culture Association, whose annual conference is always scintillating; the *Clues* editorial board, which contains many of the scholars of detective fiction I admire most; the Waterford Public Library Speculative Fiction bookclub, organized by Jill Adams and regularly attended by a diverse and energetic group of insightful readers; and my newest research and writing community, the organizers and participants of the 2023 NEH Summer Institute on Climate Futurism.

I've also found great inspiration and expertise at the University of Connecticut, where I've been privileged to work with students and scholars from many departments and to engage in ongoing conversations about what we're reading and how we're writing. I'm grateful for lots of energizing morning walks, work lunches, and writing dates with my friends and colleagues Dan Burkey, Tony Dasta, Michael Finiguerra, Serkan Gorkemli, Holly Kasem Beg, Jamie Kleinman, Karen McDermott, Jay Murzyn, Alison Paul, Ken Perez, John Redden, Erin Scanlon, Lauren Schlesselman, Jennifer Terni, Kathleen Tonry, Lyn Tribble, and Sherry Zane. Equally important have been the undergraduate, graduate, and honors students who have shared their perspectives on so many of the novels discussed in this book.

For getting me and my family through the early months of the pandemic, I thank Steve Fodor and Chip Hessenflow, the inimitable co-hosts of my favorite podcast, *Too Much Scrolling*, who are kind enough to allow me to talk with them about books once a month even now.

For organizing the always delightful—not to mention delicious—Firehouse writing retreats, I thank Helen Rozwadowski and Daniel Hornstein, as well as fellow attendees and friends Anita Duneer, Susan Lyons, and Rebecca Troeger.

For reading every word of this manuscript, from draft proposal to final version, I thank Anita Duneer, who is the best writing buddy any girl could dream of.

For substantial feedback on tricky portions of the manuscript, I thank fellow Canadians and lifelong friends, Graeme Campbell and Phyllis Mancini.

For quick and accurate reference work at multiple times, I thank Richard Bleiler.

For excellent editorial assistance and generosity, I thank Charlotte Kading as well as Bryony Reece and E. Abigail from Routledge.

And, of course, I could not have completed this project without my Canadian and American families: Claire Ross, Jim Bedore, Jenny, Martin, and Nico Hyland, Jean and Gary Phelps, and Caitlin Phelps and Bryan Flowers.

For being outright awesome, I thank my inspiring, creative, and hilarious children, Izzy and Zoe.

For being awesomely fluffy, our dear feline friends, Spring and Chai.

And for always asking the right questions, providing the right feedback, and giving the right kind and amount of support, my husband Andrew Phelps.

1
NEGOTIATIONS OF NATIONAL IDENTITY IN CANADIAN CRIME FICTION

In 2006, *Bon Cop, Bad Cop*, a fully bilingual buddy cop film, became a box office phenom in Canada, purportedly beating out teen sex comedy *Porky's* (1981) as Canada's top-grossing domestic box office hit (although this claim does not take inflation into account). What explains the enormous appeal of *Bon Cop, Bad Cop* to Canadians? Bilingual movies—this one available with several subtitle variations for French, English, and bilingual viewers—are not typically mainstream blockbusters, even in Canada or by Canadian standards. *Bon Cop, Bad Cop* is a good film—it has a good script, good actors, a good soundtrack, and good production values—in a popular genre, but I would argue that its success arises not despite but because of its potential weakness: its bilingualism. Opening with the comedic and outlandish premise of a murder victim found draped over the Welcome sign between Quebec and Ontario—a jurisdictional nightmare—the film leans into many of the stereotypes held by Quebecois and Ontarians in order to disrupt them, all while simultaneously mocking and embracing the one thing French and English Canadians can all agree upon: hockey belongs to Canada, and not to the United States.

Bon Cop, Bad Cop is hardly a monument of Canadian cultural analysis, and of course, Canadian national identity is made up of more than a reverence for hockey and all it represents (a love of cold weather, early mornings at the ice rink, bruising and bruised masculinity, etc.). And yet, the film has much to tell us about twenty-first-century Canadian mores and anxieties. The setting of the opening crime on the border between Ontario and Quebec (and the even more extensive scene in the sequel at the border between Canada and the United States) speaks to the

DOI: 10.4324/9781003125242-1

centrality of questions of borders—and, relatedly, liminality—to both crime fiction and Canadian literature. The use of the buddy cop trope, with a buttoned-up Ontario cop and a passionate non-rule-following Quebecois cop, highlights the complexity of political and cultural tensions between what Hugh MacLennan famously coined as Canada's "two solitudes" in his 1945 novel *Two Solitudes*, about the historical and ongoing tensions between English and French Canada. The buddy cop genre convention both exaggerates the tensions between mismatched detectives and provides a means for resolution. The prevalence of humor, including dark humor, encapsulates the importance of laughter to Canada's self-perception. And finally, I think it is important that the film is extremely popular within Canada and yet not especially exportable because so much of it is in French; this speaks to Canada's constant attempt to distinguish itself from the other—and specifically the United States—in its own self-definition.

Canada has long defined itself in relational terms. Perhaps most famously, we can look to Prime Minister Pierre Trudeau's 1969 trip to Washington to meet with President Richard Nixon, where Trudeau coined a phrase that has come to characterize relations between Canada and the United States: "Living next to you is in some ways like sleeping with an elephant. No matter how friendly and even-tempered is the beast, if I can call it that, one is affected by every twitch and grunt." "Sleeping with an elephant" has led to other animal metaphors to characterize the relationship between the two countries, including the first major collection of essays on the influence of American popular culture on Canada, titled *The Beaver Bites Back?* (1993), playing on Canada's national animal, the beaver. The relationship between the elephant and the beaver, as the title suggests, is a nuanced one in which Canada characterizes its popular culture industry as filled with hard-working people who need government protection in order to get a fair market share when competing with the behemoth to the south. Just a few years after Trudeau's use of the elephant metaphor, Canadian literary luminary Margaret Atwood, then just starting out, figured the United States in an even more frightening way. In *Surfacing* (1973), the narrator automatically categorizes some hunters she sees at a lake as Americans, only to learn that they are actually Canadians:

> It doesn't matter what country they're from, my head said, they're still Americans, they're what's in store for us, what we are turning into. They spread themselves like a virus, they get into the brain and take over the cells and the cells change from inside and the ones that have the disease can't tell the difference.
>
> *(129, quoted in Langer 7)*

This passage again speaks to the nuances of the relationship between the two countries. The virus metaphor suggests the silent but powerful inevitability of American hegemony, while the narrator's mislabeling of the hunters as Americans highlights the prejudice that many Canadians hold toward their closest neighbor and largest trading partner (of economic as well as cultural products).

Against this backdrop, it is no surprise that Canadian crime and detective fiction both draws upon and speaks back to the American genre. At the same time, the standard history of crime and detective fiction does not include Canada. Instead, it focuses on American and British movements, with the standard story of the genre beginning with Edgar Allan Poe's C. Auguste Dupin stories (America, 1840s) and coming to prominence with Arthur Conan Doyle's world-famous Sherlock Holmes tales (England, 1887–1927), with two more stops in America for the hardboiled fiction of the 1930s and 1940s (Dashiell Hammett, Raymond Chandler, Ross MacDonald, etc.) and the police procedurals of the 1950s and 1960s (Ed McBain's 87th Precinct series in print and National Broadcasting Company (NBC)'s *Dragnet* on television), and then an acknowledgment by the 1980s that crime fiction thrives on its variety, with classical, hardboiled, and police procedural subgenres being constantly refashioned through what Kathleen Gregory Klein has called "detectives of diversity" (1999) as well as postmodern renderings that have challenged the epistemological and ethical foundations of the genre. After such an American-English focus on crime and detective scholarship, the early twenty-first century has seen a panoply of books devoted to exploring national crime literatures of other countries. The most studied international area has been the Scandinavian countries, which have revitalized crime fiction with a new subgenre known as Nordic Noir, delved into by scholars such as Barry Forshaw, Wendy Lesser, and Jakob Stougaard-Nielsen. Other countries, too, have received attention for their national crime fiction, including Australia (Stephen Knight's *Australian Crime Fiction: A 200-Year History*, 2018), Germany (Katharina Hall's *Crime Fiction in German: Der Krimi*, 2016), Ireland (Brian Cliff's *Irish Crime Fiction*, 2018), Italy (Barbara Pezzotti's *Politics and Society in Italian Crime Fiction: An Historical Overview*, 2014), Japan (Saturo Saito's *Detective Fiction and the Rise of the Japanese Novel, 1880–1930*, 2012), and Turkey (David Mason's *Investigating Turkey: Detective Fiction and Turkish Nationalism, 1928–1945*, 2017). Canada has so far been the subject of one excellent essay collection, Jeannette Sloniowski and Marilyn Rose's *Detecting Canada: Essays on Canadian Crime Fiction, Television, and Film* (2014). With several major writers contributing to the genre in the young twenty-first century, Canadian crime fiction will certainly continue to be an area of interest to literary and cultural critics.

4 Negotiations of National Identity in Canadian Crime Fiction

Crime fiction provides a powerful perspective on key questions of social, cultural, and political identity for any national literature. As Catherine Ross Nickerson argues, crime narratives "represent the most anxiety-producing issues and narratives in culture" (744–745). Crime, at its most fundamental, represents an act of subversion, a marker of some kind of sociocultural breakdown. What is considered a crime and what constitutes criminality? Who commits crimes and why? What kinds of crimes are most offensive? What kinds of punishments are meted out for various types of crimes? And meted out by whom? How a society deals with crime—with preventing, investigating, punishing, and representing crime—serves as a kind of touchstone to understanding that society's central values, beliefs, tensions, and aesthetic investments. Canada is a large, diverse, and complex country built on a series of potentially contradictory assumptions. As Rachel Haliburton argues in her insightful exploration of the role of crime and detective fiction in investigating Canadian identity and morality, Canadians hold a self-image as "good people living in a relatively egalitarian society" ("Expressive" 71)—an image that is both distorted and worth fighting for. Using the work of Giles Blunt, Gail Bowen, and Wayne Arthurson, Haliburton looks specifically at the treatment of First Nations peoples in Canadian crime fiction, reminding readers that Indigenous people of Canada today continue to suffer from historico-cultural wrongs. Blunt, Bowen, Arthurson, and others address this dark reality—of past and present—in detective fiction that "challenges readers to alter their thinking and perhaps even their behavior" (71). For Haliburton, as for me, crime and detective fiction in the hands of Canadian writers is ultimately an optimistic genre that critiques the dark side of current society in a way that highlights Canada's potential to become a safer, more ethical, and more equitable place.

Canadian Facts and Stats: A Primer

Canada is a relatively young nation. The land that now makes up Canada was populated for thousands of years by Indigenous peoples before European explorers first arrived in the late fifteenth century. Politically, though, Canada was rather late to develop as an independent nation. The land was explored and then settled by French and British expeditions that were often in conflict with each other as well as with the Indigenous people and eventually the Americans. While the United States traces its origins as a nation to the Declaration of Independence in 1776, Canadian Confederation did not occur until 1867. Importantly, Confederation did not denote independence; rather it marked the creation of Canada as a Dominion with four provinces: the three English-speaking provinces of Ontario, Nova Scotia, and New Brunswick, along with the French-speaking province of Quebec. Other provinces and territories joined until 1949, at which time Canada had ten provinces and two territories. Confederation was achieved through bureaucracy rather than revolution, a historical fact that may explain the characterization of Canada by Northrop Frye as a "Peaceable Kingdom"—an idea since debated by cultural and intellectual historians and critics (see, for example, Lecker).

After Confederation, Canada was a self-governing nation of the British Empire, eventually joined in this status by Australia, New Zealand, Newfoundland, South Africa, and the Irish Free States. This position between autonomy and allegiance is articulated in the Balfour Declaration of 1926, which describes these six nations as "autonomous communities … united by a common allegiance to the Crown and freely associated as members of the British Commonwealth of Nations." In 1931, the Statute of Westminster increased the sovereignty of the Commonwealth nations. However, it was not until 1982—a time I remember well as an elementary school student—that the queen and prime minister signed the Constitution Act that enacted the Canadian Charter of Rights and Freedoms. To this day, Canada remains a constitutional monarchy, meaning that the elected prime minister is the head of government and the English monarch (at this time King Charles III) is the head of state. Technically, "Royal Assent" must be given to all new bills in order to enact them, and that comes from the Governor General or Lieutenant Governor, who officially represent the Monarch. 1999 marks the most recent political change to Canada's map with the creation of Nunavut, a third territory independently governed by Indigenous peoples.

Canada is a large, diverse nation with a high standard of living and a strong sense of itself as a multicultural society. It has the second largest landmass in the world, after Russia. It has an abundance of national resources and a relatively small population (approximately 38 million in 2022, making it the 39th most populous country in the world). Canada has an advanced economy and is a member of the G7 and of the North Atlantic Treaty Organization (NATO). It has the 18th largest nominal Gross Domestic Product (GDP) and the 11th largest per capita GDP (International Monetary Fund, 2022 estimate). It is generally considered a desirable place to live, with the US World and News Ranking of 2022 placing it as third (behind Sweden and Denmark) for Quality of Life, and third (behind Switzerland and Germany) for Best Countries to Live In. The 2021 Canada Census report released by Statistics Canada opens with the statement:

> Canada is known for its ethnocultural and religious diversity, a characteristic of the country valued by the vast majority of Canadians. According to the 2020 General Social Survey, 92.0% of the population

aged 15 and older agreed that ethnic or cultural diversity is a Canadian value.

("Canadian" 1)

The report goes on to note that Canadians claim over 450 ethnic or cultural origins (the largest groups reporting as Canadian, English, Irish, Scottish, and French, respectively). Approximately 70% of Canada's population identifies as White and 6% identifies as Indigenous. What Statistics Canada refers to as "the racialized groups" are led in number by South Asian (7.1%), Chinese (4.7%), and Black (4.3%). Racialized groups in Canada are experiencing growth, while religious ones are declining; in 2020, just over one-third of Canada's population reports having no religious affiliation.

Canada's large geographical size means it has several regions. Statistics Canada divides the country into six regions. Ontario, which holds about 44% of Canada's total population, includes Canada's largest city, Toronto, as well as its capital city, Ottawa; it also produces the most crime and detective fiction. Quebec, at approximately 25% of the total population, is characterized by its use of French as the official language, and also contributes substantially to crime fiction. Although Ontario and Quebec both stretch north—Ontario to Hudson Bay and Quebec to the Hudson Strait—the majority of their populations are located fairly close to the border with the United States. The Prairie provinces—Alberta, Saskatchewan, and Manitoba—contain about 18% of Canada's population and are made up of a mix of smaller urban centers as well as rural land rich in agricultural and mineral resources. The West Coast, made up of the province of British Columbia, contains about 14% of the population. Vancouver is a major metropolitan area with a great deal of cultural and ethnic diversity; it is also, along with Toronto and Montreal, a major hub of movie and television production. The Atlantic provinces—New Brunswick, Newfoundland, Nova Scotia, and Prince Edward Island—all have small populations, together making up only 6% of Canada's total population. With its legacy of fishing and shipbuilding, Atlantic Canada is characterized by its Celtic and Gaelic traditions, its friendly people, and its anxieties about the climate crisis. The final region, the North, is made up of three territories: the Northwest Territories, Nunavut, and the Yukon. The region is vast, but each territory has a population of just over 40,000 people, meaning that the entire North contains only about 0.33% of Canada's population. This sparsely inhabited area serves as a dark reminder of the destructive policies toward Indigenous peoples before Canada even became a modern nation-state.

Next to its neighbor to the south, Canada is often seen as socially liberal, tracking with the European Union on topics such as capital punishment, abortion, and gun control. On a world stage, though, Canada is quite moderate, more a center-left country than a purely progressive one. Canada has a parliamentary system that is more similar to the British system than the American. Citizens do not vote directly for the Prime Minister, or leader of Canada. Instead, they vote for a Member of Parliament from their local constituency, and the Prime Minister is the head of the party that controls the House of Commons. Canada has more than two political parties. Americans often think that the Liberals and Conservatives are roughly equivalent to the Democrats and the Republicans that make up the United States's bipartisan system. Similarities exist. But these are just the center-left (Liberal) and center-right (Conservative) parties. Other parties with federal representation in recent memory include: the Green Party, which focuses on environmental issues; the New Democratic Party, to the left of the Liberals; the Bloc Québécois, representing Quebec's unique interests as the only officially French province; and the Reform Party of Canada (1987–2000, and then briefly the Canadian Reform Conservative Alliance 2000–2003), to the right of the Progressive Conservatives. A majority government is in place if a single party controls the majority of the 338 seats in Parliament. A minority government, in which two or more parties must work together, occurs if no single party controls 170 seats. Few Canadians belong to a party, and parties realign vis-à-vis each other and ongoing issues quite often; a 2006 study found that only 1–2% of Canadians belong to a political party (Cross and Young). In its history since 1867, Canada has had 44 federal elections resulting in 23 different prime ministers; 15 of the 44 parliaments have been minority governments.

Canadian federal elections occur as needed and, by statute, provide only a short window (36–50 days) for campaigning. The twenty-first century has seen efforts to regularize the timing of elections. Some of the provinces have passed legislation to this effect, but the federal stance on this issue is representative of Canada's electoral nimbleness. In 2006, Parliament passed An Act to Amend the Canada Elections stating that general elections would occur on the third Monday of October every four years beginning in October 2009. At the same time, the Prime Minister remains free to request an election at any time, and Parliament can always be dissolved by a vote of nonconfidence. The most recent Canadian federal elections have not been especially regular, as evidenced by their dates: October 2008, May 2011, October 2015, October 2019, and September 2021.

Canadians often think of our crime as quite low, but that may be in part because we so often compare ourselves to the United States. Given that the Canadian media market is saturated by American news, often featuring crime news, most Canadians would not be surprised to learn that Canada's homicide rate is 3.2 times lower than the American rate, and that homicides are committed by different means in each country. In 2020, Canada had 759 homicides, and 278 (38%) of these were shootings (Statistics Canada); that year, the United States had 24,576 homicides, and 19,389 (79%) were shootings (Center for Disease Control). The UN finds that 54% of homicides worldwide are by firearm, so Canada has far fewer firearm deaths, while the United States has far more. At the same time, Canada's homicide rate is far from desirable, especially when compared to its other metrics. According to the World Population Review's 2018 murder rate by country, Canada is 69th for lowest per capita murder rate (at 1.76 per 100,000), between Sierra Leone (1.71) and Malawi (1.81). Canada's homicide rate is also undesirable from an equity perspective, given that almost one-quarter of all homicide victims are Indigenous people, who make up only 6% of the population.

Crime and Detective Fiction: A Primer

The idea of *genre* has a storied history within literary and cultural studies. In French, where the term originated, the term *genre* translates as both *genre* and *gender*, and is meant to delineate a category or kind. The slipperiness of this term was made clear to me when I was a graduate student explaining to my French-Canadian mother (in French) that I was writing my dissertation on gender and genre in popular literature (or, *le genre et le genre en litérature populaire*). In the hands of early twentieth-century thinkers like Soviet folklorist Vladimir Propp in his *Morphology of the Tale* (1928) and Canadian literary critic Northrop Frye in his *Anatomy of Criticism* (1957), genre is a way of classifying elements of text, with a focus on recurring formulas. This formulaic approach to genre initially appeared well-suited to the popular forms that emerged from the nineteenth-century boom in the publishing industry that resulted in dime novels in the United States, penny dreadfuls in the United Kingdom, and *feuilletons* in France, where we saw the development of what we now sometimes classify as genre fiction (as opposed to literary fiction), namely detective fiction, fantasy, romance, science fiction, and the western. Using a formula-based approach, it is possible to identify several key subgenres of crime and detective fiction.

The 1980s and 1990s saw a new approach to genre with scholars like Charles Bazerman, Richard Coe, Janet Giltrow, and Carolyn Miller approaching genre through the perspective of rhetoric rather than formula. In her landmark essay, "Genre as Social Action" (1984), Miller argues that genres arise as responses to recurring rhetorical exigencies:

> To base a classification of discourse upon recurrent situation or, more specifically, upon exigence understood as social motive, is to base it

upon the typical joint rhetorical actions available at a given point in history or culture.

(158)

Using this model of genre, we ask not what various genres or subgenres look like, but rather, what they accomplish rhetorically. What sociohistorical context led us to need a specific type of crime and detective fiction? What does that subgenre explore or even argue within that context? Why do some genres flourish at specific times and places and then fizzle out, while others are steadily produced and consumed regardless of changing sociohistorical realities? Questions like these can lead to contentious and exciting arguments such as the one Rachel Haliburton makes in *The Ethical Detective* (2018), that detective fiction "can offer a profound ethical education to its readers" (56) and even that excellent detective novels "provide a description of the moral life that is largely unrivalled in moral philosophy as it is currently practiced" (77). *Canadian Crime Fiction* draws upon both formulaic and rhetorical models of genre in exploring how Canadian crime and detective fiction participates in and contributes to the various subgenres, namely the whodunit, the hardboiled, the police procedural, the thriller, and the postmodern detective narrative. Although each of these subgenres arose at a different time and place, tendrils of all were present in the dime novels of the late nineteenth century (Bedore *Dime* 4), and all remain vibrant in today's tapestry of Canadian crime and detective fiction.

The whodunit, codified in Golden Age detective fiction and sometimes referred to as the drawing-room mystery, is told from the detective's perspective and generally follows the rules articulated by Ronald Knox in his "Detective Story Decalogue" (1924), also known as the Ten Commandments of Detective Fiction, and by S.S. Van Dine (Willard Huntington Wright) in his "Twenty Rules for Writing Detective Stories" (1928). The rules point to a central narrative structure articulated by Tzvetan Todorov: the story is made up of two stories, with the present-day narrative the detective's story as he uncovers the preceding story of the crime (46). This kind of mystery is constructed as a game between reader and writer that follows the rules of fair play, meaning that the reader has access to all the same information as the detective, and may thus attempt to compete with the writer in solving the mystery before the solution is revealed, likely in a drawn-out drawing room scene in which the detective gathers the interested parties—suspects all—and expounds upon his (or, less often, her) process of reasoning. Expected formulas include a (not very graphically described) body on page one, a closed setting with a limited number of suspects, one or more family secrets and/or characters whose identities are not as they seem, plenty of red herrings to distract the detective (and the reader), and, constitutively, a solution based on rational analysis at novel's end. Unsurprisingly, the rhetorical impact of the genre is more complex and thus more debated. George Grella's classic essay, "Murders and Manners: The Formal Detective Novel" (1970), remains an apt analysis of the genre with its argument that Golden Age detective fiction basically tells a conservative story, where the crime is always figured as a disruption to the society, and the status quo is always restored by the detective's work, indicating an eradication of the disruptive element (41).

Hardboiled fiction is associated with 1930s California and the Prohibition Era (1920–1933) that turned millions of Americans into criminals when alcohol was nationally banned and led to underground networks of alcohol production, distribution, and consumption. The formulas of the hardboiled include terse dialogue, little character interiority, a sordid setting (what Raymond Chandler famously termed "the mean streets"), graphic sex and violence, and a possibly corrupt police force. The hardboiled protagonist—usually a private investigator and as likely to be an antihero as a hero—is traditionally male, and the female characters are generally easily divisible into damsels in distress and *femmes fatales*. The prototypical hardboiled novel, in my opinion, is Dashiell Hammett's *The Maltese Falcon* (1930, further popularized in the film starring Humphrey Bogart in 1941), in which private dick Sam Spade constantly displays his tough-guy credentials while ostensibly hunting down the killers of his detective partner and becoming involved with their beautiful client. Other notable early hardboiled writers include Raymond Chandler with the Philip Marlowe series, and Canada's own Kenneth Millar, who wrote the Lew Archer novels as Ross Macdonald. Rhetorically, the hardboiled posits a very different social exigency than the whodunit. The hardboiled narrative does not assume a rational world in which all can be known as long as a brilliant detective asks the right questions of the right people and then logically arranges the evidence. Furthermore, there is no fair play between reader and writer in the hardboiled, a point famously—and perhaps apocryphally—made with Chandler's *The Big Sleep* (1939, film in 1946) when the novel was being adapted to film and the writers could not figure out who killed the chauffeur. According to a letter Chandler wrote Hamish Hamilton in 1949, "They sent me a wire (there's a joke about this too) asking me, and dammit I didn't know either" (MacShane 155–6). In the hardboiled, the reader is drawn into a fast-paced plot full of moral ambivalences in which both ethical and epistemological questions may be raised without being answered.

The police procedural genre is also associated with the American detective tradition, although it has been adopted and developed in many national detective fictions, perhaps most notably in England, the Scandinavian countries, and Canada. The police procedural has many recognizable features. Most importantly, the detective work is done by professionals working as a team that includes police officers at various ranks, forensic specialists, and often profilers and/or lawyers. The setting is generally urban, and most police procedurals focus on one or two central cases but also acknowledge that a homicide department is handling several open investigations simultaneously. As the subgenre name suggests, there is a focus on procedures: the response to the initial call, the identification of the victim, the notification of the family, the gathering of evidence at the crime scene, and the procedures for protecting the chain of evidence, the postmortem, the interviews with witnesses, loved ones, and suspects, and always, the paperwork. Initially popularized by Evan Hunter (writing as Ed McBain) in his decades-long 87th Precinct series (1956–2005), the police procedural includes bureaucracy as a constitutive feature. McBain even provides copies of standard documents like Q&A transcripts, evidence forms, and witness statements in each of his novels. Most detective fiction subgenres invite serialization, but the police procedural does so most forcefully. After all, police work is shown to be at once fascinating and repetitive, so the reader of this subgenre naturally wishes to repeat the experience of reading about it. The rhetorical impact of the police procedural is complicated. McBain's long series has been read as support for the state: as a way to celebrate the work of police detectives and to humanize them to citizens who might otherwise be skeptical of their authority (Dove, Panek). If we consider another prototypical police procedural series that started just a decade later—Maj Sjowall and Per Wahloo's Martin Beck decalogy, opening with *Roseanne* (1965) in Sweden—we find exactly the opposite rhetorical thrust, as this series provides a clear and compelling critique of Sweden's socialist state in what Barry Forshaw characterizes as an act of "introducing genuinely radical elements into what was at the time an unthreatening form" (17). Given the centrality of the police procedural to Canadian crime fiction, we will return to the multiple rhetorical potentials of this subgenre several times through our analysis of a number of different police series.

Unlike the whodunit, the hardboiled detective story, or the police procedural, the thriller formula does not necessarily include Todorov's dual narratives, with the motivating crime occurring before or very early in the detective's story. In the thriller, the main crime may occur late in the novel, with the first part of the narrative exploring the context leading up to the crime. Further, the thriller often includes a serial killer, so a number of new crimes are committed and investigated throughout the novel. As the subgenre name suggests, the thriller is characterized largely by the visceral and emotional reactions it evokes in readers. Common features include an unreliable narrator, dark gloomy settings, cliffhanger chapter endings, and graphic, often sexualized violence. Rhetorically, the thriller shares much with the hardboiled in positing an irrational world in which good people—especially innocent and attractive young women—may become victims of torture and sadism through nothing more than chance. And yet, as Patrick Anderson notes,

> Most thrillers manage some sort of happy ending. They have it both ways, reminding us how ugly and dangerous our society can be and yet offering hope in the end. Thrillers provide the illusion of order and justice in a world that often seems to have none.
>
> *(7)*

Representations of the police vary across thrillers: they may be heroic, ineffective, or even corrupt. The genre of the thriller can further be subdivided based on the profession of its protagonist into such categories as crime thriller, legal thriller, medical thriller, psychological thriller, spy thriller, techno-thriller, etc.

Although the postmodern detective narrative shares with the thriller an underlying belief in an irrational world, it is far more playful in its approach to dealing with crime, and in some ways resembles more closely the whodunit, with its competitive and intimate relationship between reader and writer. Always a global phenomenon, this subgenre draws upon postmodern aesthetic and philosophical features, such as intertextuality, self-referentiality, metafiction, and parody. The postmodern detective is just as unreliable as the world they inhabit, and the reader's pleasure derives from recognizing references, seeing them redeployed in new ways, and knowing there is little chance of predicting the next step of the story. The precursor of postmodern detective fiction in English is, perhaps, E.C. Bentley's *Trent's Last Case* (1913), also, incidentally, Trent's first case—in which every feature of the Golden Age whodunit is evoked only to be unconventionally played out. The prototypical English-language detective novel in its postmodern form is Paul Auster's *New York Trilogy* (1987), which rewrites several classics of American literature through a highly problematic detective whose investigations into mysteries end up being so labyrinthine that they traverse regularly between the real and the fictional. Rhetorically, the postmodern detective story explores uncertainty—epistemological and ethical—and leaves the reader with a sense that no boundary is secure. Not the boundary between criminal, victim, and detective, as a single person can occupy—temporarily or permanently—two or even all three of these positions. Not the boundary between good and evil, as these concepts are continually interrogated without resolution. Not even the boundary between reality and fiction, as the real world—and fictions from the real world—regularly intrude upon the fictional text. The clever play of questions of truth and knowledge render the postmodern story redolent of meaning for some readers; for others, it seems entirely and frustratingly meaningless. Perhaps for the ideal reader of this subgenre, with its small but esoteric canon, the postmodern detective story is both overflowing with and stripped of meaning at once.

Each of the subgenres has developed over time, with periods of special prominence that can be connected to specific historico-cultural events and anxieties. But generally, the subgenres all exist simultaneously, and many avid detective readers have a preferred subgenre but are open to others. Although all the subgenres initially tended to feature white, male, able-bodied, cis-gendered protagonists, the past decades have seen a substantial increase in detective characters with a variety of ethnic, gender, and ability-based identities. Women detective writers and characters have been far more common since the 1970s across all subgenres. For critic Anne Cranny-Francis, women writing genre fiction can bring feminist perspectives to genre readers who might not otherwise choose novels with female protagonists (3). Carolyn Gold Heilbrun (who wrote detective fiction as Amanda Cross from 1964 to 2002) goes even further and characterizes detective fiction as allowing feminist writers to "dabble in a little profound revolutionary thought" (7).

Certainly, not all women writers of detective fiction explicitly engage in feminist writing, and many male writers do. At the same time, the influx of women writers has notably expanded each subgenre. The whodunit includes the cozy, a very popular subgenre that has just recently begun to receive sustained critical attention. The cozy's features generally suggest comfort and escape: a female protagonist in a supportive community with a possible romance plot and little graphic violence as the crime is solved through conversation and deduction. However, as Marty Knepper compellingly argues, the cozy provides more than escape:

> While cozies reflect the neoliberal spirit of our times in the emphasis on entrepreneurship, they embody values that run counter to the dominant paradigm of the last forty years by providing a model of engaged citizenship, not disengagement and demoralization.
>
> *(38)*

The hardboiled women writers of the 1970s—Marcia Muller, Sue Grafton, and Sara Paretsky—introduce a new physical and emotional vulnerability with attendant resilience to the tough, physical protagonist that we now see in most male as well as female private investigators. The police procedural tracks with real-world changes in policing with an emphasis on a more diverse police force that more accurately represents the communities being policed and more explicitly engages with ongoing questions of how investigations are pursued by the state. Thrillers have also developed new frameworks in the hands of women writers, with a relatively new subgenre of the thriller—domestic noir—specifically exploring the issue of domestic violence in a multitude of ways that often include unclear reader identification, unreliable narrators, and complicated revenge plots. Popular writers in this subgenre include Julia Crouch, Gillian Flynn, and Tana French.

Canadian crime fiction is deeply indebted to the detective and crime writing of America, England, and France. Like these storied literary bodies, it is diverse in its approaches to representations of crime, detection, law, order, and social justice, and it productively draws from and contributes to ongoing critical conversations about representations of crime and detection around the world. Although Canadian writers have explored all the subgenres in a multitude of ways, Canadian crime fiction is unusual in national literatures in its preponderance of police procedurals. In his examination of Irish detective fiction, for example, Brian Cliff asserts that the police procedural is used only ambivalently by Irish crime writers because of "Ireland's historical mistrust of authority" (14). Canada is in the opposite situation, a point David Skene-Melvin makes in his comprehensive bibliography of Canadian crime fiction texts when he contrasts the American interest in the private eye to the Canadian preference for the police detective, arguing that "Canadians want the rule of law and the presence of law and order" (xvii) and that "Canadians rest easy, knowing that professional policemen are out there protecting us from the things that go bump in the night" (xvii). As Daniel Francis has noted, Canada is the only country to have a police officer—the Royal Canadian Mounted Police officer in his distinctive red serge dress uniform—as a national symbol (29). And, as Sloniowski and Rose suggest in their essay collection, *Detecting Canada*, Canadian crime fiction might appear to fall clearly into the conservative category of popular literature, since "Mounties," or Royal Canadian Mounted Police, are a potent national symbol of law and order that is much more often celebrated than interrogated when represented aesthetically (xiii). I would argue that Canadian crime fiction tends toward the moderate rather than the conservative or the subversive, but certainly, the police character is central to the national crime literature. Even in novels in which main characters are lawyers, professors, or political speechwriters, the police are neither absent nor filled in by stock characters. They are fully developed, complex characters who represent the rich, nuanced history of representations and understandings of law and order in a country that was founded by the bureaucratic action of Confederation.

Text Selection

With the exception of the postmodern detective narrative—a small but important subgenre since its parodic thrust delineates both the features and investments of detective fiction more broadly—much detective fiction is serial. This has been true since the earliest nineteenth-century examples, and seriality was a key feature of the dime novels (1860–1917) that served to establish many of the subgenre conventions we still see today. Seriality has many affordances. On a practical level, it is desirable to publishers and authors for economic stability; serial novels are often written rather quickly, perhaps because they do not require constant development of new detective characters. On a rhetorical level, the series offers a capacious form through which authors can explore complex questions and problems with all the nuance they deserve. As Jean Anderson, Carolina Miranda, and Barbara Pezzotti argue in their investigation of serial crime fiction, "what ultimately distinguishes the series is the tension between sameness and difference, familiarity and strangeness, repetition and progression" (4). Canadian crime fiction is in many ways a subtle genre, and the tensions described by the editors of *Serial Crime Fiction* are, in my opinion, at the center of its rhetorical investments. Therefore, most of the texts I read in this book are series. I focus most chapters on two or three novels for close reading, but I try to account for the entire series in my final analysis.

In any study of a genre, it is challenging to select enough writers to showcase the genre's features and tensions without selecting so many that analysis becomes shallow. This challenge is exacerbated when we add "Canadian" to the mix. As Garry Sherbert argues, Canada is an especially difficult nation to pin down: "Since there has always been a plurality of cultures competing for national attention, Canada has been characterized by the lack of a single, national identity" (2–3). I have settled on 14 authors, most of whom are still living and writing. These are intended as a representative set of established Canadian popular and literary authors who would appear in most courses on Canadian crime and detective fiction. My sample includes seven male and seven female writers. Most are white, with the exceptions of Ausma Zehanat Khan (born in Britain to Pakistani immigrants) and Thomas King (First Nations). Five are known largely for their literary fiction (Margaret Atwood, Timothy Findley, Thomas King, Carol Shields, and Emily St. John Mandel), and nine are best known for their crime and detective writing. Perhaps unsurprisingly, given Canada's strong commitment to immigration, five were not born in Canada: Ausma Zehanat Khan and Peter Robinson were born in the United Kingdom, and Linwood Barclay, Timothy Findley, and Thomas King were born in the United States. In associating authors with Canadian provinces, I consider the author's residency and the setting of their fiction, finding the sample to be skewed toward Canada's most populous provinces. We might associate six with Ontario, two with British Columbia, two with Quebec, two with Saskatchewan, and one with Nova Scotia. Thomas King writes about borders as a social construct and might better be associated with Canada's First Nations than with a specific province or territory. Clearly, the authors analyzed are an attempt at a representative group rather than a comprehensive one, and I mention many other crime and detective writers, Canadian and otherwise, throughout the book.

Who Dies, Who Kills, and Who Detects?

It is my belief that crime and detective fiction reveals underlying assumptions about the time and place in which and about which it is being written. After I selected the texts through which I would explore Canadian crime fiction, I undertook a quantitative analysis of the works under study; my findings are meant to be suggestive rather than conclusive, as they are based on my somewhat eclectic sample of writers. I conducted a similar study of detective dime novels in an earlier monograph, reading 100 dime novel endings in order to codify which detective conventions were firmly in place, which were nascent, and which were not yet present in 1880s American popular detective fiction (*Dime*). For *Canadian Crime Fiction*, I coded the gender and race of the detectives, victims, and criminals that appear in my sample of novels. The two postmodern writers (Findley and Shields) have one novel each. Seven writers have detective series of three to eight novels in length (Barclay, Bidulka, Blunt, Callow, Khan, King, and McFetridge) at the time of this writing. Three writers have a series of 20 or more novels: Bowen, Penny, and Robinson. I do not include Mandel or Atwood because they do not provide the kind of murders with a clear victim, killer, and detective that would lend themselves to this kind of analysis. This makes a sample of 103 novels.

All but one of these novels include murder. I count as murder a killing that is investigated and solved within the narrative (although sometimes questions remain, especially in postmodern works); most of these are current murders, but if a murder from the past is pertinent to the current investigation and is solved, I count it. If a solved murder from the past provides a motive but is not investigated, I do not. Only one novel in the sample contains no murder, and that is one of Callow's thrillers, in which

TABLE 1.1 Murders per novel

Author	# of Murders	# of Novels	Avg. murders/novel
Barclay	27	4	6.75
King	24	6	4.00
McFarland	10	3	3.33
Blunt	20	6	3.33
Khan	15	5	3.00
Robinson	79	27	2.93
Callow	10	4	2.50
Bowen	37	20	1.85
Bidulka	13	8	1.63
Penny	22	18	1.22
Findley	1	1	1.00
Shields	1	1	1.00

the detective is able to foil a planned attack. When I counted the number of murders, I realized that Barclay's four-novel Promise Falls series skewed the data, since he has 182 unidentified people die as a result of the poisoning of the town water supply. Given that these victims cannot be identified by race or gender, I leave them out. This leaves 259 murders, for an average of 2.87 murders per novel. Even leaving out the 182 poison victims, Barclay leads the pack for average murders per novel, as seen in Table 1.1.

To me, the surprise here is Louise Penny. One would expect the police procedurals and thrillers—which often have at least one serial killer—to have more murders than the novels featuring amateur detectives, which basically bears out. Penny's police procedural series, however, has just one or two murders per novel. This is because Penny's detectives never investigate a serial killer, and they twice foil major plots. Penny's lower-than-average murder rate is consonant with the idea that this police procedural series has a strong utopian bent (Bedore, "Aesthetics").

The detectives in the sample are mostly police detectives, as the scholarship on Canadian crime fiction suggests they should be. Of the 12 individual writers, Barclay is the only one to mix detective types, including a police detective, a private investigator, and an amateur detective (journalist). This leaves us with seven authors presenting police detectives, four presenting amateur detectives (Barclay, Bowen with her long series, and Shields and Findley with their postmodern detectives), two presenting private investigators (Bidulka and Barclay), and one presenting a lawyer detective (Callow). Novels featuring police make up the majority of the sample, since these are part of a series.

I had expected detective genders to track with author genders, but this was not always the case. Male detectives predominate in my sample, despite my attempt to include an equal number of male and female writers (although the sample contains seven male and five female writers after the removal of Atwood and Mandel from this study). There are 11 male and 4 female central detectives. Five of the male writers—Barclay, Bidulka, King, McFetridge, and Robinson—have central male detectives. The first four regularly place their central detective with other (largely male) detectives, but focalize exclusively or almost exclusively through the central character; Robinson includes a great many female detectives, including focalization through their perspectives, but Banks is the only detective present for all 28 novels. One female writer, Penny, has a detective duo, both male. Two of the female detectives are part of mixed-gender detective duos; the female writer's duo—Khan's Khattak and Getty series—is listed that way. Blunt's Cardinal and Delorme series is often referred to as the John Cardinal series, and the TV adaptation was called simply *Cardinal*, but I believe that Lise Delorme is very much an equal within the series if not the advertising, and her perspectives are given in each novel. Shields' postmodern novel, which investigates the meaning of art as much as it does the murder of Mary Swann, includes a mixed-gender team of academics who act as detective figures. That leaves only two series that center a female detective: Gail Bowen's Joanne Kilbourn series and Pamela Callow's Kate Lange series. My small sample nonetheless substantially overrepresents women detectives, with 37% female detectives, in contrast to 22% of female Canadian police officers (Pablo).

In the real world, homicide involves far more men than women. Statistics Canada crime data from 2017 to 2021 track between 662 and 778 homicides per year (Table 35-10-0060-01, for this and all statistics about homicide in this chapter). Within Canada, there is a remarkably consistent rate of 25% of homicide victims being female. Within the detective fiction sample, however, female victims slightly outnumber male victims, with an average of 53% female victims across all series. Findley's single victim is male. Otherwise, every single writer has female victims exceeding the real-world statistic (see Table 1.2).

The most striking data point here to me is that Pamela Callow's thriller series presents 10 female victims and 0 male victims. I had the opportunity to interview Pamela Callow in 2021 and asked her about her use of only female victims. She responded that her novels are about power dynamics, and that is one way she explores questions of unequal power between men and women.

Women in crime fiction are also over-represented in the killer position, despite their relatively small numbers. My fictional sample includes far

TABLE 1.2 Gender of murder victims

Author	Female	Male	Total	Avg. female (%)
Findley	0	1	1	0
Real world (2017–2021)	871	2,674	3,565	24.4
Robinson	35	44	79	44
Khan	7	8	15	47
Barclay	13	14	27	48
King	12	12	24	50
Bidulka	7	5	13*	54
Blunt	11	9	20	55
Bowen	21	16	37	57
McFetridge	6	4	10	60
Penny	14	8	22	64
Callow	10	0	10	100
Shields	1	0	1	100

* Bidulka includes 1 trans victim, explaining the total of 13 murders.

more male than female killers (109 males to 31 females), but the 22% number for female killers is nonetheless larger than the Statistics Canada report that 14% of people accused of homicide (again, 2017–2021) are female. Interestingly, male writers tend to be close to the portion of women killers, while female writers have far more female killers, as seen in Table 1.3.

I discuss these gender trends more in the individual chapters, of course, but I would note here that the killer position is a complex one. The killer is obviously an outlier of society, committing an unsanctioned act. At the same time, the killer has also seized ultimate power in at least one situation, depriving someone of their life; the killer is also elevated to the position of a rival—and sometimes even a double—of the detective. The over-representation of female killers could thus be seen as a strange empowering of female characters. Although I have not actually done a qualitative analysis (and am not sure such an analysis would even be possible), I believe there is also a trend where female killers are more likely to be more justified in their actions than their male counterparts, especially by male writers. We see especially clear examples of this in women killers penned by male writers, like Findley and Robinson.

I would note that my sample of 103 novels included only 2 trans characters in detective, victim, or killer positions, both from Bidulka, one of only two authors in the sample to identify as gay (the other being Findley). I would expect that as trans issues become more prevalent in

TABLE 1.3 Gender of fictional killers

Author	Female	Male	Total	Avg. female (%)
McFarland	0	6	6	0
Shields	0	1	1	0
Real world (2017–2021)	401	2,696	3,126	12.8
Barclay	2	13	15	13
Blunt	1	6	7	14
Khan	1	6	7	14
Robinson	6	36	42	14
King	1	5	6	17
Penny	6	16	22	27
Callow	1	2	3	33
Bidulka	3	5	9*	33
Bowen	9	13	22	41
Findley	1	0	1	100

* Bidulka includes one trans killer, explaining the total of nine killers.

society, we will see more trans characters in all forms of popular fiction, including detective fiction, within the next decade or two.

My notes about the race of characters are far less extensive than those about gender for the simple reason that most authors in my sample stay within their own racial identities. Central detective figures always share the race of their author; the ten white authors have white detectives and the Indigenous writer Thomas King has an Indigenous detective. The one exception is that Ausma Zehanat Khan (herself of Pakistani descent) writes a detective duo that includes a Middle Eastern man and a white woman. The vast majority of victims and killers in the fictional sample are also white. This does not at all track with Canadian statistics, where 6% of the population identifies as Indigenous, but Indigenous people make up 25% of homicide victims and 33% of people accused of homicide. In Khan's sample of murders, investigated by a branch of police devoted to race-based murders, most victims and killers are non-white. Thomas King, himself Indigenous, sets his Thumps DreadfulWater series in Montana, and includes two Indigenous and two East Asian victims, as well as several victims whose race is not clearly marked. He also includes one racialized killer, who tries to pass as Indigenous but is actually Cuban. Two white writers—Giles Blunt and Gail Bowen—include one or two Indigenous victims or killers, as discussed in their chapters. With increasing attention to Indigenous issues, especially in the wake of the Truth and Reconciliation Commission report of 2015, I would expect to also see increasing representation of racialized characters across writers.

Organizing Principles

The book is organized into three parts, each exploring a dimension through which Canadian crime fiction can be examined.

Part I is titled "Historical Confrontations" and consists of five chapters. Canada's relatively short history as a nation is defined largely by its complex relationships with the countries most involved in the development of crime and detective fiction: the United States, England, and France. Culturally, tensions with the United States have been most relevant to constructions of Canadian national identity in the twenty-first century. Within its own borders, Canada has long negotiated three conflicts whose legacies continue to define key elements of national identity today: the often bloody conflicts between European settlers and Indigenous peoples; the long-standing, sometimes bloody, feud between the French and the English; and the complex of legal and cultural tensions around race and multiculturalism. Part I of *Canadian Crime Fiction* provides a historical overview of these conflicts and makes the case for their centrality to the contemporary Canadian imagination with a close examination of five twenty-first-century authors who use crime fiction's ability to embody and grapple with the past in understanding representations of relatively recent and ongoing faultlines in Canadian identity. John McFetridge's Eddie Dougherty series (2014–2016) is set in 1970s Montreal and uses the police procedural as a means to explore how the legacy of 1960s and 1970s French-English tensions in Quebec continue to inflect twenty-first-century representations of crime in Canada. Giles Blunt's John Cardinal series (2000–2012) takes on what Manina Jones characterizes as a Nordic Noir ethos as it examines the knot of complex relationships in northern Ontario as police officers and citizens of English, French, and First Nations backgrounds must work together to address crime. Thomas King's Thumps DreadfulWater series (2002–present) infuses the conventions of the police procedural with both pathos and humor in order to explore contemporary Canadian culture's grapplings with the legacy of colonial/Indigenous encounters. Ausma Zehanat Khan's Rachel Getty and Esa Khattak series (2015–present) addresses the racialization of criminality in Canada through its setting in the Community Policing Services branch of the Toronto Police Department, a group responsible for consulting on investigations into race-based hate crimes. Linwood Barclay's *Promise Falls* series (2015–2017) provides insight into the sometimes fraught relationship between Canada and the United States through its dystopian exploration of twenty-first-century sociocultural anxieties around the decline of the mid-sized city.

Part II, "Canadian Genre Play," examines crime and detective fiction through the subgenres, noting the frequent genre hybridization that characterizes Canadian genre fiction. The section again consists of five chapters. I use Peter Robinson's Alan Banks series (1987–2023) as a representative police procedural, analyzing its increasingly complex representations of sex crimes over more than three decades to argue that the police procedural can register changing cultural mores through its examination of crime. Gail Bowen's long series (1990–present) presents Joanne Kilbourn (eventually Shreve), an amateur detective who explores and revises epistemological and ethical questions as an academic detective and mother detective. Anthony Bidulka's Russell Quant series (2003–2012) is a rare example of a Canadian private investigator series; it draws upon conventions from the hardboiled and the cozy in a fascinating exploration of lesbian, gay, bisexual, transgender, queer, and/or questioning (LGBTQ+) issues, as Quant is, in his own words, "a particularly gay detective" (*Tapas* 20). Pamela Callow's Kate Lange series (2010–present) provides insights into the Canadian legal thriller and especially the ways trauma theory is becoming increasingly important in understanding the ethico-legal analyses of the modern thriller. Finally, a chapter on postmodern detective fiction features two well-known literary authors, Carol Shields and Timothy Findley, focusing on their forays into detective fiction with Findley's *The Telling of Lies* (1986) and Shields' *Swann* (1987).

Part III, "Futuristic Explorations," makes the argument that Canadian crime fiction, with its optimistic bent, will continue to embrace hybridity as it explores the twenty-first century's greatest challenges. Increasingly, the new century has seen a mixing of genres, a move that can be seen as synergistic or contaminating, depending on one's perspective on genre purity. Within Canadian popular writing, I see the blending of detective and crime tropes with future-looking approaches to science and technology (in science fiction and literary fiction alike) as the most exciting new direction for writers of popular fiction. In this final section, I put together three very different writers in thinking about ways that crime fiction can speak to critical questions of futurity. Namely, I investigate: Louise Penny's *Bury Your Dead* (2010), from her long-running Three Pines series (2005–present), which examines eco-terrorism within an oddly utopian police procedural series; Margaret Atwood's *Madd Addam* trilogy (2003–2013), which presents a post-apocalyptic scenario precipitated by a genocidal maniac against the backdrop of technophilic excess; and Emily St. John Mandel's loose trilogy of *Station Eleven* (2014), *The Glass Hotel* (2020), and *Sea of Tranquility* (2022), which provides a postmodern, sometimes post-apocalyptic examination of noncriminal mysteries and nonfatal crimes in order to examine existential questions including what it means to be human and what kind of life is worth living.

A Note on Methodology

I am generally committed to using gender-neutral language and naming conventions. Given this, I played with the idea of consistently using either first or last names for all detective characters. I was especially reluctant to refer to male detectives by their surnames and female detectives by their given names, as this might seem to make me complicit with a long history of sexual discrimination in which professional women are subtly demeaned by more familiar monikers than would be employed for their male counterparts at the same rank. In the end, however, I decided to follow the pattern of each author. That means that many solo detectives like King's Thumps DreadfulWater or Bowen's Joanne Kilborne—eventually Joanne Shreve—are referred to by given name, while in some cases partners have different conventions, as in Ausma Zehanat Khan's Esa Khattack—almost always Khattak in the novels—and Rachel Getty—equally prevalently referred to as Rachel. This maintains the author's voice rather than substituting a perhaps unneeded corrective.

I also try, whenever possible, not to spoil endings. Detective fiction writers often spend a great deal of time crafting surprising and satisfying solutions to the mysteries they narrate. Detective fiction readers often get deeply invested in trying to reason toward—or to guess at—these solutions. As much as possible, I do not disrupt that delightful game between writer and reader that continues to provide momentum to these stories even as we understand that detective narratives provide much more to readers than a puzzle to be solved. In some cases, unfortunately, the identity of the killer is germane to my analysis, and in those cases, I am forced to reveal it. Even if you read my discussion before you read some of these delightful novels, I hope you will nonetheless find that their exploration of cultural, political, aesthetic, epistemological, and ethical questions make them very much worth the read.

And now, on to a discussion of 14 fascinating Canadian crime and detective fiction writers.

PART I
Historical Confrontations

2
JOHN MCFETRIDGE AND THE LEGACY OF FRENCH/ENGLISH TENSIONS

On May 20, 1980, the people of Quebec voted on the Quebec Independence Referendum Question, which was crafted into the following long sentence:

> The government of Quebec has made public its proposal to negotiate a new agreement with the rest of Canada, based on the equality of nations; this agreement would enable Quebec to acquire the exclusive power to make its laws, levy its taxes and establish relations abroad—in other words, sovereignty—and at the same time to maintain with Canada an economic association including a common currency; any change in political status resulting from these negotiations will only be implemented with popular approval through another referendum; on these terms, do you give the Government of Quebec the mandate to negotiate the proposed agreement between Quebec and Canada?

I was seven years old then, and I wore my hair in braids in honor of both Anne Shirley and Laura Ingalls. In April of that year, I participated in my first act of political activism. This was not a personal choice. In advance of the referendum, my grade two class engaged in a letter-writing campaign in which Ontarian students wrote directly to Quebecois students to tell them how much we wanted their province to remain a part of Canada. I was the only child in my class who wrote my letter in French. As the child of a Quebecois mother and an Ontarian father, I'm sure I wrote a fine letter. After all, we went to neighboring Quebec once a year to visit my prodigious extended family, and I could not imagine Quebec being a different country. That would make it like the United States, which I knew even then was very

DOI: 10.4324/9781003125242-3

different from Canada, and perhaps even a little scary. It was with great relief that my family took in the news that the 1980 referendum failed by a comfortable margin (40.44%–59.56% with an 85.6% turnout). The referendum of 1995 failed far more narrowly (49.42%–50.58% with a 93.52% turnout). Although no other referenda on sovereignty have been undertaken despite the close vote of 1995, the vexed relationship between French and English Canadians remains a central tension of Canadian identity, even for a twenty-first-century crime writer.

In his Eddie Dougherty series (2014–2016), John McFetridge uses detective fiction—specifically the police procedural subgenre so popular in Canada—to revisit crucial moments in Montreal history and to explore the French–English tensions surrounding them. By setting the series in the 1970s, McFetridge is able to investigate—historically, culturally, and aesthetically–the complex set of political and cultural forces that led to the two referenda on Quebec sovereignty. In these novels, McFetridge takes advantage of the pedagogical potential of detective fiction, using the narrative momentum of the police procedural to provide a series of engaging and situational history lessons. For most Canadians in 2014, the term "terrorism" would have evoked the September 11, 2001, attacks on the World Trade Center in New York City. Many Canadians even then would have had limited knowledge of the FLQ (*le Front de libération du Québec*), a guerilla movement that conducted over 160 violent attacks between 1963 and 1970, culminating in the kidnapping and murder of a prominent Canadian politician. McFetridge provides readable historical context as well as cultural analysis as he raises the concept of "two solitudes" from Hugh MacLennan's novel of the same name to interrogate the notion that French and English Canada are so distinct as to be unbridgeable. He embodies the limitations of MacLennan's metaphor through Constable Eddie Dougherty, a bilingual Montreal beat cop who interacts with a wide variety of people through his work. In so doing, McFetridge presents a rich tapestry of perspectives that draws from both the experiential and the philosophical. He also uses liminality—a concept central to detective fiction—to figure out French–English tensions as well as some of their possible resolutions, ending his series on the hopeful note that is almost a hallmark of Canadian crime and detective fiction.

Rewriting History through Philosophical Anachronism

The Eddie Dougherty series provides a new take on detective fiction's foundational investment in temporality. As evidenced by Tzvetan Todorov's classic essay on the genre, "The Typology of Detective Fiction" (1971), detective fiction always contains at least two narrative strands separated by time, with the detective's story of investigation uncovering and to some degree constructing an anteceding story—the story of the criminal and the victim and how the crime came to occur (46). Detective writers often explore important moments in history through crimes that require their detective to visit the past. For example, Peter Robinson's *In a Dry Season* (1999) requires Inspector Banks to revisit events from World War II, and Louise Penny's *Bury Your Dead* (2010) requires Chief Inspector Gamache to go even further back to the history of Samuel Champlain and the founding of Quebec. McFetridge undertakes a rich, nuanced reading of Montreal history through the detective genre, but using a different technique. He sets the novels four decades earlier than they are written in the complex sociopolitical decade in which violence and bureaucratic change exist alongside each other in setting the stage for the two referenda. In this way, McFetridge writes the Eddie Dougherty series—and we read it—with all the insights gained from the knowledge that the referenda are to be proposed and to fail. McFetridge provides substantial details of the temporal as well as physical setting through music, media reports, and character conversations about the politics of the time, presenting discussions with a sometimes tongue-in-cheek gesture to the hindsight shared by writer and reader.

The relationship between English and French Canada has been a fraught one going back at least as far as the Seven Years' War between France and Britain (1756–1763). In his influential study of the major cultural myths underlying Canadian national identity, Daniel Francis argues that the ongoing tensions between English and French Canadians can be traced to the aftermath of that eighteenth-century conflict:

> Unlike Americans, who celebrate unreservedly their victory in the War of Independence, English Canadians have never been allowed to feel that the Conquest was a moment of triumph which set the clock ticking on a great national destiny .... And so was born the myth of unity: that French and English were partners, co-operating in building the same Canada.
>
> *(96)*

Is there one unified Canada? Francis cites W.L. Morton, Governor-General-Award-winning Canadian historian, who vehemently supported the idea of Canadian unity in the 1960s: "There are not two histories, but one history, as there are not two Canadas, or any greater number, but one" (quoted in Francis 108). The Quiet Revolution, during which Quebec became a more secular society focused on modernizing its economy, revealed fractures between the English and French that had long been present. For

Francis, as for many historical and cultural critics of Canada, the notion of unity between Quebec and the rest of Canada is a myth growing out of contradictory stories. "For the Quebecois," Francis writes, "history describes a struggle to survive the assimilationist intentions of the English majority. For English-speaking Canadians, history describes the evolution of political freedom in a framework of British justice and parliamentary democracy" (105).

Tensions between French and English Canada, as well as within Quebec, played out at many levels before the referendum of 1980. Quebec nationalism—the feeling that Quebec should be celebrated as an autonomous nation distinct for its French language and culture, and separate from the rest of Canada—is generally traced to 1960 and the start of the Quiet Revolution, a period marked by substantial secularization and modernization of the province (1960–1976). In 1968, René Lévesque, who left the Quebec Liberal Party to found the Parti Québécois, wrote an essay, "Option Québec" ("An Option for Quebec"), outlining a proposal for Quebec to become an independent nation and create a new economic union with Canada (the basis of the first referendum for sovereignty). As tensions grew between federalists and separatists, the FLQ—a separatist guerilla group—gained force and was declared a domestic terrorist group by the Canadian government. Regularly planting bombs around the city of Montreal, the FLQ gained special notoriety with the Montreal Stock Exchange bombing on February 13, 1969, which destroyed much of the trading floor and injured 27 people. The group's breaking point came during the October Crisis of 1970, when the FLQ kidnapped Deputy Premier of Quebec Pierre Laporte and British Diplomat James Cross. This prompted Prime Minister Pierre Elliot Trudeau (father of Justin Trudeau, who would become prime minister in 2015) to invoke the War Measures Act, which allowed police raids of FLQ members and affiliates without warrants. October 1970 marks the only peacetime use of this Act in Canada's history.

It is in this fraught sociopolitical period that McFetridge sets the three Eddie Dougherty novels. As McFetridge outlines in the author's note at the end of *Black Rock* (2014), most of the events in that novel are based on historical facts from 1970, including the regular police searches for FLQ bombs; the kidnapping and murder of Pierre Laporte; and the multiple murders Dougherty investigates (420). *A Little More Free* (2015) references several historical events from 1972: a nightclub fire at Montreal's Blue Bird Café in which 37 people died as a result of arson; a major robbery at Montreal's Museum of Fine Arts; and a nail-biting hockey extravaganza, the Summit Series, in which Team Canada finally beat the Soviet national team in Game Eight. Against this backdrop, Dougherty investigates the fictional murder of David Murray, an American draft dodger, learning, among other things, that word choice can influence cultural understandings of history, since David and his ilk prefer the terms "deserters" or "war protesters." *One or the Other* (2016) jumps to 1976, when Montreal hosted the Summer Olympics, a Brinks truck was robbed of three million dollars (which was never recovered), and the streets of Montreal were filled with a party atmosphere that included cocaine and disco. As McFetridge writes in the author's note that follows this novel,

> Dorian Lynskey's book, *33 Revolutions Per Minute*, has a great chapter on disco as protest music, bringing gay rights to the forefront. In retrospect, this is easy to see. At the time [when McFetridge was 16] it was not.
>
> *(394)*

It is with these perspectives in mind that the final novel of the Eddie Dougherty series addresses the investigation of a double homicide with implications for gay rights.

McFetridge repeatedly raises—and challenges—a model for French-English relations that resonated in the 1970s but has been rethought in the twenty-first century. For decades after its publication in 1945, Hugh MacLennan's novel *Two Solitudes* was read as a representative anecdote for the complex history of French-English tensions as Paul Tallard and Heather Methuen, the novel's main characters, stand in for the French and English communities central to the formation of Canada as a nation-state. MacLennan figures the chasm between the two as almost unbridgeable, and yet leaves space for love to unite the two even as their families and communities continue to disapprove. McFetridge's main detective character, Constable Eddie Dougherty, grapples with MacLennan's metaphor as part of his lived experience in 1970 Montreal as he is the perfectly bilingual son of an Anglophone (Irish) father and a Francophone (Quebecois) mother. As McFetridge has said in interviews, there is a substantial autobiographical element to the Eddie Dougherty character, who resembles the author's older brother: "Eddie's parents live in the house I grew up in and Eddie's younger brother, Tommy, is exactly my age and going to the high school I went to" (Pierce). In the novel, Dougherty's parents have recently moved from one neighborhood to another and he reflects upon their similarities in *Black Rock*:

> [Greenfield Park] felt a little like the Point, a tight-knit community surrounded by what people felt were outsiders, people they never really associated with, separated by language. The two solitudes, like that book Dougherty was supposed to read in school but never finished.
>
> *(93)*

Both neighborhoods—Greenfield Park and Point St. Charles—feature an insider/outsider ethos based on the dichotomy between the French/English language and culture. While Dougherty brings to mind what seems a relevant literary reference, he also notes that he has never finished the novel, a fact possibly attributable to his mediocre performance as a high school student, but also perhaps a challenge to MacLennan's formulation. As Jeffery Vacante notes, MacLennan's vision as an explanatory model of French-English relationships in Canada was problematized as early as the 1960s, in part due to a "larger disengagement from Quebec on the part of English-Canadian writers, who came to believe that they lacked the legitimacy to write about Quebec" (43).

Black Rock reprises the MacLennan reference later in the novel when Dougherty sleeps with Ruth Garber, a graduate student in the Sociology department at McGill University who is studying multiple murderers. After sex, Dougherty has the uncharacteristic desire to learn more about Ruth and her heritage. He speculates about where she is from:

> "English Montrealers don't move into the east end," Dougherty said.
> "It's that two solitudes thing, remember?"
> "What about a guy like you who's both?"
> "I think my name's a bit of a giveaway."
> "You think you have to choose to be one or the other?"
> Dougherty shrugged. It wasn't something he'd thought about and not something he wanted to be thinking about at the moment. He really wanted to know more about Ruth, and then it hit him. "You're American."
>
> *(160–1)*

As an American, even one living in Montreal, Ruth may or may not be familiar with MacLennan's novel despite its place as a cultural touchstone for Canadians in the 1970s. Her response to Dougherty's literary reference is to immediately note that he does not fit into the model, as he is "both"—the genetic and cultural product of the melding of the two solitudes. Dougherty does not want to reflect upon his own dualities, preferring to delve more into Ruth's background. This sets up Dougherty's personal qualities. He is intelligent, as he is able to eliminate the possible Canadian identities with which Ruth might identify and thus guess correctly that she is American. At the same time, he is not gifted with Sherlock Holmes-level observational or deductive talents. Nor is he a philosopher or a cultural critic. Instead, he is dogged in pursuing the information he wants, and he cares about individuals. Although the Montreal police are overwhelmed by responding to constant bomb threats from the FLQ throughout *Black Rock*, Dougherty is able, from his lowly position as a beat cop, to weigh the importance of the ongoing political conflict and its security implications against the need to protect vulnerable young women from a vicious serial killer. This allows McFetridge to engage in historical exploration while also providing a compelling crime narrative. It also might remind readers that history is made up of individual personal stories happening in tandem with and sometimes in counterpoint to the broader political stories of their day. Crime fiction can open a window into both.

Despite his interest—and even obsession—with helping Étienne Carpentier, a senior detective, to investigate the murder of Brenda Webber, Dougherty cannot escape political news. His music listening on the radio is regularly interrupted by news breaks that often include details about possible terrorist activities. For example, as he drives around Montreal on his day off, he hears a report of a plane crash in Toronto that has apparently left 190 people dead:

> Then the news guy said that there wasn't much information yet but it was bright and sunny with excellent visibility in Toronto and they were checking into the possibility the plane had been hijacked or that a bomb was onboard.
>
> *(235)*

The casual shift from a horrifying socio-political tragedy with global implications to a local weather report bespeaks the routine nature of terrorist attacks in the 1970s as well as how they were reported. This point is underlined the next morning when Dougherty is looking at the paper as he eats breakfast with Ruth. Dougherty shows her an article about a kidnapping in Uruguay, asking "Does every country have terrorist groups these days?" to which Ruth replies, "It comes with American imperialism, I think" (263).

Such cultural analysis of American hegemony, more easily articulated in the twenty-first century than in 1970, is only one example of the power of philosophical anachronism. After a typically awkward dinner at his parents' house, Dougherty comments idly that he is surprised that his younger brother is not going to French high school as he did, which leads his Anglophone father into an uncharacteristic riff on politics:

> [Dougherty's father]: "They're talking about a wage freeze, about inflation, everybody's going on strike. And the only thing we talk about is language politics, as if it would be okay if we all lost our jobs as long as we speak the right language."

"I think the idea," Dougherty said, "is that when they get rid of the English bosses everything will be great and we'll all get raises."
"We, *kemosabe?*"

(278)

There is much to unpack here. Dougherty's father's reference through "Kemosabe" to the 1950s American Western, *The Long Ranger*, is a complex one. In 1970, this would have been a typical pop culture reference, suggesting that the speaker and his interlocutor (Tonto and the Lone Ranger) may not have the same interests. Within the context, the senior Dougherty is noting that their surname marks them both as more closely affiliated to the English bosses than to the French workers purportedly blinded by their obsession with language politics and with whom his son clearly identifies. In 2014, however, the use of "Kemosabe" will remind many Canadians of a well-publicized Canadian court case from 2004 that questions whether the term is racist to First Nations people. The Nova Scotia Human Rights Commission ruled against the grievance of a Mi'kmaq woman, who complained that her boss referred to workers as "Kemosabe." The Nova Scotia Court of Appeal upheld the ruling, and the provincial Human Rights Commission referred the case to the Canada Supreme Court, which declined to hear it ("Highest"). The potential cognitive pleasure of a reader noting this dated reference and possibly considering its implications does nothing to change the insight of Dougherty's explanation of how language politics relate to economic issues.

The conversation then turns to René Lévesque (1922–1987), the founder of the Parti Québécois who was to serve as Quebec's premier from 1976 to 1985, reminding the reader even more forcefully of the hindsight that underpins McFetridge's novel. In October of 1970, sitting at the kitchen table, Dougherty's father states that he is concerned that Lévesque will prompt violence:

[Dougherty's father]: "Because the separatists got twenty percent of the vote but only six seats. Lévesque is supposed to be the level-headed one, and he says some people will be tempted to destroy democratic institutions."

Dougherty thought, Shit, more bombs. He liked René Lévesque with his comb-over and a smoke always in his hand, the way he tried to shrug everything off, but since he'd left the Liberal Party and started up the Parti Québécois and made separation a priority, there was a whole gang with him that Dougherty wasn't sure Lévesque could control.

(279)

Dougherty's analysis may seem deceptively facile with his focus on Lévesque's hairstyle and casual demeanor, but it is actually quite astute, given that the militant separatists of the FLQ are about to undertake the action that will lead to the October Crisis.

Indeed, when McFetridge covers the kidnapping and murder of Pierre Laporte in *Black Rock*, he does so from the perspective of Dougherty the beat cop, leaning into the intersection of the personal and the political. As Dougherty and his colleagues get briefed on the kidnapping, they learn that the War Measures Act has been implemented, meaning that they need no warrants to round up anyone possibly connected with the FLQ. McFetridge captures the enormity of this change:

> Dougherty was looking at the other cops, no one smiling, no one joking around, no gung-ho comments, nothing like the charged-up dressing room before heading out onto the ice feel it usually was before nightclub raids or strapping on the riot gear.
>
> *(388)*

The Captain fails to give his usual rousing speech, and Dougherty and his fellow cops get to work. After a double shift, Dougherty heads back downtown in his own car to pursue a lead in the Brenda Webber case. As he drives, he listens to an announcer reading Pierre Trudeau's address to the House of Commons, which speaks of Canadian resilience and justice:

> "... Through justice we will get rid of the perversion of terrorism. Through justice we will find peace and freedom."
>
> Dougherty listened to the whole thing, unconvinced. He'd spent the day shoving people into police cars, not telling their families where they were going or when they could ever see them again, people screaming at him, calling him a fascist pig. Didn't seem like the kind of thing that was going to bring people together.
>
> *(390)*

The analysis here is compelling. As a smart guy who has not studied concepts like fascism and American imperialism in university, Dougherty provides an experiential perspective on the October Crisis. His matter-of-fact assertion that arresting people with no link to the kidnapping is unlikely to lead to unity echoes the analysis of historians like Guy Bouthillier and Édourd Cloutier, who bring together a number of essays by politicians, historians, and journalists who make similar points in their anthology, *Trudeau's Darkest Hour: War Measures in Time of Peace, October 1970* (2010).

Liminality as a Response to the Two Solitudes

Why is the police procedure an especially effective genre for McFetridge's brand of historical analysis? The history of detective fiction is full of liminal characters whose detective prowess is tied to their ability to successfully negotiate boundary crossings of class, race, ethnicity, and even morality. We see this in each of the three nineteenth-century traditions foundational to the early development of detective fiction. In France, we have Eugene François Vidocq (1775–1857), a thief turned detective whose memoirs of his adventures on both sides of the law inspired Edgar Allan Poe's creation of C. Auguste Dupin (1840–5), widely considered the first fictional detective. In the United States, Allan Pinkerton, the famous real-life detective and founder of the first major American detective agency, was also a fictionalized character in his 18 memoirs (1874–1900), which speak repeatedly to his ability to transcend his working-class roots as a cooper and to negotiate such diverse places as Civil War battlefields, passenger trains, and upper-class households. In England, Arthur Conan Doyle's most recognizable character, Sherlock Holmes (1887–1927), embodies the fictional detective's ability to fully inhabit various disguises as he plays a sort of confidence game with those he surveils and investigates. As I have argued elsewhere, the detective's ability to pass—sometimes explicitly as when in disguise but often more subtly by taking on, chameleon-like, appropriate postures and speech patterns when dealing with people from different social echelons—goes far in explaining the appeal of detective fiction to readers as well as writers. As a character with a certain amount of power—juridical and epistemological—the detective's liminality places them in a position to contain dangers on behalf of their society, but also makes them vulnerable to potential contamination from their dealings with the dark underbelly of society (Bedore *Dime* 4–5).

Eddie Dougherty is a liminal character in this tradition. His liminality as bilingual and bicultural, and also as caught between the professional identities of beat cop and homicide detectives, is highlighted by the title of the first novel, *Black Rock*, a historical monument that McFetridge uses to showcase both Montreal's diversity and the detective character's complex place within it. Midway through the novel, Dougherty cruises the streets of Point St. Charles, the Montreal neighborhood in which he grew up, hoping to make a drug buy from one of his former high school classmates in order to get an in with "the Point Boys" so he can contribute to the solution of the Brenda Webber case and hopefully be promoted to detective. His car radio comes on, tuned to the French station, and he listens to two popular songs by Canadian artists that showcase American influence on Canadian culture: "Plattsburgh Drive-By Blues," a bilingual song by Chantal Renaud (who would in 2004 marry Bernard Landry, Parti Québécois leader from 2001 to 2005 and Quebec premier from 2001 to 2003) and "American Woman," by The Guess Who, a Canadian rock band whose success has included the much larger American market. McFetridge subtly highlights the complex cultural history evident in Montreal street names as Dougherty turns off St. Patrick (Irish) to Laprairie (French), then takes Hibernia (the Latin name for Ireland) and the underpass at Grand Trunk (the Canadian railroad headquartered in Montreal), finally driving on Wellington (evoking the nineteenth-century Anglo-Irish prime minister of Britain) and parking on Sébastopol (named after a street in Paris). As he psychs himself up for his first undercover action, Dougherty reflects on the history of his city's urban development, looking at the little-used Autostade left over from Expo 67 and thinking about the bulldozing of Goose Village while hearing "his father's voice saying it was because Drapeau [mayor of Montreal] couldn't stand the idea that the first thing American tourists could see when they got onto the island of Montreal was an Irish slum" (144). Having successfully navigated the neighborhood, Dougherty then manages the delicate social negotiation of the undercover drug buy, convincing a now-criminal high school classmate that he is acting as a private citizen rather than as a cop.

Smiling at his success and imagining how he will tell his superiors about the new relationship he has just forged, Dougherty pauses and reads the inscription on the Black Rock monument. The epitaph, erected in 1859, memorializes 6,000 Irish immigrants who died of typhus in 1847–1848. Realizing that he has passed this rock hundreds of times without stopping to read the words, Dougherty recalls his father telling him about the brutal conditions of early Irish immigration to Canada, and the fact that in 1859, Irish workers had found a mass grave of their countrymen from just over a decade earlier. As he considers this history from a century ago, Dougherty has a kind of epiphany that tracks with McFetridge's concerns:

> Dougherty stood there on Bridge Street, practically in the shadow of the Autostade, cars coming and going from the city, and tried to imagine what it was like for those Irish workmen—men and probably boys, who probably looked like he did and like his father and his little brother Tommy and every other man in his family—when their shovels hit the first bones.
> *(150)*

He wonders how the immigrants from only 12 years earlier could have been forgotten and imagines that the workers who erected the monument were probably docked a day's pay for their action. As he gets back in his car, The Beatles' "Let It Be" comes on, reminding Dougherty and the reader of the colonial approach of letting complex questions lie. Dougherty thinks about the woman whose murder he is trying to solve and makes a resolution: "Not six thousand bodies, just one. One he wasn't going to let be forgotten" (151).

Dougherty's ability to see and understand the interstices of his city and his job offers as many challenges as affordances, as is typical in detective fiction. His Anglo name makes it just as difficult for him to fit in with his colleagues as with the citizens on the streets he polices. For example, at an FLQ rally in which he and several other police officers provide security, Dougherty is reminded once again of his liminal status:

> One of the cops said to Dougherty, 'So, when we get our police union, you don't get to join, Dog-eh-dee,' and he laughed. Another cop said, 'No, Dog-eh-dee is half French, half of him gets to join.'
> *(377–8)*

Against the backdrop of separatist chants by the crowd ("*Le Québec aux Québécois!*"), Dougherty chats with an older Francophone cop, the two agreeing that microaggressions among colleagues are not funny ("*Ce n'est pas drôle*") and that the student strikes at colleges and universities are not a game ("*Ce n'est pas un jeu*") (378). Despite this shared understanding with an unnamed colleague, Dougherty realizes that nothing will be gained by confronting Francophone cops who see as detrimental his half-English heritage (which he sometimes but not always corrects, since he is actually half-Irish). This inaction places him in contrast with contemporary Quebecois revolutionaries—the militant FLQ faction and the student strikers—whose activism marks the historical moment. Dougherty's relative passivity is represented as both pragmatism and uncertainty.

Approaching detective work from his marginal bicultural position, Dougherty is often beset by doubts, some resulting from childhood trauma. Early in *Black Rock*, Dougherty enters a bar from his old neighborhood, where he can feel the patrons, many of whom he recognizes from his teen years, staring at him:

> It wasn't that different from being the scared kid cornered between the sheds in the back lane, Buck-Buck and his friends giving him a beating, telling him his father knocked up a French whore and nobody wants the stupid half-breed kid.
> *(23)*

From this recollection of childhood abjection, Dougherty finds himself questioning the very same people who had once abused him. After a confrontation with one of the bullies (now a witness) in which Dougherty surprises himself by successfully intimidating his former tormentor into providing information, he finds himself shaking as he processes the new power that comes with his position. Carpentier, his detective mentor, insists on discussing, albeit briefly, the dangers of contamination:

> "You liked it in the store when he was afraid of you."
> "I liked that he told us what we wanted to know."
> "Be careful not to like that too much."
>
> *(58)*

The difficulty in performing the authority of the police detective without too deeply internalizing its inherent inequities is one Dougherty struggles with throughout the series.

Dougherty also struggles to maintain distance from criminals with whom he shares commonalities, another productive trope of detective fiction. The detective genre often employs the *doppelgänger* (dark double), pointing up the similarities between criminal and detective in order to explore the potentially perilous ways the detective can exploit those similarities in the morally justified task of identifying and capturing the criminal. McFetridge uses this technique, pressing down on Dougherty's anxieties as much as on his tendencies toward the morally dubious. For example, in *One or the Other*, Dougherty goes to Ontario to interview Martin Comptois, a low-level drug dealer in police custody. Dougherty immediately sees the similarities between himself and the criminal:

> Dougherty figured Comptois was in his mid-twenties, a few years younger than Dougherty, and he also figured they were at about the same place in their stalled careers. Comptois was likely looking to impress a boss by not saying anything during his incarceration just as much as Dougherty was looking to impress his by working this investigation.
>
> *(240)*

During the interrogation, Dougherty can't shake the feeling of doubleness as he lays out Comptois' options:

> "But everybody moves on, Martin. Nobody waits for you. You fall behind, you get stuck where you are. You get out of jail, you go back to what you were, you start over." The way Dougherty felt every time one of his temporary assignments to detective ended and he went back into uniform.
>
> *(243)*

Detective-criminal doubling is often used to raise the stakes of an investigation, highlighting for the reader the danger that the detective might give up part of their moral authority in mimicking the criminal's thought patterns or behaviors. Here, McFetridge places Dougherty in a less dangerous and more reflective space, as his interactions with Comptois cause him to interrogate his motives for pursuing detective work when his career path is far from the linear progression he had imagined for himself. Dougherty also feels sorry for Comptois. The Ontario cops mistakenly assume (like many Ontarians) that Comptois (like every Quebecois) can speak English, which he cannot. As a liminal Quebecois, Dougherty has the insider knowledge to negotiate between detective and criminal, but also between Quebec and Ontario.

These liminal affordances are further complicated when Dougherty faces his darker tendencies more fully, and through a gendered lens. After two novels in which virtually all cops are represented as white, cisgender males, the third novel partners Dougherty with Sergeant Legault, a female Longueil cop whose gender limits her opportunities within the police system far more than Dougherty's bicultural identity limits his. Working with Legault highlights for Dougherty that his usual method of intimidating witnesses and suspects lacks not only finesse but possibly also morality and efficacy. When Legault is able to persuade Louise Tremblay, an abused woman, to find out about her abuser's whereabouts, Dougherty is impressed: "You really did get through to her," he says. To which Legault replies, with implicit criticism, "Well, I didn't punch her" (254). Legault makes her critique more explicit later, when Louise misses a scheduled meeting:

> "I practically threatened her," Legault said. "I made her go looking for him, she didn't want to."
> "It's what we do."
> "It's what you do."
> Dougherty said, "Watch it."
> "You're just a thug."
> She turned and started walking down the hall to the elevator.
> *(289–90)*

This becomes a moment of revelation for Dougherty. When Legault later attempts to apologize for her insult, Dougherty acknowledges that he *has* been a thug who has allowed his desires for solutions, promotions, and a more general sense of authority to compromise his integrity. It is with this self-knowledge—and specifically this acknowledgment that he has acted badly and will attempt to do better in the future—that Dougherty reaches the end of his short series.

Conclusion

By setting the Eddie Dougherty series in the Montreal of the 1970s and by telling the city's most resonant stories through the lens of the police procedural, McFetridge offers a nuanced perspective on Quebec's place in Canada that takes advantage of temporal distance to engage readers in either a history lesson or a fresh new look at an important historical moment. Performing cultural analysis that may perhaps only be conducted and consumed in hindsight, with the full knowledge of the Quiet Revolution, the October Crisis, and the two failed referenda on Quebec sovereignty, McFetridge creates a character with much hopeful potential in managing tensions between French and English Canada. As a bicultural Canadian, Eddie Dougherty—like McFetridge, like me, and like many other Canadians—stands as a clear symbol that Canada's "two solitudes" can, must, and to some extent have been overcome. Playing up Dougherty's liminality in the fashion of detective fiction—on terms of cultural knowledge, professional standing, and even ethical stances—McFetridge effectively uses the police procedural to explore retroactively a crucial and sometimes overlooked period of Canadian history.

McFetridge also ends the series on the note of optimism we will see in most of the Canadian crime fiction in this volume. *One or the Other* concludes with Carpentier telling Dougherty that his promotion to homicide detective is imminent. As he drives home to tell his fiancée Judy McIntyre, whom he met in the second novel of the series, Dougherty realizes that he and Judy have developed a good routine of late, and he is satisfied with what the twenty-first-century reader might term his work/life balance:

> They were going to be married.
> He had no idea what he'd say to her.
> But when he walked into the apartment and saw Judy sitting at the dining room table eating breakfast he knew it would be okay.
> *(391)*

3
GILES BLUNT AND THE CANADIAN NORTH

Canada has a complicated relationship with its North. As Garry Sherbert argues in explaining Canada's lack of a unified national identity, a "kind of ambivalence in Canadian identity arises from the manner in which Canada treats its northern territories as both frontier and homeland" (12). In his influential 1997 account of various key elements of Canadian national identity, Daniel Francis explains that Canadians have an image of themselves as a Northern people, drawn to what he calls "the hockey version of history," where "Canada has always been a superpower, and its citizens all enjoyed an idyllic childhood playing on frozen ponds and dreaming of a career in the NHL" (168). For Francis, the North has served in the Canadian imaginary as a "source of spiritual strength" (170), a kind of pristine space to colonizers who treated it as if it was always devoid of people, and that has thus come to represent both a storied European past (complete with the romantic figure of the *coureurs des bois* [early French Canadian fur traders]) and a possible utopian future of stillness, beauty, and communion with the land. Francis closes his chapter on the North with a sobering (and, it turns out, prescient) statement: "As the North gains its own voice, and ceases to be exclusively a place about which people in the south fantasize, the master narrative will have to change to accommodate it" (171). A national motto is not exactly a master narrative, but we do see a clear articulation of Francis's insight in recent discussions of Canada's official motto, "From sea to sea," referring to the stretch of Canada's land from the Pacific Ocean to the Atlantic. The twenty-first century has seen proliferating discussion of a new motto that would include the Arctic Ocean, with its increased economic importance in the face of global

DOI: 10.4324/9781003125242-4

climate change. Indeed, the proposed expanded motto, "From sea to sea to sea," is now appearing in official speeches and texts.

At the same time, the Canadian North remains remarkably separate from—and not especially accessible to—the rest of Canada. In a 2016 *Maclean's* article, Scott Gilmore (a journalist married to Canada's Minister of the Environment) asserts: "Canada is not a proud northern nation. Its Arctic is undefended, undeveloped, and socially fraught." Gilmore provides much evidence for his claim, and challenges the federal government to attend to its Arctic regions as do those of other Arctic nations, citing a Finnish economist who finds that "the Canadian Arctic makes up approximately one-quarter of the circumpolar region, yet its production there accounts for less than 2% of that entire region's aggregate economy" (Gilmore). One might argue that the success or failure of the Canadian North is not to be measured only in economic terms, but might also be measured by the creation in 1999 of a third northern territory, Nunavut, that is governed—by consensus—entirely by First Nations people. For better or worse, the place of the North within Canada's national identity has always been—and promises to continue to be for some time at least—a matter of some contention.

My favorite fact about myself is that I was born in South Porcupine, Ontario. This tiny municipality is purportedly so named after a nearby island shaped like a porcupine, but I've always thought, whimsically, that the porcupine—an unofficial symbol of the American Libertarian Party— is also the perfect emblem for Canada's Near North. The Far North, sometimes called simply the North, refers to the part of Canada above the 60th parallel that includes the three territories and the northern portions of Quebec and Labrador. The Near North is the region containing North Bay, Ontario (whose motto is "Gateway to the North") and surroundings, a large geographic area marked by its lack of deciduous trees. With a population density between that of the Far North and of Southern Ontario, the Near North attempts to capture the narrative and perhaps spiritual power of the North, but is easily accessible by road and train, and offers many organized summer and winter activities to showcase the natural beauty of its coniferous forests and lakes. The porcupine belongs to the Near North: hardy, slow-moving, not aggressive, but perfectly capable of self-defense. And also, perhaps, a bit outlandish. The Near North revels in the outlandish, with a plethora of giant roadside attractions appearing in thousands of Canadian photo albums, including a giant cow (New Liskeard), bison (Earlton), goose (Wawa), and nickel (Sudbury), alongside charming road signs like "Latchford, The Best Little Town by a Dam Site." While this region takes pleasure—and pride—in its unconventionalities and its resilience in the face of a challenging climate, it is also an important site of some of the socio-political tensions that shape Canadian identity. In his John Cardinal series (2000–2012), Giles Blunt captures the cold beauty of the Canadian North as well as some of the complexities and eccentricities of its peoples.

The title of the first John Cardinal novel, *Forty Words for Sorrow* (2000), evokes the (questionable) claim attributed to anthropologist Frank Boaz that the Inuit language has dozens of words for snow. Boaz's claim, widely repeated in the popular imagination even as it is challenged by anthropologists and linguists, exoticizes northern First Nations people, suggesting they have such a distinct relationship with the landscape that their language provides a granularity about winter weather conditions that would seem excessive by Indo-European linguistic standards. Cardinal, a police detective, thinks about Boaz's popularized notion as he is notifying the mother of a murdered child that her daughter's body has been found:

> Eskimos, it is said, have forty different words for snow. Never mind about snow, Cardinal mused, what people really need is forty words for sorrow. *Grief. Heartbreak. Desolation.* They were not enough, not for this childless mother in her empty house.
>
> (37)

Even as he processes his own guilt and inadequacy for not finding Katie Pine before she was killed, Cardinal reflects on the insufficiency of language for expressing trauma—not only the personal trauma of a mother who has lost a child, but also the cultural trauma of Canada's First Nations people and the subtle ways this trauma has been obscured through anthropological othering as well as in everyday life.

Katie's last name—Pine—evokes a moment of rupture in the relationship between Canada's French, English, and Indigenous people: the Oka Crisis of 1990. Although North Bay, Ontario is several hundred kilometers from Oka, Quebec, the relationships Blunt explores might be understood by looking at the tensions that dominated national news in 1990. I was in high school at the time, and I remember well the strong emotions that surrounded the crisis. For some, Oka was a site where a months-long road barricade over a golf course was creating unprecedented havoc with traffic in two small First Nations villages and eventually in Montreal, so protestors should be dealt with swiftly and decisively by the federal government, since Quebec's provincial police force, la Sûreté du Québec, was clearly not handling the situation. For others, the Oka Crisis was a predictable result of centuries of tensions between settler-invaders and Indigenous people, and the protests publicized an issue at the heart of Canada's national identity. Officially, the Oka Crisis lasted 78 days (July

11–September 26, 1990), included the deployment of approximately 2,000 regular police and 4,500 soldiers, and resulted in one or two fatalities (there is debate about whether a fatality due to heart failure should be attributed to the conflict) and over 100 people wounded. Culturally, it has had more lasting resonances as French–Canadians, English-Canadians, and Indigenous peoples have discussed the issues raised by what started out as a relatively small (30-person) protest and ended up mobilizing thousands of activists and hundreds of armed warriors among Indigenous and other allies around Canada and even the United States.

Blunt's Katie Pine would remind many Canadian readers of The Pines, the area at the center of the land dispute that became the Oka Crisis. The territory known as The Pines since the 1880s was assigned to the Kanienkehaka (known in English as the Mohawks) in 1721 and included cattle pasture, a forest, and an Indigenous cemetery. The land was disputed many times in Canada's early history, with treaties/agreements/disputes between the Kanienkehaka and the French, the British, and eventually the government of Canada. As early as 1869, violence erupted around this land when a small Indigenous group attacked the French seminary established there in the mid-nineteenth century, a stand-off ended with force by local authorities. Kanienkehaka people protested again in 1936 when the seminary sold the territory, and in 1959 when Oka approved the development for a nine-hole golf course adjacent to The Pines (now only 6 square kilometers from the original 165). A court case about the land occurred in 1989, and in 1990, The Pines was adjudicated to the town of Oka, which advanced a plan to clear it for the construction of new condos as well as an expansion of the golf course to 18 holes. The protests that followed began with a small barricade in March 1990 and reached crisis proportions by July. I recall well the astonished glee of teens like myself when we saw news headlines of underdog success represented by police cars repurposed as part of the barricade. I wasn't aware until much later of the suffering of Indigenous peoples in Oka and the neighboring town of Kahnawake, who had their supply lines cut and were faced with the sight of burning Mohawk warrior effigies and signs saying "Indians Not Welcome" in nearby communities. Documentary filmmaker Tracey Deer tells a devastating story of her own experience as a child during the crisis, including the day Montrealers threw rocks at a caravan of Indigenous women, children, and elders being evacuated from the crisis zone, and the trauma that recurred in filming a reenactment of the scene years later (Schneller). The crisis has become a subject for many aesthetic works, and in her excellent study of such artistic endeavors, cultural critic Isabelle St-Amand concludes that "the siege maintained by Mohawk people against police and the military reminds us that Canada as we know it is built on the marginalization, delegitimization, and, very often, interdiction of Indigenous forms of knowledge and expression" (19).

Blunt's icy crime scenes and intricate detective bureaucracy embody both the myth of the Canadian North and its darker realities. In her analysis of Blunt's *The Delicate Storm*, Manina Jones notes that the developing romantic relationship between the two main detective characters—John Cardinal and Lise Delorme—functions similarly to the dynamic in Hugh MacLennan's classic *Two Solitudes* when the personal attraction between the French-Canadian and English-Canadian detectives is "associated in the novel with what amounts to a broader desire to unite with the national other" ("Northern" 93). Indeed, *The Delicate Storm* confronts head-on the historical legacy of French–English tensions as they played out in the summer of 1970 and during the October Crisis, doing some of the same work of cultural analysis as John McFetridge's Eddie Dougherty series, as the police procedural opens up an avenue to place a historical moment in context vis-à-vis the present. But Blunt goes much further than an exploration of tensions between French and English Canada against the backdrop of the Near North. Deploying the conventions of the police procedural to create enormous stress in a small fictional northern Ontario city—Algonquin Bay, a thinly disguised version of Blunt's native North Bay—Blunt narrates the nuanced legacy of the treatment of First Nations peoples in Canada as well as fears of American hegemony, using a contamination and containment model of detection that has its roots in the American dime novels but that translates perfectly onto a twenty-first-century Canadian cultural landscape.

Confronting the Gorgeous, Perilous, Almost Supernatural North

In her reading of the Cardinal series, Manina Jones studies the novels as well as the television adaptation to argue compellingly for reading these texts as a seemingly oxymoronic "Canadian Noir." For Jones, "the dark dimensions of Canada's colonial past find their way into the crime genre's somber aesthetic, with its focus on a morally tainted hero, preoccupation with seemingly irrational violence, and fixation on unresolved past injustices" ("Canadian" 281). Indeed, the Blunt series checks all these boxes, leaving the reader somewhat unsettled at the conclusion of each novel, as Jones explores in her analysis of *Forty Words* ("Canadian Noir") and of *The Delicate Storm* ("Northern Procedures"). That unsettled reader response may be disturbing, but it also presages the possibility of hope. I believe that Blunt draws upon the conventions of Nordic Noir and also engages some of the aesthetic dimensions of speculative fiction—an umbrella term that includes science fiction, fantasy, utopia, dystopia, and apocalyptic literature—to flesh out and provide some hopeful momentum in his nuanced portrayal of the Canadian North, past, present, and future.

Anyone who has lived in Canada's Near North knows the unforgiving—and almost surreal—beauty of its winters. In *Forty Words*, Blunt draws upon iconography from science fiction to establish, descriptively and viscerally, the contradictions inherent in this setting. *Forty Words* compares the North to the moon, with the cold creating barriers between the detectives and the crime scene: "Cardinal and the others gathered on the ice like a lunar landing party, clumsy in their calf-high boots, their plump down coats" (5). The eight people at the crime scene—the coroner, several Algonquin Bay detectives, and an OPP (Ontario Provincial Police) representative who grew up on the reservation from which Katie Pine disappeared—trek out onto the thick ice of the lake to examine the body reported by kids playing. Dr. Barnhouse undertakes a formal description of the scene and its remains, but he cannot maintain his usually professional tone:

> "Christ," he said. "Just a child." Cardinal thought he heard a tremor in Barnhouse's voice; he would not have trusted his own. It wasn't just the deterioration—all of them had seen worse: victims of hunting accidents, drowning victims—it was that the remains were preserved in a perfect rectangle of ice perhaps eight inches thick.
>
> *(8)*

The extreme cold of Northern Ontario, which effaces the individual identities of the detectives by casting them as carefully bundled humans with no distinguishing features, not even gender or ethnicity, also acts to preserve the record of a heinous crime that raises the unnarratable pain requiring 40 synonyms as well as the rift between the fictionalized city of Algonquin Bay and the First Nations reservation at its outskirts.

The Delicate Storm creates an even more complex crime scene using tropes from fantasy rather than science fiction. When the body of Winter Cates, an attractive young female doctor, is found in the woods the day after a major ice storm, the description of the scene is focalized through the usually unromantic, pragmatic perspective of Lise Delorme:

> What Delorme had never seen, in all her years of police work, was a death scene as beautiful. She and Szelagy and the others stood at the edge of a scene from a fairy tale. All around them the woods shimmered as if the trees were made of jewellery. There was no sound but the click of branches, and from farther off the buzz of a snowmobile. Sunlight bounced off every surface, making the scene more appropriate for a tale

of magic, rather than a tragedy, the kind of tale in which statues come to life.

(186–7)

The magic of the weather conditions suffuses even the remains that the police have come to examine: "It was as if she [the murder victim] were under a spell—the victim of a jealous wizard, a wicked witch" (187). The North, then, is constructed as a place whose transformation by the cold evokes the supernatural. The crime scene is "beautiful" and "shimmer[ing]," the ice that makes it treacherous for the detectives to access the site also providing a magical sheen. In this scene, Delorme processes the murder of a beautiful young woman through the lens of fairy tale, as if magic, albeit dark magic, must be at play, since it is unnatural—or even supernatural—for someone to take a life in the midst of such a sublimely beautiful setting.

The cold, icy, eerily gorgeous descriptions of the crime scenes of the first two novels of the John Cardinal series set up the tensions that traverse Blunt's work. The final novel of the series, *Until the Night*, provides a culminating exploration of the third sea in Canada's "from sea to sea to sea" motto. This novel moves between two narrative strands: Cardinal and Delorme's investigation of a serial killer and a diary called "The Blue Notebook." The serial killer here uses the North as a weapon, kidnapping women, dressing them in high-quality winter gear and providing warm food and beverages in a thermos, and then binding them in an isolated location in Northern Canada so that they slowly freeze to death. Cardinal and Delorme's inquiry into this unusual and sadistic murder method is juxtaposed with an exploration of their changing relationship. After the tragic murder of Cardinal's wife in the previous novel, the two partners have become close friends and are now at the cusp of beginning a romantic relationship, a move fraught with personal anxieties for both of them. Delorme is becoming increasingly frustrated with her position as the only woman in the department where she is "automatically assigned all the sexual assaults and all the battered wife cases, and she [is] frankly sick of them" (20). As she considers dating her long-time detective partner, a man whose integrity she has long admired, Delorme is drawn to explore her darker self and engages in more adventurous—and dangerous—sexual activities. The heat of the erotic, both in Delorme's forays into a Montreal sex club and in the potential consummation of the long-developed loving relationship between the two, is in sharp contrast to the visceral cold of the murder investigation.

The Blue Notebook sections detail Karson Durie's experience as a researcher on the fictional Arcosaur project, capturing the physical and psychological perils of Northern exploration as well as the darkness of both human indifference and cruelty. As Durie writes early in the diary, the threat of mental illness is always present in the inhospitable climate of the North despite the technological innovations that allow scientific projects to flourish: "In that white desert, the only thing worse than a crack opening up beneath your feet is a crack opening up in the psyche of the man next to you" (52–3). Durie is eventually to experience both these traumas: a coworker loses touch with reality, and a terrifying shift in the ice swallows up the high-tech shelters that are essential for survival in the northern landscape that is mimicking climactic conditions on the moon. From there, Durie's story delves into the depths of human depravity. Traveling on foot for hours in an attempt to find shelter, Durie and Rebecca, the woman he loves, are pushed to the very limit of human endurance. Just as Rebecca seems fated to release her now-tenuous hold on life, Durie sees three men in the distance; he sends up their last flare and one of the men looks his way before walking away, leaving Rebecca to perish before Durie is rescued shortly thereafter. It is Durie who is, years later, kidnapping women (specifically the wives and daughters of the three men who ignored him and Rebecca) and leaving them to die of exposure on the coldest days of the year in Algonquin Bay and nearby Near North locations. The men who ignored imperiled fellow humans, it turns out, were motivated by horrifying corruption. They were in that location only because the lunar rover they were testing in the Arctic had a navigational flaw; if they revealed their location, the flaw would become public and their rover would not be chosen for an upcoming lunar mission. The quickly made decision to leave Rebecca to die and thus obscure the test data ends up sinking the project anyway, since the men are no longer able to work together. It also leads, years later, to peril for their wives and daughters when Durie kidnaps them and leaves them to die in the cold.

Durie's decision to become a serial killer is a dispassionate one that figures a nuanced relationship between human and environment. With Rebecca dead, Durie is wrongly convicted of murdering a fellow Arcosaur researcher; instead of seeking early release for good behavior, which would involve a parole officer, Durie serves the full 18 years of his sentence so that his release is unfettered. He then operationalizes his meticulous plan to track, kidnap, and leave to die the women associated with the men who abandoned Rebecca and him in their time of need. When Durie speaks with the father of his final kidnap victim, he is calm and dispassionate:

"I don't hate her. I don't even hate you. I'm indifferent. Just like you were. You were indifferent to a man and woman who were dying at your feet. Indifferent as the Crusoe Glacier, the Piper Ridge, the Steacey Ice

Cap. It's the natural state. The remarkable thing is that there was ever in the history of mankind an instance of anyone who *wasn't* indifferent."
(286)

Given his horrifying experience, which Blunt presents to the reader through an especially compelling first-person journaling perspective, Durie's dark analysis of human nature appears to be well-founded. It is perhaps no surprise that Durie breaks the social contract; no matter how justified he may be in his dark philosophical practice, he must nonetheless be punished for his vengeful behavior within the genre of detective fiction.

Cardinal and Delorme are relieved of the burden of bringing Durie to justice by the very indifferent Nature that Durie uses as an analogy for understanding the most deplorable of human behavior. After a chase through a frozen landscape, Cardinal is closest to Durie when he is punished by Nature:

> The ice gave way beneath him [Durie] and he vanished. Cardinal crawled to the hole but could see nothing beyond shards of ice. Water like ink. He plunged his arm in up to the shoulder and the pain made him shout. He rolled back from the edge, gasping.
> Durie appeared under the ice a short distance away. The surface was not perfectly clear, but the face, stunned and incredulous, was vivid, as were the gloved hands that pressed so uselessly against the ice.
> (*Until* 295)

Despite his calculations—perhaps cold and passionate at once—about the inherent indifference of nature, both ecological and human, Durie nonetheless attempts to prevent his fate by pressing against the ice with a surprised look on his face. This scene, like the entire series, speaks to the human instinct for survival, even in the face of personal heartbreak and devastating sociocultural analysis. Cardinal comes very close to being drawn under the ice with the killer, embodying the anxiety about a detective coming too close to a criminal that underlies much crime fiction.

This scene—the closing encounter of detective and criminal in the series—reprises the dynamic from the first novel. In *Forty Words for Sorrow*, Katie Pine's killer is also identified by police, but punished by the North. This killer, Fraser, enters into hand-to-hand combat with Cardinal, and the van in which they are fighting tilts and plummets into a frozen lake. Cardinal reacts to the setting in a knowledgeable way:

> He [Cardinal] jumped free, keeping arms outflung even as his legs plunged through the ice. Cold sucked the breath out of his lungs. Then

Fraser's face at the van's door. His mouth a black O, as the ice gave way under the last wheel, the water crashed in on him, and the rest of the van slipped into the black hole.

(332)

The imagery around Fraser's death assigns an almost uncanny intentionality to Nature, as the "black O" of Fraser's mouth is replaced by the "black hole" of the frozen lake that will claim his life. As Blunt deploys the Nordic Noir conventions that link the morally tainted hero to the darkness of his northern landscape, he also makes space to explore the complex past of Canada's fraught relationship with its Indigenous peoples as they play out in cultural borderlands like those found in northern Ontario.

Beyond the Two Solitudes

While the developing relationship between John Cardinal and Lise Delorme can be read as a complex but ultimately hopeful benchmark for English–French relations in the style of MacLennan's *Two Solitudes* (Jones "Northern" 93), the cultural duality thus represented is regularly complicated by the presence of a third and even more fraught solitude—that of the First Nations peoples who inhabited the land that became modern Canada in 1867 for thousands of years before that. Indeed, Algonquin Bay includes a Chippewa Reserve that is described in chilling terms. Blunt's third-person narrator always goes into present tense to describe setting, a move that is particularly poignant when it comes to the reservation: "There are no signs to Chippewa Reserve, no gates; the Ojibwa have suffered so much at the hand of the white man that to lock the door against him now would be pointless" (33). The dispassionate, present-tense voice of the narrator evokes both history and the immediacy of the injustice that underlies settler-colonial relations before the focalization returns to Cardinal. One of Cardinal's first girlfriends lived on the Chippewa Reserve, we are told, and Cardinal had been surprised by how similar it was to any other lower middle-class Canadian neighborhood. Indeed, for Cardinal,

> The only visible difference from any other part of Algonquin Bay was, well, the place was full of Indians, a people who for the most part moved through Canadian society—or rather, alongside it—as silent and invisible as ghosts.

(33)

This characterization of First Nations silence just ten years after the Oka Crisis was front-page news for several months is telling. The narrative of

Canada's Indigenous people as mostly unseen and unheard is explored throughout the series as various crimes cause Cardinal, Delorme, and other police presences to walk over the invisible line between the Reserve and the rest of Algonquin Bay.

The reader is introduced to the intricate lines of cultural power and production early in the first novel of the series when Cardinal sits in the office of his superior, Detective Sergeant Don Dyson, seeking additional resources for the investigation into the murder of the Chippewa child Katie Pine. In this four-page scene, the reader gets a running mental commentary of Cardinal's sociocultural analysis of the various power dynamics at play in Algonquin Bay. When Dyson reminds Cardinal that the department had limited ability to investigate Katie Pine's disappearance before her body was found, Cardinal's interior monologue is scathing:

> Well yes, Cardinal thought, Katie Pine's disappearance had been a mystery. Sorry—I had a fantasy that policemen were occasionally called upon to *solve* mysteries, even in Algonquin Bay. Of course the girl was Native, and we all know how irresponsible *those* people can be.
> *(19)*

By defining himself mentally as a cop who is just as committed to solving the disappearance of a Native child as a white one, Cardinal is also aligning himself against Dyson, who is represented as a far more legible sign of law and order (as evidenced by the meticulous order of his desk) than is his subordinate:

> "Let's face it," Dyson said, inserting his letter opener precisely into a small scabbard and laying it neatly beside a ruler. "The girl was Indian, too. I like Indians, I really do, there's a calmness about them that's practically supernatural. They tend to be good-natured and they're extraordinarily fond of children, and I'd be the first to say Jerry Commanda was a first-rate officer, but there's no point pretending they're just like you and me."
> "God, no," said Cardinal, and he meant it. "Different people entirely."
> *(19)*

Dyson's racism here will be familiar to many readers: he would not see himself as racist and would doubtless protest that seeing First Nations peoples as "practically supernatural" is a compliment that ties them to the land. Cardinal's protest of his boss's—and by extension the police force's—racism is at once silent and resounding. By agreeing with Dyson on the surface, Cardinal demonstrates that he has the social skills to get along within his department. By showing Cardinal's angry thoughts, Blunt assures his readers that his main character regularly performs a more nuanced reading of Canadian identities than do most of his fellow detectives.

In the first novel, two First Nations characters present contrasting views on the present and potential future of white-Chippewa relations. Dorothy Pine, the mother of the murdered child, suggests an impenetrable wall between two cultures. During the weeks Cardinal has looked exhaustively for her missing daughter, their relationship has never moved past the strain of their cultural histories:

> [Cardinal] had hoped that Dorothy Pine would come to trust him. She never did. For the first two weeks, she telephoned daily, not only identifying herself every time but explaining why she was calling, "I was just wondering if you found my daughter, Katharine Pine."
>
> *(37)*

Months later, when Cardinal rings Katie's mother's doorbell, his finger shaking, the distance between them is even greater:

> "Okay," she said, when he told her Katie's body had been found. Just the one word, "Okay," and she started to shut the door. Case closed. Her only child was dead. Cops—let alone white cops—could be of no assistance here.
>
> *(36)*

Cardinal's reading of Mrs. Pine's internal monologue is at once poignant and devastating. The reader knows that he has worked tirelessly on the Katie Pine case, facing professional consequences for far exceeding the resources Dyson has allocated. Not only is Dorothy unaware of his efforts, but they have been completely ineffective. Cardinal is impotent not only in bridging the divide between Algonquin Bay and the silent presence of the Chippewa Reserve but also in preventing the murder of a kidnapped child.

Jerry Commanda, a fellow police officer, presents a more hopeful figure in the possibility of healing the three distinct solitudes that mark the Canadian Near North. A liminal figure who easily moves between the Chippewa Reserve and the rest of Algonquin Bay, Commanda has hidden depths: "Jerry was extremely thin, almost frail-looking, a deceptive morphology because he also happened to be a four-time provincial kickboxing champion" (*Forty* 33). Cardinal never underestimates the First Nations cop. Indeed, he reflects on something McLeod, a close colleague, once told him about being partnered with Commanda: "had they lived two hundred years earlier, he [McLeod] would have probably turned on his ancestors and happily fought the white man at Jerry's side" (*Forty* 34). Jerry commands loyalty and friendship from his white colleagues, even when he leaves the Algonquin Bay Police Force to join the OPP, a provincial organization often caught up in jurisdictional tangles with the local authorities. As an OPP officer, Jerry chooses to work exclusively on reserves: "He got the same pay as the municipal police, except—a point on which he was as infuriatingly verbose as his race is said to be silent—he was exempt from income tax" (*Forty* 34). Jerry is a good cop who works tirelessly to improve the lot of Northern First Nations communities, but also the relationship between those communities and the white-dominated societies alongside which they live. At the same time, he draws attention to his tax-exempt status as a First Nations citizen of Canada, reminding white colleagues of the legacy of abuse between their ancestors as well as of the feeble reparations that have thus far been made.

The personal relationships between detectives representing three of Canada's solitudes—Cardinal as an English-Canadian, Delorme as a French-Canadian, and Commanda as a First Nations person—resonate with the larger question of cultural relationships within the Canadian North. Like most twenty-first-century police procedural writers, Blunt does not simply use the detective novel's ending to indicate resolution—of a national tension or even of a case. Indeed, in several novels, including *The Delicate Storm*, Cardinal is dissatisfied with the resolution, a dynamic common to police procedurals, which narrate an ongoing battle between criminals and detectives, and so do not often provide the kinds of happy— or at least complete—endings we might expect of descendants of Golden Age detective fiction like the cozy. The ongoing nature of conflict in the Cardinal series goes beyond the repetitions of crime and the associated sociocultural tensions that generate narrative energy in the procedural. Indeed, Blunt prefers to raise fraught relationships within Canadian cultural groups without providing a clearly artificial closure.

The Contamination and Containment of the Compromised Cop

In the John Cardinal series, Blunt draws upon a convention that goes back to American dime novels in creating a highly sympathetic detective figure who nonetheless embodies the model of containment and contamination that explains the appeal of American detective fiction and brings it to a Canadian context. In a move that presages Noir, early American detective fiction regularly uses the compromised detective as a central figure, generating narrative momentum by raising the anxiety that the detective might succumb to corruption and might even die (Bedore *Dime* 4-5). The twenty-first-century detective genre only rarely proffers detective death as a viable narrative move, but Blunt, like many Nordic Noir writers, explicitly constructs Cardinal as a morally compromised character.

Forty Words for Sorrow leans heavily on Lise Delorme to detail Cardinal's corruption. In this novel, Delorme is introduced as a cop who recently led a successful investigation into corruption in the Algonquin Bay mayor's office, so Cardinal fears she may be investigating him (which she is). She is a true believer in not only justice and procedure, but also in an image of Canadian policing that is to be somewhat tarnished as we move through the series:

> Delorme had grown up revering the Mounties ... They had negotiated treaties with the aboriginals, sent American raiders hightailing it back to Montana or whatever barbaric pit they had crawled out of, and established the rule of law before settlers had even had a chance to think about breaking it. The RCMP had become an icon of upstanding law enforcement around the world, a travel agent's dream.
>
> Delorme had bought the image wholesale; that's what images are for, after all.
>
> *(26)*

Delorme's enthusiastic faith in the traditions of the RCMP and the respect and heritage evoked by this national symbol seems to mark her as the opposite of the much more cynical Cardinal. And yet, the third-person narrator's sly aside—"that's what images are for, after all"—suggests that Delorme's worldview may no longer be as unnuanced as when she was first introduced to the Mounties.

Cardinal, on the other hand, is a man wracked by guilt at his one act of corruption as a police detective. Years earlier, anxiety-ridden when his bipolar wife first struggled with a prolonged bout of clinical depression, Cardinal stole money from a criminal who was going to jail. He is constantly haunted by his guilt:

> For a time Cardinal had told himself that's why he had done it, that his wife's insanity had broken him. But the Catholic in him, not to mention the cop, could never accept that. He gave himself no excuse.
>
> *(245)*

The reader might—and probably does—excuse a smart, dedicated, caring detective who has used the money he stole from a despicable man in order to obtain experimental medical treatment for his wife and to pay his daughter's university tuition. Indeed, the first few novels in the series play on the reader's emotional investments in the detective's moral conflict, confronting Cardinal first with danger to his reputation through police investigation and then with bodily danger when the criminal from whom he has stolen is released from prison and demands the return of his ill-gotten gains. The reader's likely forgiveness of Cardinal in the face of his otherwise enormous integrity and compassion is in contrast to Cardinal's own assessment: "Cardinal was a Catholic—a lapsed Catholic—and like all Catholics lapsed or devout, he retained an almost gleeful ability to accuse himself of sin, though not necessarily the sin he had actually committed" (*Forty* 15).

Cardinal is an evocative name for the central character of a Northern Canadian detective, suggesting three elements in tension within Canada's history: Cardinal is a common First Nations name, a highly placed leader within the Catholic Church, and an ordinary songbird native to North America. Indeed, Cardinal carries the inflated sense of guilt common to those of us raised in the Catholic tradition—and his lapsed faith, more cultural than religious, helps him to deal with the deaths of his father and, more tragically, his wife, but in a way typical of many twenty-first-century Catholics, whose solace comes more through community than spiritual comfort. The use of a First Nations surname for a character who identifies solely as white also suggests the intermingling of cultural and genetic material in the centuries of interactions between settler and Indigenous peoples, especially in the North. The evocation of a songbird recalls the importance of Nature, seen as much in small common creatures as in startling weather events in Canada's North.

Conclusion

Throughout the six-book John Cardinal series, Blunt uses tropes from the police procedural—infused with the dark, cold energy of Nordic North, as Manina Jones so aptly points out—to provide a satisfyingly complex investigation of Canada's tangled relationship with its North, touching upon the dark and ongoing history of oppression of First Nations peoples, the beautiful and unforgiving landscape, and its mythic/spiritual resonances. Despite the dark vision pursued in these novels, Blunt ends with characteristically Canadian hope. In *Until the Night*, the last novel of the series, the traumatized killer is reclaimed by the cold that he has weaponized, and the police are able to rescue his would-be final victim. The closing scene is between Cardinal and Delorme, when they go out to dinner to celebrate the successful conclusion of their case and they end up also professing their love for each other:

> "Kind of weird, isn't it," she said, "after all these years."
> "It certainly is. It's good, though."

"I definitely like it. But I have to say, I'm also scared, still. I mean, it's great. We love each other, but ..."
"Uh-oh," Cardinal said. "We love each other. Now what?"
"Exactly. Now what?"

(299–300, original ellipsis)

Although the "now what?" ending is on its surface an open invitation to imagine that the future for Cardinal and Delorme—as for English and French Canada, and even for Canada from sea to sea to sea—might go in any of a number of possible directions, the conclusion is clearly structured as a happy ending. For Blunt, confronting the North and respecting both its dark power and its almost supernatural beauty is a key move in grappling with Canada's settler-colonial legacy and its complicated but hopeful futures.

4
THOMAS KING AND THE LIMINAL INDIGENOUS DETECTIVE

In "Godzilla vs. Post-Colonial," a 1990 essay, Thomas King does a deep dive into the perils of considering Native literature through the lens of postcolonial theory. For King, such an approach is predicated on a progressive notion of literature that starts with "the advent of Europeans in North America" and that assumes that Native literature is fundamentally about "the struggle between guardian and ward" and thus cuts off Native writers from their precolonial traditions (185). King approaches the complex question of evaluating the affordances and challenges of postcolonial theory with his usual mix of tonal accessibility and philosophical complexity. The title of the essay itself is evocative and complicated. "Godzilla vs. Post-Colonial" evokes "Bambi Meets Godzilla" (often mistitled "Bambi vs. Godzilla"), a 1969 animated short by American-Canadian Marv Newland, then a film student. The 90-second film has a simple plot. Pastoral music plays as Bambi hangs out in a meadow during the lengthy opening credits (all roles are filled by Marv Newland except for the production of Marv Newland "by Mr. and Mrs. Newland"). As the credits end, Bambi is interrupted—and obliterated—by Godzilla's giant foot thoroughly squashing him, accompanied by a loud crashing chord. The words "the end" appear, followed by a single credit: "we gratefully acknowledge the city of Tokyo, for their help in obtaining Godzilla for this film." Godzilla's toe claws then retract and extend, ending the film. "Bambi meets Godzilla" ran as an opening feature in movie theaters for several years and has been viewed by millions. How do we read King's title's riff on this cartoon cult classic? One isn't sure if Godzilla even recognized that Bambi was in his way before stepping on the little deer. Is that how colonialism functioned? Also, Godzilla (the Colonial?) is moved from the second position (predator) to the first (victim). Is King suggesting that the Post-Colonial will obliterate the monster of the Colonial ... as long as whoever owns the Post-Colonial gives permission and obtains the Post-Colonial for the film?

Not exactly. King's essay title, like the essay itself and like much of his other writing, provides musings and images that deliberately evade straightforward readings. At the same time as it's hard to completely pin down, "Godzilla vs. Post-Colonial" is nonetheless an accessible and humorous essay, including a funny anecdote about the mismatch between King's height and his basketball skills as well as a charmingly casual statement of a counterargument he goes on to rebut: "A friend of mine cautioned me about this stridency and pointed out that postcolonial is a perfectly good term to use for that literature, which is, in fact, a reaction to the historical impositions of colonialization" (185). In the end, King leaves behind the conflict between Godzilla and the postcolonial and suggests a different, far more hopeful path forward. With a refreshing humility ("I am not a theorist," he repeats, 183, 184), King provides four terms I personally find very useful in considering Native literature in Canada. The "tribal" refers to literature produced and consumed within a tribe or community, in a Native language and with no intention of going outside that context. The "polemical" is concerned with clashes between Native and non-Native communities, and "chronicles the imposition of non-Native expectations and insistencies" as well as Native resistance to such (185). The "interfusional" focuses on the blending of oral and written literature.

The "associational," the fourth term, is perhaps most relevant to our analysis here of King's Thumps DreadfulWater detective series. On the surface, the associational seems very much at odds with the conventions of detective fiction. In King's lexicon, the associational mode focuses on the everyday, deliberately avoiding "the ubiquitous climaxes and resolutions that are so valued in non-Native literature," and focusing instead on a group rather than an individual, being "a fiction that de-values heroes and villains in favor of the members of a community, a fiction which eschews judgements and conclusions" (187). Detective fiction would appear to contrast with the associational on three grounds. First, detective fiction has traditionally been a literature of heroes and villains, pitting the detective (perhaps with sidekick) against the criminal, explicitly noting the exceptional nature of both detective and criminal. The police procedural has been open to a more communal approach to the detective hero, although Thumps DreadfulWater is no longer an official member of the police force, so the generic investments of King's story would be expected to tend towards the individual. Second, detective fiction is very much based on the climaxes and resolutions that King identifies as decidedly non-Native; after all, the precipitating event of a detective story is a murder, an emphatically climactic act that calls upon the detective genre to provide a resolution. Finally, detective fiction traditionally embraces judgments and conclusions rather than rejecting them, with the detective in some sense standing in for the reader and making discernments throughout the investigation with a final almost cliched judgment (guilty or innocent) at the conclusion.

Despite the apparent contradictions between associational Native literature and the detective genre, Thomas King produces a delightful hybridization of the two in his Thumps DreadfulWater series. Perhaps best known for his postmodern novel *Green Grass, Running Water* (1993), Thomas King is a truly liminal writer. A dual citizen of Canada and the United States, King is the son of a Cherokee father and a Greek/Swiss mother. A writer of fiction and nonfiction, across and especially in between genres, King has also taken on many other roles (filmmaker, photographer, performer, even briefly, politician) while constantly challenging conventions—political, cultural, and aesthetic. King's recent foray into detective fiction brings us Thumps DreadfulWater, which embodies the notion of contemporary Canadian culture grappling with the legacy of colonial/Indigenous encounters in a series currently at seven novels (2002–present). Thumps, a former California homicide detective, ends up in the fictionalized town of Chinook, Montana trying to make a living as an artistic photographer while also trying to escape the ghosts of his past—the unsolved murders of his lover and her daughter. Despite the horror and grief inherent in Thumps' situation, King nonetheless uses humor as a rhetorical structure to manage, interrogate, and even imagine a better future for Thumps and the legacy of cultural conflicts and abuses he represents. The Thumps DreadfulWater series explores the trickster detective as a liminal, critical, and yet fundamentally optimistic figure in understanding Canada's past, present, and future trajectory around Indigenous rights and national identity.

No Heroes or Villains

On the face of it, detective fiction is a rather formulaic genre, containing the dual narrative—the story in the present of a detective uncovering the story of a crime in the past—that Tzvetan Todorov identified in his work of classic genre fiction criticism, *The Poetics of Prose* (1971). It also has recurring roles—the detective, the criminal, the victim, and the falsely accused suspect—as John Cawelti notes in his equally classic analysis of "formula stories" (1976). Because of its highly identifiable recurring formal structure, detective fiction has served as a rich playground for exactly the kind of postmodern play Thomas King delights readers with in *Green Grass, Running Water*, which includes genre hybridity, gender-bending, hero-sidekick switching, etc. From E.C. Bently's *Trent's Last Case* (1913) through Paul Auster's *The New York Trilogy* (1987), the conventions of detective fiction have been raised only to be subverted in a small but highly acclaimed body of postmodern works that frustrate and satisfy at once. When Thomas King characterizes associational Native literature as that which "de-values heroes and villains in favor of the community," one might imagine associational detective fiction as falling within the postmodern project, deliberately interrogating the social construction of roles like hero and villain—detective and criminal—in order to subvert the categories and the characters who appear to occupy them. It would be easy to imagine the use of postmodern detective fiction as an incisive critique of North American settler colonialism in which the singular crime that propels each novel stands in for the much larger historical crimes committed against Indigenous peoples. King, however, generally eschews direct criticism of the past, instead shrouding critique in postmodern play. Within the Thumps DreadfulWater series, he approaches the "devalu[ing] of heroes and villains" not by subverting those central roles, but rather by treating them with humor and by valuing the community.

The Thumps DreadfulWater novels are suffused with humor despite— or perhaps because of—the difficult subject matter they tackle. The humor resonates with the simultaneously critical and optimistic feeling of the writing. In an insightful article on the multiple functions of humor in First Nations artworks ranging from paintings to photographs to comedy skits, Kahente Horn-Miller traces several rhetorical functions of laughter for Kanienkehaka (known as Mohawk in English) people. Some will be familiar: laughter promotes community and well-being, and it can be used as a disruptive tactic against oppression (signaling either happiness and belonging or anger and resistance). Horn-Miller goes deeper in analyzing humor specifically in a First Nations context, arguing:

> For First Nations cultures and more specifically the Kanienkehaka people, humor serves to turn colonization on its back exposing its fleshy underside .... Beyond exercising the belly muscles, humor serves as a survival mechanism meant to bring about balance in an unbalanced world.
>
> *(22)*

The notion of balance is central to Thumps' worldview, and also feeds into his preference not to be a central hero even of his own narrative.

Thumps is a reluctant detective. Although we know he was once a professional detective and he undertakes one solo investigation between books, his detective work is narrated only when it unfolds as part of a community effort. He has settled in Chinook as a fine-arts photographer. When difficult cases arise—as they often do—Sheriff Benjamin (Duke) Hockney calls upon Thumps to help out, unofficially or as a deputy. For Thumps, these cases seem not to define him. As a middle-aged man actively grieving the loss of his lover and her young daughter to a serial killer he could not identify, Thumps focuses on the many small struggles he experiences, and these daily irritants are described in some detail. His life is highly routine-oriented, as he eats breakfast at Al's Diner, feeds his cat Freeway (or thinks about Freeway during the long period in which she is missing), chats with various townspeople, and regularly daydreams about untroubled sleep. With this focus on the routine matters of everyday life that usually get left out of novels—eating, sleeping, picking up prescriptions—King creates both humor and realism. In her analysis of *Green Grass, Running Water*, Hannah Green argues that King relies on repetition in bringing oral storytelling into his writing, and in so doing he "creates a future space in which the reader synthesizes new meanings and interpretations" (22–3). This is equally true in the Thumps DreadfulWater series, where repetition allows readers to imagine Thumps' interactions with each of the charming, memorable, and often outlandish people of Chinook.

Sheriff Benjamin "Duke" Hockney is repetitively connected to John Wayne through the eventual use of simply "Duke" as his moniker. The Duke provides an excellent example of King's tendency to present readers with complex symbols to unravel, perhaps always a little uncertainly. John Wayne (Marion Robert Morrison, 1907–1979) is a well-known conservative and possible white supremacist whose movie career was built on highly problematic cowboy vs. Indian stories. Is the reader to connect Chinook's sheriff with such a fraught public figure? For Thumps, the answer is no. As is explained the first time Hockney appears, it is his wife who gave him his nickname because of his resemblance to the famous actor:

> Thumps had to admit that Hockney did look a little like John Wayne. He even sounded like him when he talked, and Thumps wondered whether the sheriff had always talked this way or whether he had taken on the slow, easy drawl to please his wife.
>
> *(42–3)*

The possibility that Hockney is committed to pleasing his wife takes the sting out of the notion of a John-Wayne-style masculinity and also connects him to Thumps, who regularly muses to himself and discusses with friends ideas for ways to do nice things for his on-again off-again girlfriend, Claire Merchant.

While Hockney is easy to remember because of his repeated connection to a movie star, Beth Mooney, the town's only doctor and therefore coroner, is made memorable by the physical space she inhabits, which incorporates realism and humor. When Thumps approaches her three-story dwelling, he is filled with dread, for he knows that when he presses Beth's intercom button, he will hear one of three things: "second floor" would indicate that Beth will see him in the lovely residence she shares with her colorful lesbian lover, Ora Mae; "first floor," however, would point him to Beth's doctor's office, where she is likely to subject him to necessary but deeply undesired medical examinations or procedures; or, even more terrifyingly, "basement" would reveal that Beth is in the town morgue, where she always assumes that Thumps has the physical and emotional fortitude to witness an autopsy. Thumps' interactions with Beth are filled with gentle humor, as the third-person narrator—never dispassionate in a Thumps DreadfulWater novel—subtly indicates sympathy with Thumps' fear of Beth's basement. "Don't be a baby," Beth scoffs at Thumps in *DreadfulWater Shows Up*. " 'It's a dead body, not a snake.' Thumps wasn't sure what a dead body and a snake had to do with each other, but all things considered, he was more inclined towards the snake" (125).

Thumps is equally afraid of Chintak Rawat, the town pharmacist who moved to Chinook "straight from Toronto" (*Cold* 54) and who serves as evidence not only of the ethnic biases prevalent in the United States but also of the most effective means for combatting them. "At first, folks in Chinook had been cold to Rawat," we learn in *Cold Skies*,

> and rather than support a local business, they drove to the big-box stores in Great Falls and Helena to get their drugs. But then the price of gas had gone up and economics had proved to be more powerful than prejudice.
>
> *(54)*

Rawat simply waits out the reality of "cultural diversity being an alien concept in this part of the civilized world" (*Malice* 126). He is polite, knowledgeable, and professional. His personal tagline speaks to both deference and good judgement as he offers pharmaceutical advice that is helpful and uncomfortable, followed quickly by: "I shall say no more about it" (*Cold* 216, *Malice* 126, and elsewhere). Readers soon learn that it is the things Rawat "shall say no more about" that most often invite reader engagement, sympathy, and even perhaps activism. At the same time, Rawat cheerfully shares his liberal perspectives, clearly shaped by his life experiences in Canada. When Thumps arrives at the pharmacy with a prescription for a diabetes kit, Rawat shocks him with the cost of the lifesaving medication. When Thumps says that people like himself without drug plans could die from the cost of diabetes, Rawat opines liberally: "Yes,' said Rawat. 'Many people do [die]. It's unfortunate you do not live in Canada. In Canada, many of these costs are covered" (*Cold* 217).

In a later conversation about the price of drugs, Rawat becomes even more political, referencing the political differences between Canada and the United States that come up frequently in King novels:

> Thumps looked at the figure in disbelief. "What do I pay my taxes for?"
> "Bombs," said Rawat. "And missiles. You cannot keep the world safe with enlightened social programs and good health care."
>
> *(Obsidian 144)*

This transparent reference to the United States' military might and Canada's contrasting socialist agenda recalls contemporary news stories. *Obsidian* was published in 2020, shortly after Democratic presidential hopeful Bernie Sanders very publicly escorted a busload of American diabetics across the border between Michigan and Ontario to purchase insulin—a nonprescription drug in Canada—at one-tenth of the price they would pay in the United States. Sanders' arguments as well as his exposure of the health risks American diabetics face due to high insulin prices in the United States are put in the mouth of Rawat as he counsels Thumps on his options with his new diabetes diagnosis. King walks a fine line with this character, since Thumps, always the detective, listens to Rawat's opinions but does not respond with any kind of political comment.

Moses Blood is another colorful character to whom Thumps always listens carefully, often without a verbal response. Moses, the town's First Nations elder, is a study in contradictions who embodies a point Joanna Daxell makes in an early reading of the series. Noting that Thumps does not rely on spiritual knowledge in the tradition of many Native American detectives, Daxell argues that "King is not interested in teaching his reader about Native spirituality, but rather, he wants to show that Natives are part of contemporary America and that they are able to mediate the two worlds" (56). Moses makes this point far better than does somewhat technophobic Thumps. Although Moses often acts as a representative of the past, he also believes in contemporary technology, and is a skilled computer user as well as the owner of the largest television on the reserve. Daxell points to a compelling passage from the opening novel of the series, *Dreadfulwater Shows Up* (2002) that combines insight and humor. Thumps asks for Moses' advice and the old man reaches for his computer:

> "Some people are suspicious of computers because we didn't have them in the good old days."
> "Nobody went buffalo hunting with a laptop."
> "That's right," said Moses. "But it's best to be up-to-date. Even in the good old days, the smartest Indians were the ones who were up-to-date."
>
> *(184–5, cited in Daxell 56)*

With his ability to mediate seemingly conflicting epistemological frames and his always-welcoming catchphrase of "I've been expecting you," Moses regularly provides Thumps with a new way of looking at a problem. From simple yet profound statements like "Always hard to understand the present if you don't understand the past" (*Red Power* 123) to quietly humorous reminders like "when the women are talking, people need to listen" (*Cold* 285), Moses serves as a kind of wiseman figure without at all becoming a stock character. At the end of *The Red Power Mysteries*, a complex story in which the murders—one from the past and two from the present—force Thumps to confront old friends and colleagues who are far more politically active in fighting for First Nations rights than he is, Thumps buys a new coat with which to prepare for an active storm incoming from Canada:

> He considered driving over to Moses's place to see if the old man knew why people expected so much of themselves, and how it was a person could wind up with so little. Moses would probably make a pot of tea and tell him a story. And maybe that was it, maybe in the end a good story was the best anyone could do.
>
> *(499)*

The reader never finds out if Thumps ends up seeking out Moses's counsel, but we leave the novel knowing that Thumps is part of a community in which each member contributes vitally to the epistemological and ethical questions at the center of detective fiction.

Although the ethnic and cultural diversity of Thumps' community may seem at odds with the typical demographic make-up of a small American town in the mountain region, Chinook is presented as an "everytown." For example, when Thumps thinks about the different places he's lived, he realizes that he always ends up in small towns: "Central California, the Northwest Coast, the High Plains. Towns like Chinook. All of them, just like Chinook"

(*Malice* 151). This statement, late in the series, invites readers to look for and acknowledge the fascinating stories in the ordinary people they know, a point King makes explicitly in his essay collection, *The Truth About Stories* (2003). Each member of the Chinook community—simultaneously unique and ordinary—provides Thumps with a perspective that is helpful to his investigations, but also to his constant development as a dynamic character. In *Cold Skies*, the deep connections Thumps has made—almost against his will—are displayed by the concern of many townspeople as he experiences a health decline. In the opening pages of the novel, Thumps is asked about his health and encouraged to visit his doctor by such diverse characters as Al, the curmudgeonly female diner proprietor, Archie, the Greek bookstore owner, and Sheriff Duke Hockney, among others. Thumps muses about the indignities of small-town life in which everyone knows one's business even as the reader sees that it is these interpersonal connections that keep Thumps sane as well as make him an effective detective.

This model of community support is at odds with the individualistic nature of most hardboiled detection, a contrast that Jennifer Andrews and Priscilla L. Walton explore in their reading of the first two novels of the series and that King stresses in the fifth novel, *Obsidian*, when the characters explicitly refer to Robert B. Parker's classic hardboiled detective, Spenser. When Thumps returns to Chinook after a roadtrip to Northern California to unofficially reopen his investigation into the murders of his lover and her daughter, he takes some time before finally going to visit his sort-of girlfriend, Claire. Thumps arrives with an offering of take-out Chinese food:

> "But now that you're here with food," said Claire, "you're thinking that we should eat."
> "We'd be fools not to."
> "Robert Parker," said Claire. "The Spenser mysteries."
> "It worked for him."
> "So, I'm Susan?" Claire smiled with just the edges of her mouth. "and you're ... Pearl?"
> "Isn't Pearl the dog?"
>
> *(70)*

There is much to unpack in this intertextual reference. On the surface, there are many similarities between the set-ups of Thumps' and Spenser's inner circles. Robert B. Parker's Spenser, a Boston private investigator, works closely—usually informally—with police captain Martin Quirk, much as Thumps works with Sheriff Duke Hockney. Spenser's dog, Pearl, is just as important to him as is Thumps' cat, Freeway. Spenser has a committed relationship with his long-term girlfriend Susan Silverman, but the two do not live together, much like Thumps and Claire. The conversation between Thumps and Claire reveals that, like Spenser and Susan, they share literary references and, in the manner of close middle-aged couples, they enjoy performing their intellectual intimacy for each other.

At the same time, Spenser—perhaps the best-known hardboiled detective after the original early-twentieth-century trio of Dashiell Hammett's Sam Spade, Raymond Chandler's Philip Marlowe, and Ross Macdonald's Lew Archer—is raised in order to emphasize the ways Thumps diverges from the literary traditions of the white male American private eye, a point made humorously and emphatically by Claire's comparison of Thumps to the hardboiled detective's dog. Spenser is an avid boxer who enjoys dominating other men physically. Well-versed in Elizabethan and Romantic poetry, he is quick with verbal quips and barbs, and his interior monologue seldom includes doubts of any kind. This is in stark contrast to Thumps, who is neither white nor white-passing. Trained in fine-arts photography as well as detection, Thumps is mildly embarrassed that he enjoys the more elite sport of golf, and he is regularly beset by self-doubt as well as ill health. Although the specter of the hardboiled detective is present throughout the series, it is no surprise that the explicit reference to Parker occurs in the fifth novel, since Spenser's tough black sidekick, Hawk, shares some features with Thumps' *Obsidian* sidekick, Leon Ranger, who mirrors Hawk in openly discussing potentially sensitive questions of race with the primary detective. Leon and Thumps, perhaps unsurprisingly, address race and racism in a more nuanced way than do their predecessors. For example, when they discuss whether a potential suspect is Indian or White, they discuss their mandatory training:

> [Leon:] "You remember that seminar on race and gender we had to take?"
> [Thumps:] "Sure."
> "Dr. William Brock," said Leon. "He said that race and gender were constructs. That they didn't really exist."
> "What about him?"
> "Man was White," said Leon. "And he was male."
> "I think he was speaking theoretically."
> "Problem is we don't live in a theoretical world." Leon took out his cellphone and snapped a photo of the passing panorama. "If he had been Black and female, he might have had a different theory."

(224)

Indeed. King reveals, through Thumps' simultaneously ordinary and profound conversations with members of his community, that the detective's perspective is never the only one. Thumps' skill is not in solo ratiocination, but in listening to others and discerning not the most relevant facts, but the most pertinent *stories*, whether they are about crime, ethnicity, identity, or simply relationships.

No Climaxes, Conclusions, or Judgments

How does one write a detective story without climaxes, conclusions, or judgments? King accomplishes this repeatedly. Perhaps the most delightful example is found in *A Matter of Malice* (2019), the most postmodern of the Thumps DreadfulWater novels, and thus the one that plays most explicitly with the conventions of detective fiction. It opens like a pale echo of a country song, with a decidedly non-heroic Thumps having lost his car, his cat, and his woman (as opposed to a younger, fitter, sexier country singer, who would be lamenting the loss of his truck, his dog, and his woman). Thumps has been out of town for two months, supporting Claire in her breast cancer treatment in Seattle. When they return, Claire needs some time alone, leaving Thumps to wonder if he has inadvertently pushed her away. In the meantime, his car has been in a write-off-level accident, leaving Thumps reflective: "Now that Thumps thought about it, the Volvo was probably his longest-standing relationship. What did that say about him?" (48). Further, his cat Freeway, under the care of his neighbor during his absence, has disappeared. Thumps, who lives alone, often speaks to his cat, and the reader feels the cat's absence keenly despite Thumps's attempt to manage the loss philosophically: "But he didn't own her, had no claim to her other than the friendship they shared" (224). Against the backdrop of these small tragedies as well as Thumps's ongoing struggles to control his diabetes, the novel is plotted around a self-reflexive popular culture product: true crime.

A true crime TV show, *Malice Aforethought*, is filming in Chinook, attempting to solve a murder through a cold case reenactment. Thumps, always a reluctant detective, is especially resistant to the idea of participating as a consultant on the show, finding repugnant the use of real tragedy for entertainment. The murder of Trudy Samuels, which occurred before Thumps lived in Chinook, is soon mirrored by an active case, the murder—in the same place and using the same method—of Nina Maslow, one of the producers of the show and the woman who claims to have a lead on the Obsidian Killer, who killed Thumps' lover and her daughter, and who is to be the subject of Nina's next crime-entertainment venture. The producer's death acts as a climax of sorts, with its implications that her death, spectacular in its repetitiveness and its publicity, may cut off an avenue for Thumps to pursue in his obsessive, relentless hunt for the Obsidian Killer. However, the reality is that Thumps is not obsessed or relentless in his quest to find the man who killed his lover, her daughter, and nine other people. Indeed, Nina's murder is not represented using the pursuit metaphor that naturally builds up to a climax and is so often employed in detective fiction. King conceptualizes this potentially hardboiled situation through non-climactic metaphors more closely associated with the cozy: the puzzle and the game.

Edmund Wilson's famous quip from 1950 that "the reading of detective stories is simply a kind of vice that, for silliness and minor harmfulness, ranks somewhere between smoking and crossword puzzles" (395) speaks to the notion that detective fiction is a kind of game between the writer and the reader, where the reader's pleasure comes from trying to solve the mystery before the writer reveals the solution. The plot, then, acts as a kind of puzzle for the reader to navigate, recognizing red herrings, calling upon specialized knowledge when needed, and keeping straight all the characters' testimony, with different mental arrays based on which characters are telling the truth, which are deliberately lying and why, and which are working with incomplete or falsified information. Ronald Knox laid out the rules of the detective game in 1929, and numerous critics have since traced the cognitive pleasures of the genre (most notably, in my opinion, Charles Rzpeka in 2005 and Lisa Zunshine in 2006). This approach is in contrast to Robert A. Rushing, who declares emphatically,

> *There is no hermeneutic component to the detective novel.* The reader simply waits for the effortless dissipation of the problem, albeit misrecognizing his own waiting as some other activity, finding enjoyment like the hunter precisely in his "repeated circulation around the unattainable, always missed object."
>
> *(161, original italics)*

King's approach places him squarely in the Rushing camp as he addresses the metaphors of game and puzzle explicitly in *A Matter of Malice*, simultaneously revealing their power and limits. When Thumps gets drawn into the investigation of the modern-day murder, he reflects on the problem of detection: "Thumps had always imagined crimes to be rather like the puzzles you found at thrift stores, where there was no guarantee that all the pieces were still in the box" (252). Even as Thumps realizes that the detective does not always have all the pieces, as evidenced by the failure of his own detective team to identify and apprehend the Obsidian Killer, the reader might recognize that Thomas King is the kind of postmodern writer who may not set up a fair contest between the detective and the reader, since neither necessarily has access to all the pieces.

The puzzle metaphor is embodied within the narrative when the sheriff finally decides to arrest Tobias Rattler, the only suspect he has. Rattler, Thumps informs Sheriff Hockney when he arrives to detain the First Nations man, is doing a jigsaw puzzle with Moses and Cooley. Hockney hates jigsaw puzzles:

> "Me, I don't see the point. All those little bits of cardboard. You spend days putting the thing together and then when it's finished, you take it apart, put it back in the box, and stick it in a closet," to which Thumps replies helpfully, "The puzzle is a Bierstadt painting ... An Indian village with mountains in the background."
>
> *(310)*

Given that Thumps has already likened the case to a puzzle—albeit one with a high likelihood of missing pieces—Hockney appears here to lack respect for the work of investigation and, if all goes well, prosecution and perhaps justice (not that King represents "justice" as a foregone conclusion or even always a desirable one). This is consonant with other depictions of seasoned police detectives who know that each case will be followed by another, and the tide of crime cannot be substantially impacted even by the most accomplished police force. Thumps' response is telling, though. The picture that Moses, Cooley, and Rattler are putting together is a painting that could be of Chinook, by Albert Bierstadt (1830–1902), a member of the Hudson River School whose work has been seen as facile by some and as sublime by others. To my untrained eye, Bierstadt's use of luminism—a technique that removes the brushstroke from sight in leaving a cool hard light on an element of the landscape—appears to evoke a sense of optimism and respect for the landscape. At the same time, the Indian village is in the background of the scene, acting as nothing more than a feature of the landscape, so Hockney's lack of interest in the puzzle may be appropriate. And yet, there is a sense of community and camaraderie built through this shared focus, which draws together the white sheriff and four First Nations men, including the one Duke is to arrest ... after the pizza and the puzzle, of course.

On the night of the jigsaw puzzle, Thumps solves three cases: the cold case at the center of the *Malice Aforethought* recreation, the active case of the murdered TV producer, and another cold case, apparently a murder-suicide, that wasn't even under investigation. He does this by leaving Hockney with the puzzlers while he goes across town to share evidence with the TV people and ostensibly to get their perspectives. There is no pleasure in this decision for Thumps, who does not enjoy the company—or the menu—of the *Malice Aforethought* producer and host. In fact, he imagines his community as he drives toward the investigation:

> By now, the sheriff and Deputy Lance would have taken Rattler into custody. Or the five of them were standing around the kitchen table, eating deep dish and playing humpty dumpty with the Bierstadt landscape. Thumps was betting on pizza and puzzle.
>
> *(313)*

Of course, Thumps is right in his imagined scenario. He is also right to look beyond his community and at the TV crew and cast in understanding and eventually solving the case.

As is typical of Thumps DreadfulWater novels, *A Matter of Malice* provides some resolution—the case is solved—but also opens up other questions that go beyond the tease for the next novel. The novel ends in the morning, with Thumps leaving town after he has said goodbye to Claire, who is heading off for a month-long tour of New Zealand, and to Archie, who says his journey is a bad idea. Thumps now has a new car—a Honda Element—but his cat remains as elusive as his lover:

> He looked up and down the street in case Freeway had had enough of small children and was looking for sanctuary. Then he climbed into the Honda, put the promise of dawn at his back, and began the long drive to the coast.
>
> *(392)*

Freeway remains absent, a loss the reader feels keenly. The next novel, *Obsidian*, opens in reverse, with Thumps pausing to look at the "orange glow" of Chinook under the night sky, a little too late to drive into the sunset of a happy ending:

> Years ago, he had stopped at the same turnout and looked out across the same panorama.
> That time, he had been escaping. Running away.
> This time, he was coming home.
> Whatever that meant.
>
> (1)

The final line of this opening description, "Whatever that meant," emphasizes the associational nature of these novels, signaling that meaning is always elusive, is always, in fact, deliberately deferred, in an acknowledgement of the power not of readers or of writers, but of stories themselves.

Conclusion

In *The Truth About Stories*, King writes about his good friend Louis Owens, a Choctaw-Cherokee-Irish writer who died by suicide. After a touching memorial to Louis's art and to their friendship, King talks about his commonalities with Owens:

> We loved fly-fishing and the solitude of quiet places. We understood in each other the same desperate desire for acceptance. And we were both hopeful pessimists. That is, we wrote knowing that none of the stories we told would change the world. But we wrote in the hope that they would.
>
> *(92)*

I really appreciate this memorial to Owen's optimism, which was surely meaningful to his loved ones and his readers given how hard it is to accept the death of a writer—and their stories—before their time. This "hopeful pessimism" is, in my opinion, one of the most compelling elements of the Thumps DreadfulWater novels.

Of all the hopeful moments throughout the series, the one that stays with me involves Freeway. After her initial disappearance in *A Matter of Malice* (2019), I thought she might return, but her continued absence throughout *Obsidian* (2020) had even a hardcore optimist like me losing hope. *Deep House* (2022) opens with Thumps suffering from insomnia:

> He didn't think the insomnia was tied to his cat …. He had always been ambivalent about the cat, and Freeway certainly hadn't exhibited any filial fondness for him, at least not the kind of affection Thumps associated with small children and dogs. But he and the cat had lived together for a number of years, and there was something to be said for the familiar.
>
> *(9)*

And then, it happens. One evening Thumps is washing a red pepper in the kitchen sink when he hears a shuffling sound in his bedroom. We are privy to a plethora of his thoughts ranging from hopeful ("The best outcome would be to find Claire in his bed, waiting for him" [102]) to pessimistic ("Thumps had read about racoon infestations and how they never ended well" [102]). Thumps enters his bedroom with a club in one hand and a knife in the other. There is a hiss from the closet and he tumbles onto his bed:

> "It doesn't have to end this way."
> He tried to put some real commitment into his voice, but it was just for show. Standing there on the bed, he had already decided to get out of the room and call an animal-removal service.
>
> *(104)*

By now, Thumps is the only one not aware of who is in the closet. Even after he hears the meow, "It took a moment to register" (104). Even his most hopeful scenario (Claire surprising him in his bed) is less than the reality. Freeway is back, she has four adorable kittens, and now his insomnia involves tiny kittens burrowing into his neck. The narrator spells out Thumps' complex emotional palette: "He had had one cat and had been ambivalent about that. Now he had five and was enchanted. He knew it wouldn't last" (107).

Thumps, like King, is a hopeful pessimist, and this worldview is memorably explored not in a great climactic scene that pits the detective against the serial killer, but rather in the mundane relationship between a detective and his cat that unfolds over several novels and that blends gentle humor, pathos, and dare I say, joy. The morning after the great reunion of Thumps DreadfulWater and Freeway the cat, Freeway shows Thumps that a fifth kitten had died in the closet. Later, at the diner, Thumps tells Al the whole story:

> [Al]: "How many did she have?"
> "Five," said Thumps. "But one died."
> "That's always heartbreaking." Al started back to the grill. Halfway there, she stopped and came back in a rush. "I hope to hell you didn't throw it in the garbage."
> "No."
> "I hope you buried it in the backyard."
> "I did."
> "You and Freeway, right?" Al looked at Thumps hard. "Freeway was there when you buried her child?"
> "She was."
> "Okay," said Al, "then I'll make you breakfast. With kittens, you're going to need your strength."
>
> *(111)*

There is a clarity to the stories King tells—a simultaneously ordinary and extraordinary nature to his characters and his occurrences that suggests the narrative and epistemological power of the everyday as well as the importance of community and relationships over individuality. No heroes or villains. No climaxes, conclusions, or judgments. These are signs of a fundamentally hopeful approach to telling stories that begin with murder and end with something less than a complete resolution. These are signs of the potential of detective fiction to create new associations and perspectives. In many ways, King summarizes his own aesthetic approach to crime fiction in *The Truth about Stories*: "Want a different ethic? Tell a different story" (164).

5
AUSMA ZEHANAT KHAN AND MULTICULTURALISM IN CANADA

Esa Khattak and Rachel Getty are not afraid to cry. Throughout Ausma Zehanat Khan's series, these two detective characters regularly confront the physical manifestation of their own sorrow and their empathetic sorrow for others in the face of both personal tragedy and cultural trauma. In *A Dangerous Crossing* (2018), the fifth novel of the series, for example, Khattak reads through a file of documents relating to the Syrian conflict and specifically to Assad's politicide over a number of years. He reads a translation of an interview with a detainee:

> *My cellmate couldn't last. He screamed for his mother. When that didn't help, he cried for the Prophet Muhammad. So the guards brought the Muhammad stick, and then they beat him with that.*
> The Muhammad stick.
> Named for the messenger of peace. Used in the name of terror.
> His face gray, his mouth pinched with horror, [Esa Khattak] put his head in his hands and wept.
>
> *(257)*

The narration of detectives crying recalls nineteenth-century arguments about the dangers of both sentimental and sensation fiction, those literatures that were known to evoke visceral bodily reactions in readers (sadness and sensuality, respectively). Although we are mostly past fears of the printed page (perhaps only because our anxieties have been displaced onto video games and increasingly immersive electronic entertainment products), the power of the novel to evoke emotional reactions remains high, and Khan fully utilizes the potential of the form. When I notice tears in my own eyes as I read Khan's evocative descriptions of horrific moments in recent history—generally moments I have thought about only briefly when faced with cursory media coverage of international news—I am reminded of Richard Wright's famous statement in "How Bigger Was Born," an explication of his rhetorical and aesthetic project in one of the most influential crime novels of the twentieth century, *Native Son* (1940). In reflecting upon his earlier short story collection, *Uncle Tom's Children* (1938), Wright reflects:

> I found that I had written a book which even bankers' daughters could read and weep over and feel good about. I swore to myself that if I ever wrote another book, no one would weep over it; that it would be so hard and deep that they would have to face it without the consolation of tears.
>
> *(454)*

As a lumberjack's daughter (Canadian cliché, but it's true), I am hardly of the class Wright was concerned would find unearned and unproductive catharsis in his work. And yet, I still take his point that a reader's tears at the plights of fictional characters based on real people experiencing the most appalling of human rights abuses might blunt the rhetorical edge of the analysis. It might, in fact, prevent readers from getting angry. Wright's approach in 1940 to telling stories of the legacy of slavery in the United States is very much a product of his time, his country, and his own personal identity, as is Ausma Zehanat Khan's. Born in Britain to Pakistani immigrants, Khan was raised in Toronto as a Canadian citizen and has recently become a US citizen; she has accompanied her husband, Nader Hashemi, to Northwestern University in Illinois and now to the University of Denver, where he directs the Center for Middle East Studies. With a PhD in international human rights, Khan has worked as an immigration lawyer (Toronto), an international human rights law professor (Northwestern), and a magazine editor (*Muslim Girl*) before turning to a career writing fantasy and detective fiction. She has clearly articulated her purpose in writing the Khattak and Getty series:

> In the entire Muslim world, the picture is bleak, particularly with Iraq and Syria, but all over. A tremendous darkness on what was once such civilizational beauty, and elegance, and grace. That's the darkness that I'm trying to describe.
>
> *(Bethune)*

In describing both the current darkness and the complex historical light, Khan regularly provides opportunities for readers to cry, often through italicized accounts from the perspectives of victims of genocide or other human rights abuses interspersed with the account of the detectives' story (as in the example that opens this chapter).

Characterized as "a potent antidote to the simplistic and stereotypical portrayal of Muslim citizens of the West" (Ayoob), Khan's series addresses the fraught tensions around Canada's ability, as a nation-state and a cultural construct, to engage productively with questions of religion and multiculturalism. In each novel of the series, she uses a murder mystery as an entry point to a nuanced sociopolitical situation that she has carefully researched and explores in depth through narrative. The opening novel of the series, *The Unquiet Dead*, uses a classic detective trope: a wealthy middle-aged man has plummeted to his death over a cliff near his home on a dark and stormy night; although it is conceivable that an outsider has made their way to this deserted place, it is far more likely that Christopher Drayton either died by suicide (perhaps pressured by a letter-writing campaign against him?) or has been pushed by one of his neighbors. This scenario, familiar to readers of the cozy, promises a small cast of intriguing characters, each with their own reasons—financial, romantic, or vengeful—for wanting Drayton dead. In Khan's hands, the scenario is complicated, however, by the fact that brings this case to Esa Khattak and Rachel Getty at the Community Policing Section: the victim was quite possibly in Canada under an assumed identity and is actually Dražen Krstić, an escaped war criminal from the Bosnian genocide of the 1990s.

Khan makes the move of referencing real-world global crises within the frame of individual mysteries repeatedly throughout the series. *The Language of Secrets* (2016) explores the policing of domestic terrorist threats in Canada when an undercover cop in a Muslim terrorist cell is killed in Algonquin Park. *Among the Ruins* (2017) takes Khattak and Rachel to Iran, where they interact with various dissidents in pursuing the recent murder of a Canadian-Iranian filmmaker in an Iranian prison. In *A Dangerous Crossing* (2018), Khattak and Rachel go to Syria, where they investigate the disappearance of a Canadian aid worker and discover some dark truths about the Syrian refugee crisis. *A Deadly Divide* (2019), the most recent novel at the time of this writing, is set in Quebec in the aftermath of a mass shooting in a mosque that is the culmination of a series of anti-Islamic hate crimes. In each case, Khan presents two possibilities: (1) a murder might be motivated by the personal, or (2) a murder might be motivated by the political. As activists of various stripes have often articulated, the personal often *is* political, and the motives—and punishments, in most cases—for the crimes explored in the series often mimic the complexity of the socio-historical situations being explored.

In Canada, this is a very complex socio-historical situation indeed. On one hand, Canada can and does take pride in being the first country to adopt multiculturalism as an official national policy, with the Canadian Multiculturalism Act, a law aimed to preserve and enhance cultural diversity, passed in 1988. On the other hand, the real-life understanding and enforcement of that law is far from straightforward. In an essay on media representations of crimes involving Canadian women of color, Yasmin Jiwani makes a sobering point that captures this contradiction within Canadian self-representation and reality. As Jiwani argues,

> At an official level of government discourse, Canada is characterized as a multicultural society .... Yet this multiplicity is also structured hierarchically, with the cultures of the two "founding" nations—the English and the French—being accorded greater dominance and legitimacy, albeit to varying degrees depending on one's geographical location.
>
> *(99–100)*

It has been my experience that we as Canadians pride ourselves in official venues but also in casual conversations on our multiculturalism, often with the metaphor of the "cultural mosaic" or "tossed salad" where many cultures exist harmoniously alongside each other in contrast to the "melting pot" of the United States, with its singular national identity. Examining Canadian crime fiction analytically, and especially quantifying the ethnic identities of detectives, criminals, and victims within a representative sample, has emphasized for me exactly the point Jiwani makes: despite our (I believe genuine) stated commitment to multiculturalism and diversity, Canadian writers affiliated to the dominant (English and French) groups tend to represent almost exclusively characters from those groups. With the exceptions of many characters created by Thomas King and Ausma Zahanat Khan (two writers of color) and a few characters penned by Giles Blunt and Gail Bowen, only a tiny proportion of characters in Canadian crime fiction—detective, victim, or criminal—are from racialized groups. This means that multiculturalism gets little fictional exploration within the popular genre perhaps best poised to investigate it.

Jiwani examines media coverage of crimes in documenting the normalization of the dominant culture. For example, she studies a prominent crime story from 1996 known as "the Vernon massacre," in which a man drove to Vernon, British Columbia, and used a gun to kill his estranged wife, eight other members of her family, and then himself.

Jiwani shows that media reports underscored the ethnicity of the killer and victim in a number of ways ranging from describing the victims as members of "a prominent Indo-Canadian family," and "founding members of the Vernon Sikh temple," to mentions of the practice of arranged marriage as a potential explanatory framework for the murders (106). Jiwani persuasively contrasts this story to another crime in Vernon in 1995 in which Sharon Velisek, a white woman, was shot (not fatally) by her ex-boyfriend, who then killed himself. Both women had been in touch with police to complain of threats from their eventual assailants, but concerns about gun violence and the limitations of police action to prevent violent crime dominated coverage only of the white woman's story (107–8). Jiwani concludes that

> The absence of a cultural explanation as a cause of violence in the Velisek case may have to do with her "unmarked" appearance—she is not a racial minority belonging to a community or religious tradition that constitutes the popular and common-sense notion of a cultural "other."
>
> *(108)*

Khan repeatedly uses classical detective scenarios as a backdrop for exploring Canada's roles and reactions to a fraught global sociopolitical issue, demonstrating that an individual murder can serve as a key to unlocking a cultural trauma for readers. In portraying a multicultural Toronto in which numerous national histories interweave and collide, Khan opens up conversations about how twenty-first-century Canada may act as a productive space for dealing with individual and cultural trauma, grief, and injustice. She uses an extremely effective classic detective duo formula in Khattak and Getty and has been recognized for her nuanced representations of complex global conflicts. For example, Pilar Cuder-Domínguez argues that "Western readers, through Khattak, are brought into close relationality with those who are made vulnerable and even disposable by current political and economic practices" (54). Marcia Lynx-Qually compares Khan's positive centering of a Muslim detective to a trend Phyllis Betz has identified in lesbian detective fiction, arguing that Khan

> takes characteristics viewed as abnormal and criminalized in the bulk of popular detective fiction—such as Muslim prayer, the use of the Arabic word Allah for God, visiting a mosque for congregational prayer, and the like—and renders them normal and conventional, and safe.
>
> *(192)*

In addition to capitalizing on these affordances of the genre, Khan also explores love in its many facets. Taken as a whole, the series suggests that by investigating global humanitarian crises through a Canadian lens—and that might mean leaving the United States out of the representation—readers can gain a deeper, more nuanced perspective on Canada's path forward into the culturally interconnected and sometimes labyrinthine twenty-first century.

Grappling with Liminality, Empathy, and Contradiction

Detective fiction has a complicated relationship with questions of justice, equity, diversity, and inclusion. On one hand, the genre's generic investments appear to be quite conservative, with the criminal representing the forces of disorder and revolution, and the detective standing in for a return to the status quo (Grella). On the other hand, as Carolyn Heilbrun has famously asserted, the formal structure of the genre leaves the writer "free to dabble in a little profound revolutionary thought" (7). Canada's history with diversity, equity, and inclusion has been equally complex. In a detailed exploration of the eponymous question, *Is Canada Postcolonial?*, Laura Moss gathers together a number of leading and emerging scholars of Canadian literature and culture who grapple with Canada's historical and contemporary relationship to postcoloniality and multiculturalism. For Stephen Slemon, the very notion of Canada is incommensurate with the postcolonial. " 'Canada' can no more *be* 'postcolonial' than patriarchy can be feminist, or homophobia can be queer" (322), he argues provocatively, making reference to Canada's long history as a relatively powerful country on the world stage where white privilege has long been the dominant mode culturally, politically, and economically. At the other end of a spectrum of responses to what is clearly not a yes-or-no question, Diana Brydon makes what is for me an equally persuasive case that although Canada is certainly not a straightforward example of a postcolonial nation and postcolonial theory is certainly not a straightforward approach ("As frameworks for understanding the world, both postcolonialism and Canada require continual vigilance and renovation" [50]), there is nonetheless much to be gained from viewing Canadian culture through a postcolonial lens. Much of Canada's postcolonial literary criticism has, understandably, focused on Canada as a settler-invader society and on questions of indigeneity. For some, like Brydon, postcolonial theory also offers tools to think about Canada in a more global, social-justice framework, as when she explains,

> In stressing the need to move beyond a politics of representation toward a politics of accountability, I am drawing on that strain of postcolonial

theory that seeks to renew commitment to the well-being of humanity as a whole, based on a revised understanding of what it means to be human.

(73–4)

I would suggest this is very much what Khan is doing in the Khattak and Getty novels, as she approaches a series of conflicts and human rights abuses from around the world through the perspective of two Canadian detectives.

Khan sets up her detective duo with an eye to subtly educating her audience on some of the difficulties faced by a multicultural twenty-first-century Canada. Each of the writers I investigate in this section on "Canadian Confrontations" takes a different approach to constructing the detectives' cultural identities. John McFetridge's Eddie Dougherty is a deeply liminal character—a perfectly bilingual and bicultural cop whose mother is French and whose father is Irish. Giles Blunt provides three police officers, each representing a different cultural perspective: the English-Canadian John Cardinal, his partner and eventual love interest, French-Canadian Lise Delorme, and the less central but still important Ontario Provincial Police officer, Jerry Commanda, a member of the First Nations. Thomas King creates an even broader sense of community for his Cherokee ex-cop, Thumps DreadfulWater, whose family lineage is little explored but whose friends and colleagues represent a wide swath of cultural perspectives. Barclay, meanwhile, includes three models of American male detectives: the police detective, the private investigator, and the journalist. On the surface, Khan's approach most closely resembles Blunt's, as she uses a fairly typical male–female detective duo, with the older male detective in a leadership role. At the same time, there is a distance—cultural, aesthetic, and spiritual—between Khattak and Rachel that creates a space for readers to both identity with and watch the detective characters as they develop throughout the series.

Khan provides an effective set-up for a Western reader unfamiliar with the Middle Eastern tensions and conflicts that act as a backdrop to her detective stories. Esa Khattak, a liminal detective if ever there was one, is a Pakistani-Canadian man who heads up Community Policing Services (CPS), a new police branch responsible for consulting on investigations into race-based hate crimes. Khattak is intimately familiar with the cultural, linguistic, and religious practices of the people he polices; indeed, he is first presented on his prayer mat in *The Unquiet Dead*, creating a distance for many readers who might not be familiar with the rituals of Islam. He is paired up with Rachel Getty, a younger white Canadian Torontonian (fully bilingual in English and French, we learn in *A Deadly Divide*), who is constantly learning about Islam as well as about the sociopolitical backgrounds of the sensitive cases handled by CPS. As a progressive, open-minded person who seeks to fill in the knowledge gaps common to many white Canadians, Rachel is a clear stand-in for many readers. Her stance on learning about new cultures is explicitly articulated in *The Unquiet Dead*: "Nothing about multiculturalism antagonized Rachel. She liked all kinds of food, clothing, cultural customs, and music. The one thing that held her aloof was a fear of offending through ignorance" (97). Khan avoids a hierarchical Holmes–Watson dynamic in which Khattak has the knowledge and mental acuity to do the detective work while Rachel looks on admiringly and narrates for the less gifted reader. Rachel is more than a sounding board for Khattak, even though he is always far more familiar with the social, political, aesthetic, and theological features of the communities into which the two venture. Indeed, Khattak is sometimes too close to a case, and it is Rachel's outsider perspective that reveals the missing piece of the detective puzzle. In *A Dangerous Crossing*, when someone Khattak has known for years in suspected, Rachel reflects: "She didn't dismiss the possibility of Audrey's guilt—she knew Khattak wouldn't want her to. Their different perspectives on a case were the key to their partnership's success" (28). Rhetorically, this suggests that a person learning about a new culture or religion with an open mind, like Rachel, can function effectively in a new space as long as they take care not to offend members of the community and to review evidence with the mix of rational analysis and personal intuition that so often marks the most successful fictional detectives.

The complexly drawn Khattak faces many pressures and contradictions. As a widower, a Pakistani-Canadian, and a literary policeman whose best friend is famed novelist Nathan Clare, Khattak is clearly a liminal character. He is also established from the series opening as a nuanced thinker. When he is first introduced on his prayer mat at twilight (the most liminal of times), Khattak is not bothered when his prayer is interrupted by a police call:

> He no longer possessed the hot-blooded certainties of youth that a prayer missed or delayed would bring about a concomitant judgment of sin. Time had taught him to view his faith through the prism of compassion: when ritual was sacrificed in pursuit of the very values it was meant to inspire, there could be no judgment, no sin.
>
> *(1–2)*

This introduction provides the reader with a sense of Khattak's struggle to bring together the disparate parts of his life. He sees the value of compassion—for himself as well as for others—and has come to recognize that he must approach his faith openly, without excessive rigidity, understanding policing and prayer as based on the same values and working toward the same ends. We also get a sense here that Khattak has a more storied past than his affect as a calm, poised officer of the law in his late thirties might suggest. The "hot-blooded certainties of youth" evoke the inherent tension between the passionate activism of the young and the more measured approach of experience that is investigated repeatedly throughout the series.

Although Khattak manages to resolve some of the potential contradictions between his work and his religious practice, he continues to struggle with his professional tasks at CPS, a problem of which his boss is cognizant:

> She [Martine Killiam, Khattak's superior] was well aware of the risks inherent in Khattak's position. He would always be accused of failing some constituency or mandate—either the minority communities he'd been tasked to represent or the law he was meant to uphold. Only in rare cases would these objectives work together.
>
> *(Language 13)*

In an interview with Khan, Brian Bethune asks about her decision to always place Khattak in difficult personal situations in addition to the intricate crimes he investigates. Specifically, Bethune notes that Khattak often faces suspicion from other Muslims as well as from white Canadians. Khan's response reveals the intellectual and personal complexity of her representation of Khattak's liminality, a liminality she shares in many ways:

> I was exploring the idea of being squeezed ... that on the one hand there are the people who have subverted their own tradition and turned to violence, and on the other inflammatory rhetoric that generalizes the entire faith community to this extremist fringe. Khattak, like the rest of us, feels that pressure all the time, having to defend yourself against extremists within and assaults from without, having to prove a negative, proving you're not an unindicted co-conspirator.
>
> *(3)*

Khattak, then, feels enormous pressure as he tries to represent the interests of his marginalized ethnic and faith communities at the same time as he mediates between the white-male-dominated police establishment and the communities of color (which include criminals as well as victims) involved in whichever crime he is trying to unravel. Using a third-person focalizing narration, Khan provides Khattak's perspective in a sensitive and compelling way.

Khan regularly moves between Khattak's point of view and that of Rachel Getty, who, though younger, already has the open-mindedness and maturity that Khattak is hinted to have achieved only later in his life. Rachel's deep engagement with and interest in the culturally fraught situations she encounters model both an intellectual and aesthetic openness. For example, in *Among the Ruins*, Rachel joins a tour group visiting the sights of Shiraz, Iran, in order to discreetly assist Khattak in his investigation into the murder of a Canadian journalist. As a person with "no decided form of worship" (298), Rachel is nonetheless awed by the sublimity of the Nasir al-Mulk mosque: "Her thoughts of Iran had been limited to a scowling Ayatollah, to a region in turmoil, and lately to the nuclear negotiations. What she hadn't imagined was this ample tranquility, this amphitheater of joy" (299). This is a point Khan makes repeatedly: the twenty-first-century media environment leads to a situation where even well-meaning, open-minded Canadians tend to reduce cultures outside their immediate experience to a series of geopolitical conflicts and problems. It is only when she visits Iran and *feels* the beauty of the mosque that Rachel is able to see beyond her own limited information, previously restricted to the intellectual.

Rachel's experience in the mosque is discussed using the language of pedagogy: "The dignity of the mosque tore at Rachel's heart. Her lens was *correcting* itself. There was something *to be learned* from the cosmic radiance of her surroundings" (299–300, emphasis added). What is to be learned is quickly described as an even deeper empathy than that which has already been ascribed to Rachel: "Her mind was seized by a painful imagining: what must it be like to have your civilization possessed of such celestial beauty and to find yourself the object of diminishment?" (300). The brief shift to the second person ("you") here emphasizes that Rachel is doing more than observing the disjunction between the representation of Iran to the outside world and the sublimity of one of its places of worship; she is attempting to take on—in her imagination— the perspective of an Iranian aware of this disjunction. She continues her musings by considering the perspective of her partner, one of the few Muslims she knows personally: "She was roaming the deep places of the soul. And she wondered if this soaring elevation of spirit was the essence of Esa Khattak, or if it was an epiphany personal to her" (300). Although Rachel never explicitly returns to this question, Khan shows repeatedly that, by inviting a moment of sublime contemplation about the mélange of the cultural, the aesthetic, the spiritual, and the sociopolitical, Rachel has indeed tapped into the strengths and challenges at the center of Khattak's worldview. Shortly after her epiphany, Rachel meets Khattak with some relief, avoiding his questions about her sightseeing and pleased to be back in a realm she understands: "To investigate a death was her safe and comforting reality" (300). The abrupt transition from the sublime to the workaday only serves to emphasize the ways in which Khan's stories of crime and detection are meant to evoke—sometimes contrapuntally and sometimes mimetically—the rich geopolitical and sociohistorical backdrops of her settings.

Rachel and Khattak work on one mystery per novel. In most cases, they arrive at a solution by identifying the killer. Despite this performance of one of the basic features of the detective genre, the novels do not always commit to the kind of closure associated with more traditional detective fiction. For example, the aptly named first novel of the series, *The Unquiet Dead*, ends with Khattak and Rachel being quite sure of the killer's identity but unable to prove it. The novel's closing scene makes clear that the value of the work is separate from the case closure rate. After the suspect says something that could be interpreted as a confession (although certainly not adequate for a court of law), Rachel asks Khattak what they should do now. As occurs frequently, Rachel's interior monologue may well represent the reader's perspective: "She wanted Khattak to know. She wanted to believe he had the bedrock certainty of right and wrong, truth and falsehood, that she herself lacked" (319). Indeed, this desire—for order, for clarity, for closure—has often been seen as central to the appeal of the detective genre. Although Khattak cannot provide the epistemological certainly Rachel—and, perhaps, the reader—seeks, he does know what to do next: they report their findings to the agency that asked for the investigation and allow its members to act on the information as they see fit.

This conclusion might feel unsatisfactory in some contexts. Given the impossible, contradictory position of the CPS, however, it is sensible. And Khan makes the conclusion more palatable by ending on an evocative image that echoes but also advances the opening image of Khattak on his prayer mat. In the end, as Khattak reflects on what he thinks he knows—that an imam has killed a Bosnian war criminal—he muses on the possible death scene:

There had been a tumble in the dark on the edge of Cathedral Bluffs.
Justice had found the butcher of Sebrenica.
And the shadow of the mosque was no consolation.

(320)

The idea of murder as justice is a complex one that draws together the themes of liminality, empathy, and contradiction that resonate throughout the series. In so doing, the mystery provides a perfect generic opportunity for Khan to explore the pressures of liminality on Muslim Canadians as well as the need for other Canadians to face questions of multiculturalism with an openness that goes beyond the intellectual.

Centering Love

In a rare scathing review of *A Dangerous Crossing* (Khan is usually very positively reviewed in major outlets for both her project and her writing skills), Maureen Corrigan critiques Khan for providing too many personal details external to the investigation under consideration: "Overwhelmed? I was too. The personal histories of Khan's characters are so enmeshed that tracing back their connections is like trying to untangle a hair ball." Corrigan's critique is valid only if we see the detective novel either as a puzzle that the reader is trying to solve ahead of the fictional detective, or as an exposé of a human rights violation that should not be sidetracked by its characters. In either case, I would argue that the personal details are vital to Khan's project in this series, which is much bigger than narrating a series of murder mysteries. Not only do these details provide depth to the central characters, turning them into fictional constructs whose adventures and ongoing work matter to readers, but they also show the expansive nature of victimhood that follows any crime, from a solitary murder to a genocide. By focusing on the personal histories of her characters, Khan explores a concept that may at first seem in diametrical opposition to crime but that she posits as necessary for effectively processing crime: love. Khan investigates love in many forms—familial, collegial, romantic, and cultural. It is through these investigations that she develops the ethos and pathos that accompany the logos to make her rhetorical analyses work as detective narratives and as pieces of sociocultural critique.

Familial love is central to the main characters of the series. At the series opening, when Rachel is in her seventh year as a police detective, the only person she has ever really loved is her little brother, Zach, who disappeared as a teenager. Rachel has difficult relationships with her parents. She is traumatized by her father's toxic masculinity, which is exacerbated by his position as a police officer; she is equally appalled by her mother's selfishness when she learns that her mother has long known Zach's whereabouts, but has chosen not to share them with her frantic, grieving daughter. Twenty-first-century nonreligious Canadians with Rachel's background might be expected to have only modest ties to their families, creating new communities (sometimes explicitly referred to using kinship terms) in a family of friends or, in a detective story, a fraternity of police colleagues. Rachel and Khattak, however, are bound together by their shared commitment to putting family first. Khattak and his best friend Nathan Clare deploy the same model of defensive (almost paternalistic) masculinity as they repeatedly seek to protect their younger sisters, even when those very capable grown women explicitly state that they need no protection. Although the novels acknowledge that the protectiveness of the elder siblings (Rachel, Khattak, and Nate) is not always appreciated by younger siblings, the narratives generally show this selfless love, which occasionally includes risking their lives, as a positive force.

From these strong familial ties grow bonds of enduring friendship that are shown as vital to the important work Khattak and Rachel undertake. *The Unquiet Dead* articulates each detective's devotion to the work as a potentially unhealthy obsession that prevents the kind of work-life balance that benefits not only the detective but also the communities with whom the detective interacts. As Khattak completes a prayer, he muses upon the centrality of his work to his identity: "Lately, he'd come to accept that there was no separate place. His work, and the harshness of the choices he had made, bled into everything" (4). When Rachel interviews a witness who has been planning a wedding, she realizes how far such concerns are from her own mind:

> When she thought about what the future might hold, she saw only her work. Instead of the promise of love and companionship, there was the constant presence of loss. And work was the one thing that could make her forget, the one place she could do something that mattered, that healed.
>
> *(47–8)*

As the series progresses, however, Rachel and Khattak develop a platonic but loving relationship that brings added value to the work as both a personal and professional enterprise. This friendship, which also involves saving each other's lives, is based on Rachel's and Khattak's mutual sense of empathy. "It was Rachel's habit of getting inside the skin of a case, the skin of another's pain," the narrator proclaims in *The Unquiet Dead*. "It was what Khattak most respected about her" (254). Although the early novels hint at possible attraction between the two, which would tap into a common trope of detective fiction, Khan does not pursue that avenue. Instead, the dedication to police work—and thus to a cherished colleague in the field—is elevated as superior to mere romantic love.

In the later novels, Khan finally allows her main characters the pleasure of erotic love. Khattak eventually falls in love with Sehr, a lawyer specializing in international human rights cases who had been a close friend of his late wife. Rachel, in the meantime, meets Quebecois detective Christian Lemaire, and appears to be developing a promising romantic relationship with him by the end of *A Deadly Divide*. Like tears, signs of loving and caring are represented as positives in Khan's richly drawn fictional world. Rachel and Khattak are both intelligent, competent detectives skilled in interrogation and ratiocination, but even more importantly, they are both good at mediation, communication, and empathy. It is the centrality of these qualities that makes Khan's series such a compelling entry into representing Canada's current and potential role as a global player.

The Nearly Absent Elephant

In 1944, W.P. Wilgar expressed a sentiment that remains relevant to many Canadians today:

> The Canadian is sympathetically British .... But at the same time, he finds himself in the curious and awkward position of respecting all that is British while he has to admit to himself that he has a far more advanced understanding of the American mind than he has of the Old World mentality.
>
> *(270–1)*

The cultural and philosophical connections many Canadians feel with Western Europe (with France as well as England, I would argue) are often a point of pride, especially for those of us living in the United States. Indeed, many Canadians deliberately downplay our deep and sometimes inextricable connections to what Pierre Trudeau famously characterized as the "elephant" beside which Canada sleeps. "Living next to you," Trudeau declared in a Washington Press Club Speech in 1969, "is in some ways like sleeping with an elephant. No matter how friendly and even-tempered is the beast, if I can call it that, one is affected by every twitch and grunt." In Canadian crime fiction, as we have seen in our explorations of John McFetridge (Dougherty dates an American woman and has detailed conversations about their two countries in *Black Rock*), Giles Blunt (Cardinal and Delorme's investigation in *A Delicate Storm* begins with the murder of an American), and Thomas King (the Thumps Dreadfulwater series is set in Montana), writers often deliberately address the relationship between Canada and the United States even as they use crime and detective tropes to explore sociocultural issues in Canada.

Khan has many opportunities to do the same. The United States brokered the Dayton Peace Accords that ended the Bosnian War of 1992–1995, but, like Canadians, most Americans have little knowledge of the details or the aftermath of that conflict (*The Unquiet Dead*). US intelligence agencies have had substantial experience dealing with—and infiltrating—radicalized domestic terror cells (*The Language of Secrets*).

The United States, like Canada, has had journalists executed in the Middle East (*Among the Ruins*). Americans, like Canadians, exhibit a number of different sentiments regarding the Syrian refugee crisis and to what degree Syrian refugees should be welcomed in North America. It would have been reasonable for Canadian Audrey Clare to work with American NGOs in her Syrian relief efforts (*Dangerous*). And certainly, mass shootings—including in places of worship—are far more common in the United States than anywhere else in the world (*Deadly*).

And yet, Khan seldom mentions the cultural hegemon that shares the world's largest undefended border with Canada. Even when the United States is briefly mentioned, it is in conjunction with a worldwide phenomenon, as, for example, in *The Unquiet Dead*: "Everywhere the radical right was rising: Sweden, France, Belgium, Denmark, Holland. While a steady stream of vitriol drifted north of the U.S. border" (255). The relative absence of the United States in Khan's series has two rhetorical impacts: it allows for a direct representation of Canada and it gives Canada more responsibility on the world stage. The United States tends to have an outsized impact on many global conversations and their representations in media and culture. By mostly leaving out the United States, Khan is able to portray a form of globalization that includes many players, which means that Canada must take on an important role (as it often does, including in the Syrian refugee crisis). Having grown up in Toronto, Khan is committed to capturing the city's cultural intricacies. As she told the CBC's Ryan B. Patrick,

> It's not just geographical: There's an attitude or a sensibility from having lived in Toronto where you understand you're one of many different communities currently negotiating how to happily live together. It's a feeling I wanted to set as the baseline for the book series.

Khan captures Toronto's multiculturalism directly instead of by comparison.

Indeed, Canada is often compared to the United States when it comes to both human rights abuses and humanitarian aid. These comparisons are often favorable to Canada, whose rhetoric on human rights issues tends to be more globally palatable, generally aligned with the approaches of major world organizations such as the United Nations. This can provide Canada with a built-in justification for not participating as fully as many activists feel is needed. In an argument about the placement of Syrian refugees, for example, someone arguing that Canada should welcome more refugees might be met with the note that Canada has already accepted more Syrians than the United States, with its far larger population. Khan sets the stage to avoid such faultlines, presenting historico-political situations in which Khattak and Rachel muse about the importance of countries such as Canada getting involved to combat human rights abuses throughout our increasingly globalized world.

Conclusion

In *The Unquiet Dead*, Rachel looks on as Khattak takes the lead in interviewing an imam, noticing that that two men share cultural background, attributing shared significance to each other's name and birthplace, "names that mean something to Khattak, if not to Rachel" (99). Rachel reflects that she has learned much from Esa Khattak about Muslim names: "The name Esa could be found in the Arab world, the Indian subcontinent, the villages of Turkey and Persia, or further east in Malaysia and China. It simply meant Jesus" (99). Khan is not given to wry humor, but this last line of Rachel's reflection might prompt a reader to grin. There is nothing simple about giving a detective a name that means Jesus; the move is further complicated when it is a Muslim detective working in a unit that specializes in mediating between law enforcement and minority communities in the aftermath of violent crimes. "Jesus" is a complex symbol with different meanings for different communities, and explicitly having a main detective character bearing a Muslim version of this name invites readers to perform as much exegesis as they would like in reading the Khan novels. Notably, Rachel is also a name with biblical significance who is honored in Christian, Judaic, and Islamic traditions. A reader who wishes to learn about recent global conflicts and human rights abuses will find in Khan's novels a series of compelling murder mysteries with strong character development that provide well-researched information about the socio-politics of the situation, including an author's afterword with primary sources for further reading. At the same time, a reader with expertise in world religion and/or global conflict will be rewarded for delving further into Khan's carefully chosen names and metaphors. In either case, the detective duo of Esa Khattak and Rachel Getty provides readers a nuanced and compelling perspective on Canada's relationship to multiculturalism at home and its potential to make a difference in standing up for human rights on the world stage.

6
CANADA AND THE AMERICAN DREAM

Linwood Barclay's *Promise Falls* Series

I recently told a Canadian colleague at my American university—also a green card holder and not a US citizen, as we are both quick to point out—that I am writing a book about Canadian crime fiction.

"Isn't that an oxymoron?" he quipped.
We both laughed.
"But seriously," he said. "We have so much less crime in Canada."

I hesitated. Certainly, Canada's rate of violent crimes and especially homicide is considerably lower than that of the United States, but Canada has plenty of crime, much of it revealing systemic injustices that Canadians living outside Canada may prefer not to talk about, or even think about. "Well, it's crime *fiction*!" I said brightly, and we moved on to other topics.

I share this anecdote to highlight a reality of Canadians living in the United States (and perhaps of all people living outside their homeland). Just as I would hesitate to complain seriously about a beloved family member outside my family, I virtually never speak ill of any aspect of Canada with friends and colleagues in the United States. I—and my colleague and countless other Canadians living in the United States, no doubt—prefer to imagine and represent our native land as a crime-free, almost utopian space. And we often do this by contrasting Canada to the United States.

Canada and the United States have a long history of peaceful alliance represented metonymically by the phrase "the longest undefended border in the word." And indeed, the two countries have had no military conflicts since the War of 1812. Each country's national character can be illuminated in part by its origin story, each of which might prefer not to delve too deeply into the treatment of the First Nations people who numbered in the millions before European invasion. The creation of the United States articulated in the famous foundational document, the Declaration of Independence, on July 4, 1776, was defended by the American Revolutionary War. Canadian Confederation almost a century later, on July 1, 1867, was a more bureaucratic affair, and the stereotype of the aggressive, independent-minded American and the peaceful, orderly Canadian remains to this day. The United States and Canada are by far each other's largest trading partners and have several important bilateral ties in areas of trade, human rights, security, environment, and global affairs. Culturally, the two countries resemble each other more than they resemble any other nation.

The relationship between Canadian and American popular culture has been theorized—mostly by Canadians—in a number of different ways. Frank Manning argues against the well-known metaphor of "a masculine America's penetration of feminine Canada" (4), finding instead a dialectic that is "both conflictive and complementary" (27) in the two nations' cultural exchange. Bernard Ostry posits that the relationship between the two countries "would be easier if the differences were more dramatic and clear-cut" (37); indeed, Americans and Canadians alike are sometimes unsure of the nationality of our writers and other artists. For Andrew Wernick, the United States is associated with the modern and Canada with the postmodern: "America, the incarnation of centralizing and homogenizing industrial progress, is still *modernity*. But Canada, a dispersed society of margins without a center, now becomes a figure for *post-modernity*" (300). Certainly the self-reflective irony and pastiche that characterizes many Canadian cultural products connects it to the postmodern (although many American texts can be similarly situated). As Reid Gilbert notes in his analysis of the Canadian Mountie figure, "It is the highly satirical nature of the Canadian sense of self that is finally the most interesting and the most complicated aspect of the Canadian national character" (192). Indeed, humor has been much discussed as a central feature of Canadian identity, and Danielle Deveau's analysis of Canadian comedians is persuasive in arguing that "the paradoxical outsider/insider relationship that Canadians have with American popular culture is integral to Canadian comics' ability to 'pass' within the dominant US culture" (172).

I would add another metaphor to this list based on my experience of living in the United States and knowing a lot of leftist American academics: the US seems like a dystopia and Canada like a utopia. As has been reported in both countries, in times of political turmoil in the United States, Google searches for how to immigrate to Canada often increase substantially (Noor) and recent years have even seen a mild uptick of such immigration (Gilmore). The dystopia/utopia lens will seem familiar to many readers. The United States is the most powerful, influential country in the world, and yet it is plagued by features found in many modern-day dystopias: gun violence, substance abuse, an increasing wealth gap, and, recently, a curtailing of reproductive rights. To American liberals, Canada might look like a utopia, with even the harsh winters recently (and regrettably) softened by global climate change. To scholars of utopia, however, the label is hardly a compliment. The "perfect place" (u-topos) is always "no place" (eu-topos), as built into the genre's origins with Thomas More's *Utopia* (1516). Indeed, the rhetorical purpose of a utopia is not to outline an ideal society but rather to do the same work as a dystopia: to engage in the critique of contemporary society in order to imagine a better future and activate readers to avoid the perils identified by the critique. Canadian writer and literary critic Margaret Atwood has coined a new term to show the inextricable links between utopia and dystopia: *ustopia* (*Other* 66).

Linwood Barclay sets his crime thrillers in a ustopian space that uses fast-paced plots to engage readers in sociopolitical critique. Barclay (b. 1955) is an American-born Canadian who moved from Darien, Connecticut to Toronto as a young child and has since studied and worked in several smaller Ontario towns and cities, namely Bobcaygeon, Peterborough, and Oakville. He claims Ross Macdonald (1915–1983), an earlier Canadian crime fiction writer whom Barclay met when he was 21, as one of his main literary inspirations. Macdonald is known for his 18 novels featuring California private investigator Lew Archer, and is celebrated for bringing psychological depth to the figure of the hard-boiled hero as articulated by Raymond Chandler: "But down these mean streets a man must go who is not himself mean, who is neither tarnished nor afraid" (59). As Barclay has noted in an interview, "[Macdonald] was the writer who showed you could use the conventions of the detective novel to tackle big issues. Family dysfunction, environmentalism, disaffected youth" (Penzler). Macdonald never attempted to construct Canadian spaces as "mean streets" needing a tough yet untarnished hero. Barclay, similarly, sets his thrillers across the border, using an American backdrop for his multi-perspective novels, which move between criminal, victim, and detective viewpoints in order to provide a substantial critique of twenty-first-century socio-technological mores, apparently in the United States, but also relevant to Canada.

Jeannette Sloniowski and Marilyn Rose rightly note that "To demand that Canadian writers write only about Canada is, of course, limiting and terribly prescriptive" (14). And yet, Canadian writers who set their works elsewhere are often confronted with exactly that demand. Barclay defends his decision to use an American setting with humor and perhaps a little indignation in responding to a Goodreads question:

> Hi Janet. Why not? No one ever asks Peter Robinson why he sets books in the UK, or Rohinton Ministry why he sets books in India. But if you set a book in the US, that sometimes gets questioned.

After explaining that he was born in the United States, has dual citizenship, and has spent considerable time in the United States, he concludes with a typically Canadian elucidation: "I think a US setting suits my stories slightly better. I like to say that many of my characters are so nasty, they couldn't possibly be Canadian anyway." This tongue-in-cheek statement reflects the idea of a utopian Canada sitting next to a dystopian United States. A close examination of Barclay's novels, however, reveals that the dystopian critique he sets in the United States can—and should—be applied to readers' analysis of Canadian culture as well.

Rewriting the American Dream: Promises Rise and Fall

The American Dream is a vexed proposition. When the term was popularized by historian James Truslow Adams in 1931, it was described as an ideal reminiscent of precepts in utopian writing: "that American dream of a better, richer, and happier life for all our citizens of every rank which is the greatest contribution we have as yet made to the thought and welfare of the world" (viii). Even as Adams claims this contribution for the United States, he also argues that the American Dream is in peril in the 1930s. Indeed, the notion of the American Dream, like any good utopian term, is more often used as an imagined ideal for figuring a better-imagined future than as an accurate descriptor of the present. Canadians might claim that the Canadian Dream (if such a concept exists) is more modest, or at least more modestly articulated, than the American dream, since the Canadian version leaves space to acknowledge assistance from a socialist government. However, recent research suggests that Canadians and Americans have many of the same utopian longings for their countries. As Miles Corak reports, 2019 public opinion polls comparing American and Canadian respondents found remarkably similar attitudes in the two populations. Respondents identify similar factors as contributing to upward mobility, privileging elements relating to individual choice rather than causes beyond an individual's control. Corak identifies a statistically significant but not overwhelming difference between attitudes about the role of government, with 35% of Americans and 47% of Canadians agreeing or strongly agreeing with the statement "Government's responsibility is to reduce the gap between high and low incomes" and a similar proportion feeling that governmental action is generally positive. Although Canada does not clearly articulate a "Canadian Dream," Corak persuasively shows that "if there is such a thing as the 'Canadian Dream,' it would look very much like what Americans say is the 'American Dream.'" In other words, it would hold dear principles of equality and opportunity while also being subject to ongoing interrogation.

Linwood Barclay's Promise Falls series engages in a dystopian project that suggests, like Adams almost a century earlier, that the American Dream is in peril, or perhaps has already perished. Promise Falls is a fictional municipality, so named in honor of an attractive geographical feature. The name provides a juxtaposition, though, with "Promise" (hope) sitting next to "Falls" (decline). By the end of the first novel, *Broken Promise* (2015), the falls has become the site of a death by suicide with the narrator musing darkly: "She wasn't the first person to die from going off the bridge that spans that rushing cliff of water, and she probably wouldn't be the last" (487). In *Broken Promise*, we meet a series of characters who each represents a different major institution in a state of decline. David Harwood is a journalist returning to work on his hometown newspaper after a stint with the Boston Globe, only to find out on his first day back that the smaller paper is closing permanently due to insolvency. Agnes Pickens, David's aunt and the local hospital administrator, worries about the state of health care in the community in the wake of the news that Promise Falls General Hospital has recently fallen to below average in rankings of regional hospitals, due in part to a recent *c-diff* outbreak. Agnes thinks, sourly, "Too bad the *Promise Falls Standard* was still printing at the time [of the outbreak in the hospital]; it was front-page material for the better part of two weeks" (57). Gloria Fenwick, the administrator in charge of overseeing the closure of the Five Mountains Theme Park just outside the city, ruminates about the reasons such an entertainment investment has not paid off: "Building in that location was a miscalculation. Traffic patterns were misjudged. Promise Falls is too far from Albany. There are no other attractions, like a discount outlet mall, to make this a logical destination point" (138). Detective Barry Duckworth, a 20-year veteran representing the police force, is uncomfortable in his body, reflecting often on his slow and steady weight gain over 20 years of literally eating donuts, part of his strategy for keeping ties with his local community. Clive Duncomb, the new head of security at Thackeray College, engages in dangerous policing practices, citing as justification the need to prevent reputational harm like that done several years ago "with the college president and that plagiarism scandal and the shooting"

(74–5). The slow breakdown of major institutions—media, health care, entertainment, law enforcement, and education—occurs in tandem with a familiar story of political corruption. Randall (aptly nicknamed Randy) Finley is Promise Falls' disgraced mayor, not re-elected after a scandal involving an underaged prostitute. Promise Falls thus seems representative of many mid-sized cities in the United States—and Canada—that were built on the promise of post–World War II manufacturing but are now in a state of economic and cultural decline.

Promise Falls' dystopian potential, however, is much greater than that of the average run-down city with limited prospects for its young people, as it is to become known in social media circles as a "Revenge City." In the weeks narrated by the original trilogy—*Broken Promise* (2016), *Far From True* (2016), and *The Twenty-Three* (2016)—the small city is awash in a wave of crimes. Some are reversible, like a chilling adoption scam, a foiled child kidnapping, an attempted murder for hire, and a prison break. Others feature criminals of various kinds: a thief who is murdered when he attempts to rob the garage of a domestic terrorist, an arsonist who commits a hate crime against a Muslim bookstore owner, and a serial killer targeting young women with long dark hair (who turns out to be a cop, expanding the critique of institutions). These side stories provide a dystopian backdrop for the central plot, which involves a series of bizarre and very public misdemeanors: 23 dead squirrels strung up in a row, three naked mannequins with a warning painted across their chests in carriage 23 of an abandoned Ferris wheel, and a young man wearing a hoodie with the number 23 attempting to assault young women on the college campus. The central culprit, it turns out, is driven mad by grief and rage, and perpetrates two horrifying acts of domestic terrorism: an explosion at a drive-in movie theater that kills four random patrons in *Far From True*, and the poisoning of the town water supply in *The Twenty-Three*, an act that kills almost 200 of the town's inhabitants.

In this onslaught of crimes, Barclay references—subtly or openly—real-world cases, a technique that does the utopian/dystopian work of engaging readers in real-world critique. The deadly poisoning of the water supply will remind many Canadians of the Walkerton *E. coli* outbreak of 2000 and the subsequent Walkerton Inquiry that resulted in two Public Utilities Commission operators pleading guilty in 2004. Walkerton is a small town west of Toronto that became famous in Canada and around the world for an *E. coli* outbreak caused by improper water treatment that led to 7 deaths and 2,000 people becoming ill, some with long-term effects. Although there was apparently no criminal intent in the Walkerton incident, the Inquiry revealed a problem as familiar to readers as it is to characters in dystopian novels. Brian Gover, a commissioner in the Inquiry, recounts an interaction with one of the water treatment operators:

> One of the ... answers that Stan Koebel [the operator] gave has always stayed with me. He was asked—what happened? It didn't have to do with falsifying lab tests necessarily, although it did, or underchlorinating the water, although it did—he said "complacency." Overall that was the problem. Complacency among the legislators, the regulators, and the operators.
>
> *(Burrowes)*

The prevalence of complacency—in all the major institutions of Promise Falls, and perhaps other real-world municipalities—is both dystopian and realistic. As is the tragedy at the heart of the domestic terror that frames the first three novels.

The tragedy that haunts Promise Falls raises the kind of epistemological and ethical questions common to both crime fiction and dystopian literature. Three years before the chain of events that begins in *Broken Promise*, the town saw the murder of Olivia Walden, a young woman whose boyfriend was late to meet her and whose screams were heard by 22 town residents, none of whom reported them to police. The domestic terrorist leaves clues about the 23 (including the tardy boyfriend in the list of the culpable) so the town can make sense of his rage as he seeks an expansive revenge given that the singular murderer remains unidentified. The events of Olivia's death are rare; she is the first victim of a serial killer, a statistically unlikely form of murder despite its popularity in fiction. But the notion of the bystander effect—that people are inhibited from helping someone in need if others are also present—is as controversial as it is well-known. Indeed, characters in the novel mention the Kitty Genovese case that popularized the bystander effect as an alleged psychological phenomenon. Genovese was raped and murdered in New York City in 1964, and the *New York Times* published an article claiming that 38 witnesses saw or heard the attack and that none attempted to help or call for help. This well-known and dramatic representation of the bystander effect has since been disproved (the number of witnesses was exaggerated, and several people did call the police), forcing social scientists to rethink the dark version of human nature it appears to reveal. And yet, the notion that people will be complacent and apathetic in an emergency—and that social institutions may participate in that apathy—remains familiar to twenty-first-century readers. This duality—that the bystander effect is both well-known and inaccurate—may point to a fundamental flaw in the utopian project of the American Dream.

American Guns: Police, Journalists, and the Broken Family

The Promise Falls series registers a deep concern in the Canadian public as well as in a sizeable portion of the American public with gun violence. Although guns appear frequently throughout the series, I will focus my analysis on two incidents that engage readers in thinking through the ethical implications of "justified shootings": the killing of alleged rapist Mason Helt by campus security chief Clive Duncomb and the killing of escaped convict Brandon Worthington by journalist David Harwood.

Duncomb is first introduced in *Broken Promise* through the perspective of detective Barry Duckworth as an arrogant security chief who eschews the local police when Thackeray College experiences a series of attempted sexual assaults. Duncomb explains that he has set up his own sting operation without involving the police, citing his former experience on the Boston Police Department as justification. Duckworth is appalled that Duncomb is sending out an armed female security guard without appropriate training or backup to lure what appears to be a dangerous sexual predator, and orders Duncomb to end this unauthorized operation. The character sketch of Duncomb is then built out by Joyce Pilgrim, the security guard whose safety concerns Duckworth. As the only female member of the five-person Thackeray College security team, Joyce regularly experiences a hostile workplace characterized by sexual harassment. She has considered reporting her situation to the human relations department, but

> Even though the [sexual harassment] policy, which was there for everyone to read on the college's Web site, stressed that no individual's employment would be placed in jeopardy by lodging a complaint, she knew the real world was very different.
>
> *(230)*

When ordered to act as a lure, Joyce considers discussing the situation with her husband, but he is between jobs, so she doesn't want to put him in a situation of choosing between her safety and her much-needed income. Duncomb's arrogance and continued disrespect of his only female colleague, coupled with the systemic reasons she cannot easily escape, speak to a dystopian element of Promise Falls that too often mimics the real world.

The sting operation, as Duckworth and Joyce Pilgrim have both predicted, goes very badly. The surveillance on Joyce breaks down, so that none of the other security guards on watch actually witness the man in the hoody grabbing Joyce and pulling her into the bushes. Her earpiece comes out, but she still has the gun. The man pins her to the ground and then tells her he isn't actually going to hurt her. Joyce manages to pull out the gun, still without backup, and the surprised assailant knocks it from her untrained hand. He grabs the gun from the ground, and the scene unfolds:

> "Goddamn it," the man said. "I was never going to do anything." He angled the gun away, so that if it went off, it wouldn't hit Joyce. "It's all for show, a gig, a kind of social experiment, he called it."
> "What?" Joyce said.
> "No one actually gets hurt or anything, so—"
> There was a stirring in the bushes to the left. Then a deafening bang. One side of the attacker's head blew clean off.
> Joyce screamed.
> Clive Duncomb emerged from the brush, gun in hand.
> "Got the son of a bitch," he said.
>
> *(235–6)*

Mason Helt, a student from the drama department, was hired to frighten female students under the guise of performing a social science experiment, although we eventually learn that it's part of the vigilante's plan to frighten the town and provide a clue through the number 23 on Mason's hoody. Duncomb's fatal shooting of Mason, which is ruled as justified despite the predictable failure of the sting operation he was not authorized to supervise, provides a dark vision of the private security industry and its uneasy relationship to state authority. The breakdown of the legal system here is emphasized in the next novel when Duncomb is revealed to be involved in a scheme to drug and rape the college girls he is employed to protect.

The other example of a "justified shooting" is more morally complex. David Harwood clearly introduces Barclay's concern with a changing media landscape as well as with a preponderance of guns in America. Harwood, formerly a *Boston Globe* reporter, has come home to Promise Falls after the murder of his wife in order to seek a better life for his young son. When the local newspaper closes on his first day of work, Harwood is forced to use his rhetorical and communications skills in a distasteful way, as the Public Relations (PR) expert for disgraced ex-mayor Randall Finley, who is running again for his old leadership position. Harwood stands in for the decline of the newspaper industry, a problem that deeply concerns Barclay, a long-time newspaper editor and humor columnist. In a recent interview, Barclay notes: "If there's any kind of trend that concerns me, it's been the death, or the decline, of newspapers. Also this kind of embracing of ignorance, and real fake news" (Donaldson). As a journalist who has become a PR expert, Harwood himself represents a move from real to fake news. He also exists in a liminal personal space. He is caught between the needs of his son and his parents, with his son being bullied at his new school as he grieves his mother, and Harwood's own mother dealing with health issues that may include cognitive decline. As a relatively young widower, he is also caught between his grief for his murdered wife and some reluctant enthusiasm for dating Samantha, the divorced mother of the boy who has bullied his son.

In *The Twenty-Three*, when Harwood uses a gun to kill an unarmed man, the scene is set up to maximize ethical complexity. Harwood is dating Sam, whose ex-husband Brandon Worthington is in jail and whose son Carl has already been a victim of a kidnap attempt by Brandon's parents. Now Brandon has escaped from prison and Sam has taken Carl away to hide until her ex-husband is back in police custody. Harwood and Brandon both know Sam well enough to guess which campground she will take Carl to, and focalization moves between Harwood and Sam as the scene unfolds. Sam and Carl are in a tent when Brandon appears, begging for five minutes to talk to them. He explains that he has turned a new leaf and escaped from police custody when the opportunity presented itself because he wanted them to know they had nothing to fear from him or his family, and he will not bother them again. Harwood, meanwhile, arrives at the campground intent on saving Sam and Carl from the escaped convict. He sees that Brandon is already in their tent and realizes that he doesn't have time to get help, but he isn't sure he will be able to fight Brandon. When he sees Sam's shotgun in her unlocked car, he reaches for it, gingerly and inexpertly:

> He realized he had the barrel pointing straight at his chest, so he shifted a few inches to the left so that he wouldn't kill himself if the damn thing went off.
>
> He didn't even know if it was loaded. But then, maybe it wouldn't have to be.
>
> Just having it would be enough to defuse the situation, if it came to that.
>
> … David didn't know a lot about guns.
>
> *(388)*

As Barclay is about to make clearer, David certainly does not know a lot about guns if he thinks having one will diffuse a situation he also does not know a lot about.

After apologizing to Sam and Carl, Brandon turns to leave in order to turn himself in to the authorities. Carl goes to hug his father, and trips. When Brandon turns to help his son regain his footing, David erroneously reads the gesture as threatening: "It looked pretty clear to David that Brandon was going to grab his son and make a run for it" (424). Since David cannot really see what is going on behind the tent, he yells at Brandon to get away from the kid and runs toward the scene brandishing Sam's shotgun. Brandon, who has never met Harwood before, grabs a cooking pot in an attempt to protect his family. The scene is devastating.

> David felt his finger on the trigger of the shotgun.
> Sam cried, "David, no!"
> Carl wailed, "Dad!"
> David fired.
>
> *(425)*

As a person who has never held a gun before and who is described as having little intentionality ("felt his finger on the trigger"), David nonetheless takes a single fatal shot. The scene ends with Sam hugging her shocked and grieving son as she berates David:

> "You idiot!" she yells at him over the cries of her son. "You stupid fucking idiot."
> "But ..."
>
> *(425)*

This feels to me like a clear representation of what many Canadians believe to be an overly permissive gun culture in the United States. Sam's gun, lawfully purchased, was unlawfully stored in the backseat of an unlocked car (somewhat understandable, given that she is on the run and so comfortable with guns that she is not constantly thinking about the location of her weapon). David—as uncomfortable and unfamiliar with guns as Sam is comfortable and familiar—nonetheless believes the weapon is necessary to diffuse a potentially volatile situation. In a misguided attempt to save Sam and her son, David ends up causing extreme trauma to them both and accidentally preventing the potential salvage of their family. And in the end, when faced with the proof that his inexperienced use of a gun in a time of crisis (perhaps caused by the prevalence of gun culture in the United States) was wrong, David can do nothing but sputter "But ...."

Barclay's *Parting Shot*: Revenge in the Age of Social Media

Although Barclay explores his concern with declining journalism through David Harwood's shifting career in the first three novels of the series, it is in the final novel that he most explicitly addresses what has now come to replace the newspaper in informing the public: social media. After the single narrative arc of the first three novels of the series, *Parting Shot* narrates the dark yet predictable impact of the city's reputation as a revenge town in an age of social media. The novel is fast-paced and exciting, but it is also suffused with the deep sadness that characterizes much dystopian fiction. Promise Falls is no longer a city in decline; it has become a full-blown dystopian space as Barclay once again presents a series of situations that invite readers to weigh and consider various perspectives on media, crime, and family relationships when negatively skewed by social media addiction.

In this novel, Cal Weaver, a private investigator, is hired to protect Jeremy Pilford, a wealthy, white, 18-year-old man who has recently received a sentence of probation for the crime of vehicular manslaughter with the defense that he had been so pampered throughout his life that he did not understand his own wrongdoing. Pilford is known as "The Big Baby" on late-night talk shows as on social media. Pilford's propulsion to national news because of his high-priced defense lawyer's tactics and his paltry sentence may remind readers of the Stanford Rape Case that prompted a national outcry when Brock Allen Turner, a wealthy, white, 20-year-old Stanford University student-athlete received a sentence of 6 months county jail time and 3 years' probation for the sexual assault in January 2015 of an intoxicated, unconscious woman, a crime whose punishment carries up to 14 years in state prison. The judge's comment that a harsher sentence would have had a "severe impact" on Turner's athletic aspirations (Koren), and Turner's father's highly publicized letter, which includes the much-quoted line that jailtime would be "a steep price to pay for 20 minutes of action out of his 20 plus years of life" (Samuels) brought national attention to this case and to broader concerns about rape culture on college campuses. According to Jennifer Tisdale, Turner is now living quietly in Dayton, Ohio, where women very publicly use social media to track his movements and warn others of his activities. Barclay's use of a similar situation for the fictional Jeremy Pilford draws attention not only to inequities within the US juridical system but also to the complex sociocultural and moral landscape created by social media trends fueled by viral courtroom moments.

Cal is hired by Jeremy's great-aunt, Madeline Plimpton, whose family had been long-time owners of the town's recently shuttered newspaper. Plimpton offers a jaded analysis of social media trends that includes mention of several cases from immediately before the novel's publication, including the Stanford Rape Case:

> "Social consternation over [Jeremy's] sentencing will last a few months at most, I would think. The world is always waiting for the new thing

to be outraged by. A hunter who kills a prize lion in Africa. A woman who tweets a joke about AIDS. A dimwitted politician who things a woman's body knows how to shut down pregnancy following rape. That other judge, who gave the light sentence to the boy who raped that unconscious girl. We are so thrilled to be angered about something that we want a new target for our rage every week."

(18–9)

This condemnation of human nature ("We are so thrilled to be angered") provides a pointed critique of social media's ability to repeatedly raise outrage and even motivate dangerous and criminal behavior through the power of viral storytelling. This fictional newspaperwoman's analysis closely matches recent scholarship on social media by such scholars as New York Times reporter Max Fisher in his book, *The Chaos Machine: The Inside Story of How Social Media Rewired Our Minds and Our World* (2022).

Jeremy Pilford's mother, Gloria, is constructed as being very much part of the problem. She agreed to the defense strategy of painting her son as a boy whose moral compass never developed in part due to poor parenting on her part, and she receives almost as much social media venom as does Jeremy. Surely Cal represents the reader when he looks askance at the threats and vitriolic comments on her Facebook page:

"How did these people become your friends in the first place?" I [Cal] asked. "Don't people have to ask, and then you accept?"
  Grant Finch [Gloria's fiancé] gave me a tired look. "We've talked about this."
  "I like to know who my enemies are," Gloria said defiantly.
  "It's like you've opened the front door for them," I said.

(40)

Gloria's refusal to remove herself, even temporarily, from the social media spotlight is representative of a chasm in contemporary society—in both the United States and Canada, and perhaps globally. Those who seldom or never use social media, like the two main detectives in the Promise Falls series, cannot understand the compulsion of others to continually immerse themselves in a network of virtual relationships and communications that are both destructive and addictive. And yet, the result of social media immersion sometimes erupts in crimes that must then be investigated by detectives who may not have a basic understanding of social media; detectives used to thinking of perpetrators as either known to the victim or not must now face the possibility of perpetrators known to the victim only through online contact.

The policing of social-media-fueled crimes is especially complicated in Promise Falls given recent events. As Weaver learns,

> Incredibly, [the killer from the first three novels] had become something of a folk hero in certain communities once it became known that his monstrous crime was intended as a lesson. The people of Promise Falls had gained a reputation for not caring when no one came to the aid of a woman being murdered in the downtown park. Now we had a new reputation. We were the national capital for retribution.
>
> *(41–2)*

As Barry Duckworth investigates a malicious tattooing incident, he visits the repulsive Craig Pierce, a pedophile who was exonerated of his crime because the mentally handicapped girl he molested was unable to testify against him. Pierce has been the victim of a horrifying revenge plot and provides Duckworth with a great deal of information about Just Deserts, a website that reports on—and indirectly promotes—especially creative or visually memorable revenge plots. As Pierce explains, "So you've got people all over the [expletive] planet inspired to exact vengeance on people who've got it coming, hoping like crazy that what they do is nasty enough to be honored on this website" (159). Pierce, now disabled from the vengeance plot against him from the year before, shares with Duckworth his own detective work—superior to any the Promise Falls police department has undertaken—in gathering clues and analyzing evidence in attempting to identify some of the real-world perpetrators posting their vengeance trophy pictures on the website.

Pierce's research uncovers Cory Calder, a bright young man from a stable middle-class family whose obsession with social media leads him to create increasingly extravagant vengeance plots. Barclay's analysis of Calder's transformation is chilling. Calder's parents were advocates for a variety of social justice causes until his mother died a few years earlier. His brother is a marine scientist researching ways to transform oceans into potable water, and his sister is a doctor working with other humanitarians on the European refugee crisis. Calder's rivalry with family members is especially fueled by media coverage of their exploits, and Cory Calder ends up seeking to compete for fame by uploading pictures of horrifying revenge schemes to Just Deserts. The reader is given Cory's perspective after he uploads information and pictures documenting his vile revenge on Craig Pierce: "Seeing the response was without question the most exciting thing that had ever happened to Cory Calder" (347). And later, to press the point, "Very quickly, the online adulation became addictive" (348). Cory reframes his actions in an especially competitive manner:

> Well, you didn't need a medical degree or a PhD in whatever it was his brother had to make your mark in the world. There were other paths to greatness. In many ways, Cory considered what he had been doing more noble, because it was anonymous. He wasn't on CNN. He wasn't getting quoted in the *New York Times*.
>
> *(349)*

The Promise Falls series provides a nuanced view on vigilante justice that may well be one of the reasons Barclay has set it in the United States, where opinions about state-sanctioned capital punishment vary by state (the last execution in Canada was in 1962, and the death penalty was federally abolished in 1976). As Cal works to protect Jeremy from potential revenge plots that can be organized and will doubtless be celebrated on social media, he also takes on a paternal role toward the young man, even accidentally calling him by his deceased son's name when he teaches him how to drive with a standard transmission. Eventually, he discovers that Jeremy has been gaslighted all along. He was not driving the car involved in the vehicular manslaughter and was in fact set up to take the fall by powerful middle-aged men including his lawyer and his mother's fiancé. The final scene of the novel recalls the earlier, less technologically complicated times of Golden Age detective fiction when the detective is fully in control of a rational explanation for the crime and can reveal it pleasurably by gathering the key players and explaining his admirable reasoning. Promise Falls, of course, does not belong in the epistemologically ordered world of the Victorian era that gave rise to that scene, and Cal quickly loses control of the narrative when several key players gather in the kitchen of Madeline Plimpton's house and Cal reveals his solution to the crime for which Jeremy has already been tried and received a suspended sentence.

There is Jeremy, his great-aunt, his mother, his mother's fiancé Bob Butler, and Cal the private detective (waiting for Barry Duckworth the police detective to come to arrest Bob). Cal reveals to all that Jeremy did not commit the crime and that an associate of Bob's was actually driving the car, a fact Bob knew when he stepped in to pay for the expert legal counsel that devised the defense that would spare Jeremy prison time but that would cause irreparable reputational harm. Faced with the truth, Bob tries to escape, forcing Cal to manhandle him onto the floor. In the midst of this chaotic reveal scene, Jeremy learns that his mother, Gloria, knew he was innocent of the crime. Gloria defends her decision to her devastated son, tearfully:

> "If it hadn't worked," she said weakly, "I told them, that if they sent Jeremy to jail, then I'd have to say ... I'd have to say something ..."
> "You let them do this to me," Jeremy said.
> "But I let them humiliate *me*," she told him. "I let them make a laughing stock of me, because I *love* you. I was willing to do anything to save you. I didn't care. I did it for you."
>
> *(483, original ellipses and italics)*

The full force of Gloria's betrayal of her son can be seen in Jeremy's reactions as he processes the fact that his mother allowed him to face not only public ridicule and scorn but also personal guilt. As evidenced by Gloria's weak defense of her actions, she is just as—and perhaps far more—obsessed with surface reputational identity as her son and his generation.

When Duckworth arrives, angry that Cal attempted a reveal scene without proper police protection and procedure, the situation goes even further awry. While Duckworth and his colleague handcuff Bob, a shot is heard in the kitchen. The novel ends with Jeremy exiting the kitchen in which he has shot his mother:

> Jeremy walked calmly out of the kitchen, stopped, looked at me [Cal Weaver], and managed to make his quivering lips smile ever so slightly.
> "I did it," he said. "I take full responsibility." He paused. "I own this."
> I took him into my arms, while Duckworth ran into the kitchen to see how bad it was.
>
> *(486)*

This conclusion to the novel—and the series—leaves the reader to determine "how bad it was." One presumes that Jeremy is now a killer for real, and he will not have access to expensive lawyers who can fashion elaborate defenses that will prevent state-sanctioned punishment while inviting social-media-fueled threats. At the same time, he has also taken control of his life for the first time ever. In a dark way, his decision to take action—and responsibility for that action—may be read as simply the most complex in a series of cultural investigations of revenge. Jeremy's parting shot represents one possible reaction to a chaotic world in which misinformation and vengeance are the most prevalent features of a town called Promise Falls.

Conclusion

The past few years have seen the circulation of a meme that shows a sandwich board at a bookstore that proclaims: "Dystopian Fiction has been moved to the Current Events Section." Barclay, in the tradition of other writers of dark detective fiction, represents a world with markedly dystopian features: a declining city, declining social institutions, and problematic replacements to those institutions. Is Barclay's series simply a reflection of the real-world conditions south of the border? Or of how Canadians (want to) see conditions in the United States? Or is it participating in the dystopian literary project of creating an exaggeratedly dark world in order to critique—and hopefully positively affect—current events?

Barclay's perspective leaves much of the interpretation to readers, as evidenced by the series' closing scene, which does not tell the reader whether the gunshot was fatal or how to interpret Jeremy's act. To me, this is evidence of Barclay's activist dystopian leanings. It is typical of dystopian fiction to leave an open ending that engages readers to answer the questions that are posed by the text and to reflect on the problems illuminated therein. By creating crimes that reference real-world, highly publicized cases from the United States and Canada—the Kitty Genovese case that came to (erroneously) stand for the bystander effect, the Walkerton *E. coli* water crisis, and the Stanford rape case—Barclay highlights dark realities that threaten contemporary North American daily life. In this way, his dystopian series can be paired with another Canadian series—Louise Penny's Three Pines series, discussed in Chapter 12 and elsewhere as combining detective fiction with utopian leanings—to show that we stand at an important moment in twenty-first-century North American and global contexts. Although anxieties abound (in the real world as in Barclay's fictional text), readers still have time to act in order to enact the kinds of policy and legal changes that will effectively prevent the creation of a real-world Promise Falls.

PART II
Canadian Genre Play

7
THE POLICE PROCEDURAL
Registering Change with Peter Robinson's DCI Banks

Peter Robinson's DCI Banks series is all about perspective. With chapter segments moving regularly between the protagonist's perspective and those of other characters—bystanders, victims, criminals, and other detectives—Robinson's novels explore a variety of crimes and attendant issues in complex ways that invite readers to think through the ethical, psychological, and sociological implications of a crime. Banks is a detective prone to self-reflection, and he recognizes that as he interacts with different people, he sees different parts of himself. When he is with his coarse, abrasive, and yet usually effective colleague Sergeant Jim Hatchley, Banks seems almost radical. As he muses in *Gallows View* (1987), the first novel of the series, "Why was it, he wondered, that talking to Hatchley always made him, a moderate socialist, feel like a bleeding-heart liberal?" (13–4). When, on the other hand, he is with Dr. Jenny Fuller, the psychologist who does profiling for his department and who has actual radical friends, he feels almost conservative. As a moderate socialist who welcomes and tries to understand the perspectives of others, Banks in some ways serves as an embodiment of an idealized version of Canada—a complex thinker who believes that much of the present can be understood through an analysis of the past.

An English-born writer who earned his MA and PhD from Canadian universities, Robinson (1950–2022) lived and worked in Toronto, but sets his most famous series (the 28 novels featuring Inspector Alan Banks) in the United Kingdom, and *DCI Banks*, the TV series based on these novels is produced for Britain's ITV and features an almost entirely English cast. Nonetheless, Jeanette Sloniowski claims Robinson as "Canada's most

DOI: 10.4324/9781003125242-9

distinguished crime writer" (123), arguing that he writes about a fear of American cultural encroachment on British culture, an anxiety certainly familiar to Canadian readers. In her excellent analysis of Robinson's *In a Dry Season* (1999), Sloniowski examines a novel that focuses on the past in order to articulate the importance of questions of genre and gender to Robinson's project. As Sloniowski ably demonstrates, Robinson's novels are replete with a "complex and extensive postmodern use of references to other writers, books, films, and in particular names of songs or musicians to evoke emotions, ideas, or a particular ambiance" (129). Characterizing Robinson's style as palimpsestic, Sloniowski highlights his nuances as a writer, focusing on the generic hybridity of his narratives as well as the complexity of his characters' perspectives on gender. Working from the notion that Robinson's worldview "can most certainly be seen as Canadian in nature" (Sloniowski and Rose xvi) despite the setting of his series in Yorkshire and its surroundings, I examine Robinson's developing notion of how to represent the gender dynamics around sex crimes by reading the first novel of the series, *Gallows View* (1987), as well as the 27th, *Not Dark Yet* (2021).

Canadian crime and detective fiction centers the police procedural as its dominant subgenre. This is perhaps no surprise given the country's use of a police official—the Royal Canadian Mounted Police officer, or "Mountie"—as a national icon. As Daniel Francis notes, "Canadians are the only people in the world who recognize a police force as their proudest national symbol" (29). The embracing of the police procedural also resonates with Canadian self-identity as a country of rule-followers who believe in the benefits of a strong government, including for security. It also speaks to Canadian writers' interest in realism, since this is the subgenre most closely connected to the real world, given that most real-world crimes are processed by police, and few real-world police officers consult with the town librarian or baker or other amateur detectives for help in solving cases.

The police procedural rose to prominence in the 1950s in the United States and in the 1960s in Sweden. Alternately characterized as conservative and subversive by scholars, the form is now so pervasive that one can find examples of the police procedural with all kinds of different rhetorical goals making all kinds of different critiques. As George Dove found in his early writings about Ed McBain, the police procedural's momentum comes in part from its seriality, representing over many novels a team of detectives working together, building friendships as well as enmities as they face head-on the grind of constant crime in the city. Robert Winston and Nancy Mellerski see the police procedural as enacting a form of conservative social control, arguing that "By shifting reader identification from the criminal element to the state apparatus which opposes it, the procedural reshapes the potentially destructive impulses of individualism into successful participation in a corporate structure, the police squad" (2). Christopher Wilson, who characterizes the police as "knowledge workers" (5), sees the genre as more nuanced, suggesting that the police procedural does not focus upon "either police power or upon criminality, but on the symbiosis between these seemingly antithetical forces" (3). In examining Scandinavian police procedurals, Barry Forshaw demonstrates the early subversive potential of the form, arguing that in their Martin Beck series (1965–1975), Maj Sjöwall and Per Wahlöö introduced "genuinely radical elements into what was at the time an unthreatening form (with, they felt, distinctly bourgeois values" (17). In my opinion, the police procedural in the hands of an effective writer is the perfect genre for tracing developing public sentiment on key issues around crime, surveillance, and power. Despite its setting, Robinson's long Alan Banks series is an exemplary Canadian police procedural because it spans four decades and registers shifting views on numerous topics through representation of the police workplace as well as of the lives of police detectives. Looking at two Robinson novels—*Gallows View* (1987), the opening novel of the series, and *Not Dark Yet* (2021), the penultimate offering before Robinson's untimely death in October 2022 at age 72—allows us to examine changing ways of thinking and talking about difficult topics regarding gender and sexuality.

Gallows View: Peepers, STIs, and Independent Women

In the climactic scene of *Gallows View* (1987), Detective Chief Inspector Alan Banks finds himself in an unenviable conundrum. Within moments, he learns that two women he deeply cares about are in crisis and need his help. His wife Sandra has just been sexually assaulted in their home by the neighborhood Peeping Tom whom Banks has been pursuing, and she has hit the culprit on the head with a heavy camera and fears he may be dead. At the same moment, his attractive colleague, psychological profiler Jenny Fuller, is being held against her will by another criminal Banks is actively pursuing, and the kidnapper is demanding a negotiation specifically with Banks. The situation is made even more difficult by the fact that Banks feels some residual guilt about his ongoing attraction to Jenny and his (correct) suspicion that Sandra is aware of it. When Banks chooses to attend personally to the ongoing kidnapping and to send a trusted colleague to provide support to his wife after her traumatic victimization, his direct superior Superintendent Gristhorpe praises him for doing the right thing by putting the job first. As the narrative progresses, however, it becomes clear that Banks's decision is not made solely on the basis of the professional versus the personal, or even of the active crime versus the concluded crime. Banks goes to Jenny because he trusts and understands his wife and her strength. He predicts—rightly—that she will be in full support of his decision. Just as Robinson is a Canadian writing about English crimes and detection, so too is he a male writer addressing topics around gender and sexuality more routinely explored in detective fiction written by women. His nuanced depictions of several criminal situations involving sexual violence work together to form a provocative tapestry that invites readers to engage in gender analysis alongside the detectives.

Gallows View explores a range of complex sexual situations, some ordinary and some criminal, from multiple perspectives: marital fidelity, scopophilia (peeping), and rape. The two sex crimes investigated in the novel interrogate gendered power dynamics in a number of ways, as does the more mundane topic of marital fidelity. Like all the DCI Banks novels, *Gallows View* uses a third-person narrator with the majority of scenes focalized through Banks, and the others told through the eyes of secondary characters, be they bystanders, victims, criminals, or other detectives. Like many police procedural series, most of Robinson's novels include multiple crimes of various kinds; this provides narrative momentum as well as verisimilitude, since police departments by their nature always have several open investigations ongoing. The multiple crimes combined with the varied narrative points of view, provide the reader an engaging and nuanced perspective on gender dynamics. As Sloniowski reports, Robinson has said that his life in Canada has given him new insights into the British society depicted in his novels (124). Similarly, perhaps, Robinson's experience as a man may provide him insights into questions of gender and sexuality.

The peeper ("peeping Tom" for Canadian and American audiences) plot in *Gallows View* is explored from the criminal, victim, and detective perspectives, each engaging the reader in different ways. The opening scene of the novel is focalized through the criminal perspective as a woman (unnamed in the scene) slowly undresses alone in her bedroom, with details about her clothing and body carefully described. When she is fully naked, the woman looks towards a chink in the curtains and realizes she is being watched. It is only at the end of the short scene that the reader recognizes that this is not an omniscient narrator, but a limited narrator focalized through the criminal peeper: "His whole body tingled as he watched the shock register in her eyes. He couldn't move" (1–2). The perspective here has the potential to make the reader complicit in what Banks soon learns is called scopophilia, literally "the love of looking," but within this context, referring to a nonconsensual, objectifying gaze that dehumanizes women.

The slippery subject position of the reader is intensified as the detective perspective is provided. Detectives, as Robinson shows repeatedly throughout the series, are not a homogenous group. Within the police department, Banks and Gristhorpe take the crime seriously, recognizing a violation against the female victims, while Hatchley treats the situation as a joke, commenting jovially, "I can't see why I have to spend so much time chasing a bloke who just likes to look at a nice pair of knockers" (13). The reader presumably identifies initially with Banks, the protagonist, but Banks's perspective is soon brought into question by a complaint against Hatchley. In a scene that allows readers to identify in a variety of ways, Dorothy Wycombe, the chairperson of WEEF (The Women of Eastvale for Emancipation and Freedom) makes a complaint against Hatchley. Focalized through Banks, the situation is revealed to be complicated. Wycombe, initially unwilling to attribute a source, reports that one of the women preyed upon by the peeper found her police interview offensive, as Hatchley seemed not to take the matter seriously and even made suggestive comments about her body. Banks finds this complaint entirely plausible. At the same time, Ms. Wycombe (who brusquely berates Banks for calling her "Ma'am") is offensive in a different way, as she is here reporting street gossip without the permission of the actual complainant. When Banks approaches Hatchley to reprimand him for his inappropriate comments, the other officer claims that he was just complimenting the victim, and explains that she clearly took his comments as they were meant, since she then accepted his offer of a date. Although Hatchley's disrespectful attitude towards the women victimized by the peeper (a disrespect embodied in his habit of pasting pinup girls in his area of the office) is called out by Banks, Hatchley is rewarded within the narrative by his flirting with the victim, who even becomes his wife in a later novel.

The second—and even more complicated—situation that questions the ability of both the police and the public to make sense of sex crimes occurs when Sandra Banks, Alan's wife, becomes a victim of the peeper. Sandra, an attractive, confident woman in her thirties with a strong social support system, serves as the reader's main victim vantage point to the impact of nonconsensual voyeurism. The narrative spends time on her complex, sometimes contradictory, attempts to understand her own response to being victimized in this way:

> Apart from the immediate shock, which had made her scream, Sandra felt very calm about her experience. One minute she had been undressing for bed, as she had done thousands of times before, absorbed in her own private rituals, and the next moment that world was in tatters, would probably never be the same again. She realized that the idea of such

permanent ruin was melodramatic, so she kept it to herself, but she could think of no other way to express the complex sense of violation she had experienced.

She wasn't scared; she wasn't even angry after the shock had worn off and the adrenaline dispersed. Surprisingly, her main feeling was pity ... Her pity was not a soft and loving feeling, though; it was more akin to contempt.

(118, my ellipses)

Sandra's private musings are full of contradictions—and of recognition of those contradictions. The depth of her feeling of violation is considerable. She realizes that her reaction may be out-of-step with what is socially acceptable, but she nonetheless acknowledges her own reaction. By articulating Sandra's multi-valenced reaction as the reason she does not share her feelings with anyone, Robinson gives voice to the difficulty victims often face in reporting sexual crimes. The inadequacy of social and juridical apparatuses for processing victim experiences signals a potential danger to reporting. Further, Sandra feels both pity and contempt for her voyeur; in the absence of anger and fear, she cannot quite bring herself to report his crimes.

Sandra's experience highlights the difficult decisions involved in the reporting of sex crimes. In the end, the Bankses choose not to report the crime despite its potential value to the interrogation. Alan Banks is both supportive of his wife and troubled by her decision. On family vacation shortly thereafter, Banks, at a historic site, muses upon the various ways history can be read and reflects on his emotional reactions to the reporting dilemma:

> He hadn't reported the incident, and that nagged at his sense of integrity. On the other hand, as he and Sandra had decided, it would probably have been a lot more embarrassing and galling all round to have reported it .... And even as he worried about his own decision, Banks also wondered how many others had not seen fit to tell the police of similar incidents. If women were still reluctant to report rape, for example, would many of them not also balk at reporting a Peeping Tom?

(102)

As he continues to second-guess the decision, Banks confesses to a colleague, but now with a different motive than saving his wife and family from embarrassment:

> There would be too much unfavourable publicity all round. Not only for Sandra but for the department, too. That Wycombe woman would just

love to get her hands on something like this. If it were made public and we solved the case quickly, according to her it would only be because a policeman's wife was among the victims. No, I'd rather keep it quiet.
(109)

Banks's ability to build new justifications for the decision again invites the reader to contemplate the nuances of how sex crimes are treated in various quarters, by such diverse actors as feminist activists like Dorothy Wycombe, conservative police officers like Jim Hatchley, art gallery curators like Sandra Banks, and more moderate and sensitive men like Banks and Gristhorpe.

The novel pairs the peeper investigation with the plot of a stranger rape committed during a burglary. Once again, the reader is curiously implicated by the multiple narrative perspectives, which are, in order, the criminal's, the detective's, and (through her testimony), the victim's. The reader has been focalized through the rapist many times before the scene of the rape. Trevor Sharp is a teenager who was once a good student but has now fallen in with a bad crowd; his father, a single parent since his wife left years earlier, is unable to provide adequate guidance. Trevor has ordinary problems, such as missed homework and dental decay, but he is also embarking on a life of crime. Armed with tips from a career criminal, Trevor and his friend Mick commit burglaries in fancy homes when they know the owners are away. Reminiscent of the excessive disrespect explored in Anthony Burgess's *A Clockwork Orange* (1971), these young working-class men urinate and defecate in the living rooms of the affluent homes they are robbing. When a homeowner unexpectedly returns home early during the commission of a burglary, Trevor's disrespect toward property turns to violence and he rapes Thelma Pitt. The reader is forced to endure the scene from Trevor's perspective, which includes anxiety as well as triumph as he looks down on his victim: "Because of the scarf between her teeth she seemed to be grinning maliciously, and when he caught her eyes he thought he saw mockery in them, not just fear" (136).

The rape is then processed through the perspective of Banks as he meets with Thelma Pitt. Banks enters the interview with a sense of Thelma's past, which does not position her as a victim and is thus at odds with the horrifying scene the reader has already read: "Thelma's legendary parties, which some said were thinly disguised orgies, involved a number of prominent Eastvalers, who were all eventually embarrassed one way or another" (154). When Thelma announces that she wants to report a robbery that occurred four days earlier, Banks is puzzled by the delay. She explains that she was raped, and Banks immediately offers her the opportunity to meet with a policewoman instead. In declining this offer, Thelma provides insights into her hesitation to report the crime:

> "Inspector, I've lived with this night and day since Monday. I couldn't come in before because I was ashamed to. I felt dirty. I believed it was all my fault—a punishment for past sins. I'm a Catholic, though not a very good one. I haven't left the house since then. This morning I woke up angry, do you understand? I feel angry, and I want to do whatever I can to see that the criminals are caught. The robbery doesn't matter. The jewels were worth a great deal but not as much ... not as much."
>
> *(155, original ellipses)*

Clearly, Thelma is aware of her reputation as a woman prone to giving wild parties, and realizes that she will not be seen as a likely victim of rape. It takes her several days to move beyond her own stereotypes about who gets raped—stereotypes that are systemic in 1980s society—and toward a righteous anger.

Banks's response to Thelma's report, which clearly articulates her complex feelings as a victim, underlines the problems of the juridical system in dealing with sex crimes. Although Banks has already been shown to be a positive contrast to police officers like Jim Hatchley, who makes jokes around sex crimes, even Banks shows little compassion to Thelma as he acts (very correctly for the time) as a detective *par excellence*. The reader might focus on Thelma's shame, trauma, or anger, but Banks focuses on her pluralization of *criminal*, surprised that this is not an escalation of the Peeping Tom, but the work of two or more men. He questions her to get more details and suggests that she might see her doctor, even though it is unlikely after four days that any trace evidence would remain. Later in the chapter, Banks goes to Dr. Jenny Fuller because "it was a sexual crime and he needed a woman's advice" (158). Jenny articulates what the reader may already have noticed: Banks should have treated Thelma as a victim and not a witness. In a conversation that sets the stage for Banks to learn how to better deal with sex crimes, Jenny berates him a little:

> "Have you sent her for any help?" Jenny asked.
> "I suggested she see a doctor. Mostly for our own official purposes, I have to admit."
> "That won't do her a lot of good, Alan. There's a Rape Crisis Center in York, a place where people can talk about their problems. I'm surprised you don't know about it."
>
> *(158)*

Banks takes the number for the Rape Crisis Center and promises to give it to Thelma, apparently having learned something valuable. Jenny then proceeds to flirt with him, making the gender politics of this scene almost as difficult to track as those where Hatchley's jokes about the peeper violating Carol's privacy end up getting him a date.

As Banks—and perhaps the reader alongside—learns about the complex violations that accompany sex crimes, whether violent or not, the novel repeatedly shows women to be intelligent, pragmatic, and ultimately powerful. Even as he is investigating two separate sex crimes, Banks is also processing his own impulse to engage in infidelity for the first time in his long, apparently happy marriage to Sandra. When Banks finds out that Dr. Jenny Fuller returns his interest, he is tempted to act upon it. Jenny instigates a conversation about a possible affair, and smoothly saves the friendship when Banks, after much hesitation, turns her down. In the meantime, Sandra intuits the temptation her husband faces vis-à-vis his new colleague and discusses the situation with her friend Harriet. When Harriet asks Sandra what she plans to do, Sandra confidently says she will do nothing:

[Harriet]: "Would he tell you?"
[Sandra]: "Yes. Eventually. Men like Alan usually do, you know. They think it's because they're being honest with you, but it's really because the guilt is too much of a burden; they can't bear it alone. I'd probably rather not know, but he wouldn't consider that."

(144)

This conversation reveals how well Sandra understands her husband, his likely behavior, and his motivations. When Harriet suggests that she invite Jenny to dinner, Sandra beams at the idea. In the next chapter, from Banks's perspective, Sandra suggests a meal with Jenny, effectively disarming the threat of infidelity: "a silly argument followed, in which Banks protested that he hardly knew the woman, and that their relationship was purely professional. His nose grew an inch or two, and Sandra backed down gracefully" (152).

Sandra's pragmatism and insight regarding her own marriage previews the fact that she is no damsel in distress. Indeed, in all the sex crimes explored in the novel, the female victims show remarkable fortitude in the face of trauma, and do not need men to save them. When the peeper—a man Sandra knows slightly from her camera club—assaults her in her home, she defends herself by hitting him with a camera. When Thelma Pitt reports her rape to Banks, she also provides him a way to catch the rapist when she tells him that she has gonorrhea. The reader might recall, upon this revelation, the young rapist's feeling that his victim's eyes hold mockery as well as fear. In the end, it is the gonorrhea that leads Banks to identify Trevor and his crew as the rapist and the burglars. Once identified, Trevor's friend Mick takes Jenny Fuller hostage in a drug-addled attempt to escape prosecution. Although Banks is present, it is Jenny who takes the lead in incapacitating the criminal: "Mick reddened and looked, to Banks, dangerously near the end of his tether. But Jenny was the psychologist, and she seemed to have taken the initiative; it was up to Banks to follow" (195–6). Jenny's initiative in a physical confrontation with a criminal—seemingly more Banks's expertise than hers—and especially Banks's good judgment in following her lead, result in the safe capture of the criminal.

The denouement of *Gallows View* focuses on Banks's reflections as a male police detective and husband. In the aftermath of the simultaneous traumas Sandra and Jenny have faced in successfully fending off male attackers, the Bankses invite Jenny to stay at their home. The silly argument about inviting Jenny to dinner as a potential wedge against infidelity is far behind the three. In the face of sexual violence and the systemic inadequacies of men in understanding its violations, Sandra and Jenny are no longer rivals, if they ever were. Banks goes for an evening walk, trying to identify why he feels so disconcerted in the presence of the two women, concluding that his discomfort has

> everything to do with his sensing a strong bond between them that put him on the outside. They didn't even have to talk to make it clear. Banks had felt as if he were a clumsy, primitive beast in the presence of two alien creatures.
>
> *(201)*

Sandra confirms his analysis later, in bed, as she and Banks talk through what has happened:

> "You did the right thing," Banks said, holding her and feeling her warm tears on his shoulder.
> "I know. But that's what I mean when I said you'd never understand. You never could. There are some things men could never grasp in a million years."
> Banks felt shut out again, and it irked him that Sandra was probably right. He wanted to understand everything, and he had sympathy, feelings and imagination enough to do so, or so he had thought. Now Sandra was telling him that no matter how hard he tried, he could never fathom the bond that united her and Jenny and excluded him, simply

because he was a man .... In a way, it didn't matter how gentle and understanding he was; he was guilty by association.

(210, my ellipses)

Banks's frustration is palpable, and this reflection, in my opinion, invites readers of all genders to consider what gender gaps may exist—and need to be bridged—when it comes to sex crimes, juridically and emotionally.

Culturally, legally, and philosophically, much has changed in the three-plus decades between the publication of *Gallows View* and this analysis of it. Misogynistic jokes are no longer acceptable in the workplace. Police forces, though still dominated by men, have made an effort to more closely represent the demographic make-up of the communities they police, leading to a substantial increase in women; in Canada, women represented less than 4% of police officers in 1986 and 22% in 2019 (Pablo). Gender identity and expression are now protected categories under Canadian legislation, and there is far more awareness that not only people who identify as female are victims of sex crimes. Further, countries now work together to fight the global phenomenon of sex trafficking. In the end of *Gallows View*, Alan Banks recognizes something that is perhaps easier to understand now than it was then. Banks may feel like "a clumsy, primitive beast in the presence of two alien creatures" (201) when confronted with Sandra and Jenny, but perhaps this is an important revelation rather than an insult to his talents as a detective or a husband. As he reflects more deeply on his inability to fully understand what Sandra has experienced, he realizes that the peeper did not introduce a new gap between husband and wife; Banks was simply recognizing a chasm that had always existed. Now that he sees the chasm, he can at least try to address it:

> The human spirit was a great deal more resilient than one imagined in one's darker moments. Still, the distance between them [him and Sandra] was more apparent now than ever, and would have to be dealt with; he would have to make attempts to cross it.
>
> *(210)*

For Robinson, then, gender discrimination and sexual violence are not problems to be addressed only by women or only by police officers. They are problems to be addressed by men working alongside women.

Not Dark Yet: Human Trafficking, Revenge Plots, and Powerful Women

Like *Gallows View* 35 years earlier, *Not Dark Yet* (2021) presents a series of simultaneous investigations underway by the Eastvale Police in returning to the themes of the earlier novel with a main character far the wiser on topics of gender equality and sexual violence. Banks is now Detective Superintendent, and he works with a very different team. Gristhorpe and Hatchley have long ago retired, and Banks is surrounded by a team of strong and effective female detectives, including Area Commander Catherine Gervaise (his boss), Detective Inspector Annie Cabbot (long-time detective partner and briefly lover), Detective Sergeant Winsome Jackman (on maternity leave during *Not Dark Yet*, pointing to the ability of female detectives to balance professional and personal obligations), and Detective Constable Geraldine (Gerry) Masterson (the newest addition to the team). Once again, Banks works with Richard "Dirty Dick" Burgess, a fellow detective who has substantially changed his tune regarding questions of gender over the decades, transforming from a proud misogynist in the early novels to a far more nuanced thinker in his new position working at National Crime Agency headquarters. Thirty-five years have also led to positioning detection within a far more global context. Where *Gallows View* narrates the police investigation into a local peeper and a young rapist by a relatively young detective tempted by marital infidelity, *Not Dark Yet* presents a divorced older detective as he and his team process evidence of a rape adjacent to a murder case that ends up being part of a devastating analysis of the global problem of sexual slavery.

Banks's personal life is much changed by *Not Dark Yet*, a novel named after the Bob Dylan song by the same name whose chorus, "It's not dark yet, but it's gettin' there," has been read as an older man confronting his mortality (Ricks). Banks and Sandra have long been divorced, and the novel opens at their daughter's wedding, where Banks feels a typical mix of pride and nostalgia at witnessing his child going through a ritual of adulthood, and where he also finds awkward the small forced interactions with his ex-wife and her second husband. Banks's love life is described succinctly:

> There had been women since then [his divorce], but nothing that lasted. Commitment had never been a strong point with him after Sandra; he was dedicated to his job, and he tended to take up with women who were similarly dedicated to something other than hanging onto a partner.
>
> *(57)*

For Banks, then, his devotion to detection precludes a similar devotion to a romantic relationship. Although the series presents detective characters who balance the personal and the professional, Annie Cabbot, the detective to whom Banks is closest, has also chosen the profession over a family and partner.

It is through Annie and her partner Gerry Masterson that *Not Dark Yet* explores the rape and subsequent disappearance of Marnie Sedgwick, a 19-year-old woman who had been on the wait staff at a gangster's party and whose rape there was caught on a low-quality hidden camera feed. The police procedural formula increases the pathos of Marnie's sexual violation and its consequences. Annie and Gerry initially get the rape video as an offshoot of a murder investigation into the deaths of Connor Clive Blaydon, gangster, and his factotum Neville Roberts. It takes them several weeks to process the evidence, and once they have the video, a substantial part of their investigation is spent in identifying the victim. By the time they go to interview Marnie, she has left town in an uncharacteristic bout of depression. She has told no one of the rape. Annie understands Marnie's decision and is reminded of her own rape (by three fellow police officers) many years earlier:

> It was a long time ago now, but the pain and shame would never completely go away; they were deep down, rooted in her very being. But that didn't mean she couldn't live a normal life, couldn't function properly. She did. She wanted to find Marnie and tell her that she could do it, too, even if at first she wouldn't believe it.
>
> *(182–3)*

Tragically, Annie is not to find Marnie in time. By the time she and Gerry trace Marnie back to her childhood home in Wool, Dorset, they learn from local police that she has died by suicide and that the autopsy revealed she was pregnant. Interviewing Marnie's parents leads to a difficult moment for Annie. When Gerry reveals to Mr. and Mrs. Sedgwick that Marnie had been raped in Leeds, the reaction is telling:

> "I told you," said Mr. Sedgwick to his wife. "I told you Marnie wasn't the sort of girl to get herself into trouble."
>
> "But, Dennis," she said. "She was *raped*. Our Marnie was raped. Oh, God." She wielded a handkerchief from beneath her cushions and started to cry.
>
> Annie thought it was true that Dennis Sedgwick had made rape sound preferable to getting pregnant through consensual sex, but she didn't think he had intended it to come out that way. It had been a thoughtless statement, but not a cruel or brutal one.
>
> *(225)*

Annie's reflection on the statement is important here. Dennis, an older traditional man, is trying to process horrifying information about his daughter's final days. Although his comment is hurtful (especially to a rape victim like herself), she doesn't judge him for his reaction in a time of extreme stress. Robinson here is once again providing a nuanced representation of the array of reactions that can occur in response to sexual crimes.

The other sexual crime explored in this novel is far more extensive in its scope: sex trafficking. The narrative tells the story of the enslavement, forced prostitution, escape, and vigilante killings of a young Moldovan woman named Nelia Melnick who now goes by the name of Zelda. Previous novels have alluded to Zelda's tragic back story in the context of her part-time work with British intelligence as a super-recognizer who is able to recognize and identify Eastern European sex traffickers from surveillance photos and videos. She comes to the attention of Banks's old colleague, "Dirty Dick" Burgess, when she appears around the edges of some open investigations relating to traffickers in London. After first reminding the reader of Burgess's earlier misogyny ("Are you so pussy-whipped you can't see the wood for the trees?" Burgess asks Banks, 33), Robinson shows us a detective who has changed with the times. Burgess reveals both sensitivity and insight when he asks Banks to have an unofficial conversation with Zelda in advance of any official inquiries:

> "For fuck's sake, Banksy. I might not be as soft-hearted as you– ... I don't know this Zelda. I've never met her. But a woman like her, what she's been through, what she's suffered, it almost beggars the imagination."
>
> *(45)*

As Burgess and Banks discuss, victims of sex trafficking are not only repeatedly raped and enslaved, but they also are often without legal recourse, since police may treat them as prostitutes who have broken the law instead of as victims.

This line between victim and criminal is explored with enormous nuance in *Not Dark Yet*, which spends as much time from Zelda's point of view as it does from Banks's, giving the reader an intimate perspective on her story. The novel opens with Zelda on a trip to Moldova to confront the various men who participated in her enslavement as a teenager. She learns—and the reader learns—the various steps that went into her trafficking. She was raised in an orphanage because both her parents had died in the war. She was kidnapped just moments after she left the orphanage, having been identified by an orphanage administrator as a beautiful young woman with no one in the world to report her missing. She was then brought to a "breaking house" to be prepared, through repeated sexual assaults, for her life as a sex slave. As a beautiful, intelligent young woman with a strong instinct for survival, Zelda moved her way through various levels of prostitution, eventually servicing powerful politicians in Europe. From there, she killed her pimp and was granted a French passport by a cabinet minister who was in love with her and covered up the murder, since "the powers that be had wanted both to reward her and get rid of her" (64). She moved to London, where she became a street artist and, at age 30, began an unconventional but positive relationship with a much older artist (Ray Cabbot, Annie's father and Banks's friend).

Robinson narrates Zelda's story with an eye to both impacting the reader on a personal level and showing that her trauma is caused by a systemic crime perpetuated against some of the most vulnerable people in the world. In her trip to Moldova, Zelda confronts Vasile Lupescu, the man who sold her from the orphanage. She introduces herself to him (he is now a feeble old man) and explains how they know each other. Lupescu tries to protest that he was forced to participate in her sale by threats against his own young daughters, but Zelda stands strong in holding him responsible: "In one smooth movement Zelda stood up, picked up the infinity sculpture from the table beside her and hit him on the side of the head" (38). The infinity sculpture here is a distressing symbol of the pervasive and perhaps even timeless nature of the crime that continues to traumatize Zelda. Lupescu eventually confesses to having received $5,000 for each of the 12 isolated girls he sold from the orphanage. Zelda's reaction is simultaneously visceral and intellectual:

> Zelda felt her muscles tense and the breath tighten in her throat. So that was what her life had been worth. Five thousand dollars. They had made more than that out of her in the first few months. Multiply that by twelve. And the years. She couldn't stop herself from slapping him backhanded across the face, hard.
>
> (49–50)

Zelda has lost control of her body here, with her tensed muscles, her tight breathing, and her uncontrolled strike; she is also doing the mental math that follows from the systemic commodification of young female bodies.

The reach of Zelda's trauma into her adult perspective is narrated for maximum effect. When Zelda first embarks upon her plan to confront and possibly kill the various men who participated in her enslavement—and continue to be part of a global sex trafficking ring—she describes herself as a monster, but justifies her actions to herself: "But she had to do this. Until she did, the past would keep growing, like a cancer inside her, consuming or blotting out all that was good in her life" (27–8). Despite this evocative image of something dark and deadly growing inside her as a result of her trauma, she chooses to spare Lupescu's life (although she has already taken the life of a trafficker who personally raped her), picking up on the previously introduced cancer metaphor as she muses: "the whole encounter was fast making her feel disgusted and empty, even of hatred" (51). Confronting Lupescu with details of her experience and forcing him to admit that he profited from his role and thus bears responsibility for his part in the global problem of sex trafficking leaves Zelda empty—of hatred, but also hopefully of the cancerous past she has felt growing inside her.

Zelda is not able to turn entirely away from her vigilante project, as she is kidnapped from her home shortly after her return from Moldova by Petar Tadić, a Croatian gangster whose brother she killed before the beginning of the novel. The encounter in an abandoned warehouse between Tadić and the newly kidnapped Zelda is reminiscent of the female power displayed in *Gallows View*, but now with more nuance. Tadić has been a monster to Zelda for her entire adult life, so it is almost deflating that he knows her only as the woman who killed his brother; he does not recognize her as a girl he and his brother once trafficked. When Zelda, zip-tied to a radiator, confronts him with her reality, he is dismissive: "I don't remember you. Or Chişinău. Is that why you killed my brother?" (164). His intended punishment of her is to sell her back into slavery, sending her to an especially degrading house of prostitution in Dhaka. Left alone and confined, Zelda unsuccessfully tries to kill herself. During this time of intense stress and isolation, Zelda experiences a panoply of emotions that embody her trauma:

> Also, in some of her darkest moments, she had a strange feeling of elation out of nowhere. It was like a smell—not of the sea, but of the seaside—and a vague image of being a little girl walking with her hand in her father's at Odessa flashed through her mind. A sense of safety and warmth. But it was also neither a smell nor an image; it was an inchoate memory of total happiness she had perhaps never experienced.
>
> *(171–2)*

Perhaps emboldened by her own imagination of a childhood she never had, Zelda forms a plan when Tadić returns and forces her to fellate him. Despite—or perhaps because of—the cold knife held to her jugular, Zelda bites down. She will not be raped by this man again and she welcomes the opportunity to finally find death. Instead, Tadić falls and Zelda is able to wrestle the knife from him, killing him, cutting her zip-ties, and saving Banks (also held in the warehouse) from a fire before she escapes.

Much as in *Gallows View*, a woman's power to enact her own escape from sexual violence gives Banks pause. Not only has Zelda saved herself from the man who sold her into slavery years earlier, she has also saved him from his long-time nemesis, Phil Keane, who has recently become involved in the sex trade. As he recovers in his hospital room, Banks reflects that this is not the first time he has had his life saved by a woman:

> [Zelda] had risked her own life to save Banks from Keane, just the way Annie and Winsome had done that first time, back in Newhope Cottage. Many more instances like that, he realized, and he'd be getting worried about his masculinity. Wasn't he supposed to be the one doing that saving?
>
> *(251)*

This is an almost humorous reflection after Banks's series-long development of excellent working relationships with female detectives. As he did in *Gallows View*, when he agreed to Sandra's much less pivotal decision not to report the peeper, Banks here again chooses to protect Zelda over his professional obligations. The novel ends with Banks taking a holiday in Croatia. There he meets with Zelda, who is now referred to by her birthname of Nelia and who lives with an old friend who runs a hostel for girls who have escaped sexual slavery. Banks returns Nelia's notebook and tells her of the recent death by heart attack of her partner, Ray Cabbot. Ray has left Nelia a substantial bequest:

> "I don't want anything."
> Banks gestured to the house. "It might help. With all your work here."
> Nelia nodded, her back to him.
> "I'll see to it," Banks said. "I'll go now."
> Nelia turned to face him. "Must you go so soon?" she said. "It's not dark yet."
>
> *(320)*

Banks goes, not quite at the end of his career or his life ("it's not dark yet, but it's gettin' there"), having made a decision. He has devoted the second half of his professional life, after his divorce, entirely to his work as a detective. Zelda has killed four men—human traffickers, but still human beings. And yet, not only does he not arrest her. He ensures that she will have funding to pursue unofficial venues in helping victims of the sex trade.

Conclusion

Peter Robinson died in 2022, so there will be only one more Alan Banks novel. At 28 novels, it is an extremely fine body of work. As a highly recognizable representative of Canadian police procedural writing, Robinson balances the conservative and subversive potentials of the genre. The novels always privilege Banks's more liberal views, and in so doing represent the police as a positive force in the world. And yet, as Banks and Burgess suggest in *Not Dark Yet*, institutions are sometimes limited in their ethical options, so individual members of the force sometimes need to make decisions that go against their training. Much has changed in the world between the publication of *Gallows View* and *Not Dark Yet*, and reading these novels next to each other reminds us that sex crimes are no longer a secret that shames victims. Regular reporting on the global sex trade as well as popular movements like #metoo have made conversations about sex crimes more open and ultimately more nuanced. Through multiple perspectives that implicate the reader in an array of ways, Robinson investigates, interrogates, and ultimately gestures to a just, inclusive and equitable future for how the police and society more broadly identify, evaluate, and respond to sex crimes and gender inequities.

8
THE AMATEUR DETECTIVE

Gail Bowen's Joanne Kilbourn as Canadian Revisionist

Gail Bowen's long-serving detective, née Joanne Allard, then Joanne Kilbourn, and most recently Joanne Shreve, is a planner. As she asserts in *Kaleidoscope* (2012), the 14th novel of the ongoing series:

> I'm an orderly cook. I assemble all the ingredients before I begin. I make certain everything I need is at hand, and then I begin. It's important for me to know that if I plan carefully and follow the steps outlined in a recipe, I'll end up with the result I'm going for.
>
> *(144)*

Jo details for readers her cooking, cleaning, and exercise regimens as well as her busy family, social, and professional calendars. She wakes up early every morning, goes for a long run with her dogs (apparently at a brisk pace, since her running partners over the years include much younger, very fit men), returns home to prepare nutritious meals for her family, goes to her workplace where she is a tireless advocate for the downtrodden, goes home to make more excellent food, and then embarks either upon extensive massage and love-making with her husband or upon amateur detective investigations. With a freezer full of delicious home-cooked meals and a closet full of well-chosen outfits for any occasion, Jo can seem like an idealized personage—one some readers may aspire to emulate, and others may prefer to hate. At the same time, Jo is a complex character who pulls together features from several subgenres of detective fiction: the mother detective, the academic detective, and the much less common yet highly intriguing political detective. In exploring the possible configurations of

DOI: 10.4324/9781003125242-10

the amateur detective, Bowen ends up with a detective who can be seen, whimsically, as embodying—sometimes confidently and sometimes more uncomfortably—the nation of Canada itself.

Firmly anchored in Canada's prairies, the Jo Kilbourn series represents Canada's national identity as polite, community-minded, and ultimately moderate. As Bowen has addressed in interviews, she is committed to representing Canada fully in these novels. An associate professor of English at First Nations University of Canada in Regina Saskatchewan, Bowen began writing the series in her mid-40s. As she told Sheryl Smolkin, Jo is

> very much a Canadian woman. Most American female protagonists in mysteries are sort of lone wolves, but I think Canadians tend to be more community-minded, and Joanne is firmly rooted in her community. She has friends. Her family is so important to her …. Joanne also really is someone who, when she sees injustice or inequity, rolls up her sleeves and tries to do what she can to right what she perceives as wrong. And again, I see that as a very Canadian attitude.
>
> *(Smolkin)*

Bowen's analysis here is astute. The series addresses a number of Canada's contemporary social issues, including censorship, LGBTQ+ rights, Indigenous people's rights, the Me Too movement, addiction, prostitution, inequity, etc. And certainly, Jo always acts decisively based on what "she perceives as wrong"; and yet, the novels allow space for readers to consider the often complex ethical implications of various crimes and their solutions. In many ways, Jo—a political science professor and activist as well as a mother, grandmother, and friend to many—stands in for the nation from its center in Regina and Saskatoon.

Jo's personal history in these novels in some ways echoes the history of the nation. Over its relatively short 150+ official years as a country, Canada has done a good deal of historical rewriting. Shameful historical events such as the treatment of the Chinese through a series of discriminatory immigration acts and of the Japanese through internment during World War II have been slowly added to Canadian K-12 curricula over the years. This rewriting of historical confrontations between the nation of Canada and other nations, especially from Asia and the Middle East, has occurred simultaneously with a reconceptualization—by historians, educators, politicians, and others—of the story of Canadian First Nations. Even as twenty-first-century Indigenous women are increasingly being recognized as far more likely to be victims of sexual assault and murder than other demographic groups in Canada, so too are revelations about horrifying abuses in residential schools coming to light, often complete with the physical bones of murdered and neglected children.

Bowen explores the discrimination faced by First Nations Canadians through numerous Indigenous characters, ranging from Jo's long-time lover Alex Kequahtooway to many minor but recurring characters. She also explores the notion of rewriting history through Jo's ongoing investigations into her own marriage and childhood. As Jo says to her friend Howard in the first novel of the series, "We're all revisionists when it comes to our own lives" (*Deadly* 123). Then secure in her identity as a doctor's child and a politician's beloved—if sometimes taken-for-granted—wife, Jo learns many identity-shattering facts in later novels, including the truth about her first husband's murder, his long-term affair with a close family friend, and eventually, a revelation about her own birth.

Like the nation she represents, Jo must review this new information for accuracy, carefully consider how it changes her sense of self and her presentation to others, and integrate the new data into her identity. From the beginning of the series, she recognizes the power of stories and their necessity in building a stable sense of self. In *Deadly Appearances* (1990), for example, she undertakes a biography of a murder victim, musing:

> I had to prove somehow that life, life with a capital *L*, was a coherent narrative with a beginning, a middle, and an end. Somehow I convinced myself that if I understood Andy's life, I could make sense of his death.
> *(63–4)*

This idea of detection as "making sense"—as constructing "a coherent narrative" and locating a comforting logic to life—is central to Bowen's project in these novels. Drawing upon the underlying uncertainty of the postmodern period, she deploys the conventions of detective subgenres in order to create a series whose very ordinariness appears to provide comfort and escapism to readers, but which also invites readers to consider—and reconsider—difficult socio-cultural issues as well as fraught questions about the reality and the presentation of Canadian attitudes and even of Canadian identity. Even as she recognizes and acknowledges (sometimes slowly, but always thoughtfully) her own privilege, Jo is deeply invested in making her community and ultimately her country a better, more equitable place. We see this in her work as a mother and an academic in the first half of the series, and then as a politician's wife—deeply rewritten—in the more recent novels.

The Mother Detective: Exploring Generic and Temporal Paradoxes

The late twentieth and early twenty-first centuries have seen a marked increase in the number of fictional mother detectives. From spinster detectives (à la Miss Marple) or child detectives (à la Nancy Drew) in the early twentieth century, the detective genre saw an infusion of women detectives across subgenres in the 1970s and 80s, but most of the best-known examples are childless, like the hardboiled triumvirate of Marcia Muller's Sharon McCone (1977–present), Sue Grafton's Kinsey Millhone (1982–2017), and Sara Paretsky's V.I. Warshawski (1982–present). Of course, it might be difficult for a private detective to manage the balancing act of motherhood and dangerous contract work, but even in more sedate settings like the university in, for example, Amanda Cross's Kate Fansler series (1964–2002, penname of Victorian scholar Carolyn Heilbrun), the focus of fictional female detectives has generally been on detection rather than parenthood until quite recently. I would argue that the dearth of earlier mother detectives points to more than a plotting challenge. Generically, detective fiction was long the province of male characters, so many early female and feminist detective writers may have been showing that women detectives had much to offer the profession and the genre; they may have deliberately avoided representing the challenges of motherhood so as not to remove attention from the intellectual and physical work of detection. Philosophically, the parent detective presents a special challenge at the locus of temporality. The temporal momentum of the detective narrative is fundamentally backward-looking, as the detective looks toward the past to discover and reveal the story of the crime that predates and makes possible the story of its detection. Parenthood, on the other hand, orients people to look forward, even beyond their own lifespans to a future that places not themselves but their child in a central role. Although some prominent male fictional detectives had children before the late twentieth century, these tended also to have wives who did most of the childcare, leaving the male detective free to obsess about the crime and the criminal at hand. The mother detective, on the other hand, tends to be equally invested in both halves of her identity, and is thus caught in a place of tension between focus on past, present, and future.

Gail Bowen's series is part of a trend in the 1990s that grapples with the complexities of motherhood and detection, a tension that is now regularly explored in TV shows (for example, *The Killing*, 2011–2015, *Broadchurch*, 2013–2017, and even *Criminal Minds*, 2005–present) as well as mystery novels. Bowen does not shy away from representations of Jo's motherhood in favor of the less quotidian representation of detection. Indeed, the work of feeding, sheltering, stimulating, and counseling children is described in great detail, and the stages of Jo's motherhood serve to divide the series into sections. The early novels establish Jo as a single mother to her three teenage children: Mieka, Peter, and Angus. A busy professor and an active mother, Jo performs a typical modern motherhood as she struggles to balance her many commitments, often feeling like she is failing on all fronts. After Jo's closest childhood friend is killed in the second novel, Jo adopts Sally's daughter, Taylor Love, who is four years old and already a budding artist who will clearly follow in her mother's artistic footsteps. The middle novels explore the challenges of parenting an adopted child with a trauma-laden past and an enormous talent, still mostly as a single mother despite her ongoing relationship with Alex, an Indigenous cop with whom Jo has a long-term relationship. In the later novels, Jo learns the pleasures of co-parenting (which she never explored even in young motherhood with Ian Kilbourn, a busy lawyer and politician and an unfaithful husband), when she marries paraplegic defense lawyer Zack Shreve. Jo and Zack are very involved in Taylor's life in her young adulthood, and are active grandparents to their growing brood of grandchildren; they also babysit often for neighbors and friends, with their large social network regularly placing them in the position of surrogate parents.

An avid reader—aloud to children and quietly to herself—Jo can always be counted upon for the right quotation for any situation. The passage she cites most often is from English novelist, C.P. Snow: "the love between a parent and a child is the only one that moves toward separation" (cited in *Wandering* 18, *Killing* 221–2, *What's Left* 167, and elsewhere). This mantra does a lot of work. First, it is central to Jo's parenting philosophy and establishes her credentials as an accomplished mother, as she regularly achieves what many parents only dream of: fully supporting her children through difficult times while also promoting their independence. Secondly, the Snow reference rewards an investigation for its thematic resonances. As a chemist and a novelist, C.P. Snow (1905–1980) is best known for his academic novel, *The Masters* (1951), set in Cambridge College and exploring the politics of higher education, and for his lecture, *The Two Cultures* (1959), in which he argued that scholars from the sciences and the humanities must communicate with each other more often and more effectively in order to solve the world's most pressing problems. As such, Snow is a representative of the ideas of moderation and open-mindedness that are central to Jo's worldview. Thirdly, the Snow quotation highlights the paradox of parenthood that is somewhat analogous to the paradox of the mother detective, both of which are temporally based. Just as the mother detective must be a sort of Janus figure, looking backward at the crime to be solved even as she also looks forward at the future to be experienced by her children, so too must any great parent be able to find a love—an almost impossibly selfless love—that allows them to simultaneously look back (perhaps nostalgically but not obsessively) at the years during which the parent was central to the child's life and also look forward (fondly and acceptingly) to the years to come in which the parent will become, naturally and healthily, peripheral.

The importance of Jo's motherhood to the series is regularly highlighted by the prevalence of characters who turn out to be—in contrast to Jo— bad mothers. The opening novel, *Deadly Appearances* (1990), introduces Julie Evanson, obsessed with her son's success in all things until she determines he is below average and turns her attention away from him entirely. From there, we meet Sally Love in *Murder at the Mendel* (1991), a brilliant artist who barely knows her 4-year-old daughter and who, as Jo reflects in a later novel, has spent less time looking at her daughter than her daughter has spent looking at her mother's art (*Last* 197). Other choice bad mothers throughout the series include: Tracy Lowell, who doesn't admit to being her daughter's biological mother even after the girl's adopted mother dies in *The Glass Coffin* (2002); Lily Ryder, who might have been a more attentive parent had her daughter looked more Native in *The Last Good Day* (2004); Kathryn Morrisey, who completely ignores her own somewhat sociopathic child while she ruins the families of others through her exploitative journalistic exposés of political families in *The Endless Knot* (2006); and, in the same novel, Bev Parker, who disowns her transgendered daughter, even going so far as trying to prevent the young woman from attending her own father's funeral. And these are only the mothers who don't actually kill their children or the children of others. In a series that includes no spousal murders, we see a surprising number of dark representations of mother–child relations: children kill their mothers in two novels; mothers kill their biological children (and others) in two others; and mothers kill their surrogate children in yet two more.

The murderous mother who resonates most loudly through the series— and who thus contrasts most profoundly with Jo—is the one who is closest: Nina Love, the mother of Jo's childhood friend and now famous artist Sally, and the grandmother of Jo's adopted daughter Taylor. Jo has been close to Nina since she was a child, in part because her own mother was distant. It is thus a devastating revelation in *Murder at the Mendel* when Jo realizes that Nina is a killer. To complicate matters, the revelation comes at a terrible time, when Jo is caring for 4-year-old Taylor. In an ill-considered move, Jo tells the little girl to stay in the car as she goes into a remote boathouse to confront Nina, who admits to the crimes and, predictably, points her gun at Jo. Taylor appears behind Jo and asks in "a small voice. Clear and clearly frightened" (208) if Nina will kill everyone. Faced with her young granddaughter's curiosity, fear, and comprehension, Nina turns the gun on herself. This scene underscores the nuances of Bowen's representations of motherhood throughout the series. Fundamentally, the scene highlights the conflicts between detection and motherhood. On one hand, Jo chooses detection over motherhood, leaving Taylor alone in the car while she goes to confront a murderer in an isolated location. On the other hand, Taylor saves Jo's life by appearing at exactly the right moment, perhaps because even the murderous Nina cannot kill Jo in front of a little child to whom Jo is about to become a surrogate mother. Even the most fully explored model of sinister motherhood refuses to locate itself simply in black and white.

Despite her often heartbreaking exploration of the dark side of motherhood, Bowen generally finds an optimistic note on which to end her novels, even when the contradictions she examines are not and cannot be permanently resolved. For example, *The Gifted*, which focuses on the complex legacies of Sally and Nina, two very complicated mother figures, ends with Jo thinking back to a long period of estrangement between herself and Sally. She recalls Sally's recasting of this separation: "the distance between us was only physical. You've always been in my heart—and I was always in yours" (271). From this warm rewriting of a difficult relationship, Jo returns to C.P. Snow to conclude the novel:

> I was struck again by the painful truth of C.P. Snow's observation that the love of a parent for a child is the only love that must grow towards separation. But as Sally had pointed out, the distance between Taylor and us would only be physical. Taylor's family, including both her mothers, would be with her every step of the way.
>
> *(271)*

Sally Love was seldom physically present for Taylor even before her death, but the artistic talent she has passed onto her daughter as well as the paintings from which Taylor gleans inspiration keep her motherhood alive. In this moment, Jo is able to see and acknowledge the value of motherhood alongside her own more traditional, daily enterprise of providing Taylor all types of support. This combination of pragmatism and optimism may well capture the Canadian spirit, marked by a genuine attempt to narrate the wrongs of the past and address them responsibly toward a better future.

The Academic Detective: The Education of the Professor-Detective

Given the detective genre's engagement with epistemological questions, it is no surprise there is a long history of professors acting as amateur detectives. Pragmatically, the university serves as a productive closed system in which to set a crime with a manageable number of viable suspects. Philosophically, the university acts as a locus of knowledge production, so a criminal disruption in a place where new ways of thinking are produced, tested, and disseminated makes for a compelling narrative with potentially important socio-cultural implications. Several early Jo Kilbourn novels are set on campus, often exploring the interpersonal relationships and power dynamics of the political science department. Jo finds herself especially embroiled in questions of feminist theory and praxis in *Burying Ariel* (2000), the Bowen novel that has thus far received the most extended critical discussion. Elżbieta Perkowska-Gawlik characterizes *Burying Ariel* as "a kind of sequel to [Amanda Cross's] *Death in a Tenured Position*" (111), arguing that Bowen's novel is set in a postfeminist world and can thus explore women as not only victims but also potential oppressors. My own reading of the same novel focuses on Jo's commitment to a moderate feminism that acknowledges the celebration of moderation as a Canadian political value but that also encourages readers to make up their own minds about gender politics:

> In *Burying Ariel*, Jo again sees radical feminism as a danger to be contained, but the novel's structure forces the reader to question Jo's stance on feminism while finding her an attractive character in many respects.
>
> (Bedore "Colder" 174)

Jo's days as a political science professor with a great fondness for literature and a deep engagement with her students and colleagues in the middle novels continually place her in a position to interrogate her own assumptions and beliefs. Repeatedly, she combines her intellectual and emotional intelligences to delve into an issue and attempt to fully understand it, generally ending up at a moderate-left position characteristic of Canadian politics writ large. This is nowhere more nuanced than in her professional and personal interactions with the Kequahtooway family. In *The Wandering Soul Murders* (1992), Jo meets Perry Kequahtooway, a police constable, who tells her the meaning of his surname: " 'In Ojibway,' he said, 'it means he who interprets. You know, the guy who tries to help people understand' " (67). Perry's self-proclaimed interpreter role gives him insight into how people think and reach. When he asks Jo to assist informally with the investigation, she protests that this is the police's realm and they will also be asking questions. Perry counters: "That's right, we will, but sometimes people like you can get to a different kind of truth than the police do" (67). Perry's perception here is profound, and his policing is based on a multiplicity of epistemological frames rather than a simple black-and-white approach to truth and justice. Perry's cousin, Alex Kequahtooway, becomes an even more central character to the series as he and Jo date for several years and he continually provides a nuanced lens on questions of truth and knowledge. Alex is a liminal character who moves smoothly between Indigenous and white society, between the police and the criminal underclass, and between Jo's comfortable middle-class white existence and a tougher world to which she has little access and of which she has little comprehension. As Alex becomes a mainstay in the academic mystery portion of the series, he is central to Jo's work as a detective who explores how knowledge gets constructed, disseminated, challenged, and understood by various constituencies.

Alex's lucidity and insight into knowledge construction and identity politics are perhaps best expressed in *A Killing Spring* (1996), a classic university mystery in which the head of the journalism department is the murder victim. Alex articulates the epistemological complexity of police detection, relying on metaphors also used by professors investigating academic questions in various disciplines:

> You know, Jo, cops don't talk much about the role imagination plays in police work, but it's essential. When an investigation into a sudden death starts moving in the right direction, it's like watching a movie playing backwards. You can see what happened in those last hours and, crazy as it sounds, you can feel the emotion. We've put all the pieces of the puzzle together on this one, but I still can't see the pictures.
>
> *(Killing 114)*

Alex speaks of an investigation as a "puzzle" or a "movie," noting the importance of both imagination and emotion in the work of constructing a narrative that makes sense of all the pieces. This is much the work of a professor writing a book or article that develops a coherent narrative to explain a phenomenon in the world.

Alex understands his detective work as intrinsically imbricated with his identity as a member of the First Nations. He articulates his growing disillusionment with his deliberately liminal role to Jo in *A Killing Spring*: "'That's why I joined the force. I was going to show the public that a native cop could be as smart and as reliable as a white cop, and I was going to show the native community that the law was fair and impartial.' He laughed. 'In those days, I thought of myself as a force for change'" (42). Alex's laugh here is a dark one, as he has eventually come to view the gap between his two communities as fundamentally unbridgeable. Indeed, he notes to Jo in both *A Killing Spring* and *Verdict in Blood* (1998) that Jo's young children are far more confident than he, a middle-aged detective with a great deal of life experience and professional success behind him. His statements are as provocative as they are devastating. In explaining why Jo shouldn't date him, he states that there are consequences for her children as well as herself: "And you don't know what you're getting your kids into. Angus and Taylor are great kids, Jo—so confident, so sure that all the doors are open for them and that when they walk into a room people can't wait to welcome them" (*Killing* 124–5). Later, when he explains that dealing with his nephew Eli has brought back earlier traumas, he again reaches for the issue of unequal confidence: "On his worst days, Angus has more confidence that life's going to work out than Eli will ever have—than *I* will ever have" (*Verdict* 225). The confidence here is not self-confidence, per se, but rather a confidence that systems of power can be effectively navigated. In Alex's experience, his First Nations identity prevents him from accessing not only open doors, but also hope—the notion "that life's going to work out."

As Jo moves through the academic mysteries of the earlier novels with Alex at her side, she tries on a variety of intellectual perspectives on several controversial issues, including the complex historical and social interactions between settler and Indigenous cultures that continue to shape Canadian national identity and Canadians' personal identities today. The issue of bridging cultural difference becomes literalized on the Albert Street Bridge in an event that occurs in *A Killing Spring* and is recounted again in detail (and with further analysis) in *The Last Good Day*. The incident is first narrated as an action scene, with dialogue and terse description. Jo and Alex are walking home, Jo is cold, and Alex puts his arm around her. A man in a half-ton truck yells a racial epithet and Jo breaks free from Alex's embrace and runs away instead of ignoring the comment or standing up for her lover of several years. Afterward, she tries to laugh off the incident, but Alex is not so easily mollified:

> Alex didn't smile. I reached for his hand, but he drew away. "Alex, I'm sorry."
> "Don't be," he said. "It was just a reflex. Getting out of the line of fire is instinctive."
> "You wouldn't have done it."
> He smiled sadly. "I couldn't have done it."
> "Because you're not a coward."
> "No," he said gently, "because I'm not white. That closes off a lot of options."
>
> (*Killing* 119–20)

Despite years of working in politics and academia, Jo appears to have missed the most obvious fact about Alex's lived experience as an Ojibwa Canadian: his options are always foreclosed by his heritage, including the visible signs of that heritage in his appearance.

Academic detectives are often armed with impressive knowledge and insight on topics relevant to the crimes they are investigating, and Jo regularly demonstrates her ability to synthesize her knowledge about politics and journalism in reconstructing the narrative of the crime and identifying the culprit. At the same time, she is, like every excellent teacher, always learning new things and demonstrating the learning process to others. Jo and Alex never truly resolve the bridge incident in *A Killing Spring*, but Jo thinks back to it in detail in *The Last Good Day*, the novel that ends tragically with Alex's death by suicide. The discussion here is in long paragraphs of internal analysis as Jo acknowledges that she has "replayed the scene a hundred times in [her] mind" and notes that although she always imagines herself behaving heroically in the face of anti-Indigenous sentiment, the truth is: "I had not been brave. Obeying an impulse as atavistic as it was unforgiveable" (204). Jo's analysis here is complicated. Her use of the term "atavistic" might suggest that running away from calling out racism is acceptable because it is a natural survival reaction, built into our genes from our ancestors. In the same breath, though, she characterizes the action as "unforgivable," making clear that her experience as a privileged white woman has long left her "drawing from a shallow well of liberal decency" (*Killing* 123) in the face of anti-Indigenous sentiment, and she does not and should not forgive herself for her cowardice. Indeed, *The Last Good Day* provides a difficult story for Jo Kilbourn fans. Jo and Alex are no longer a couple, and Jo appears unable to bridge the distance between them or to interpret his words and actions, ultimately failing to anticipate his death by suicide. Like a good lecture on a complex ethical question, the novel provides a solution to the crime, and yet leaves the final interpretation to the reader.

The Kaleidoscopic Detective

The Joanne Kilbourn/Shreve series shifts—tonally and narratively—in the 13th novel, *Kaleidoscope* (2012), when Jo retires from the university where she has long been a political science professor. Not yet 60, and with a long history of becoming productively embroiled in important and sometimes controversial intellectual debates with students and colleagues, Jo is, perhaps surprisingly to some long-time readers, happy to be moving on. She is especially delighted by her retirement gift, a gorgeous hand-crafted glass kaleidoscope inscribed with the tagline Jo had written for her first husband Ian's campaigns years earlier: "*Security for any one of us lies in greater abundance for all of us*" (7). The kaleidoscope acts as a powerful metaphor for Jo's late middle age, in which she revisits the idea of Ian's motto even as she continually seeks to take on new perspectives. After a long career in academia accompanied by a series of amateur detective cases approached from an academic outlook, Jo understands the importance of nuance—of taking the time to look into the kaleidoscope and see the many different patterns that might emerge—as well as the power of art to both represent and produce these perspectives.

Throughout the series, Jo struggles to fully understand the complexities of her various roles in politics, as a speech writer, a politician's wife, a pundit (regularly appearing on NationTV), a political science professor, and finally, a second politician's wife. Her marriage to Zack Shreve forces her to constantly look through a kaleidoscope. On the face of it, Zack seems an unlikely partner for Jo. A charismatic defense attorney formerly known as "the Prince of Darkness," Zack is notorious for his formidable courtroom presence and his questionable ethics. As a paraplegic since an accident in adolescence, Zack was a single-minded lawyer deeply aware of his shortened life expectancy who only took cases he could win and who partied hard before he met Jo. Jo and Zack's marriage transforms them both. As a married man, he has a new-found respect for family and community, and has drastically reduced the number of hours he spends at the office and reconsidered the kinds of cases he will accept. Jo, too, is changed by the new perspectives Zack brings to her life. It is presumably Zack's influence that leads her to assert, quite seriously: " 'One of my retirement goals is to stop being judgmental' " (*Kaleidescope* 28).

Readers of the later novels, in which Jo encourages Zack to pause his lucrative career as a defense lawyer in order to run for mayor of Regina, might wonder why Jo does not run for the post herself. A recently retired professor and stalwart member of the community, she has none of the political baggage accumulated by Zack in his days as a hard-drinking attorney who frequented prostitutes. Jo is also an excellent public speaker and speechwriter who has shown herself to be capable of change and compromise, qualities one might value in a political leader. I would suggest that having Zack run for mayor instead of Jo doing it allows Jo to more fully rewrite herself, creating a parallel situation to her work as Ian Kilbourn's political wife decades earlier. She does not want to become a politician. Rather, she wants to be a politician's wife once again, but with a different role for herself. After all, Jo's first political marriage to Ian Kilborne forced her to reduce herself, as revealed in a conversation with politician, Howard Dowhanuik:

"You and Ian had a good marriage."
"Ian and I had a good marriage because we both lived Ian's life." I was surprised at the anger in my voice, and I was surprised at what I'd

said. Until that moment I don't think I'1d acknowledged how much everything had been for Ian.

(Deadly 121)

Jo's acknowledgment of her complicity in allowing herself to be taken for granted by her first husband is rewritten with Zack's redemption arc as he is transformed by his relationship with Jo and her family and is able to bring new meaning to the words on the kaleidoscope: *"Security for any one of us lies in greater abundance for all of us."*

As mayor of Regina, Zack is able to facilitate a major downtown renewal project built on principles of social equity that Jo has long supported and that Zack has come to recently but passionately. Zack acknowledges and appreciates Jo's contributions to his work as Ian never did. He also seems to accomplish more sustainable change because of his variegated history with the law. As Heidi Tiedemann Darroch and Manina Jones note, the later books of the Jo Kilbourn series include an earnest exploration of how "developers and urban planners can work collaboratively with residents—sometimes with a tinge of noblesse oblige—to increase the life-chances of Indigenous children caught up with intergenerational poverty and trauma." Jo's influence on Zack, along with his numerous and sometimes unsavory contacts in Regina's business committee, allows him to succeed at this kind of transformative project. It also speaks to Canada's current focus on rethinking, even revisioning the past in order to not only understand and acknowledge past unethical acts, especially in settler/Indigenous interactions, but also to think creatively about how to move forward ethically and effectively.

Conclusion

In January 2022, Gail Bowen wrote a column for CBC's Opinion section about COVID fatigue. In this piece, Bowen notes that people in her age group—over 70—are finding the regular challenges of aging exacerbated by emotional and sometimes physical fatigue caused by the ongoing pandemic. Bowen speaks to the power of resiliency by acknowledging the challenges faced by previous generations of ordinary but hardy Canadians. Like her main character, Bowen has the right quote for the moment, this time citing Albert Camus:

> In the midst of hate, I found within me, an invincible love.
>   In the midst of tears, I found there was, within me, an invincible smile.
>   In the midst of chaos, I found there was, within me, an invincible calm.

I realized through it all, that ... the midst of winter I found there was, within me, an invincible summer.

And that makes me happy. For it says that no matter how hard the world pushes against me, within me, there is something stronger—something better, pushing right back.

(her ellipsis)

Bowen explains that she keeps an old-fashioned desk diary and that this is the quotation she has chosen for her 2022 volume. It is a quotation suited to the creator of Jo Kilbourn, and relevant to her readers, who might see resilience, flexibility, and even rewriting as a mainstay of the Canadian people and even of the Canadian nation.

9
THE GAY PRIVATE EYE
Anthony Bidulka's Hardboiled Romantic, Russell Quant

In *Tapas on the Ramblas* (2005), Russell Quant wonders how a client so obviously wealthy and well-connected as Charity Wiser would choose to hire him, a relatively inexperienced Saskatchewan private investigator, to protect her life on a Mediterranean cruise. And then he realizes: "Suddenly it became clear to me why she'd obviously gone to some trouble to track me down and hire me. It wasn't because I'm a particularly skillful detective. Humph! It's because I'm a particularly gay detective" (20). Throughout Anthony Bidulka's Russell Quant series, the detective's openly gay identity is often characterized as a positive quality that attracts clients to his small but well-appointed office. In *Amuse-Bouche* (2003), semi-closeted Harold Chavell hires Quant to seek his missing male fiancé on the recommendation of a mutual gay acquaintance; Chavell's private eye selection is made partly because Quant is gay. In *Flight of Aquavit* (2004), Daniel Guest, a closeted gay man married to a woman, is being blackmailed about his sexuality. He deliberately seeks a gay private eye, explaining,

> It was important to me to learn you're gay. I know at first that might sound trite or even foolhardy, I should want someone who is good at their job, regardless of their sexuality ... but it's not about that so much as I want someone good at their job who I also feel comfortable discussing my circumstance with.
>
> *(24)*

Indeed, in each novel of this eight-book series (2003–2012), Russell is always hired specifically because he is a gay detective. The effect of this

DOI: 10.4324/9781003125242-11

repeated trope is twofold. First, it suggests that a person's sexuality—and views about sexuality more broadly—may impact whom they choose to hire, especially for the personal matters that are the province of the private investigator. Secondly, and relatedly, it suggests that the gay private eye, who may contain contradictory markers when using Chandler's classical definition of the hardboiled, is not only possible but also necessary in highly diverse twenty-first-century Canada, and thus in twenty-first-century Canadian detective fiction.

Canadian crime fiction is far less PI-oriented than its American counterpart. This may be because the fictional American private eye—often a hardboiled figure—reflects a certain anxiety about the police. Can the state be trusted to solve a loved one's murder? Are the police effective? Are they honest? As reflected by both the Mountie as a national symbol of Canada and the preponderance of police procedurals within Canadian crime fiction, police departments are generally portrayed quite positively in Canada. Indeed, Russell was a police officer before he decided to become a private detective. He does not complain of a culture of violence or disrespect within or against the police establishment. Rather, he muses that police work and private investigation have much in common, explaining that he still "[gets] to solve criminal riddles, help good guys and get rid of bad guys" (51). Throughout the series, Bidulka flirts with the difficulty that generally exists within the American hardboiled between the private eye and the police through a complex rendering of the ongoing relationship between Russell and police detective Darren Kirsch. And yet, even in this classical tension, Bidulka's series plays out the relationship between police and private detectives only to put a new spin on it marked by both Russell's nationality and his sexuality.

Bidulka's queering of the detective genre places him in a small but well-respected set of mystery writers who, like the most intriguing popular writers in all genre fictions, have introduced sexual diversity at the site of the main character in ways that reflect and sometimes even presage changing cultural norms. The hardboiled detective genre was the province of hyper-masculine detectives until the 1970s and 1980s, when the genre—always far more popular in the United States—saw a major influx of women writing female hardboiled detectives, most notably Marcia Muller with the Sharon McCone series (1977–present), Sue Grafton with the Kinsey Milhone "Alphabet" series (1982–2017), and Sara Paretsky with the V.I. Warshawski series (1982–present). Muller, Grafton, and Paretsky do not simply place female characters in "masculine" roles; rather, by exploring at length the complex challenges faced (and generally overcome) by women successfully doing the work of private investigators, they invite readers to reconsider the very notion of masculinity in the hardboiled detective space. The development of female hardboiled detectives who are capable of protecting themselves and others while also performing feminine traits when they want to has been read by critics like Anne Cranny-Francis as a means of bringing feminist ideas to an existing (and not always already convinced) readership (3). As feminist writers and theorists moved toward a more inclusive politics in the 1990s and in the new century with third-wave feminism and LGBTQ+ movements, there was another influx of fictional detectives, named "detectives of diversity" by Kathleen Gregory Klein, that included detectives of color as well as LGBTQ+ detectives. The Russell Quant series capitalizes on this movement from a Canadian perspective, as Russell interacts with many other LGBTQ+ characters throughout the series. In his insightful analysis of the series, Péter Balogh points out that Bidulka challenges heteronormative narratives, but only within very specific parameters, given that his "seemingly counterdiscursive act of writing is deployed almost exclusively to the advantage of an unmarked community of white, middle-class, and affluent gay men who can pass as straight" (186). I take Balogh's argument seriously and keep in mind his persuasive critique of Bidulka's problematic representations of racialized characters throughout the series. At the same time, I argue in this chapter that Bidulka presents in Russell Quant a liminal character who resides at the interstices between subgenres—the hardboiled, the cozy, and the postmodern—in order to show that in a Canadian LGBTQ+ context, it is possible to bring hope and even romance to the hardboiled detective.

Genre Hybridity: Queering the Hardboiled

The private-eye detective came to prominence in the American 1930s under the umbrella of the hardboiled. Students always ask me what "hardboiled" means, as the term evokes a humorous response at odds with the subgenre's inherent darkness. The hardboiled detective is in contrast to the egg-headed (soft-boiled, more physically fragile) armchair detective who can solve a mystery without leaving the room, using only what Agatha Christie's Hercule Poirot calls "the little grey cells." The hardboiled detective constantly places their body in danger, as investigating crime for these self-employed sleuths locates them on what Raymond Chandler coined the "Mean Streets" of the city. It is worth quoting Chandler's seminal essay on the hardboiled at some length to understand the ethical complexities of this subgenre:

> But down these mean streets a man must go who is not himself mean, who is neither tarnished nor afraid. The detective in this kind of story must be such a man. He is the hero; he is everything. He must be a complete man and a common man and yet an unusual man. He must

be, to use a rather weathered phrase, a man of honor—by instinct, by inevitability, without thought of it, and certainly without saying it. He must be the best man in his world and a good enough man for any world. I do not care much about his private life; he is neither a eunuch nor a satyr; I think he might seduce a duchess and I am quite sure he would not spoil a virgin; if he is a man of honor in one thing, he is that in all things. He is a relatively poor man, or he would not be a detective at all. He is a common man or he could not go among common people. He has a sense of character, or he would not know his job. He will take no man's money dishonestly and no man's insolence without a due and dispassionate revenge. He is a lonely man and his pride is that you will treat him as a proud man or be very sorry you ever saw him. He talks as the man of his age talks—that is, with rude wit, a lively sense of the grotesque, a disgust for sham, and a contempt for pettiness. The story is this man's adventure in search of a hidden truth, and it would be no adventure if it did not happen to a man fit for adventure.

(59)

Chandler's famous characterization of the hardboiled hero is one of the most oft-cited paragraphs in crime and detective studies, as it should be. It sets almost impossible expectations for the hardboiled hero, who is untarnished, unafraid, honest, and yet tough. Chandler describes here a man whose private life is not a matter to be shared with readers, and whose interiority is not only outside the narrative, but also presumably quite bland, as this character is boiled all the way through, as hard on the inside as the outside. The metaphor clearly has nuance, as an egg is by nature not only vulnerable but also associated in reproductive terms with the feminine. The most salient feature of a hardboiled egg is perhaps its resiliency; it is not made of inherently durable material, but has been rendered unbreakable through a process of boiling.

Andrew Pepper, decades later, expands Chandler's analysis of the hardboiled detective after the American neoliberal turn. Embedding his analysis in a critique of twentieth-century American cultural theory, Pepper argues that "most detectives are not, and have never been, polite cultural mediators, but rather usually violent, always conflicted figures who operate out of selfish as well as selfless motivations" (6). From this premise that the hardboiled detective is a vexed literary construction with violent potential and a conflicted core, Pepper considers the rhetorical work of the detective figure:

The genre has much subversive potential, not least because the detective's function is arguably less a palliative one—to provide insights into social and cultural problems or to mediate between individuals and groups in order to reconcile differences—than an overly aggressive one based on a desire to expose state-sponsored corruption and dismantle the hierarchies that spawned it layer by layer, piece by piece.

(7)

Pepper's argument here is pointed very much to the American hardboiled, reminding us that the hardboiled detective is often characterized as fundamentally American just as the armchair detective is generally understood to have English roots. It also reads the detective genre as posing a clear challenge to sociocultural norms in its investigation of not only a specific mystery or crime, but of the criminal justice system. Given that Bidulka's Russell Quant is an out gay detective whose clients routinely choose him because of this facet of his identity, we might also expect his adventures to hold up a mirror to the state of LGBTQ+ issues and rights in Canada.

Russell Quant is, on the surface, a private investigator with some typical hardboiled traits. He is an attractive, able-bodied man in his early thirties who owns a gun and has above-average skills in self-defense. He has a quick wit, a strong sense of pride and honor, a keen desire for adventure, and a complex relationship with the police. Certainly, Bidulka is drawing upon hardboiled conventions in the construction of his character and the situations in which Russell finds himself, which include a quest for a rare antique carpet (*Date with a Sheesha*) that recalls certain aspects of Dashiell Hammett's *The Maltese Falcon*, as well as work for a client who fears being murdered for her wealth (*Tapas on the Ramblas*) or is experiencing blackmail (*Flight of Aquavit*) in the tradition of hardboiled luminaries Raymond Chandler and (Canadian) Ross McDonald. At the same time, he seems to embody an argument Leonard Cassuto makes regarding the ability of the hardboiled to merge with other genres, showing some of the surprising similarities between the hardboiled and the sentimental:

> Hard-boiled fiction and sentimentalism require both domestic ideology to draw on, and a market-based public world to explore and criticize. Both position the home as a center of value against the public market economy, and at the same time acknowledge that the two realms aren't really separate—thus marking an unarticulated contradiction of the pervasive public ideology of separate male and female spheres.
>
> *(11)*

As a man who loves spending time at home, Russell lacks many of the constitutive features of the "hardboiled dick." He certainly has no opportunity to prowl Chandler's mean streets, as he lives in Saskatoon,

Saskatchewan, a medium-sized city on the South Saskatchewan River sometimes referred to as "the Paris of the Prairies" in homage to its many brass-plated bridges. Further, he is certainly not "a lonely man," as he has a strong social network of diverse friends and regularly basks in the warm affection of his beloved canine companions, Barbra and Brutus. Russell also lacks the overall flavor of the hardboiled man—with his hard exterior going all the way through—as he regularly shows kindness and empathy to his clients as well as reveals his insecurities to readers.

Indeed, Bidulka establishes Russell's liminal position between the hardboiled and the cozy from the opening of the series in *Amuse Bouche*: "I have to believe that Hercule Poirot and Jessica Fletcher, along with the current slate of mystery novel and television detectives, had to start somewhere" (13). He goes on from these references to well-known cozy sleuths to self-deprecatingly—and metafictionally—imagining how his own career might be fictionally portrayed: "If someone were creating a TV show about some of the cases I've had in the past year, they'd have to resort to episode titles like 'The Case of the Hiding Pussy Cat' or 'Midnight Surveillance Sucks'" (13–14). Russell, the fictional detective, often reflects self-referentially on the ways his life resembles fiction, a pleasurable feature to readers who enjoy a postmodern aesthetic. He even uses an investigative technique whose name is taken from classical mystery stories. The Red Herring file is a document in which Russell collects discoveries that do not appear to fit the potential narrative(s) of the crime that he is constructing; whenever he finds himself without viable leads, he visits his Red Herring file to see if any of these odd notes prompt a connection. The term "red herring" refers in detective fiction fandom and scholarship to an author's deliberate attempt to mislead or distract the reader, so Russell here is reclaiming a classic trope in his own investigative practice. By putting aside (but not entirely discounting) potential red herrings, Russell acts almost as a reader, engaging on the pages in the kind of epistemological "fair play" that occurs between the writer and the reader. As he flirts with the postmodern and commits to the cozy with accounts of having recently "mailed a bill for fifty-three dollars and fifty cents, for time *and* expenses, and closed the filed on 'The Case of the Missing Casserole Dish'" (*Amuse* 14), Russell's tale in *Amuse Bouche* nonetheless has many hardboiled characteristics, as the mystery is a murder that ends with Russell not only putting his body in danger in the tradition of the hardboiled hero, but eventually even shooting the killer.

The hybridization of hardboiled and cozy is perhaps nowhere more evident than in Russell's relationship with the Saskatoon Police Department, embodied in the person of Darren Kirsch. From the opening novel, Russell describes Darren as an uneasy ally, a kind of frenemy from the Police Academy who is willing to enter a pragmatic symbiotic relationship, since Russell sometimes needs insider police information just as Darren sometimes needs someone who understands police work but is less constrained by police regulations. There are hints of what Eve Kosofsky Sedgwick might term a homosocial bond between the two men. Russell repeatedly describes Darren as physically attractive but regrettably straight, and the two men have occasion to go undercover as a gay couple in *Date With a Sheesha*, leading to a characteristically bitchy exchange:

[Russell:] "You have a problem with being undercover?"
[Darren:] "Of course not. And I'm fine with people thinking I'm gay. What I'm not fine with is them thinking I settled for someone like you."

(241)

The sharp banter between a police detective and private investigator recalls the hardboiled genre to which Bidulka owes considerable allegiance, but the eventual move from fraught working relationship to full-on friendship puts a Canadian spin on this classic trope.

Russell and Darren become progressively closer as the series unfolds. After several verbal sparring matches in the early novels, they have a moment of nuanced communion in *Stain of the Berry* after Russell is the victim of attempted rape. Russell is in a hospital room, changing into his own clothes, when the door opens to reveal the constable:

"Quant," came the gruff greeting as he walked into the room in his big he-man way.

I looked away at first, an unexpected jolt of embarrassment and shame passing over me like a hot flash ....

"Quant?" he said again, this time with surprising gentleness ... I felt a hand on my shoulder. 'You're okay, you know.'

(279)

Bidulka emphasizes that Darren is stepping out of his usual mock-adversarial relationship with Russell in order to help him through a traumatic experience when Russell asks for information and Darren takes his hand off the other man's shoulder and steps back "to a safer, manlier distance" (279). The scene is touching, with its embodiment of the respect and caring between two masculine men—one straight and one gay—who can count on each other in a time of need. By series end, after Darren has helped Russell to capture a serial killer, Russell gives a final summation of the police officer: "Although I'd never admit it to his face, I always felt he was probably a pretty good cop. Now I knew how wrong I was. He was an *excellent* cop" (*Dos Equis* 218, his emphasis).

Bidulka draws upon three distinct subgenres of detective fiction in his creation of Russell Quant: the cozy, the hardboiled, and the postmodern. The genre hybridization reflects at a meta-level the theme of liminality that runs through the series as Russell simultaneously embraces and rejects various constitutive features associated with the subgenres. He loves investigating murders rather than more mundane mysteries but hates the pain that murder always causes. He hates guns and yet uses them effectively as needed. He has an enviable group of interesting, diverse friends and yet often seeks solitude, including a full year of solo travels. And as an out gay man who appears perfectly comfortable with his sexual identity from the opening pages of the first novel, he nonetheless grows throughout the series as both a detective and a person.

Gender Politics: Thinking Through the Heteronormative

In his preface to a 2011 re-issue of *Amuse Bouche* (2003), Bidulka notes that his series has frequently been read as participating in a gender politics project: "With few exceptions, the first reviews, articles and interviews all included the word 'GAY' somewhere in the title or first sentence or two, long before content or merit made an appearance" (11, his emphasis). At the time of this writing, only one scholarly article has appeared on Bidulka, and it follows the popular press in its interest in Russell Quant as a gay detective. In his insightful article on the gender politics of Bidulka's series, Péter Balogh argues that

> Bidulka's representations of the LGBTQ+ community in Saskatchewan ends up being homonormative—privileging the kind of able-bodied, attractive, middle-class, largely sexless, white gay man who can pass as straight or at least as a form of gay easily legible to and acceptable in a white heteronormative society. For Balogh, much of the cultural critique we might expect in an LGBTQ+ detective series is of an unappealing kind, amounting to what he calls "the regulation of queers and other individuals not represented by the dominant gay male voice."
>
> *(186)*

Balogh provides compelling close readings of key passages from the novels to argue that Bidulka's series engages in casual misogyny, celebrates

Queer Eye gay characters while disparaging those who do not fit into this white affluent consumerist (possibly American) model of homosexuality, avoids even passing representations of gay sex, and depicts racialized gay characters in ways that "buttress the homonationalist project" (201). Balogh's conclusion is provocative: the Russell Quant series presents "an 'imagined' mainstream gay community, which politely accepts certain domestic 'rights' in exchange for assimilation and collusion with the nation-state that ensures that queer outlaws and racialized others will continue to be scrutinized as threats to 'civil society'" (201). It is an intriguing argument. And yet, a deeper contextualization of some of Bidulka's moves might reveal that his project is more progressive than Balogh's characterization suggests. I take his point that Quant and his closest gay male friends embody a kind of privileged masculinity. However, I believe we can more fully understand elements Balogh finds problematic—alleged casual misogyny, an absence of gay sex, and racialized gay characters—if we contextualize Bidulka's project within the broader framework of the hardboiled.

In locating casual misogyny in the Russell Quant series, Balogh argues that "Bidulka appears to have staked out a post-feminist politics of depoliticization as part of his homonormalizing project, which results in an irrational misogyny and sets up a framework for the constant tension that surfaces between the masculine and feminine throughout the series" (187). Balogh supports this interpretation with a close reading of the PWC Building description in *Amuse Bouche* and with the assertion that "a comparatively high number of women are killed off in Bidulka's series" (187). I agree with Balogh that the introduction of Russell's office in the PWC Building in the opening scene of the series deserves some unpacking; however, I read the scene differently. Quant explains that in the early eighties, "when it was cool to delete the reference to 'men'" (15), one of the "old character houses" on Spadina Crescent was turned into the Professional Womyn's Centre, a business space that was successful for several years. "But as the nineties matured," Quant asserts,

> and women overall became less hung up about the 'man' thing, what was once politically correct became a bit of an embarrassment and serious-minded tenants moved out. They headed for buildings with less controversial names like the Templeton Complex or better yet, no name at all.
>
> *(15)*

What Quant describes here, in my opinion, is the move from second-wave feminism, with its focus on equality between men and women, to third-wave feminism, with its interest in intersectionality, sex positivity, and queer theory. I do not read the character as indicting second-wave feminism or as arguing that "feminist struggles are immature and that serious-minded people have outgrown them" (Balogh 187). The building in which his office is located, now called only the PWC, houses three women professionals and one gay male private investigator. The idea of retaining the initials of the original building but deleting the reference to a dated feminist movement strikes me as fairly typical of the early twentieth-first century; at this time we see similar debates around language in university departments where some keep the name "Women's Studies" while others go to "Women's and Gender Studies" or simply "Gender Studies." To me, the fact that Errall Strane, the lesbian lawyer who owns the building, accepts Quant as its first male tenant suggests that the reader is meant to see him as a progressive gay man rather than as a misogynist.

Balogh's second argument for the series' misogyny, that it kills an unusual high number of female characters, is simply not grounded in the realities of crime writing. Bidulka's victimology is certainly unusual within the genre, but not in the way Balogh suggests. In a genre that tends to represent more female than male victims, this series is actually more balanced than most in the gender of its victims. Nine murder victims appear in the present timeline of the eight-novel Russell Quant series: 4 male, 4 female, and 1 female-to-male trans person. In *Dos Equis*, there is reference to previous victims (several female) of a serial killer, but those are not part of the current investigation. Bidulka's victimology is unusual for its preponderance of gay characters. There are four novels with a single murdered character: a gay man in *Amuse*, *Flight*, and *Aloha*, and a trans person in *Tapas*. *Sundowner* has no murder, focusing instead of the bullying of one gay male teen by another in the past. *Stain* has two murder victims, both women who sang in a gay choir whose members are being targeted, and a gay male victim disfigured by acid. *Sheesha* has a gay male victim whose murder Russell is investigating, and then, at novel's end, a straight female victim who was assisting with the investigation. The exploration of the risks associate with a detective's work continues in *Dos Equis*, where the primary victim is a lesbian private investigator.

Balogh reads a lack of sex in the Russell Quant novels as a kind of shying away from addressing the full range of potential gay sexualities: "In Bidulka's storytelling, sex disappears, so much so that an ironic side effect of the author's homonormalizing project is the erasure of homosexual activity throughout his books" (190). I do not share this reading. Most subgenres of detective fiction—including the hardboiled and the cozy from which Bidulka draws most heavily—do not present graphic descriptions of the protagonist's erotic life. Quant hints throughout the series to an early heartbreak from before his career as a private investigator. He regularly shares with readers when he is attracted to someone, be it the unattainable Jared Lowe (partner and eventual husband of Russell's close friend Anthony Gatt) or Alex Canyon (boyfriend until he proposes and Russell breaks off the relationship), or Ethan Ash (the boyfriend to follow), or JP Taine (the boyfriend at series end, with the suggestion of a Happily Ever After conclusion). Russell makes clear that he struggles to maintain long-term relationships, which hardly makes him an outlier in the world of fictional detectives. He also shares—subtly but clearly—that he has an active sex life. In *Stain of the Berry*, for example, Russell describes a perfect day off, opening with "I woke up late Sunday morning, with some whisker burn (obtained long after Jared went home to Anthony), and a nice big smile on my face" (32). After he describes the rest of the day off, which includes gardening, reading, playing with his dogs, eating and drinking his favorites, and taking a nap, he reminds the reader where the day began: "The cure for summer blahs? Get laid. It puts a definite bounce in one's step" (32). I would disagree with the premise that homosexual activity is erased from the series, suggesting instead that Russell can more productively be read as a gay embodiment of Chandler's hardboiled dick, "neither a eunuch nor a satyr" (59).

Balogh's reading of *Stain of the Berry*, the novel in which Russell is a victim of attempted rape, provides many compelling points about the decision to present a killer who is a trans Asian character. Balogh approaches this reading with the nuance it deserves, asserting:

> While it might be tempting to censure the novel for its reliance on this clearly negative stereotype [gay Asian men as effeminate], I argue that by contextualizing it and looking at it through queer and post-colonial lenses, we can reveal much more complex issues that speak not only to Bidulka's marginalized gay community but also to mainstream gay culture in Canada, as well as the larger Canadian nation-state.
>
> *(195)*

Bidulka's novel, like many of the crime fiction narratives I examine, certainly highlights elements of Canadian culture that over-rely on hegemonic power relations, and Balogh's reading illuminates rifts within Canadian gay culture that reveal this to be a category of identity as heterogenous as any other, complete with problematic hierarchies whose axes of power may have intersectional roots. In *Stain in the Berry*, Bidulka almost invites critique of racist attitudes within the LGBTQ+ community when Russell Quant learns that the killer, Jinny Chau, was ridiculed and ostracized by other members of the Pink Gophers, an LGBTQ+ choir (*Stained* 281, read in Balogh 197). As Balogh perceptively shows, though, Bidulka does not push this avenue of exploring systemic oppression as a cause of criminality (*Stained* 283, Balogh 197).

At the same time, my project of quantifying demographic representation within detective, victim, and criminal positions reveals an absence of authors leaving their comfort zones. As discussed in Chapter 1, most white Canadian writers present killers who are also white, and most male writers have far more male than female killers. I imagine there is a hesitancy to cross ethnic or sexuality markers in constructing a killer; a writer does not want to inadvertently appear racist, anti-gay, or anti-trans. My personal feeling is that Canadian crime fiction would benefit from more diversity in the role of the killer. After all, the killer position can productively be construed as a place of power that draws attention to important social critiques through the breaking of social and legal mores. Although Bidulka may not have intended it, the narrative of anti-Asian stereotyping within his imagined LGBTQ+ community as revealed by Balogh's reading ends up illuminating a complex and timely sociocultural issue in a way crime fiction is often well-positioned to do.

Mentorship: The Detective as Gay Mentor

Fully acknowledging Balogh's critique that Bidulka values a white, middle-class gay aesthetic over a more intersectional approach to gay characters, I would like to offer a reading of the series—and specifically of *Flight of Aquavit*—as placing Quant in a mentor position to a fellow character, and perhaps, analogously, Bidulka in a pedagogical position vis-à-vis his (mostly straight) readers. *Flight of Aquavit* won a 2005 Lambda Literary Award, a prestigious award celebrating LGBTQ+ writing. Using the conventions of detective fiction, the novel invites readers to think about the experience of a closeted gay man otherwise possessed of the same privilege as Quant and his *Queer Eye* friends. In this novel, Daniel Guest, a male accountant married to a woman, is being blackmailed for his recent gay activity. As Russell gets to know his client, he reflects on how difficult it must be for Daniel to hide his desires not only from the people around him, but also, in some sense, from himself. An especially poignant moment of Daniel's self-denial is revealed when Russell questions him about an anonymous lover who might be the blackmailer.

> Daniel's eyes narrowed as he recalled the evening, as if suddenly understanding something he hadn't before. "You know, Russell, to him it [gay sex] wasn't something dirty, something you do quickly in

the dark without talking or smiling, it was something you do with ... rapture ... like ... real sex."

(30, his ellipsis)

Daniel here casually equates "real sex" with the heterosexual, revealing an unhealthy and alienating attitude toward his own sexual orientation.

As Russell interacts with Daniel's two recent anonymous male lovers, he finds them both unlikely blackmailers. Could there be a third man Daniel has not admitted to? It is Darren Kirsch, Russell's police friend, who provides a clue to the blackmailer's identity:

[Darren]: "Could it have been a woman?"
[Russell]: "What? A woman?" Sexistly, I had not even considered that.

(178)

Once again, Russell's apparent self-awareness offers an engaging opportunity to the reader. After characterizing himself as sexist, Russell nonetheless continues to pursue male suspects, and the reader might be quicker than the detective in identifying Daniel's wife as the blackmailer. Russell's reactions to finally recognizing Cheryl's crime are worth unpacking: "I felt sorry for Cheryl Guest. Despite all she'd done, here was a woman wronged, a victim of perfidy, outraged and filled with unfathomable sadness at the lamentable outcome of her useless vengeance" (279). Russell is able to see that Cheryl is just as harmed by Daniel's inability to express his sexual desire as is Daniel himself. The social and psychological scars of anti-gay and homophobic sentiment affect all sorts of people. As an out gay man with many deep ties to the LGBTQ+ community, Russell learns his own blind spots when it comes to a straight woman's experience of being unknowingly married to a gay man.

Even as he learns to move past his owns stereotypes, Russell also acts as a kind of mentor to Daniel, helping the other man articulate his desires and introducing him to a community of people comfortable with their LGBTQ+ identities. The novel ends uncertainly for Daniel. In the final scene, Daniel comes by Russell's bustling holiday party to thank the detective for not only completing the investigation but also for showing him that self-loathing about his sexuality may be unnecessary and detrimental. Russell is disheartened by this sincere but ambiguous thanks: "Might be? Maybe? I was disappointed. Hadn't the last couple of weeks taught him anything at all?" (298). Russell's final interaction with his client invites readers to reflect on whether or not Russell has been successful in helping Daniel accept and even embrace his identity. "I want to be happier, Russell," Daniel says haltingly, but Russell sees the other man's uncertainty: "I could see by the look in his eyes that his familiar, closeted lifestyle was luring him, tempting him with its shallow promise of safety and ease" (298). Intent on helping his client, even reminding him of a conversation they had a few days earlier about how being openly gay means being free, Russell brings out a bottle of Aquavit—a drink earlier tied to sensuality—for a toast. The two men drink, then Daniel gets into his car and drives away, the bottle of Aquavit on the roof. The novel ends with a musing on the title:

> And as the car moved away I realized Daniel had indeed taken something with him.
> A Flight of Aquavit.
> Atop the vehicle was the bottle of Aquavit. I watched as it jerked from the sudden motion of the car's departure, precariously close to falling ... and then ... it did.
> *(299, original ellipses)*

What is the reader to make of this ending? If the Aquavit is a symbol of acknowledging and embracing one's sexual desires, which embody one's true and free self, then Daniel would seem to be continuing his path of self-denial and even self-hatred. And yet, there is hope in the image of the bottle atop the car. Although it eventually falls, Daniel does not know it is there and it teeters precariously before finally tumbling. Given Daniel's articulation of his desire to live an openly gay lifestyle, I believe it is possible to read the ending as acknowledging the power of the closet; it may take a middle-aged gay man several attempts before he finally comes out, but every step he takes moves him closer to that ultimate goal.

Conclusion

The final novel of the Russell Quant series, in keeping with many of the Canadian crime fiction series examined in this book, ends with a classic comedy resolution that presents the main detective character with a romantic resolution to accompany the solution to a particularly difficult criminal case. The crime in *Dos Equis* (2012) is a dark one in two ways. The first victim is not only someone known to Russell, but also a sort of double for him—Jane Cross, a lesbian private investigator, also from Saskatchewan. Jane has stumbled upon an especially distasteful criminal: a killer who specializes in making the murder of elderly people look accidental when hired by their family members. Against this backdrop, Russell ends the series by taking a very big step. In a final scene with his boyfriend JP Taine, also a gay private eye, Russell refers to Jessica Fletcher and Hercule Poirot (as he does in the opening scene of the first novel). He then gives JP a gift: a piece of wood engraved "Quant & Taine, Private Investigators." The final paragraph of the series reviews not Russell's cases, but his personal and professional identities:

> Being a man who enjoys his time as a lone wolf is not a bad thing. I embrace it, but I'm also a man who welcomes new challenges, new desires, new experiences .... I have been Russell Quant, PI for a long time. Now, opening this new chapter, I will be one half of Quant & Taine. Together, we would hang out our shingle for all to see. Who knows where this will lead.
> Who knows.
>
> *(229)*

These words echo the conclusion of Giles Blunt's police series, when John Cardinal and Lise Delorme conclude that they love each other and ask "Now what?" (*Until the Night* 300). They also signal a kind of optimism in reflecting on changes that have happened in the past—even after a particularly difficult case—and a hopeful belief in a positive future.

10

THE LEGAL THRILLER

Trauma and Resilience in Pamela Callow's Kate Lange Series

Early in *Damaged* (2010), the first novel of Pamela Callow's Kate Lange series, we learn that Kate, a lawyer, has recently broken off her engagement with Ethan Drake, a homicide detective. The two meet on a dark, stormy night and rehash their breakup, which occurred after Ethan learned of Kate's difficult past, whose details she had never shared with him. For Kate, her secrecy, even from her fiancé, is a matter of self-preservation and epistemological identity:

> Her past was something she kept locked in a very dark, deep box. Putting voice to it made it real again.
> It had scared her. Terrified her. Admitting what she'd done to this man whom she loved so desperately. Ethan saw life in black-and-white. The only thing she saw in black-and-white was death. Everything else was shades in between.
>
> *(40)*

Kate's view here—that her perspective on the world is more nuanced than Ethan's—will be interrogated throughout the series. Her deep psychological need to bury her past, however, will only be strengthened. Kate's constant struggle to simultaneously comprehend and repress her past can perhaps best be understood through a lens of trauma theory that is particularly suited to unpacking the rhetorical moves of the thriller, which approaches the epistemological and ethical questions at the center of all crime fictions through an unusually visceral perspective.

The thriller has its roots in the nineteenth-century sensation novel, a frowned-upon form then considered to be too salacious for young readers and generally contrasted with the sentimental novel, which centered sentiment (of the heart) rather than sensation (of the body). The sensation novel was seen as perilous, especially to young women readers, who might identify with the endangered heroines of such novels, often caught up in Gothic worlds full of labyrinthine spaces peopled by dangerous forces unregulated by religious or social mores. The foundational generic impulse of the thriller, as its label suggests, is a visceral one that raises a thrill or frisson in the body. Or, as John McCarty explains, the thriller has a "single minded purpose, which is to put the reader or audience on edge and keep them there" (cited in Hoppenstand xi). The frisson of the thriller suggests a somewhat jaded worldview, pointing to a reality in which peril is always imminent, in a narrative where danger does not disappear after the body whose murder must be investigated is produced. The modern thriller explores several epistemologically distinct areas through its subgenres, which include the legal thriller, the medical thriller, the military thriller, the psychological thriller, the supernatural thriller, the technological thriller, and others. In each case, an epistemological frame or way of knowing—law, medicine, psychology, religion, science, etc.—is combined with a thrill, generally accomplished through fast-paced narration toward what appears to be inexorable peril.

Although the thriller often has the same rhetorical goals as detective fiction—to showcase a vulnerability in the social fabric and demonstrate the possibility for resolution—it uses a markedly different narrative structure. Where the detective narrative tells the story of a detective uncovering the previously occurring story of the crime (Todorov 46), the thriller tends to provide both stories in tandem, moving between a force of disorder (for example, criminal, disease, out-of-control technology) and a force of order (for example, detective/lawyer, doctor, scientist). The movement between these forces can provide readers with complex identifications. In the legal thriller, for example, the reader often moves between the lawyer/investigator and the criminal. The criminal's perspective is unmediated by the detective's point of view, and the reader often gets access to the criminal's mind and motivation even before the crime has been committed. Some thriller authors draw readers into potential sympathy with the criminal while others use the revelation of the criminal's thought processes to elicit horror. Some, like Pamela Callow, do both at various times.

I was fortunate enough to speak with Callow in November 2021 to get her perspective on how the genre of the thriller functions for her. She spoke enthusiastically about her decision to set her work in Canada. She is committed to authentic world-building and believes that having a clear sense of place is important to telling stories that engage readers intellectually and viscerally. Halifax, as she told me, has all the features a thriller writer needs in order to pursue various thought experiments: five universities, a huge medical center, a number of large law firms, a fascinating history, a fair amount of crime, and extremely variable weather. It also provides a great deal of geographic variety: the bustling downtown area includes an international harbor with much sensational potential at night, and characters are able to leave the city and quickly find themselves in more desolate rural settings. Callow has taken pieces of Halifax history in crafting her stories, including the inclusion of Creutzfeldt–Jakob disease (CJD), a rare disorder that has an outsized prevalence in Nova Scotia.

Callow has appeared at ThrillerFest, an international conference for thriller writers. She once spoke on a panel titled "Are Thrillers Society's Conscience?" and was able to respond with a very definitive yes. For her, the thriller is a genre that naturally supplies much-needed social commentary. She tries not to be preachy, but she sees herself as providing a level of education for her readers by allowing them to immerse themselves in whatever legal conundrum she is exploring. Indeed, each of the Kate Lange novels addresses a thorny legal issue, including the regulation of new biomedical techniques and technologies, the legality of assisted suicide and the role of the advocate in that question, and the protections afforded to whistleblowers. In writing about important legal challenges, Callow deploys the pedagogical potential of the thriller in engaging readers in thinking through difficult questions of trauma that are increasingly understood and discussed in contemporary Canadian society.

The Pedagogical Potential of the Thriller at the Site of Gender Equity

Priscilla L. Walton, who co-authored (with fellow Canadian scholar Manina Jones) *Detective Agency*, an important study of hard-boiled women detectives, argues that the twenty-first century has seen a movement from women detectives with outsider status, such as private detectives, to women detectives with insider status, such as those who are protagonists of legal thrillers (22). Walton identifies a trend in legal thrillers wherein "women writers and their protagonists often explore cases that relate to women specifically, as they contingently trace the problems with which female professionals are plagued" (24). Walton notes the prevalence of lawyers among the authors of legal thrillers and suggests that these female lawyer-writers often differ from their male counterparts by interrogating the very possibility of "'objective' or 'lawyerly' distance," instead tending to "involve the reader in the issue at hand through their protagonists' involvement" (25). Indeed, Callow was long a practicing lawyer before she began writing thrillers, and even now, she remains a non-practicing member of the Nova Scotia Bar. I asked Callow why she thinks so many lawyers are attracted to writing legal thrillers, and she gave me two reasons. First, many lawyers are closet writers likely to be attracted to a career in writing fiction; this resonated with me as an English professor, since my own students are often just as attracted to careers in the law as to those in writing, publishing, and editing. Secondly, Callow noted that many thriller writers come to the genre as a second career, from law, journalism, or even espionage. Given the level of expertise required to craft credible texts in the thriller subgenres—legal, medical, technological, etc.—it makes sense that skilled professionals in those areas with an interest in writing would have the credentials and skills to become successful thriller authors. A third implicit reason became clear as we spoke: activism. Many people become lawyers because they genuinely want to make a difference in protecting people's rights and making sure the law remains abreast of sociocultural and technological change. Writing fiction can be another way to achieve those goals, as popular literature can be a powerful way to introduce readers to timely and important sociocultural issues.

Like the legal thriller protagonists penned by the female authors Walton investigates, Callow's Kate Lange is often faced with unpalatable role models and choices as a woman in the legal world. At the series opening, she is a 31-year-old lawyer who has recently landed a job as a junior member of a prominent Halifax law firm. She lacks the privilege of other members of the firm and has had to fight hard to gain this prestigious placement given that she had to work part-time jobs to support herself through university and law school. She now finds herself largely relegated to "the pink ghetto" (*Damaged* 4), the family law cases often assigned to female associates. In a realistic exploration of a working-class female lawyer at a blue-chip firm, we see Kate negotiating socially complicated terrain that calls as much upon her interpersonal skills as her legal prowess. In the opening pages of *Damaged*, for example, Kate bemoans the fact that she has not yet received any litigation, insurance, or corporate cases. And now, she is handed an especially thorny custody case. The child is Lisa MacAdam, a rebellious 15-year-old whose paternal grandmother is exploring the option of taking custody away from the child's single mother, a well-known Halifax judge being considered for the province's Supreme Court. Given Judge Hope Carson's position in the community and the lack of evidence of neglect or abuse, Kate does not contact Child Protection to instigate the investigation that would be required in order to open a custody battle. She is later to question this decision—made in deference to a more powerful female in the field of law—when Lisa turns up dead, the first victim of a serial killer.

In this and other novels in the series, female lawyers face enormous challenges, especially if they attempt to pursue motherhood alongside their legal careers. Judge Carson is initially described by her mother-in-law as an unfit mother, but Kate comes to suspect that this characterization may be based on generational understandings of motherhood. As a single parent in a demanding profession, Hope indeed struggles to balance her work and family obligations, as do many (or perhaps most) twenty-first-century real-life mothers. Hope appears to be cold and uncaring, but the narrative provides some brief scenes from her perspective that show how hard she has worked to cultivate that appearance. After her return home from identifying her daughter's body at the morgue, a task she completed dry-eyed, Hope downs three glasses of Scotch before she forces herself to go upstairs to her daughter's room. The third-person focalized narration reveals the contradictions at the base of her mental processes: "Hating the weakness that threatened to topple her to the floor, she crossed the room. Woodenly. Like a puppet" (195). As she stands alone, looking down at her daughter's things, she attempts to keep her emotions at bay: "She would not weep. Because it would never stop" (196) and "She needed to lie down. But if she lay down in here she would never get up" (196). Finally, Hope breaks down as she looks at one of Lisa's prized possessions, a picture of herself at eight years old with a beloved dog. Hope sobs uncontrollably before she closes herself off emotionally by thinking about her professional aspirations: "All she had left was her career. Her own hopes. And those hopes were high, right now. The Supreme Court was within her grasp" (197). It is only the reader who has access to Hope's emotions. For the characters in the novel, she is a cold, professional woman whose murdered daughter stands as an embodiment of her inability to balance her career and her motherhood.

One could argue that Elise Vanderzell, the murder victim in the second novel of the series, *Indefensible*, functions in some of the same ways as a negative example of a woman trying to balance family with a legal career. A mother of two, she is a lawyer recently divorced from Randall Barrett, Kate's boss and eventual love interest. Brief focalization through Elise's perspective before she is killed provides some parallels with Kate in how she thinks about the law:

> Acquaintances often asked her—with a note of incredulity in their voice—how she liked being a tax lawyer. Elise knew it sounded dull and arcane, but she loved her work. She loved the elaborate structures, the

legal fictions, the satisfaction of rendering concrete an entity that was abstract. Of giving form to something intangible.

(Indefensible 38)

Elise here puts into words a love of the legal system that Kate often appears also to espouse. She sees the law as a structuring force that, while made up of nothing but words, nonetheless is able to provide comfort and order by "rendering concrete" and "giving form to" other equally abstract linguistic constructs like the tax code or the constitution. Like many women in thrillers, Elise suffers a fate that appears to punish her for transgressive sexual activity. She is killed by her psychiatrist, with whom she is having an affair. The psychiatrist, who happens to be a serial killer particularly attracted by pubescent girls, also targets Elise's daughter Lucy, although Kate and Randall together are able to save the young woman.

As victims, Hope and Elise—mother of a murder victim and murder victim, respectively—could be seen as cautionary tales for women attempting to pursue legal careers while also having a family. When I asked Callow about the possibility of reading Hope and Elise as being punished by the narrative for their ambition, she said she was trying to show the struggles female professionals—especially those with families—continue to face in the workplace. She has seen female lawyers punish others at the office for such things as taking maternity leave. She concluded our discussion of *Damaged* by saying: "I'm glad my book is authentic and accurate, but that's also depressing." Using the exaggerated plot devices of the thriller (serial killers are rare everywhere, perhaps especially in Canada's Maritime provinces), Callow explores Kate's workplace interactions with other female lawyers as well as with a range of male colleagues with varying access to authority, thus revealing the power dynamics underlying the legal side of the justice system. She accomplishes this largely by exposing her characters to trauma.

Personal and Professional Trauma in the Legal Thriller

Few, if any, legal thrillers are built around a cheerful, well-adjusted lawyer character who is living the dream by doing meaningful, well-compensated legal work that meshes perfectly with the other, equally fulfilling parts of their life. By its nature, legal work shares some of the dark perspectives built into the police procedural as well. An amateur detective can always assume that the current case marks the only time—or at least the last time, if they are a serial character—they will ever have to deal with a crime in their immediate surroundings. Such a detective figure can imagine a crime-free future. For professionals, be they investigators, forensic specialists, or members of the legal apparatus, each case, whether successfully (re)solved or not, will soon be replaced by another with all its potential for the same interaction with trauma.

Trauma theory has been increasingly used in understanding the appeal and power of crime fiction in the twenty-first century. In a recent article in *Clues: The Journal of Detection*, Mary Ann Gillies argues that "as understanding of what constitutes trauma has shifted over the last century, crime fiction has adapted as well, representing trauma in increasingly sophisticated and complex ways and, in doing so, mirroring the twenty-first century's preoccupation with it" (41). In her analysis of recent crime fiction that addresses trauma directly, she calls upon Roger Luckhurst's formulation of trauma as "a piercing or breach of a border that puts inside and outside into a strange communication" (cited Gillies 41). Luckhurst's piercing or breach can refer to a physical wound or even a mental wound; in detective fiction, it can also—and sometimes simultaneously—refer to the disruption of the cultural fabric that begins every murder mystery. As W.H. Auden observed in 1948,

> Murder is unique in that it abolishes the party it injures, so that society has to take the place of the victim and on his behalf demand atonement or grant forgiveness; it is the one crime in which society has a direct interest.
>
> *(557)*

Murder, then, is a breach of social convention that pierces the social contract codified into laws. It also traumatizes the victim, the victim's loved ones, and even the investigators who attempt to construct an explanatory narrative (police) and to ensure that justice of some sort is achieved (lawyers).

Other pioneering trauma theorists include Elaine Scarry and Cathy Caruth. In *The Body in Pain* (1985), Scarry provides the deep insight that intense pain destroys language, arguing that "as the content of one's world disintegrates, so the content of one's language disintegrates; as the self disintegrates, so that which would express and project the self is robbed of its source and its subject" (35). In *Unclaimed Experience* (1996), Caruth also works from the notion that trauma cannot be fully understood as it happens, which is why it recurs in nightmares and flashbacks. Caruth examines individual and cultural trauma, asserting that trauma includes both destruction and survival: "It is only by recognizing traumatic experience as a paradoxical relation between destructiveness and survival that we can also recognize the legacy of incomprehensibility at the heart of catastrophic experience" (58). Maria Tumarkin's *Traumascapes: The*

Power and Fate of Places Transformed by Tragedy (2005) situates locale at the center of trauma, arguing that places of trauma can be "full of visual and sensory triggers, capable of eliciting a whole palette of emotions" (cited Gillies 46). These notions of trauma as language-destroying, site-specific, and linked to both destruction and survival are threaded through Callow's terrifying representations of trauma through the Kate Lange series.

Callow explores the generalized impact of witnessing trauma on her police and lawyer characters. Quite early in *Damaged*, Kate's ex-fiancé and homicide detective Ethan Drake emphasize the fact that participation in the justice system as a service to the community takes its toll on workers. As Ethan performs his duties of bringing in Judge Hope Carson to identify her daughter's murdered body, he muses about the traumatizing nature of his job: "For some reason, the longer he worked on this unit, the harder it was getting to keep his distance. He thought he'd get desensitized. But he'd only gotten more thirsty for retribution" (84). This type of reflection underlines one of the appeals of detective fiction: the interplay of contamination and containment in the detective figure, who regularly faces the ravages of criminal activity, which serve as a threat to the detective's inherently strong ethical framework and underlying optimism. The appeal of the genre, I have argued elsewhere, lies partly in the detective's potential contamination and ultimate containment (Bedore *Dime*). Here, we see Ethan trying to develop a thicker skin around his dealing with the treatment of the victim by the justice system. This is a thought echoed later in the same chapter when he attends Lisa's autopsy and imagines the victim in life: "He could just imagine how a fifteen-year-old girl would feel to have all these strange men examining her" (85). Ethan has not become desensitized to his work, which could be read as his not becoming contaminated by the ugliness that surrounds him. At the same time, he finds himself in the potentially hazardous position of desiring retribution, a value opposed to the project of the police and legal systems in which he works. And personally, witnessing the traumatized bodies of murder victims and of their shocked, grieving loved ones, marks him with a sort of residual trauma.

For Kate, the trauma is both professional and personal. When she attends the funeral of 15-year-old Lisa Carson, Kate realizes that her teenage sister died the same year the murdered girl was born. We are privy to her internal thoughts, where she seeks hope but finds only existential despair:

> You'd like to think that the eternal circle of life was kicking in, providing some order to the universe but, as life would have it, Lisa died a tragic death too. Kate had no doubt there was another baby being born who

would face a similar tragic death in fifteen years, whose passing would rend the fabric of the family and leave them unraveled.

(Damaged 121)

Kate here clearly attempts to find meaning in tragedy with her reference to "the eternal circle of life," but to no avail. This places Callow's novels within the rich tradition of detective fiction that investigates the impact of crime on not only those close to murder victims, but also those who investigate and attempt to understand—if not make meaning—of their deaths.

Kate enters the series as a deeply traumatized person. The secret she never divulged to Ethan when they were dating and even engaged is one that continues to haunt her in the sense that Caruth identifies: "a wound of the mind ... experienced too soon, too unexpectedly, to be fully known and is therefore not available to consciousness until it imposes itself again, repeatedly, in the nightmares and repetitive actions of the survivor" (4). We learn that Kate and Ethan broke up when Ethan's ex-girlfriend Vicky told him of two things from Kate's past: that her father was a convicted embezzler and that her sister Imogen had died. The first mention of Imogen's death is not of the trauma itself but of its documentation. In a heated conversation with Ethan, Kate feels the trauma in her body:

> [Ethan]: "It only ruined things because you lied to me."
> [Kate]: "I didn't lie!" Her fingers curled into themselves.
> "Lying by omission."
> She stared at him. In the space of four months, he'd gone from being her lover to her accuser.
> *Her pulse began to pound in her temples.* "You just can't deal with the fact that the future wife of a homicide detective has a father who is a convicted embezzler."
> He crossed his arms. "It's not just your father, Kate."
> She stiffened. She knew where he was going with this. *Rage flooded her.* She welcomed it. "What do you mean?"
> "I need to know what happened with your sister."
> She raised her chin. "Vicky couldn't find the report?"

(34, emphasis added)

Kate's pulse is elevated and her body is flooded with endorphins (rage) when she is confronted with the trauma of her sister's death and, as we are about to learn, her own role in it. Her (admittedly catty) mention of the police report also speaks to the presence of trauma here as it evokes

Scarry's insight that the body in pain (physical or mental) is separated from words and can no longer access linguistic tools. For Kate, even 15 years later, it is almost insurmountably difficult to put words to what happened to her sister, so she grasps for the police report instead.

When Kate finally finds the words to tell Ethan what happened, her explanation is stark in the extreme:

> She took a deep breath. Made her voice flat. "Here's the story."
> Her eyes forced him to hold her gaze.
> "When I was sixteen I killed my sister."
> He flinched. "The report says you were driving. The car crashed."
> "I was speeding. I killed her."
> It was as simple as that. A blink of an eye. A life gone.
>
> (35)

Kate turns away from Ethan and struggles with her housekey, eventually pitching forward into her front hallway. Her body is uncoordinated as she fumbles with the dog's water bowl, splashing herself and the floor. She must reach for tools she has built over the years to calm her body and her mind: "Her fingers were shaking. She leaned against the counter, head down, breathing deeply until the anger leached from her body" (36). As the ongoing narrative makes clear, Kate is dealing with far more than anger here. The specter of Imogen's death is to haunt her in a variety of ways, as it, in Caruth's words, "imposes itself again, repeatedly, in the nightmares and repetitive actions of the survivor" (4). Ethan walks away from Kate after their difficult conversation, apparently unequipped to help her. Throughout the series, though, he too is to understand Kate as a trauma survivor. Later in *Damaged*, for example, Ethan interviews a doctor with two small children whose husband is experiencing cognitive decline. He realizes that Dr. Clare must be devastated by her situation, and later reflects upon her attitude: "And yet, she had had a desperate determination in her gaze. The stunned look of a survivor. He realized—with a shock of recognition—he'd seen that same look before. In Kate's eyes" (293). This recalls Caruth's assertion that trauma balances on a fine point between destruction and survival, since Kate, like Dr. Clare, has been threatened by her trauma but has also shown resilience in surviving it.

Callow calls upon the Gothic roots of the thriller genre in creating a trauma-inflected confrontation between Kate and the serial killer near the end of *Damaged*. The encounter occurs in the embalming room of a funeral home where the killer has murdered and dismembered other victims. Kate, kidnapped by a trusted mentor involved in a human tissue brokering scheme, awakens, naked and drugged, on a steel gurney to which she is tied hand and foot with medical tubing. Within this grotesque new trauma, Kate endures the aftereffects of Imogen's death in a way that speaks to the survivorship Caruth associates with trauma. After a seriously injured Kate cleverly figures out a way to free herself from the gurney, she attempts to escape the funeral home, crippled by the physiological effects of her experience:

> She bit the scalpel sideways between her teeth, keeping her hands free, and lowered her feet to the floor. It was icy. But where her blood spattered, the tiling was warm and slick. Vertigo tilted the room ....
> *You can do it.*
> That wasn't her voice urging her forward.
> It was Imogen's.
> A small warmth spread from inside her chest.
> *(370, original emphasis)*

Buoyed by her dead sister's presence—Caruth's repetition caused by the wound of the mind—Kate is able to navigate her way out of the room only to be attacked by the serial killer.

The killer is terrifying not only because of his past actions, but also because he is infected with CJD, a rare brain disorder that causes mental deterioration and dementia. The causes for CJD are not entirely known (some cases are hereditary and some sporadic), but a small percentage are acquired through transmission by exposure to brain or nervous system tissue. As the killer grabs Kate by the throat and she attempts to leverage the scalpel in her hand, she is again visited by Imogen's presence, this time assuring Kate that she had done all she could to help her little sister before her death. Finally, just as Kate is about to lose consciousness, she stops feeling Imogen as a presence and instead reaches for a resonant memory, of the two of them as kids, seeing who could hold their breath the longest underwater at the pool. Fueled by involuntary flashbacks of her sister in the early part of her escape, Kate is, in the end, able to deliberately grasp a relevant memory that allows her to break free of the killer's stranglehold and kill him with the scalpel. After this, Kate finds herself awash in a complex pain: "The pain was there. Deep, silent, waiting for her to approach. But not reproachful. It was the pain of having something that had been lodged deep in her flesh finally removed. It was a healing pain" (384). Accessing the trauma of her sister's death during the new trauma has brought Kate both destructiveness and survival.

The first novel ends with an embodiment of the contradictory impulses that follow trauma. Kate survives, but she bears a new wound that has just as much potential to disintegrate the self in Scarry's terms as does the guilt-laden wound of Imogen's death half a lifetime earlier. In *Indefensible* (2011), the second novel of the series, Kate has garnered substantial celebrity within Halifax legal circles as the person who took down the Body Butcher, the city's first serial killer. Her encounter with the Body Butcher has left her with several physical wounds as well as a dread of the small possibility that she might have contracted CJD from their bloody encounter. At the novel's opening, Kate is invited to a social outing that seems more exhausting than pleasurable, but she forces herself to say yes:

> She'd had a taste of her mortality. She was seizing life with both hands. Carpe diem and all that crap. And maybe she'd wear away through sheer exhaustion the imprint that [the Body Butcher] had made on her soul.
> *(38)*

Kate attempts to replace trauma with normalcy by saying yes to a one-night stand, only to find her trauma reasserting itself. In bed with the fortunately generous lover she has taken home, she cannot escape the recurrence of trauma:

> [The Body Butcher] had boxed her into a corner of shadows and fear. She'd won the battle in May when she killed him. But he was winning the war on her mind. After months of nightmares pounding at her reserves, she was ready to do pretty well anything to keep [the Body Butcher] out of her bedroom.
> *(60)*

Luckhurst's breach between inside and outside—between body and mind—is here evident in Kate's inability to focus on sexual pleasure in the face of her trauma. As the novel continues, though, she gains insight from her traumatic experience and its involuntary repetitions. She struggles with insomnia, now unable to sleep without first locking all the windows, often "held hostage to nighttime terror" (189). On one of these sleepless nights, with her heart racing, Kate remembers that Ethan once told her he had killed a man in self-defense. Kate had been sympathetic,

> But she'd never understood. Never truly comprehended what it was like to end another human's life. To see that person's life force drain in front of your eyes. To know that it would stain your soul for the rest of your life.
> *(190)*

Now that she has had the horrifying experience of killing a killer—in self-defense but also in defense of the other women he would surely have attacked if left unchecked—Kate has access to true understanding. This is a level of understanding most readers will never have, but its narration through a trauma lens at least partially articulates the ineffable toll of detective work.

Traumascape and the Dark Double

On the surface, *Tattooed* (2012), the third novel of the Kate Lange series, provides a thoughtful, well-researched, ethically complex exploration of an issue controversial to Canada before and after the 2016 Supreme Court decision striking down the prohibition against assisted death: the right to choose medical assistance in dying and the role of the advocate in that choice. Callow told me she wanted to show "the ambiguity and complexity of human motivation" on this topic, and she also wanted to position the readers as the jury, which demonstrates once again the pedagogical potential of the legal thriller in engaging readers to think deeply about complex ethical and legal questions. In tandem with this legal exploration and its attendant traumas (for the woman seeking assisted death and for her daughter), *Tattooed* also uses the Gothic trope of the dark double as it presents Kate with a traumascape of the kind Maria Tumarkin has recently revisited in an autoethnographic exploration of the importance of sites of trauma. For Tumarkin,

> Traumascapes are haunted and haunting places, where visible and invisible, past and present, physical and metaphysical come to coexist and share a common space. These are places that get to us, that affect us at the very core, that make us feel everything from awe to unease, from fear to epiphany, from a burst of involuntary memories to a sense of deep, all-powerful transformation.
>
> *("Twenty" 5)*

The sense of juxtaposition in this statement—between haunted and haunting, awe and unease, etc.—is especially embodied in *Tattooed*, which is presented as a book-length legal, mental, emotional, and eventually physical battle between Kate Lange and her dark double Kenzie Sloane.

Tattooed opens with Kate meeting with Frances Sloane, an older woman suffering from amyotrophic lateral sclerosis (ALS) who seeks legal counsel in the hopes of attaining medical assistance in dying. Kate has a complicated relationship with Frances, the woman who was away on business almost two decades earlier when her daughter Kenzie threw the out-of-control party from which Kate picked up her little sister on the night of the fatal accident. Kate's last encounter with Frances was in the receiving line at her sister's funeral, when Frances had told 17-year-old Kate how sorry she was, not only in condolence for her sister's death, but also in guilt for Frances's own role in allowing her teen daughter to throw the fateful party. For Kate, Frances's dualistic "sorry"—both condolence and apology—had led to the kind of conflicting impulses so often identified in trauma theory: "Kate's eyes had welled with tears. Frances' words were a form of absolution; a recognition that the blame for Imogen's death did not reside solely on Kate's seventeen-year-old shoulders. And Kate's rage melted into liquid warmth, spilling down her cheeks" (14). Now Frances is seeking death and has chosen Kate from among all of Halifax's lawyers to take her case. As Frances laboriously explains the symptoms of ALS, Kate recognizes the horrors of the disease, in which the victim remains mentally sharp while slowly losing all bodily function. Her insight into that horror is earned in part by her own trauma, evidenced when she reflects, "Unlike the Creutzfeldt-Jakob disease that could be lurking in her own cells. That disease robbed its victim of all cognitive function" (18).

Although Kate tells Frances that she needs a lobbyist, since the 2016 Supreme Court decision on medical assistance in dying had not yet been delivered, Frances insists that Kate—well-known for her bravery in standing up to a serial killer—take on a public role in the case. This leads to Kate revisiting Frances's home for the first time since the night Imogen died, raising excruciating memories for the main character that provide the reader with the first full picture of the circumstances that have, until this point in the series, been described only in terse, stark sentences and phrases. In her review of 20 years of research on traumascapes in 2019, Tumarkin provides eight bullet points that distill her thinking about the kind of cultural work traumascapes can provide. Each of these gestures to a potentially transformative function. For example, "Traumascapes can crystallise identities and meanings," "Traumascapes can act as focal points or catalysts for truth-seeking and justice-seeking," and "Traumascapes can become portals for individual experiences of shame, brutalization, loss of meaning, and humiliation, to become reconfigured as socially shared experiences" (11). For Kate, driving to Frances's home 17 years after her sister's death crystallizes her memories and provides meaning: "Strange how time blurs so many memories, and then driving down a driveway in the early morning May sunshine brought back, in vivid detail, the dark May night when Kate was seventeen" (121). When she walks into the house, Kate is beset by uncontrollable memories of a Cranberries' song, "Salvation," the anti-drug anthem that had been ironically playing when she had taken the same walk 17 years earlier (123). As she prepares for her meeting with Frances, Kate continues to look at the back porch of the Sloane house as "The memories that had been crowding at the gates of Kate's subconscious now surged through the barrier" (125). Kate's memories of that night are presented over several pages as the first clear narrative of events that describe how she found her little sister expertly snorting cocaine with Kenzie Sloane, had an altercation with Kenzie, insisted that Imogen come home with her, and then, while fighting with her intoxicated sister, lost control of the car, leading to the fatal crash. Callow's presentation of details over several novels mirrors the fraught relationship between understanding a trauma in the moment and the involuntary echoes that appear, often only partially, over time. There is the police report, Kate's brief description of the crash to Ethan, and now the much fuller story.

As a classic dark double figure, Kenzie Sloane occupies a significant place in that fuller story. Kate and Kenzie battled for the affection of Imogen Sloane when they were teens, Kate with sisterly concern and Kenzie with the intention of grooming the younger girl in conjunction with a male lover. *Tattooed* reveals that Kenzie and her boyfriend had actually targeted Imogen as a potential murder victim only to have her die in Kate's car before their plan could be realized. Kate and Kenzie both love dogs, with Kate's pure white husky Alaska a stark contrast to Kenzie's black pug Foo Dog. As Callow told me, "Kenzie is the dark part of Kate's soul. She's the person holding up the mirror." A harrowing encounter between the two women in *Tattooed* includes Kenzie holding up a very dark mirror indeed. The two meet at a storage locker that includes some of Imogen's things, and the scene turns deadly as Kenzie's old boyfriend, who has been in prison for the past ten years, tries to kill Kate. After Kate kills him—a trauma we know will haunt her—Kenzie accuses Kate of having driven her little sister to Kenzie through controlling behavior. Kenzie pulls the trigger to kill Kate, but Kate rushes her and the two grapple for the gun, Kate coming up with it. She points the gun at her dark double, feeling the viscerality of the thriller genre as her rival taunts her:

> A chill ran along Kate's scalp.
> Kenzie's gaze locked onto hers. *Do it. I want you to do it.*
> "You can do it, Kate. You think you are so high-and-mighty, a frigging hero to the masses, but underneath that pure white skin [i.e. not tattooed, unlike Kenzie's], you are just like me." She raised a brow. "It takes guts to do this, Kate. Not anyone can be a killer."
>
> *(334)*

As Kate lowers the gun and runs out, she hears Kenzie's taunts in her mind, slightly reframed: "*Not everyone can be a killer. But you can. I see it in your eyes. You are just like me*" (334). Although Kate chooses—in a heightened and traumatized state—not to kill Kenzie, she is, of course, a killer. Even though her killings have been committed in the most desperate of self-defense scenarios, their trauma remains with her, to be re-experienced—often involuntarily and sometimes insightfully—as she continues her legal/detective career.

Conclusion

Tattooed ends with reflections on the toll of detection on those who are part of the justice system, such as detectives or lawyers. Despite the altercation at the storage locker, there is not enough evidence to convict Kenzie of a crime, and Ethan, the homicide detective, reflects upon Kate's role in the case:

> It made him sick to think Kenzie was getting away with murder.
> He wished Kate had shot her.
> An eye for an eye.
> But he knew Kate would never have gotten over it.
>
> (342–3)

As a detective who has killed in self-defense before, and as a former lover of Kate's who has watched her deal with the trauma of her teen years as well as with the trauma of her killing of the Body Butcher, Ethan can stand in for the reader in providing a perspective on the personal price paid by detectives, official and otherwise, in representing the public when it comes to dealing with the crime of murder. Given Canada's propensity for embracing police as a national symbol, thrillers like Callow's that center trauma are crucial to our understanding of crime fiction.

They also reveal the same optimistic impulse as much of Canadian crime fiction. *Tattooed* is the most personal of Kate's stories, revealing much about her character as well as her place in the world with its reliance on the classic detective tropes of liminality and doubling. The ending, therefore, gives readers a sense of both her personal resilience and that of her community: Kate ends up having tea with her elderly neighbors Muriel and Enid, sisters who act as surrogate wise-woman grandmother figures to her throughout the series. With them, she processes her encounter with her dark double:

> "I wanted to *kill* Kenzie. I had the gun. It felt so good in my hand, Enid."
> "Don't punish yourself over this, Kate. You are not a machine."
> Muriel added a sugar cube to Kate's mug of tea. Then another.

Kate's eyes searched Enid's. "What am I, then?"
A killer?

Enid gave a small smile. "You are a survivor." She glanced at Muriel. "We are all survivors."

Muriel handed Kate the mug of tea. By now it held at least three sugar cubes.

Kate took it, her hands clasped around its warmth.

A survivor.

I can live with that.

(349)

Drinking her overly sweetened—or perhaps perfectly sweetened—tea, Kate finds herself at peace with her trauma, knowing that its aftereffects will occur, but also that she has the resilience and support to survive and even thrive.

11
THE POSTMODERN DETECTIVE
Literary Detection in Timothy Findley and Carol Shields

Literary fiction and genre fiction in Canada, as elsewhere, are not always marked as entirely separate by the publishing industry or the academy. Indeed, tropes from crime and detective fiction feature prominently in some of Canada's most acclaimed literary works. This chapter elucidates the relationship between crime fiction and Canadian literary fiction by the use of two postmodern texts by leading Canadian writers. Timothy Findley's *The Telling of Lies* (1986) examines the photographer's aesthetic and critical gaze around the murder of a pharmaceutical mogul representing exploitation and disparity, while Carol Shields' *Swann* (1987) explores the convergence of aesthetics and investigations at the site of the murder of an obscure poet. Both novels serve to situate Canadian crime narratives at the junction of literary and genre fiction, where they participate in the postmodern project that has productively advanced both detective fiction and Canadian literature.

Detective fiction has a long tradition of intersecting with the concerns of literary writers, as is to be expected by the genre's deep investments with epistemological and ethical questions. American literary writers from realism to postmodernism, including such luminaries as Mark Twain, William Faulkner, and Paul Auster, have explicitly borrowed from the genre of detective fiction in many of their novels, and have even penned full-length detective works (*Pudd'nhead Wilson* (1893), *Knight's Gambit* (1949), and *The New York Trilogy* (1987), respectively). Postmodern writers from around the world, including Jorge Luis Borges, Umberto Eco, and Alain Robbe-Grillet, have likewise taken up the form of postmodern detective fiction, or what Patricia Merivale and Elizabeth Sweeney call the

DOI: 10.4324/9781003125242-13

"metaphysical detective story" in the title of their survey of the genre. Indeed, Michael Holquist sees detective fiction as a backbone to the postmodern project, going so far as to argue that "what the structural and philosophical presupposition of myth and depth psychology were to Modernism ... the detective story is to Post-Modernism" (135).

Holquist's claim is a provocative one. Postmodernism, often seen as a post–World War II response to Modernism, features a constellation of approaches to representation that challenge twentieth-century meta-narratives: self-referentiality, metafictional commentary, intertextuality, and playful parody. In her groundbreaking study, *The Politics of Postmodernism*, Linda Hutcheon references a number of theoretical approaches to postmodernism (by Brian McHale, Fredric Jameson, Jean Baudrillard, etc.) before making a typically postmodern philosophical move by naming what she calls "my own parodic postmodernism of complicity and critique, of reflexivity and historicity, that at once inscribes and subverts the conventions and ideologies of the dominant cultural and social forces of the twentieth-century western world" (11). Hutcheon's approach does not place detective conventions at the center of the postmodern project as Holquist's does, but it refers to many of the questions central to the detective narrative, with its examination of crime as a space that allows for an articulation of critique of dominant ideals as well as interrogation of the very construction of knowledge. As Merivale and Sweeney argue in their exploration of postmodern detective fiction, narratives in this subgenre of crime fiction "explicitly speculate about the workings of language, the structure of narrative, the limitations of genre, the meanings of prior texts, and the nature of reading" (7). Whether or not detective conventions are constitutive of postmodern writing, the intersection of the two clearly share central approaches to questions of knowledge and morality.

Like most postmodern detective narratives, Timothy Findley's *The Telling of Lies* and Carol Shields's *Swann* both self-reflexively mix genres and rewrite existing fictional tropes. Findley's novel presents as a classic murder mystery, but it actually resides in the interstices—between Can Lit and genre fiction, between mystery and magical realism, between the diary and the detective story, and even between Canada and the United States. Shield's novel, on the other hand, presents as a classic academic narrative whose axes involve two mysteries: the brutal murder of Mary Swann by her husband Amos decades earlier and the present-day enigma of how and why all the documentation surrounding Swann—from personal collections as well as from official library holdings—is disappearing. There is no singular detective figure in *Swann*, perhaps because detection here is not conceptualized as a solo activity, but as a collaborative enterprise akin to scholarship that requires multiple perspectives, none of which is elevated above others. Shields' novel is equally present in interstices—also between Can Lit and genre fiction, between the scholar and the detective including the scholar *as* detective, between the series of third-person focalized narrations and the film script, and also between Canada and the United States. Liminality, the quality of existing in between, is central to the power and appeal of detective fiction in general and perhaps especially of postmodern detective fiction. Findley and Shields both present mysteries that have no easy answers—ethically or epistemologically—and that occupy liminal spaces—temporally, culturally, generically—in order to fashion slippery, contingent, yet oddly satisfying conclusions that are as much beginnings as endings. In short, they represent two major Canadian writers embodying the postmodern project.

The Study of Lies in Findley

The text of *The Telling of Lies* is made up of the problematic diary of Vanessa Van Horn, who, early in the novel, asks a familiar postmodern question: "What do we really know of one another—even after all these years, I wonder" (7). One's answer, given the priming of the title, might capture the slippery uncertainty of postmodern epistemology: no one really knows another person, since our main means of communication—language—is always inadequate to representing the nuances of the human heart. After raising the possibility that humans remain largely unknown and unknowable to one another, Vanessa provides an answer to the question "what do we really know of one another" that might surprise the cynics among us: "More, I suspect, than any one of us has said of who we are and what we've done" (7). She goes on to explain that the beautiful leather notebook in which she is writing the text that we are reading was given to her, completely unexpectedly, by Lily Porter, the flightiest of the four friends who have met at the ASH (Aurora Sands Hotel) in Maine almost every summer of their lives. Through the gift of the well-designed and aesthetically pleasing journal, along with a beautiful Japanese greeting card, Lily shows not only that she is more perceptive than Vanessa has given her credit for, but that, more broadly, people *can* know one another, *can* discern each other's supposedly hidden depths.

For Lisa Zunshine, who uses cognitive science research in her literary analysis, the appeal of modernist and postmodernist writing, as well as of detective fiction, lies in fiction's ability to embody the problem of human connection and to solve it in a way that is often difficult or impossible in real life. Zunshine explores levels of intentionality, showing that while it is difficult for people to cognitively process four or five levels of intentionality (I know that you know that I think that she is thinking …), readers are often able to process complicated intentionality in story (132). In using the affordances of the mystery genre, Findley explores just such cognitive complexity around lies, truth, and knowability. In musing about Lily's unexpected gift, for example, Vanessa slips into the process of attributing intentionality, thinking that Lily has read "The me behind the me ... the absolutely private me I didn't realize she knew—whose solitude must surely have seemed, for all these years, so self-engrossed, self-satisfied and unnatural because it has been so disciplined" (7–8). Vanessa here sees herself through Lily's surprisingly astute perspective, using the physical gift as a kind of philosophical gift that reveals the gaps in not only the public self she has shown to others, but also in the solitude she has always claimed to need. Lily's insight is even more dramatic when it comes to the Japanese greeting card that accompanies the perfect journal. When Vanessa asks about it, Lily is vague but perceptive: " 'You like things Japanese,' she said, adding—embarrassed; 'in spite of ... everything' " (4, his ellipsis). Lily, we learn, is right. Despite Vanessa's childhood years spent at a prisoner of war (POW) camp in Bandung, Indonesia directed by a Japanese colonel, she has a deep appreciation for Japanese landscape architecture and philosophy. In fact, she ends her reflections about Lily's surprisingly insightful choice with a nod to her POW experience: "I will dedicate this book to Colonel Norimitsu—who, with one hand, killed my father and with the other made of my father's grave a garden. Death before life. So very Japanese" (8). Death before life. And lies before truth, as this novel's epigraph by John Cheever suggests: "The telling of lies is a sort of slight of hand that displays our deepest feelings about life." Although Brent MacLaine calls Findley "a reluctant or cautious postmodernist" (92), I would argue that *The Telling of Lies* repeatedly engages with the epistemological slippages, intertextuality, metafictionality, and generic hybridity that are hallmark strategies of the postmodern project.

In true postmodern fashion, Findley draws upon a number of different genres in *The Telling of Lies*. The murder mystery is a classic one. Calder Maddox, an elderly drug magnate—the type of powerful wealthy white man who has surely made a good number of enemies over his lifetime—is found dead on the beach of an exclusive hotel, providing what David Lehman calls "The Corpse on Page One" in his study of traditional detective tropes (2). Foul play is suspected and soon confirmed. The detective figure, Vanessa, is a middle-aged spinster who does not appreciate this characterization: "A spinster," she tells a police officer who questions her, "is a person who spins. For money" (66). An avid photographer, Vanessa documents many important moments while attempting to unravel the mystery of Maddox's death, only to repeatedly find, in classic detective fiction fashion, more mysteries behind the initial one. Other mysteries intersect with the primary one to various degrees: the case of the suddenly appearing iceberg may seem largely metaphorical; the question of why several high-level American politicians are having a secret meeting at the other exclusive hotel that shares the beach with the ASH may seem coincidental; and the mystery of the unexpected disappearance and eventually discovered brainwashing of Lily may seem tantalizingly pertinent but difficult to connect.

Although the mystery genre is the primary narrative vehicle, Findley's use of the diary form signals an innovative take on this classic genre. As Anne Geddes Bailey persuasively shows, the diary form creates Vanessa as an unreliable narrator, especially as she announces to the reader that she is running two days behind while recording events, which means (as Bailey points out) that she actually knew who the murderer was when she was recording her own confusion. As Theo D'Haen observes, the novel also draws upon conventions of magical realism, a genre whose interests overlap considerably with those of postmodernism. I would add that the novel also alludes quite obviously to the great English dystopias of the early twentieth century, namely Aldous Huxley's *Brave New World* (1932) and George Orwell's *Nineteen Eighty-Four* (1949). Vanessa's discovery of Lily's sleep tapes, which attempt to hypnotize her into believing an alternate explanation for Calder's murder, remind the reader of the sleep-hypnosis codified into the upbringing of standardized clones in Huxley's famous novel. The program of disinformation practiced by the CIA in the torture and medical experimentation that has left another regular guest of the hotel, Michael Riches, physically and mentally crippled, along with the present-day secrecy around American government officials, alludes to Orwell's Ministry of Truth, whose officially sanctioned business is lies. Although mysteries rarely hybridize with dystopian literature, these intertexts are consonant with Findley's project here and elsewhere. Although Vanessa is intrigued by the question of who killed Calder Maddox and why—as is the reader—her bigger concerns are with how the world works, how knowledge is constructed, and how a person who spent a substantial part of her childhood in a POW camp is to understand the late twentieth century, with all its ethical and epistemological complexities. To understand Maddox's death, it turns out, we must understand The Telling of Lies—the way humans communicate with each other, and perhaps also with the self, using a matrix of truth and lies that continually provide both cognitive challenges and pleasures.

Perhaps the most engaging conundrum in Findley's novel is the iceberg. The entirely unexpected, somewhat outlandish appearance of a massive iceberg off the coast of Maine in early summer acts as an enigmatic and constantly proliferating backdrop to the murder mystery we read in Vanessa's journal. She explains that people stream from the hotel and/or look out their windows ("trapped by age or nakedness in their rooms" [27]) when the iceberg appears. She describes the scene using the language of performance: "'What is it? What' said all the voices together—singing in *sotto voce* like a choir. 'What is it? What?'" (27). This chorus—surely an accurate rendition of words people would say when faced with the unknown, but also organized by Vanessa as a kind of performance evoking Greek tragedy—carries through her description of how she contextualizes the iceberg within her own professional and personal experiences:

> The only images I've ever created in all of my professional life—consciously and with a vengeance—have been the studied shapes of gardens. And in my photographs? What *is*. But never accidents; never the overturning of reality. Not anarchy.
>
> And now this; just as the prison rose around me out of the garden of my parents' lives—an iceberg rises out of the trusted sea before my eyes. Meaningless and awesome—but only meaningless because of its absurd and incomprehensible presence where it should not—cannot possibly be.
>
> *(27)*

Vanessa here speaks to the disruptive potential of crime and to her almost pathological avoidance of the disorderly. She creates only order—"with a vengeance"—and focuses on reality. She compares the unexpected and seemingly inexplicable appearance of the iceberg to her childhood trauma in the POW camp. Vanessa refers to the pre-prison existence as "the garden of my parents' lives," making clear that her professional work in landscape architecture is invested in the garden as a symbol of order. The iceberg, she explains, is "meaningless" because it is outside of its ordered place, because its presence is "where it should not be—cannot possibly be."

Vanessa sees the iceberg as a sign of disorder—generically connected to the murdered body that marks the disruption that is to be ordered by the detective in a classic murder mystery. At the same time, she recognizes disorder's potential for hope later on when she compares the iceberg to the open gate that signaled the end of the war for the inmates of Bandung:

> It felt like that: escape; recovery; rescue. The long, eccentric column of people in assorted states of dress making its progress towards the absolute safety of the porches [of the hotel] reminded me of the day we were released from prison: Bandung, 1945. Though of course not so desperate, the sense of confusion—the sense of bewilderment was just the same; the violation of reality.
>
> *(29)*

Some of the guests note that the iceberg bears "an eerie likeness to the Capital Building in Washington, D.C. (28) that serves as a highly recognizable symbol of American democracy. An elderly woman who had been on board the Titanic raises the specter of that famous disaster with its underpinnings of hubris by claiming that this iceberg is larger than that which destroyed the Titanic (28). Given that Vanessa and her friends are spending their last summer at the ASH, which will soon be closing its doors forever, it is tempting to view the iceberg as representing the end of an institution, perhaps even the end of an era of privilege for these wealthy Americans and Canadians.

Findley invites multiple readings of the unexpected iceberg, and critics have been happy to oblige. For example, Catherine Hunter reads the iceberg as "a postmodern version of Poe's purloined letter" (101), an intertextual reference to the object in plain sight that references the American origin of detective fiction in Edgar Allan Poe's three C. August Dupin tales (1840–1845), and also the legacy of scholarship by such critical luminaries as Jacques Lacan and Jacques Derrida, who have used Poe's story, "The Purloined Letter," as a means of exploring the theoretical potentials of detective fiction. Hunter also explores the etymology of "iceberg." She notes that

> It derives from the German *berg*, which refers both to the "mountain" above the surface and to the "mine" below; it is linked with the words "borrow" and "bury". It is associated with another German paradox as well—the verb *Bergen*, "to hide, conceal" or (mysteriously) "to salvage, to excavate"—to uncover, to bring to light
>
> *(100)*

Hunter sees the iceberg as "an invitation to write in the rest of the story" (101), a kind of playful project common in postmodern writing, where the writer often explicitly invites readers to join in the construction of knowledge, which is always slippery and proliferating.

Indeed, the iceberg also thematizes the novel's title, suggesting the depth of the unclear and the unknown (unknowable?) that lies beneath the surface. Hemingway's "iceberg theory of writing" is laid out in *Death in the Afternoon* (1932), when he states:

> If a writer of prose knows enough of what he is writing about he may omit things that he knows and the reader, if the writer is writing truly enough, will have a feeling of those things as strongly as though the writer had stated them. The dignity of movement of an ice-berg is due

to only one-eighth of it being above water. A writer who omits things because he does not know them only makes hollow places in his writing.

(154)

For a modernist like Hemingway, the writer must know what lies beneath the surface—and the reader must know that the writer knows. For a postmodernist like Findley, the "hollow places" in the writing are not a fault as much as a commentary on the structure of knowledge. The iceberg is at once unreadable and multiply readable. One could argue that it is meaningless—and perhaps even a symbol of a meaningless world (although, of course, this latter would ascribe meaning in a common postmodern paradox). Or one could argue that the iceberg provides one of a number of comments on the mystery, some harmonic and some contrapuntal. The notion that seven-eighths (or nine-tenths, as Findley and the US Geological Survey both report) of the meaning lies beneath is at once a challenge to the certainty of classic detective fiction and a potential direction for the genre in the postmodern play and uncertainty of the late twentieth and early twenty-first centuries.

To twenty-first-century readers, an iceberg in Maine might draw one's thoughts to the impending climate crisis. Whether or not Findley had climate change (or global warming, as it was called in the 1980s) on his mind when composing the mysterious iceberg is, in my mind, irrelevant. The construction of a symbol that can take on new meanings in new decades speaks to the innovative temporality of Findley's novel. Indeed, partway through the novel, after working with her friend Lawrence Pawley to solve the murder mystery and find the missing Lily Porter, Vanessa realizes that Lawrence is afraid and will no longer be pursuing the investigation. She is in this alone. As is typical when Vanessa is stressed or anxious, she reflects on her time, decades earlier, in Bandung, thinking specifically of "a phrase I learned in prison: *only the brave can achieve the certainties*" (260). Vanessa is caught here between past and future as she tries to draw upon the bravery built by her childhood trauma in pursuing the investigation. Interestingly, she links her own struggle with the iceberg's:

> I feel, at once, a kinship with the iceberg. I, too, am cold. I, too, am stranded. I, too, am nine-tenths hidden. And now, I, too, must become a *stabilized renegade*.
>
> I peered out through the screens. I could see the iceberg out in the bay.
> I raised my hand.
> Be well.
>
> *(260)*

Vanessa's "kinship" with the iceberg travels beautifully through history, since the analogy resonates even more powerfully when considered in the face of the climate crisis of the twenty-first century. The iceberg is stranded and out of place as a result of not only human activity but also human failure to acknowledge scientific findings and to change carbon-emitting behaviors that have led and will continue to lead to increasingly unpredictable weather patterns. Vanessa's trauma, like the iceberg's, sets the stage for her inability to restore order as a classic detective of the late nineteenth century would certainly have done.

In the end, Vanessa learns that the murder of Calder Maddox is related to CIA activity that was at least nine-tenths under the surface. In the novel, Vanessa eventually discovers that a close friend's husband was the victim of medical experimentation in brainwashing in Montreal, and this is why a Canadian woman Vanessa has known all her life has killed Calder Maddox, creator of the pharmaceutical Maddoxin. The medical abuses being avenged in this fictional crime were, in fact, real abuses, and Sherrill Grace, Findley's biographer, notes that Findley did substantial research on Canadian and American medical experiments during the Cold War (Grace 300-1). Alluding to the controversial work of Dr. Ewer Cameron, conducted in Montreal's Allan Memorial Institution and sponsored by the CIA, Findley grounds his novel in the uglier sides of twentieth-century history, abroad with the Bandung POW recollections and at home with unethical medical experimentation. The postmodern strategy of exploring historical continuities and discontinuities with fiction joins the detective genre's ability to explore real-world ethical and political controversies in the aptly if darkly titled *The Telling of Lies*.

Findley's novel ends with a final nod to the stranded iceberg—the *stabilized renegade* (260)—that provides such a strong metaphorical embodiment for Findley's postmodern detective project. Vanessa's final diary entry, number 190, begins with a declaration of a slippery ending: "It ends like this, for now" (358). Vanessa does a personal reflection that accomplishes the work often found in the denouement of a classic detective tale, where the detective gathers everyone in one location to do the great reveal. In postmodern contradiction, Vanessa catalogs the many people to whom she has not revealed the truth about Maddox's death, reflecting that although she has joined the cover-up, she does not believe this to be ethically wrong. Her diary ends with the four women who have spent so many summers together in this hotel:

> I think of who we were and what we wanted. And I think of who we are and what we got.

> I think of this Hotel, its being where we met, and I think its rise and fall have been our rise and fall; the lot of us together. Someone sold us out—but only when we ceased to pay attention.
> Yes. It is time the icebergs came.
> And they are here.
> And so I pull the shade.
> And the shade is green.
>
> *(359)*

Grace reads this evocative ending as an address to readers, arguing that "Now it is our turn to read Vanessa's journal and take heed of the frightening connections she makes between torture in war and secret crimes against humanity in peacetime" (302). I agree and would further connect the ending—with its contrast between icebergs and verdancy—with the hopeful project that underlies many postmodern as well as Canadian writings. Vanessa reflects here on the importance of sociopolitical engagement (bad things happen when we cease to pay attention) and nuanced ethical choices. In the end, the iceberg, I think, is a utopian symbol of sorts, a reminder that we need to know pain in order to understand pleasure, that we need to know disorder in order to understand and appreciate order, which can be pleasurable but is always just one lens, one green shade through which to process the world.

The Study of Art in Shields

Carol Shields' *Swann* is the product of its author's practical knowledge about academic endeavors as well as her substantial reading and thinking about literary theory, and especially the postmodern project. Shields was a sessional (adjunct) English lecturer at the University of Ottawa and a creative writing professor at the University of British Columbia before she became a full-time writer. In *Swann*, she compares the work of the literary scholar to that of the detective, embodying through a series of fascinating characters her appreciation of the affordances and limitations of postmodern theory that she has spoken about elsewhere. In an interview with Eleanor Wachtel, for example, Shields states that postmodernism "can take you around some sharper corners that you didn't even know existed. It gives you permission to let the story go in curious angles" (cited in Ramon 61). *Swann* is indeed a novel full of curious angles, engaging with deep aesthetic questions even as it explores the many roles imagined by, performed by, and withheld from women in the history of literary production and criticism.

Mary Swann is the absent center of Shields' novel. Swann would have been a perfectly ordinary—and by now forgotten—middle-aged farm woman from rural Ontario except for two distinguishing features: her sensational death and her luminous poems. These raise questions that prompt the subtitle in some editions of the novel, *Swann: A Mystery*. Swann has been murdered 20 years before the novel's opening in a gruesome manner: her husband shot her in the head, bludgeoned her with a hammer, hacked up her body, and hid her dismembered corpse in the grain silo, where it was discovered after his death by suicide. The mysteries surrounding this grisly death are not those typical of detective fiction, as the perpetrator's identity was known immediately, so questions of motive would not have been especially pertinent to the investigation, and police were presumably able to quickly clear the case shortly after the bodies were found. In some ways, the details of Swann's unexpected death might act more as a clue than as a mystery. After all, the inquiry pursued by the "detectives" (read: literary critics) of the novel relate to Swann's poetry. An unschooled poet from rural Ontario, Swann somehow found wonderful modernist images without ever studying or even reading the great Modernist poets. The novel, then, poses three major mysteries: (1) why did Mary Swann's husband kill her on the night she came home from seeing Frederic Cruzzi, her publisher (who assaulted his beloved wife for the first and only time in their long marriage at much the same time)? (2) why are Mary Swann's manuscripts and scant personal belongings, held in library and personal collections, disappearing in 1985 in the build-up to the first symposium held in her honor? and (3) how do we explain Mary Swann's incredible poetry given her lack of access to the influences literary scholars usually trace in understanding fresh new aesthetic works?

Shields explores these three linked mysteries using innovative narrative techniques as well as genre blending. She uses the mystery form as a base, but immediately combines it with the academic novel, building the narrative around the preparations for and eventual performance of a literary symposium on the work and life of Mary Swann. Told in five distinct sections, the novel presents four "detective" figures, each representing a different branch of literary production, consumption, and critique. Sarah Maloney, writing in the first person, is the English professor most often credited with discovering Mary Swann, although, as Sarah reflects, "In truth, no one really discovers anyone; it's the stickiest kind of arrogance even to think in such terms" (31). Morton Jimroy, the second narrator, is a well-known literary biographer; he holds only honorary doctorates, and thus lacks the PhD that gives Sarah and several other academic characters their prestige. Jimroy's section is written in third person, perhaps reflecting in part that this grumpy, middle-aged man does not often access his own interiority. Rose Hindmarsh, the small-town librarian from Nadeau, Ontario, represents the public-facing side of literary consumption, and her section includes whimsical subtitles ("Rose's Hats," "Some Words of Orientation," or "Here Comes Rose Now," for example). As Alex Ramon notes, Rose also occasionally slips into second-person narration in order to "implicate the reader more directly in response to Rose" (Ramon 78). Frederic Cruzzi's section is perhaps the most innovatively told. An eighty-year-old retired newspaper and small-press publisher, Cruzzi is an avid letter- and journal-writer, and his section is largely epistolary, including excerpts from his correspondence that are referenced in the other sections. The final section of the novel breaks with convention entirely and is presented as a film script, complete with playful Director's Notes, camera instructions, and scripted conversations, including those with unnamed characters identified only as "Blue-Spotted Tie," "Woman with Turban," "Wistful Demeanour," etc.

Throughout the novel, the characters attempt to solve the three big mysteries, but do so with varying degrees of success, largely because, as is made especially evident by the focalization through the four characters deeply involved with the publication, transmission, and analysis of Mary Swann's work, everybody lies. The current-day (1985) mystery of the disappearing items from the Mary Swann collection seems the most answerable. As the various characters prepare for the symposium, several of them realize that objects held in their homes, offices, or even library collections, have disappeared. Because it is embarrassing for a researcher to lose an original document or item relating to an object of study and, therefore, they are slow to report to others what they fear is personal carelessness, it is not until the symposium that the characters become aware that there is a pattern of disappearance of Mary Swann artifacts. The culprit has a straightforward motive (profit) and is finally caught during the symposium, although Shields wastes no time considering if and how the thief shall be punished. Far more interesting to her project is the fact that the theft of collectibles is only the tip of the iceberg when it comes to misuse of Swann artifacts by the scholar, the biographer, the librarian, and even the publisher. Throughout the novel, after all, Shields has shown that the entire Mary Swann narrative is made up of an intricate web of lies, including many that relate to the tangible (and thus seemingly "real") physical objects from Swann's life.

Professor Sarah Maloney discards Mary Swann's rhyming dictionary as something embarrassing to the dead poet's reputation, and lies by omission by never mentioning it to another scholar. Further, she refuses to share Swann's personal journal because it is made up of nothing but quotidian details about the farm and weather (again, embarrassing to the construction of the poet Sarah has helped to build and perpetuate). Biographer Morton Jimroy brashly steals two pieces of Mary Swann memorabilia (the only clear photograph of the poet and her surprisingly fancy writing pen), knowing that he can easily lie if confronted. Librarian Rose Hindmarch stretches the truth almost accidentally, initially embellishing on her relationship with Mary Swann and eventually engaging in outright lies until she is widely considered the person who knew Mary best. She also fails to note that the Mary Swann Room at Nadeau's public library is furnished with items from the period of Mary Swann rather than with the contents of her own home. Rose justifies this to herself: "the charm of falsehood is not that it distorts reality, but that it creates reality afresh" (163).

Publisher Frederic Cruzzi has perpetrated what is surely the biggest lie of all when it comes to the construction of Mary Swann, poetess. The reader learns only late in the novel—and the other characters not at all—that Frederic's wife and publishing partner Hildë threw fresh fish bones in the paper bag containing the only copy of Swann's 125 unpublished poems, so the two reconstructed a good deal of the language that constitutes the definitive first edition of *Swann's Songs*. The narrative draws attention to the problematic nature of this reconstruction:

> By now—it was morning—a curious conspiracy had overtaken them. Guilt, or perhaps a wish to make amends, convinced them that they owed Mrs. Swann an interpretation that would reinforce her strengths as a poet. They wanted to offer her help and protection, what she seemed never to have had. Both of them, Cruzzi from his instinct for tinkering and Hildë from a vestigial talent never abused, made their alterations with, it seemed to them, a single hand.
>
> *(223)*

The poems of Mary Swann, then, were to some degree co-written by the unknowable poetess and the two publishers.

Unsurprisingly, the question of why Mary Swann was killed is unanswerable. After all, Swann and her husband had little contact with their neighbors and the only documents they left behind were Mary's poems, delivered to Frederic Cruzzi as a series of scraps in a paper bag on the very day of her murder. By taking his own life, Mr. Swann made it virtually impossible for anyone to ascertain his motives, although various characters speculate that his wife's unexpected trip by bus to a publisher in the much larger town of Kingston, Ontario might have somehow prompted his actions. Mr. Swann's deeply inaccessible motive prompts a related question: why did Frederic Cruzzi assault his beloved wife when he realized that she had thrown fish remnants in the paper bag containing

Mary Swann's poems, the only time in his life he has ever committed an act of violence? The scene is frighteningly described. When Hildë sees Frederic looking at the soaked scraps of paper with sorrow, she goes to embrace him:

> It was a mistake, though not one she could have foreseen. He threw her off violently with the whole force of his body, and an arm reached out, his arm, striking her at the side of the neck. They both knew it was a blow delivered without restraint. It sent her falling to the floor, slipping on the fish guts, out of control, banging her jaw on the edge of the table as she went down.
>
> *(220)*

Frederic is immediately mortified by this uncharacteristic action, and tries to justify it in his mind, first as a result of his two loves ("the written word and his wife, Hildë" (205)): "He had not, he said, now firmly in the grasp of reason, struck out at *her*. He had struck at some fearful conclusion" (221), the conclusion being that Swann's powerful poems were lost forever. Soon, though, he turns to a more trite explanation in his mind, aware of the cliché even as he thinks it: "He knew that phrase—*something snapped*. He heard it every day, he deplored it" (221). Although Cruzzi himself does not connect his violence toward Hildë with Mr. Swann's perhaps simultaneous violence to Mary (killed the same night), the reader sees the simultaneity and is reminded of the horrifying but undeniable fact that domestic abuse, violence, and homicide are common, not only in the past and not only in households lacking material and cultural capital. The lack of explicit motives for men injuring and even killing their wives can be read as a commentary on classic detective fiction's general avoidance of these devastatingly ordinary crimes in favor of more exotic, sensational stories that engage the reader's intellect rather than their empathy.

The novel's final and most existential mystery is verbalized several times throughout the various sections. Sarah and Jimroy use gendered quest motifs in articulating what both call "the central mystery." Sarah muses: "Mary Swann discovered herself, and therein, suspended on tissues of implausibility, like a hammock without strings, hangs the central mystery; how did she do it?" (31). Jimroy lectures: "I believe ... that you must be alluding to the central mystery of art ... which is, that from common clay, works of genius evolve. That is to say, the work often possesses a greater degree of dignity than the hand that made it" (82, my ellipses). Sarah's ethereal description of creativity sits next to Jimroy's classic "genius" model in a contrapuntal relationship that highlights the gaps that arise from various readers' individualized subjectivities as characterized by age, gender, ethnicity, academic position, life experience, worldview, etc. After all, alongside the question of how Mary Swann produced her poetry within the sparseness of her life experience resides the equally important question of how various literary and academic forces would answer that question, would interpret her texts. Does literary criticism enhance or violate? Does it create deeper understanding and/or inhibit aesthetic appreciation?

Shields uses Swann's poems to explore these questions in ways at once humorous and poignant. Jimroy's narration reveals that he fabricates influences for Swann in keeping with his genius model of creativity:

> He is going over some notes covering Mary Swann's middle period (1940–1955) and making a few additions and notations with a freshly sharpened pencil. *It is highly probable that Swann read Jane Austen during this period because*
>
> *(118, original ellipses)*

These ellipses speak volumes, inviting the reader to imagine how Jimroy could possibly concoct an ending to the sentence that would support such a patently false claim. The next sighting of Jimroy occurs in Rose Hindmarch's section when Rose thinks back to her dinner with the biographer 18 months earlier. The dinner scene (complete with the double pork chop platter at the old hotel in Elgin) demonstrates the pleasures and vagaries of literary criticism. Jimroy shows Rose a baptism reference in a Swann poem that she attributes to the mundane fact that there was no well on the Swann property. Undaunted, Jimroy suggests a deep spirituality in Swann's decision not to attend Church, while Rose explains it by the country woman's lack of appropriate clothing. Their different interpretations come to a head over a poem included in the novel:

> Blood pronounces my name
> Blisters the day with shame
> Spends what little I own
> Robbing the hour, rubbing the bone.
>
> (148)

Jimroy reads the poem as "a pretty direct reference to the sacrament of holy communion. Or perhaps, and this is my point, perhaps to a more elemental sort of blood covenant, the eating of the Godhead, that sort of thing" (148). Rose is silenced by this reading. She feels confident that Swann's poem is about menstruation, but she is unable to speak this word in the presence of the seemingly esoteric male biographer. Prevented from speaking by her feelings of inferiority in both gender and profession, Rose nevertheless shares her interpretation with the reader, who thus accesses a fuller hermeneutic picture than any single character. The reader further learns in Frederic Cruzzi's narration that the Blood poem was the most damaged by the fish guts, and thus the most deeply rewritten by the two publishers. Even a reader who feels confident they can interpret Swann's poem (following Rose, Jimroy, or an approach of their own) discovers that even such a confident interpretation must surely be uncertain.

At the same time, despite the multiple levels of parody and hermeneutic uncertainty, the novel suggests, again and again, that aesthetic appreciation, like literary criticism, is a worthwhile endeavor. The final section of the novel, the film script that distances the reader by continually drawing attention to the text's fictionality with unusual filming directions and character names, nonetheless presents a hopeful ending. Clara Thomas captures the playfulness and pleasure of Shields' project in *Swann*, arguing that the author

> invite[s] her reader to enjoy the dénouement of her *writing* of the story, not with the smug "the joke's on you" tone so familiar to mystery story addicts, but with a happy, "We've all been in this together."
> *(112)*

Thomas reads the film script in the novel as a sort of smiling, almost joyful celebration of the pleasure of literature, suggesting that the director's note instructing that the final reveal scene be "played with a very slight parodic edge" (quoted in Thomas 112) places the writer in a delightful metafictional communion with the reader while watching the fictional readers in the novel strive to understand the fictional writer, gracefully and collaboratively accepting that such comprehension is both to be strived for and never achieved.

After the Mary Swann artifact thief has been revealed, the guests at the symposium gather in a circle, reassembling one of Swann's poems in an act of community. The Director's Final Note emphasizes the power of art as these scholars, who have engaged in passionate debate with one another as well as in petty insults, turn their attention toward a collaboration: "The faces of the acts have been subtly transformed. They are seen joined in a ceremonial act of reconstruction, perhaps even an act of creation" (311). The slippage in terminology where the collaborators are initially called "actors" and then referred to as having the interiority of scholars highlights the metafictional project of the text. Perhaps it is not only scholars—or detectives—who do the interpretive cultural work of understanding aesthetics or crime. It is actors. And it is readers. *Swann* ends with the recreated poem, "Lost Things." By now, the reader knows this is unlikely to be an accurate rendition of Mary Swann's poem. Despite its textual imprecisions, however, the poem is powerful. It is, perhaps, true in its metaphorical exploration of how loss works, in its arresting notion of lost things

> ... becoming part of a larger loss,
> Without a name
> Or definition or form
> Not unlike what touches us
> In moments of shame.
>
> (313)

Conclusion

The postmodern project, growing out of early twentieth-century disillusionment with the modernist belief in progress and objective truth, seems like a dark one. If "reality" is socially constructed and "knowledge" is always slippery and contingent, how are we to grasp the most basic "facts" about our lives and our worlds, let alone understand the complex ethical and epistemological questions grappled with in detective fiction? Acclaimed Canadian literary writers Timothy Findley and Carol Shields both lean into this darkness with the premises of their postmodern detective novels, which connect difficult historical occurrences to current epistemological problems, revealing the potential hollow center of what lies beneath contemporary understanding of social, cultural, and aesthetic life. And yet, the disposition of a detective narrative can often be understood by its ending, and Findley and Shields conclude with optimism. This is a nuanced, subtle optimism, to be sure, but I believe it is indicative of the hopeful yet pragmatic timber that marks Canadian literature of the late twentieth century.

PART III
Futuristic Explorations

12
LOUISE PENNY'S COZY EXPLORATION OF TRAUMA AND TEMPORALITY IN THE ANTHROPOCENE

Louise Penny's Three Pines series is fundamentally a work about love. Love between romantic partners. Love between friends. Love between parents and children. Love between humans and animals. Love of Food. Love of Literature. Love of Art. Love of Nature. As I have argued elsewhere, this series draws upon several conventions of detective fiction—including the cozy, the thriller, and the police procedural—in order to undertake a utopian project ("Aesthetics"). The Quebec village of Three Pines is marked as a utopian space by its location outside of place (it appears on no maps) and of time (it features limited internet connectivity and a cast of eccentric characters who transcend any specific decade). Penny confirms her utopian intentions in the Author's Note of *Glass Houses* (2017), the 13th book of the series:

> Some might argue that Three Pines itself isn't real, and they'd be right, but limited in their view. The village does not exist, physically. But I think of it as existing in ways that are far more important and powerful. Three Pines is a state of mind. When we choose tolerance over hate. Kindness over cruelty. Goodness over bullying. When we choose to be hopeful, not cynical. Then we live in Three Pines.
>
> *(391)*

And yet, despite the centering of tolerance, kindness, goodness, and hope in the imaginary space of Three Pines, the series is by no means facile in its exploration of twenty-first-century sociocultural issues. By following Chief Inspector Armand Gamache and his team, Penny explores many dark elements of human interactions with each other and with the Earth, repeatedly introducing cold-blooded murder to her Edenic village of Three Pines. As Rachel Haliburton argues in her use of the series to argue for detective stories as a "moral technology" (*Ethical* 108), Gamache "serves as a role model to others, demonstrating to them that a virtuous life in not necessarily a life of deprivation and hardship, but, rather, can be filled with genuinely good things" (*Ethical* 101). Working through the technique of contrast that is central to the utopian project, Penny's series explores the themes of greed, corruption, and despair that are raised by murder in order to provide a hopeful blueprint—not for a perfect society as in traditional utopian writing, but for a way of moving forward in the Anthropocene.

Utopian fiction has a long history of accomplishing a dual rhetorical function: critiquing the present day while also imagining a better future. It is possible to see the naming of the Anthropocene, which is still controversial as I write this book, as participating in a utopian venture. To officially name our current time as a geological epoch distinct from the Holocene— a project undertaken by a working group within the International Commission on Stratigraphy—would be to acknowledge that humans have had enough of an influence on the planet and its environment to prompt a distinct geological change. Such an acknowledgment would suggest both that humans are responsible for addressing the impending climate crisis and that we are capable of conceptualizing and operationalizing an approach that could mitigate the crisis. Thinking geologically also challenges our conceptions of time, moving us beyond our typical approach to temporality of considering our own lifetime as a benchmark, an idea explored in depth by Marcia Bjornerud in *Timefulness: How Thinking Like a Geologist Can Help Save the World* (2018). Detective fiction, like utopian literature and climate crisis scholarship, also has the potential to engage with questions of temporality. Tzvetan Todorov was perhaps the first scholar of detective fiction to note the genre's rhetorical investments in notions of temporality with his insight that a detective story must always contain two narratives: the present-day story of the detective's investigation and the story from the past being uncovered by the detective (44). More recently, Mary Ann Gillies and other detective fiction scholars have noted the centrality of trauma to the genre, asserting that detective texts engaging with trauma may represent "the disrupted experience of time, which is common in trauma" (Gillies 42). Penny's Three Pines series draws upon complex notions of trauma and temporality as it evokes an episodic format typical of police procedural but draws some investigations—even those that appear complete—across several novels as it performs trenchant analysis of Canada and the Anthropocene.

Penny's series has been incredibly popular, crossing into the American market, with 18 novels and counting as well as a TV series, *Three Pines*, released on Amazon Prime Video in 2022. This commercial success outside of Canada may seem surprising, given the depth of a regional topic—Quebec history and culture—explored in these novels. The stories are well-written and the detective characters are memorable, led by Chief Inspector Armand Gamache, characterized by his love of beauty, and Jean-Guy Beauvoir, his decidedly non-arts-loving second-in-command. Even so, I believe this series' success is also explained by the exotic utopian space of Three Pines, Quebec, as well as its ability to subtly address global issues, including the climate crisis. In the sixth novel, *Bury Your Dead* (2010), Penny showcases her bigger project when she twines three separate mysteries together in the most narratively, philosophically, and theoretically complex of her novels. First, there is the present-day detective story, a body-in-the-library mystery that speaks to the importance of the past when Gamache opens an investigation into Quebec's 400-year history. Second, there is the reopening by Beauvoir of a mystery from the previous novel in the series that challenges the detectives' "final" conclusions, suggesting that we must be willing to revisit and revise the past in order to address the future. And finally, there is the telling, in trauma-laden flashbacks, of the ecologically horrifying terrorist plot that has happened between the fifth and sixth novels of the series and that has traumatized both Gamache and Beauvoir. All three plots culminate in unusual reveal scenes that appear to mimic the typical conclusions of Golden Age detective stories but that, in fact, engage characters—and readers—in a project of rereading and revisioning. The innovative storytelling raises issues of ecoterrorism and climate change through a lens of trauma that reveals not only detective fiction's capacity to participate in the project of environmental writing but also speaks to Canada's fraught relationship to environmentalism and the need for Canadians to revisit and confront our past as we move forward in time to the climate challenges of the future.

Revisiting Canada's Past: The Samuel Champlain Story

The present-day throughline of *Bury Your Dead* presents an almost aggressively typical drawing-room mystery, prompted by the discovery of a body in the library. Replete with resonances to dozens of cozies as well as to the boardgame *Clue*, the mystery acts as the temporal backbone of the novel, progressing from the finding of the body, the interviews with suspects, the chasing down of clues, and the confrontation with the murderer. The body, like most in drawing-room mysteries, represents a puzzle more than a tragedy. The victim, Augustin Renaud, is a rather unpleasant Quebecois independent scholar obsessed with finding the remains of Samuel de Champlain, the purported "Father of Quebec," who died in 1635 and whose burial place remains unknown. Renaud is survived by his ex-wife, an agreeable woman who was unable to continue supporting her husband's obsession, and is spoken of kindly by only Alain Doucet, a rare books dealer who understood Renaud's fascination with the past. Renaud has been murdered in an Anglophone space, the library of the Literary and Historical Society of Quebec, known as the "Lit & His." Given that Renaud had no business being in the basement of Quebec City's best-known Anglophone archive, the classical murder mystery has a limited group of suspects, since only the five members of the board of the Lit & His reasonably had access to the site.

In informally investigating this classical mystery while on medical leave, Gamache finds many opportunities for reflection—on Quebec history, on French-English relationships, and on murder in general. Throughout the series, Gamache often tells younger detectives to look deep into a person's history to understand the motives for a murder. In *Bury Your Dead*, he has similar conversations about the nature of murder with two different priests. Early in the novel, he interviews Père Sébastien, a senior Francophone priest from the Notre-Dame Basilica, to learn more about the victim. The priest suggests there are a lot of motives for murder, but Gamache disagrees:

> "I've found there's only one. Beneath all the justifications, all the psychology, all the motives given, like revenge or greed or jealousy, there lies the real reason. … Fear. Fear of losing what you had or not getting what you want."
>
> *(133–4)*

This notion of fear comes up again when Gamache interviews the much younger English priest, Tom Hancock. Hancock explains that the English community in Quebec City is shrinking, so institutions are more important than ever, since they provide safety:

> Safe, thought Gamache. How primal that was, how powerful. What would people do to preserve a safe harbor? They'd do what they'd done for centuries. What the French had done to save Québec, what the English had done to take it. What countries do to protect their borders, what individuals do to protect their houses.
>
> They kill. To feel safe. It almost never worked.
>
> *(232)*

In both these interviews, Gamache returns to fear as the central motive for individual murder, expanding that fear to a motive for larger conflicts like the ongoing one between the French and the English in Quebec.

As Penny announces in the Acknowledgements statement that precedes the novel, she is exploring the impact of Quebec's history on both its French and English populace: "Like the rest of the Chief Inspector Gamache books, *Bury Your Dead* is not about death, but about life. And the need to both respect the past and let it go" (vii). Quebec's motto, *Je me souviens* ("I remember") comes up often throughout the novel. The idea of remembering is constructed as important, but the danger of placing too much emphasis on the past is also explored. As Gamache muses during an interview with a brusque archeologist, "For them [archaeologists and historians], the past was as alive as the present. And while forgetting the past might condemn people to repeat it, remembering it too vividly condemned them to never leave" (250). Gamache also finds a distinction between how the French and English remember the past, a distinction he is able to make because he is fully bilingual—a Francophone Quebecois who studied in England and speaks perfect English with a beautiful accent. As he interviews the secretary of the Lit & His, he learns that she knows the names of all the society members by heart:

> It struck Gamache for the first time what an interesting English expression that was. To commit something to memory was to know it by heart. Memories were kept in the heart, not the head. At least, that's where the English kept their memories.
>
> *(177)*

Shortly thereafter, still in the same scene, someone asks "Which way?" and Gamache freezes in trauma. This was a question he had been asked during the case that has placed him on medical leave and whose story the reader does not yet fully know. The language for the trauma places Gamache in a liminal space: "Gamache could feel his *heart* thumping from the *memory* and had to remind himself it was just that. It was past, done. Dead and gone" (179, my emphasis). He initially feels the memory in his heart (the English approach) but then must use his head (the French approach?) to process it and remind himself to remember, but not too much.

The English and French of Quebec City are represented in the novel through two groups of mostly elderly people: the board of the Lit & His and the Société Champlain. The Lit & His members are perhaps best represented by Elizabeth MacWhirter, a member of "a venerable and moneyed family" (7) who is now in straightened circumstances but nonetheless carries herself with a deportment befitting her roots. She is passionate about preserving the English history of Quebec, and Gamache finds himself both drawn to her project and repulsed by it. When the board members tell him of their mission *"to discover and rescue from the unsparing hand of time the records which yet remain of the earliest history of Canada,"* he finds himself "deeply moved by the simplicity and the nobility of them. He suddenly felt an overwhelming desire to help these people, to help save them from the unsparing hand of time" (195). At the same time, he is frequently reminded that despite the small size of the English community in Quebec, it nonetheless holds substantial power.

Quebec City's French community, represented in the novel by the Société Champlain and by Gamache's friend and mentor Émile Comeau, provides a metaphor that exemplifies Penny's larger concerns about history. René Dallaire, a member of the Société, characterizes Quebec as a "rowboat society" explaining: "It's why Québec is so perfectly preserved. It's why we're all so fascinated with history. We're in a rowboat. We move forward, but we're always looking back" (108). Gamache has an opportunity to recall this comparison later in the novel when he and Émile discuss the violence at the heart of Quebec City's history and Gamache realizes for the first time that his mentor is a separatist. Their decades-long ease with one another is suddenly disrupted: "They'd never talked about it before. It hadn't been exactly a dirty little secret, just a private subject they'd never broached. In Québec, politics was always dangerous territory" (173). As an Ontarian with family in Quebec, I can attest to the truth of this statement, as can millions of other Canadians who have experienced the tension—"Already the atmosphere was becoming charged" (174)—of friends and loved ones discussing the issue of separatism from different perspectives. Within the scene, the two men review the history of the Quebec Independence movement, complete with the October Crisis and kidnapping and murder of Pierre Laporte investigated in John McFetridge's *Black Rock* (discussed in Chapter 2). Gamache eventually reaches for the rowboat metaphor:

> "*Je me souviens*," said Gamache. "What was it René Dallaire called Québec? A rowboat society? Moving forward but looking back? Is the past ever really far from sight here?"
> Émile stared at him for a moment, then smiled and resumed eating ...
> *(174)*

The recognition that Quebec—Francophone and Anglophone, as it turns out—may be too focused on the past allows the two men to traverse the tension generated by the conversation's turn to Quebec's role within

Canada. It also highlights the potential faultlines in a mentor/mentee relationship that will also be explored in this complex novel.

Émile, as Gamache's mentor at the Sûreté du Québec (Quebec's provincial police force), is the one who has taught him the four sentences he tells his own mentees that homicide detectives must be willing to utter: "I'm sorry. I was wrong. I need help. I don't know" (*Bury* 170 and many places throughout the series). As a man approaching 80 who lost his wife five years ago, Émile also reminds Gamache of the healing properties of time. "*Avec le temps*" ("With time"), he tells Gamache early in the novel to reassure him that the tremble in his hand will eventually disappear or at least lessen (2). Gamache will think back to this insight later when mental trauma buffets him: "'*Avec le temps*,' Émile had said. With time. And maybe he was right. His strength was coming back, why not his sanity?" (28). But despite Émile's years of support for Gamache, their relationship is threatened by the case that requires looking closely at Quebec's history, distant (with Samuel Champlain's missing body from almost 400 years ago) and near (with Augustin Renaud's recently murdered body in the library). There comes a moment when Gamache is to visit the Société Champlain and he realizes that Émile has lied to him about not only the meeting's start time but also about the Société's relationship to the murder victim. Gamache reacts with uncharacteristic impetuousness:

> Émile stared. "I'm sorry, I should never have lied to you. It won't happen again."
> "It already has," said Gamache getting to his feet and putting down a hundred dollars for the water and the use of the quiet table by the fireplace.
> *(307)*

Gamache walks out, ignoring Émile's calls for him to wait. But then, with the mature judgment of one who has moved from mentee to mentor over a long career, Gamache remembers Émile's crucial lessons about balance: "That was the danger. Not that betrayals happened, not that cruel things happened, but that they could outweigh all the good. That he could forget the good and only remember the bad" (308). Gamache stops and turns to listen to his old friend. By novel's end, in fact, Gamache suggests to Émile that he may want to call Elizabeth MacWhirter, from the Lit & His, so the two elderly Quebec City natives—one French and one English—can pursue a new friendship, yet another example (along with those in McFetridge and Blunt) of a move to bridge Canada's "two solitudes."

Mentorship and Revisions: The Olivier Story

The historically inflected body-in-the-library mystery unfolds in tandem with the revisiting of a past mystery from the previous (fifth) novel of the series, *The Brutal Telling* (2009). In that book, Gamache and his team investigate the murder of an unidentified hermit who lived in a small hut in the woods near Three Pines. The hut is as unlikely as the utopian village. Filled with magnificent antiques and priceless artworks, it serves as an aesthetic oasis, simultaneously cosmopolitan in the breadth of presumably stolen art it contains and yet also at one with nature given the coherent vision underlying the organic interactions of the hermit, his modest domicile, and his environment. The fifth novel ends with Gamache regretfully concluding that Olivier Brulé, who runs Three Pines' delightful bistro with his long-time partner Gabri Dubeau, must have murdered the hermit. In the sixth novel, Gamache receives a daily missive from Gabri, who refuses to accept his partner's guilt. "Why did he move the body?" Gabri asks repeatedly, pointing to the one unsatisfactory detail in the police account of the crime, which was nonetheless accepted by a jury and has led to Olivier's conviction and imprisonment.

In an unusual move within detective fiction, Penny narrates Gamache's decision to revisit the old case, essentially overturning the detective work of a seemingly complete murder mystery, and thus unraveling the uncovered narrative the reader has observed being constructed by the detectives. This move is one of restoration but also of mentorship. Gamache does not reopen the case himself, but instead asks his long-term mentee, Jean-Guy Beauvoir, also on extended leave to recover from his traumatic injury, to revisit Three Pines and unofficially review the evidence in a new way. Gamache's instructions are counterintuitive to Beauvoir: "Maybe the thing to do is look at it from the other direction. ... Go to Three Pines and try to prove Olivier didn't murder the Hermit Jacob" (51). The challenge is, in part, an attempt to bolster the past solution; if Beauvoir seeks to prove Olivier innocent and fails, Gamache can move on from the niggling doubt caused by the very reasonable question posed daily by Gabri. But this moment also registers a shift in the series from epistemological certainty to uncertainty. Gamache is the head of homicide at the Sûreté du Québec, repeatedly touted as the top detective in the province. His strength—as a detective and as a fictional character—is in being able to admit when he is wrong. If Gamache has been wrong in imprisoning series regular Olivier Brulé, the reader can no longer expect any Three Pines novel to tell a singular tale with clear beginning, middle, and ending.

Bury Your Dead marks the first time the reader spends an extensive period of time with Beauvoir without Gamache. As Beauvoir gets to know the people of Three Pines in unfurling the work of the previous case, he gains new insights into Gamache as well as himself. After his first real conversation with Clara Morrow, a talented visual artist of the village, he reflects on Gamache's interactions with the residents of Three Pines:

> Somehow [the Chief had] managed to become friends with most of them but Beauvoir had never been able to pass through that membrane, to see people as both suspects and humans. He'd never wanted to. The idea repulsed him.
>
> *(153–4)*

The image of passing through a membrane here evokes the notion of liminality, a space Gamache occupies easily but that Beauvoir resists. Eventually, though, Beauvoir takes Clara into his confidence and tells her he is unofficially reopening the hermit case. She talks through the case with him as they wash and dry the dishes after dinner in her modest home, and Beauvoir sees even more clearly that he has been wrong not to more closely follow his Chief's investigative techniques:

> He [Beauvoir] was beginning to appreciate why the Chief Inspector insinuated himself into the communities they investigated. It had long perplexed Beauvoir and privately he didn't approve. It blurred the lines between investigator and investigated. But he now wondered if that was such a bad thing.
>
> *(205–6)*

Indeed, it is through this re-investigation that Beauvoir opens himself up to blurring lines and occupying more liminal spaces. And in the end of *Bury Your Dead*, despite the hostile relationship that has long existed between nonliterary Jean-Guy Beauvoir and celebrated poet Ruth Zardo, it is to Ruth that he tells the story of the trauma that has haunted him and the Chief throughout the novel.

The Brutal Telling is a sad novel. It moves toward the identification of Olivier as a murderer and, relatedly, toward the incipient and inevitable ecological threat to the utopian community of Three Pines. The almost surreal cabin where the hermit lives in the nearby woods is imperiled by the new spa that has opened in the village, which suggests the inevitable march of "progress" marked by the development that endangers both the woodland ecosystem and the unlikely aesthetic and historical treasures hidden therein. Although *Bury Your Dead* is by no means a happy novel given its focus on the trauma of the series' main characters, it *does* provide a kind of blueprint for returning the utopian space to the reader. This return is perhaps most clearly seen by comparing the final scenes from *The Brutal Telling* and *Bury Your Dead*.

The final scene of the earlier novel is filled with pathos and reflection. When Gamache arrests Olivier, confident in his belief that he has correctly identified the murderer, he is touched by Gabri's equally steadfast belief in his life partner. "'What a magnificent man' Gamache says to Myrna, the village's bookstore owner, as they walk towards the village green" (370). Myrna agrees, predicting that Gabri will wait forever for Olivier to come back. In an echo of this unconditional love between the two men, we are presented with another kind of love as Gamache and Myrna see Ruth Zardo feeding her duck Rosa. Unexpectedly, Rosa is without the clothing Ruth has long provided for the little creature, whom she rescued as a duckling. As Myrna and Gamache watch the scene emotionally ("'Oh my God,' breathed Myrna" [371]), Rosa flies up into the air, away from the bread that Ruth offers, and joins a V formation of ducks flying south for the winter. Myrna marks the solemnity of the moment by pulling out a gorgeous poem on a crumpled piece of paper (attributed to Ruth in the novel but penned by Canadian poet Mike Freeman) to share with Gamache. "*She rose up into the air and the jilted earth let out a sigh,*" the poem begins (371). As Gamache watches Ruth start to come to terms with Rosa's predictable and yet heartbreaking departure, he thinks of Olivier's murder of the hermit. "But there was no hiding from Conscience," Gamache muses.

> It would find you. The past always did. Which was why, Gamache knew, it was vital to be aware of actions in the present. Because the present became the past, and the past grew. And got up, and followed you.
> (372)

After this dark reflection, the novel ends, as do all Penny's novels, with a more positive scene. As Gamache watches, Ruth hobbles to the bench on the green, where she meets Gabri, who takes her hand and murmurs "there, there" as the two heartbroken people find solace in each other—the youngish gay man whose partner has been arrested for murder and the elderly poet whose animal companion has returned to nature. The pathos and hope of the scene are cemented by a final quotation from the Mike Freeman poem, "Gravity Zero": "*She rose up but remembered to politely wave good-bye ...*" (372, original ellipses).

Bury Your Dead ends with Gamache's only visit to Three Pines in the whole novel. It takes place on a Sunday afternoon in the bistro, where all the main characters from the village are sitting in their pajamas, an act of sympathy for Gabri, who struggled with depression after Olivier was arrested and agreed to open the bistro on Sundays only if everyone agreed to join him in not getting dressed all day. A Volvo arrives in the village, and Gabri stares out the window from behind the bar, pausing for a moment to savor his recurring fantasy that it will be Olivier coming home. And this time, it is: "Gabri, unable to speak, opened his arms and Olivier fell into them. The two men hugged and rocked and wept. Around them villagers applauded and cried and hugged each other" (370). After the scene of rejoicing, the place goes quiet and Gamache speaks to Olivier, loudly enough for everyone to hear. In front of his own mentee, Beauvoir, he speaks two of the four sentences Émile taught him were most important: "I was wrong" and "I'm so sorry" (370). Olivier says he cannot forgive Gamache, but Gamache continues, echoing another line from Émile, this time in English: "Maybe, with time" (370). The novel ends with Gamache alone on the village green, reflecting on his recent trauma, but also hearing the joyful sound of children playing in the snow. Given all that he has learned about the importance of both processing and moving on from the past, this ending feels hopeful, even when one considers the third and final strand of the novel.

Fragments of Time and Trauma: The Eco-Terrorist Plot

The eco-terrorist plot, which encapsulates the real-world eco-anxiety raised by the recent naming of our current geological period as the Anthropocene, cannot be presented in a linear fashion, and is instead related through interruptions into the other two plots. Like the climate crisis itself, the eco-terrorist narrative—the anticipation, the crisis, and the aftermath—intrudes into ordinary life regardless of our attempts to suppress it; in the case of the novel, it intrudes into both the classical murder mystery and the revisiting of a previous mystery, demanding attention. Although the Three Pines series is not usually regarded as climate fiction (cli-fi), I would argue that environmental themes pervade the series as part of Penny's utopian project. Indeed, I would go further and argue that this series—and especially *Bury Your Dead* with its innovative narrative techniques—showcases the potential for detective fiction to participate in an activist cli-fi agenda embraced by many twenty-first-century writers.

In *Don't Even Think About It: Why Our Brain are Wired To Ignore Climate Change* (2014), George Marshall argues that one of the reasons humans around the world are not single-mindedly and collaboratively focused on solving the existential threat of climate change is that we are driven by narratives that tell good stories, ideally those that include perpetrators and heroes; climate change, by its nature, has no built-in villains (106–7). This means that people are forced to create antagonists, be they greedy oil company executives or tree-hugging environmental fanatics. Writers of various ilks have attempted to dramatize the climate crisis, often finding considerable commercial success in novels and films exploring futuristic or present-day climate disasters. However, as Amitav Ghosh argues in *The Great Derangement* (2016), these fictional narratives have resided almost exclusively in the domain of science fiction, in some ways constructing the climate crisis as analogous to alien invasion or time travel, rather than to the subjects treated by realist novels or literary fiction (7). Furthermore, as E. Ann Kaplan suggests in *Climate Trauma: Foreseeing the Future in Dystopian Film and Fiction* (2016), cli-fi texts, as they are usually conceived, may lead to what she calls pre-Traumatic Stress Disorder, a debilitating form of eco-paralysis, an "immobilizing anticipatory anxiety around the future" (xix). Given the generic ghettoizing and psychological trauma thus identified, the effectiveness of climate disaster texts in leading to eco-activism is an open question. To date, most climate fiction has been in the subgenre of the thriller, but I expect we will see more engagement with climate issues in the police procedural as we begin to better understand the criminal impacts likely to accompany the crisis in the real world.

Penny hints at her interest in climate issues in the second novel of the series, *A Fatal Grace* (2006), when a pair of baby sealskin boots central to the murder plot also become a symbol of Canada's fraught relationship with the environmental movement. When Beauvoir explains that the boots acted as a conductor of electricity in the complicated murder-by-electrocution scenario, Gamache's reaction goes far beyond satisfaction at finally having an answer to a difficult forensic question:

> Armand Gamache felt his jaw clench. Who would wear such boots? The Inuit, maybe. In the Arctic. But even they wouldn't kill baby seals. The Inuit were respectful and sensible hunters who'd never dream of killing the young.
> ...
> Armand Gamache wondered whether CC de Poitiers [the murder victim, wearer of the boots] was at that very moment trying to explain herself to a perplexed God and a couple of very angry seals.
>
> *(112)*

Penny clearly connects CC's personal malevolence with the anti-environmentalist movement, carving out an exception to the hunting of protected animals for First Nations peoples, and then clarifying that such hunters are too respectful to target the young for sustenance, let alone fashion. CC, thus, is severely judged by Gamache and his team, providing a representation of Canadians as strongly adverse to environmentally irresponsible fashion choices. Gamache's closing thought—his whimsical image of CC facing the dead seals along with "a perplexed God"—emphasizes that stewardship is more than a cultural, social, or political value; it is consonant with the chief inspector's ethico-theological perspective, which represents the common twenty-first-century Quebecois attitude of retaining a nondenominational monotheistic belief while rejecting the Catholic Church long dominant in Quebec.

The powerful symbol of the sealskin boots is reprised later in the series by reference to "La Complainte du phoque en Alaska" ("The Complaint of a Seal in Alaska"), a popular Quebecois song written by Michel Rivard and performed by Beau Dommage (1975) and mentioned in *A Fatal Grace* (274), *The Brutal Telling* (2009, p. 12), and *The Beautiful Mystery* (2012, p. 6). "La Complainte" provides a deep reflection upon the relationship of Canada to the United States, articulating a simultaneous Canadian longing and anxiety about being more like its neighbor to the south. Rivard's ballad, characterized by Penny's narrator as "about a lonely seal whose love had disappeared" (*Beautiful* 6), can be summarized as follows: a seal in Alaska is missing his mate, who has gone to the United States to perform in a circus. The seal's own glistening pelt reminds him of iconic American images—of the streets of New York after a rainstorm, of Chicago, of Marilyn Monroe—as he wishes he could witness his mate's performances. And yet, he bemoans the empty fame that accompanies a seal, performing for others who do not appreciate her true value. "La Complainte" speaks to the ongoing tensions in the relationship between Canada and the United States regarding both the natural environment that the two nations share in many ways and the role of environmentalism in both countries. In recent years, Alaska—with its seal population—has become a site of tension for Americans and Canadians; after all, it is home to the Arctic National Wildlife Refuge coveted by oil companies, it contains the controversial Trans-Alaska Pipeline System, and it is, like the Canadian Arctic, a locale undergoing enormous environmental changes whose impacts—environmental, economic, and socio-political—are not yet known. The seal itself has been used as a symbol of environmental exploitation that may well contribute to the eco-paralysis identified by Judith Williamson's analysis of the polar bear's symbolic use in environmental visual rhetoric as nostalgically and ineffectually pointing backward rather than forward (cited in Marshall 137).

A Fatal Grace presents a simple yet effective eco-critique through its very serious postmodern play with the seal as a symbol. *Bury Your Dead* provides a far more complex exploration of this theme through the ecoterrorist plot as well as its relationships with the two other mysteries that share the novel. This plot, which borrows its pacing from the genre of the thriller, is revealed in fragments that play with temporality, explicitly through jarring shifts in scene and verb tense, and implicitly as Gamache reflects upon the scheme, his efforts to subvert it, and the unauthorized YouTube video that documents these actions and serves as a kind of reveal scene at the end. In the first 300+ pages of the novel, the reader gets frequent but incomplete access to Gamache's memories of the day that has left him with a facial scar as well as a right hand that trembles uncontrollably in moments of high stress, whether the stress is triggered by memories of the past, tensions in the present, or anxieties about the future. Gamache's memories focus on the long day during which his acolyte Paul Morin was physically held captive in an unknown location and Gamache psychologically held captive by the kidnapper's threats of killing Morin if Gamache were to end his 24-hour phone call with the young detective. The day culminates in the raid of a factory that prevents a domestic terrorist plot from blowing up an enormous Quebec dam that would cause devastating power outages in Maritime Canada as well as in the much more populated Eastern Seaboard of the United States. Poignant details from the conversation frequently interrupt Gamache's present-day train of thought, bringing with them memories of the cat-and-mouse game happening in the interstices of the conversation. As Gamache and Morin converse, covering topics ranging from childhood memories to hopes for the future, another agent attempts to discover Morin's location by isolating and analyzing tiny background signals. As the narrator reports: "In listening to the spaces between words they'd found him" (352).

    Finding Paul Morin is not the end of the story, since his kidnapping has been a ruse, a distraction to occupy the police while the much larger plot is carried out. It is through a lifelong commitment to intensive listening—technologically with Yvette Nichols and interpersonally as always—that Gamache and his team discern the ecoterrorist plot. In the ensuing police action, the two main detective characters of the series—Gamache and Beauvoir—are shot. As the novel's innovative storytelling makes clear, though, recognizing the plot's existence and eventually preventing its execution are not the same as fully understanding it. Penny provides her reader with an experience that mimics the fragmented trauma time of the main detectives by giving only shards of memory, including many mundane exchanges from the long phone call between Gamache and Morin, until the last few chapters of the novel. The full story is told only when Gamache and Beauvoir view an anonymously posted YouTube video that has been pulled together from police cam footage and that provides the first linear, coherent, revelatory—yet profoundly mediated—account of the factory raid.

    Although the YouTube video is described as surprisingly comprehensive in its presentation of the story, the reader nonetheless accesses it only incompletely. Reading about a video is an example of ekphrasis—the textual representation of a visual or audiovisual artwork—and is, by its nature incomplete. However, Penny draws even more attention to the gaps that always exist in even the most carefully documented historical accounts by revealing the video through several different perspectives. Beauvoir learns of the video's existence and can tell that others have seen it before he has:

> Something had changed. Jean-Guy Beauvoir could feel it. It was the way people looked at him. It was as though they'd seen him naked, as though they'd seen him in a position so vulnerable, so exposed it was all they could see now. Not the man he really was. An edited man.
> *(317)*

And then, with the power of the video to change people's perceptions of Beauvoir, the reader's access to the now-viral text is provided only over the shoulders of Beauvoir (watching in Three Pines with irascible poet Ruth Zardo) and of Gamache (watching in Quebec City with his mentor Émile Comeau).

The first view is from Beauvoir:

> As he suspected, the images were cobbled together from the tiny cameras attached to the headsets of each Sûreté officer. What he hadn't expected was the clarity. He'd thought it'd be grainy, hard to distinguish the players, but it was clear.
> *(340)*

After this promise of painful clarity for the character, the reader is buffeted from one short segment to another, always with a switch of perspective between. Each segment opens on a visceral character reaction that guides the reader's experience. For example:

> Armand Gamache watched, unblinking, though all he wanted to do was look away. Close his eyes, cover his ears, curl into a ball.
> *(341)*

> Beauvoir watched the screen through his fingers clutched to his face, his eyes wide.
> *(342)*

> Émile hadn't moved since the video began.
> *(342)*

> Ruth stared at the screen, her Scotch untouched.
>
> (345)

The description of the video pauses on the violent trauma suffered by Gamache, Beauvoir, and several other detectives, highlighting the human cost of the plot to characters we know and love. Beauvoir is shot first, and Gamache tries to staunch the younger man's wound before returning to the fray, where he himself is shot. Four Sûreté officers are killed in the raid, and the video includes footage from their funeral procession, lingering on an anguished yet heroic portrayal of Gamache standing behind the column of police officials and the four coffins: "It became the image of grief. The image on every front page and every news program and every magazine cover" (349).

The move from the convolution of the video assemblage to the iconic still image of Gamache highlights the rhetorical complexity of both the act of representation in a postmodern world and the plot that led to the raid of the abandoned factory. Penny's narrative moves to longer segments as it delves into the tensions that have led to this plot's development in Canada, and specifically in Quebec. Embroiled in a power struggle with his superior, Chief Superintendent Francoeur, Gamache is limited in his response to the plot to destroy the dam almost equally by the kidnappers who are keeping him on the phone and by his own police bureaucracy. Through the intelligence, persistence, and leadership skills that have served him throughout the series, Gamache eventually uncovers the story. The plot recounts an asymmetrical attack, since fairly simple explosives are intended to deploy an enormous human-made power source against millions of people, highlighting the ways that electrification has altered the natural environment, making us increasingly reliant on technology and increasingly separate from Nature.

Gamache explains the foiled scheme to Tom Hancock, an Anglophone minister in Quebec City, on the historic Plains of Abraham in the midst of a white-out snowstorm. Gamache references the flaws of Canadian police and intelligence officials that made possible the plot: "Hidden inside their own hubris, their certainty that advance technology would uncover any threat" (356). He tells Hancock that the plotters came so close to succeeding because they avoided modern technology altogether:

> "They did it by working where they knew we wouldn't look." [Gamache explains]
> "And where was that?"
> "In the past."

... The two men's voices were low, like conspirators or storytellers. It felt as it must have millennia ago, when people sat together across fires and told tales.

(356–7)

This passage evokes the importance of time and of story, both key concepts in considering the questions around the climate crisis that drive so much utopian thought today. As Gamache tells Hancock the story—also telling the reader the full story for the first time—the narrator reminds us of the importance of narrative in structuring our understanding of the world, a point that has been made repeatedly about the problematic, often lackluster, narratives that get told about the existential threat of climate change.

For Penny, attending to the environment means attending to Canada's history, and specifically, to the contrasting attitudes and perspectives that undergirded early interactions between settlers and Indigenous populations. As Daniel Francis argues, the Canadian celebration of its elite police force, the Royal Canadian Mounted Police (RCMP), ignores the historical fact that this force's early work was in "protecting" white settlers and thus suppressing First Nations peoples. Francis debunks the myth of the RCMP with an almost laughably Canadian tact: "The image of the Mountie is a fabrication, which does not mean that it is untrue, just that its 'truth' is psychological, not historical" (50). Penny, whose narrator regularly describes the Sûreté du Québec as an "elite" police force, is not so gentle in her analysis of the relationship between white Canadians and First Nations peoples. The drivers of the explosively rigged trucks that are to blow up the La Grande Dam are young Cree men. In telling Hancock the story, Gamache never refers to them as terrorists or even criminals. In an extension of the series' preoccupation with addiction and with the drug trade between Canada and the United States, including its devastating impact on Indigenous communities, the blame for the ecoterrorist plot is place squarely on privileged white Canadian criminals. The plight of Indigenous youth is laid out starkly: "Agent Lacoste's reports started to form a picture. Of a generation on the reserves without hope. Drunk and high and lost. With no life and no future and nothing to lose. It had all been taken. This Gamache already knew. Anyone with the stomach to look saw that" (359).

This critique of contemporary Canadian culture—an important rhetorical aim of the utopian genre from which Penny's series draws much of its energy—is sharpened in its connection to ecoterrorism. Gamache and his team discover that the young Cree men on the reserve have been radicalized over many years by white English-Canadian teachers who have been developing the plot against the dam. Already suicidal, two Cree youth have agreed to drive the trucks in an attempt to regain some lost aspect of their First Nations identity: "[the alleged teacher] had also taught their students that they need not be victims any longer. They could be warriors again" (359). The tragic death of the young Cree men, along with the fact that the white instigators are not identified let alone captured by novel's end, emphasizes this novel's generic hybridity. Not only does it reside between the conventions of the cozy and the police procedural, like most of Penny's works, but it also evokes the complex, multi-faceted thriller narratives that today are so closely tied to our understandings of the climate crisis and the many discourses around this existential threat.

Penny's story of the ecoterrorist plot and the factory raid is deeply layered in its presentation, effectively mimicking the tentative, multifaceted accounts of the global climate crisis. Traumatized by his part in this story—a story that calls up the exploitative history of interactions between settlers and Indigenous peoples—Gamache the detective is unable to perform his usual epistemological work of unraveling the mystery and clearly identifying and communicating the identity of the guilty parties. Instead, he is so traumatized by individual moments in the plot that he cannot see the larger picture or its implications, again evoking the cognitive gaps people often experience when thinking about the Anthropocene and the temporal disjunctions of past, present, and future in addressing questions of climate crisis. This novel, I believe, tells a compelling story of potential ecological disaster while avoiding the paralyzing anxiety feared by both Marshall and Kaplan in their efforts to understand the psychological barriers to climate activism. Because hers is a fundamentally utopian project, Penny manages to make a rhetorically effective critique of Canada's vulnerabilities in the face of the global climate crisis, but in a way that prompts reader reflection and activism, that performs what Lucy Sargisson calls utopianism's "transformative function" (12).

Conclusion

Louise Penny's Armand Gamache series is fundamentally a utopian project, using the conventions of detective fiction in deploying a trenchant yet hopeful critique of contemporary Canadian culture and politics. Working through some of Canada's most vexed historical relationships—including those between English and French, settlers and Indigenous peoples, and Canadians and Americans—Penny repeatedly examines expansive issues critical to Canada's place in the world today. By juxtaposing the historical vibrancy of very real Quebec City with the Edenic stillness of fictional Three Pines in *Bury Your Dead*, Penny examines the tenuousness of both time and place in constructions of reality, a move that demonstrates the power of crime fiction to interrogate the most pressing sociocultural and philosophical concerns of the twenty-first century. The theme of environmentalism pervades many of the novels in the series, but it is in *Bury Your Dead* that Penny provides her most complex and compelling exploration of this theme, ultimately showing that we need to acknowledge both the past and the future in order to live responsibly in the Anthropocene.

13
STORYTELLING, GUILT, AND GAMES IN MARGARET ATWOOD'S POST-APOCALYPTIC CRIME FICTION

Spoiler Alert: Everybody Dies

This is the premise of Margaret Atwood's cheeky yet sublime short story, "Happy Endings" (1983), in which she pushes her metafictional tendencies to the extreme in six versions of the story of John and Mary, each of which ends with the death of the two main characters. After a sketch of several possible scenarios (introduced with letters A through F) for two people who meet and embark upon a romantic relationship, Atwood concludes in a way that deliberately recalls her good friend and frequent intellectual antagonist, Ursula K. Le Guin. In "The Ones Who Walk Away from Omelas" (1973), a brief yet brilliant short story that has come to define utopian writing and criticism, Le Guin articulates the trade-offs of utopia, arguing that happiness is always paid for by suffering, although the sufferer may not be the same person who experiences the happiness. In describing her utopian city of Omelas, the narrator acknowledges different reader preferences, but notes that these have no impact on her main point: "I fear that Omelas strikes some of you as goody-goody. Smiles, bells, parades, horses, bleh. If so, please add an orgy" (*Wind* 279). Atwood makes the same narrative move—and the same basic point—at the end of "Happy Endings": "If you think this is all too bourgeois, make John a revolutionary and Mary a counterespionage agent and see how far that gets you. Remember, this is Canada. You'll still end up with A, though in between you may get a lustful brawling saga of passionate involvement, a chronicle of our times, sort of" (*Murder* 50). By stepping outside the story and inviting the reader to imagine different permutations, Atwood is, like Le Guin, claiming metafictional status for her story, drawing attention to its commentary on the nature of all stories. Her tongue-in-cheek reference to Canada, with its allegedly rule-following populace, only cements the universality of her final claim: "That's about all that can be said for plots, which anyway are just one thing after another, a what and a what and a what. Now try How and Why" (51).

Classical detective fiction, with its sobriquet of the *whodunit*, is fundamentally interested in the *how* and *why*, the means, opportunities, and motives that make possible the crime or disruption that begins a detective narrative. As Jackie Shead has shown in her excellent analysis of Atwood's many forays into the world of crime writing, Atwood repeatedly employs the tropes of detective fiction, often combining these with conventions from other genres in order to both celebrate and write back against classic mystery writers like Arthur Conan Doyle and Agatha Christie. As Atwood herself notes in *In Other Worlds: SF and the Human Imagination* (2011), "When it comes to genres, the borders are increasingly undefended, and things slip back and forth across them with insouciance" (7). Shead carefully documents several of the interventions Atwood makes vis-à-vis the traditional detective narrative as it is laid out by Tzvetan Todorov, who argues that the detective story always contains a dual narrative: the story of the crime and the story of uncovering the crime. Atwood's literary fiction often includes crimes and even detective figures, but she moves away from the detective genre's common practice, in which it "circulates suspicion but finally pinpoints blame" (Shead 54). Instead, Atwood's stories tend to disperse blame, never tying it to a single character, expanding it over social and cultural forces, and often asking even the reader to question their own potential complicity. Further, Atwood does not stop telling the story when the mystery is solved (and, in typical postmodern detective fashion, does not always solve the mystery); rather, she explores the ramifications of crime, including its epistemological and ethical impacts on individuals and their communities. As Shead concludes,

> Atwood transforms crime fiction not simply to create a corrective parody of some of its influential mythologies (such as, the criminal is always another, never ourselves), though she certainly does that. She also uses the genre as a tool to deconstruct other mythologies: the romance narrative, the virtue of self-sacrifice, the belief we can be ideologically neutral or exploit natural resources with impunity.
>
> *(196)*

Atwood is not alone in her use of detective and crime fiction as an entry into larger philosophical questions that test the boundaries of traditional detective fiction. Indeed, "postmodern" or "metaphysical" detective fiction, a relatively small corpus of work associated with a post–World-War-II postmodern project, evokes generic tropes from detective fiction in order to interrogate, problematize, and parody the epistemological and ethical assumptions that have shaped the detective genre. Such works include E. C. Bentley's *Trent's Last Case* (1936), Alain Robbe-Grillet's *The Erasers* (1952, translated from French), Manuel Puig's *The Buenos Aires Affair* (1973, translated from Spanish), Umberto Eco's *The Name of the Rose* (1983, translated from Italian), and Paul Auster's *New York Trilogy* (1987). These texts present mysteries that seem appropriate fodder for detective strategies, but then withhold solutions in a way that suggests that "solutions" to mysteries are always already incomplete, as they are based on reductive understandings of "truth" and "reality." Such texts luxuriate in metaphysical uncertainty, suggesting that knowledge and morality are both always best understood as slippery, contextually specific concepts. Through a postmodern commitment to self-reflexivity, metafiction, intertextuality, and parody, metaphysical detective narratives avoid closure in a way that resonates with the utopian project that is central to both utopian and dystopian—and what Atwood calls *ustopian*—writing (*In Other Worlds* 66).

The *MaddAddam* trilogy takes an expansive approach to telling and understanding an enormous crime: the bioterrorist attack that is designed to usher in the death of the human race and thus end the human destruction of the natural environment. Using several narratives and narrative modes across three novels (*Oryx and Crake* [2003], *The Year of the Flood* [2009], and *MaddAddam* [2013]) that Atwood calls "siblings" rather than "sequels" (*In Other Worlds* 92), this trilogy highlights the epistemological and ethical conundrums that inhere in a postmodern world facing an existential environmental crisis. Within the socio-economic frame of late capitalism and the aesthetic frame of reality TV and virtual reality gaming, *crime*, like *detection*, becomes a multi-valenced term. In keeping with her career-long interest in expanding understandings of guilt and complicity, Atwood uses games and stories in the *MaddAddam* trilogy to show that crimes in the future will be neither understood nor contained by detective figures. Rather, they might require communities of thoughtful people with multiple epistemological approaches—the scientific (Crake), the aesthetic (Jimmy and Amanda), the spiritual (Toby and the God's Gardeners), and even the posthuman (the Crakers)—to work together in identifying, articulating, and responding to existential threats.

Genocide, Guilt, and Complicity

Questions of guilt underlie crime and detective fiction. For classic theorists of detective fiction like George Grella, the detective story is a fundamentally conservative genre, narrating a disruption to the social order that is addressed by the detective figure so that the status quo is restored in the end. John Cawelti, another pioneer in popular culture studies, argues that the detective story explores the dynamic among not only the central triangle of characters—the criminal, the victim, and the detective—but also includes the suspect as a fourth term in considering possible ways of assigning guilt (90). In typical postmodern detective fashion, Atwood raises these traditional narrative structures and tropes in her exploration of the biggest crime in human history. In one sense, the bioterrorist plot at the center of the story lays the guilt fully at Crake's feet. He has spent years observing and cataloguing the weaknesses of humanity, as evidenced by his many discussions on the topic with his friend Jimmy. He has analyzed data, recruited personnel (various scientists as well as Jimmy for advertising), developed a replacement for humanity that attempts to overcome a series of identified weaknesses, and then deliberately bioengineered a pandemic hemorrhagic supervirus designed to exterminate the human race. The genocide is a result of years of meticulous planning and thus would appear to easily meet the criteria for a crime against humanity. And yet, as the novels develop the story of the cataclysm, we wonder if perhaps Crake alone does not bear full culpability for the genocide. Working within a philosophical framework consonant with that of the more extreme proponents of deep ecology who treat environmental issues today, Crake's actions raise several complex questions, including: (1) how do we most equitably and accurately assign guilt for the genocide? and (2) are there ways to see the genocide as a productive next step, perhaps not for humans, but for the planet?

In treating these and other questions, Atwood places her trilogy in the "increasingly undefended" borders between crime fiction and ustopia. As Atwood explains in *In Other Worlds*, "*Ustopia* is a word I made up by combining utopia and dystopias—the imagined perfect society and its opposite—because, in my view, each contains a latent version of the other" (66). In some ways, Atwood's neologism is a doubling down on the paradox already inherent in *utopia* (*u-topos* is "the perfect place" and its homonym *eu-topos* is "no place"), and yet it is useful in drawing attention to that central contradiction in a twenty-first-century context in which etymologies are not always well-known, especially to younger readers, an important target group for any utopian project. Atwood pushes the duality inherent in utopian and dystopian writing even further when she explores the narrative momentum of ustopia:

> As ustopia is by definition elsewhere, it is almost always bracketed by two journeys: the one that transports the tale-teller to the other place and the one that transports him (or her) back so he can deliver his report to us.
>
> *(71)*

In the *MaddAddam* trilogy, the journey that transports the tale-teller to the other place (the future in which most humans are dead and the Earth is inhabited largely by their hybrid creations including the Crakers) is narrated largely in *Oryx and Crake*. This novel relies on a bildungsroman element in which Jimmy, by telling his own coming-of-age story in flashbacks, ends up providing a detailed narrative of the creation of Crake and his bioterrorist plot, as well as an exploration of its aftermath. The journey that delivers the report to readers develops through *The Year of the Flood* and *MaddAddam*, epistolary novels made up of documents constructed by various characters (Toby, Ren, and Adam One in *Year*; Toby and Blackbeard in *Madd*). The report to readers is thus highly complex, as it encompasses a number of different perspectives, including the posthuman point of view of the Crakers. It is a report that interrogates questions of guilt and hope, largely through a postmodern interest in games and storytelling.

The complex dispersal of guilt away from the individual and toward larger cultural forces (a move Shead identifies as typical in Atwood's crime fiction) can be seen in *Oryx and Crake* when Jimmy visits his best friend in college at the prestigious Watson-Crick Institute and Crake considers the problems of the decaying world with incisive analysis. Seen through Jimmy's post-apocalyptic eyes, Crake's rational examination of the interlinked problems of human nature and environmental degradation is presented in a way at once chilling and humorous:

> "Let's suppose for the sake of argument," said Crake one evening, "that civilization as we know it gets destroyed. Want some popcorn?"
>
> "Is that real butter?" said Jimmy.
>
> "Nothing but the best as Watson-Crick," said Crake. "Once it's flattened, it could never be rebuilt."
>
> "Because why? Got any salt?"
>
> "Because all the available surface metals have already been ruined," said Crake. ... Want a beer?"
>
> "Is it cold?"
>
> "All it takes," said Crake, "is the elimination of one generation. One generation of anything. Beetles, trees, microbes, scientists, speakers of

French, whatever. Break the link in time between one generation and the next, and it's game over forever."

"Speaking of games," said Jimmy. "it's your move."

(Oryx 223)

The juxtaposition of two young men playing a game while eating superior-quality snacks with their deadly earnest conversation about how to rid the Earth of its dominant species encapsulates Atwood's complex representation of Crake's genocidal plot. Crake recognizes the practical limits of using HelthWyzer's existing system for secretly creating and distributing new diseases that require costly medical interventions provided by HelthWyzer (" 'This would be really evil,' said Jimmy" [211] when Crake explains the scheme), since not every human can be infected by a single pathogen, no matter how lethal and infectious. There are always humans living off the grid through which disease distribution takes place. By Crake's analysis, however, the elements of civilization that are most destructive to the environment cannot be maintained beyond a single human generation, so his plan—not so much to kill the humans as to save the Earth—is secure. It is the result of a game theory analysis that plays out different potential responses to different stimuli, highlighting the analytic potential of games that also underlies crime and detective fiction.

Games and Game Theory—Violence, Achievement, and Subversion

The use of games to represent epistemological and ethical questions has a long history in detective fiction, including postmodern responses to the genre. Indeed, Atwood has impressive precedents in her use of games to figure the relationship among criminal, victim, and detective; these include Edgar Allan Poe's "The Purloined Letter" (1845), with its treatise on the game of odds and evens, as well as William Faulkner's *Knight's Gambit* (1949), which uses chess to explore questions of history, love, morality, and American identity. For Poe, Faulkner, and others, games have acted as a secondary representational medium that supports and comments on the representative medium of the story to articulate questions and anxieties around crime, criminality, deviancy, and culpability. As Jackie Shead notes, Atwood's *Bodily Harm* (1981) uses the board game *Clue* to explore the doubled perspective so commonly considered in detective fiction. *Clue* provides an especially apt metaphor for Atwood, since the players are at once onlookers and game pieces, with one player (unbeknown even to themselves) being the murderer. *Clue* is premised on the notion of a clearly guilty party (Colonel Mustard, with the lead pipe, in the library, for instance), but the player with the yellow token (enacting the Colonel Mustard role) is unaware of their own guilt (Shead 66).

In *Oryx and Crake*, Atwood has Jimmy and Crake play a number of games, real and invented, to explore the many potentials of games in figuring relationships and power dynamics in postmodern crime fiction. In classical detective tradition starting with Poe's Chevalier Dupin and moving through Chandler, Faulkner, and Borges, chess has been used to figure the detective-criminal relationship as a battle of wits between two equally matched players. The criminal plays first, with equal resources and all information available, and the detective responds, trying to see more steps into the future than the opponent in order to best the opponent, all while maintaining at least the polite fiction that the battle is a gentlemanly contest in which no brawls will occur. As teenagers, Jimmy and Crake play computer chess when they should be doing their homework, leading to a postmodern commentary of the simulacrum that manages life in the pleeblands (poor neighborhoods) and compounds (affluent, gated neighborhoods) even more fully than it does for us today:

> "Why don't we use a real set?" Jimmy asked one day when they were doing some [computer] chess. "The old kind. With plastic men." It did seem weird to have the two of them in the same room, back to back, playing on computers.
> "Why?" said Crake. "Anyway, this *is* a real set."
> "No it's not."
> "Okay, granted, but neither is plastic men."
> "What?"
> "The real set is in your head."
> "Bogus!" Jimmy yelled. It was a good word, he'd got it off an old DVD; they'd taken to using it to tear each other down for being pompous. "Way too bogus!"
> Crake laughed.
> *(Oryx 77)*

The notion of reality here is delightfully deferred as Crake makes the reasonable observation than although a physical chess set has tactility, it lacks reality in some of the same ways as does a computer chess set, in that chess is already a metaphor for power dynamics rather than the "real" power dynamics that would be explored if there were two knights on horses facing each other in battle rather than jumping on a board in a prescribed and limited way. Crake argues that the reality of an elegant, storied game like chess resides in your head, in the insights the game provides, while Jimmy refuses this insight as too pompous or, again, lacking "reality."

Crake's laugh, like the humor that pervades the novel, sometimes in uncomfortable ways (see, for example, Bouson or Traub), reminds the reader that many of the MaddAddam games, like all the representations in dystopian and apocalyptic literature, are at once deeply earnest and hopefully avoidable.

Two of Atwood's more memorable games in the trilogy—Barbarian Stomp and Blood and Roses—are presented as both humorous and deeply disturbing. Barbarian Stomp explores the relationship between civilization and savagery by pitting wealthy cities against vicious barbarian hordes. Jimmy's explanation of the match-ups explored in the game reveals the perspective play that Atwood so enjoys: "Rome versus the Visigoths, Ancient Egypt versus the Hyksos, Aztecs versus the Spaniards. That was a cute one, because it was the Aztecs who represented civilization, while the Spaniards were the barbarian hordes" (77–8). When Jimmy beats Crake at Barbarian Stomp as a result of his love of historical research, Crake switches his loyalties to Blood and Roses, a game committed to creating an odd fungibility in its commodification of historical and aesthetic products. Blood and Roses is a trading game in which the Blood side plays human atrocities, while the Roses plays achievements. Given Jimmy's strengths in arts and humanities, and Crake's in calculation, this game favors Crake with its focus on numbers:

> "The exchange rates—one *Mona Lisa* equaled Bergen-Belsen, one Armenian genocide equals the *Ninth Symphony* plus three Great Pyramids—" are paired with the need "to know the numbers—the total number of corpses for the atrocities, the latest open-market price for the artworks".
>
> *(79)*

Jimmy concludes the description by calling it a "wicked game" (79). After all,

> The Blood player usually won, but winning meant you inherited a wasteland. This was the point of the game, said Crake, when Jimmy complained. Jimmy said if that was the point, it was pretty pointless. He didn't want to tell Crake that he was having some severe nightmares.
>
> *(80)*

The game's focus on reducing aesthetic and political events to commodifiable pieces provides a pointed critique of emotional shallowness, raising concerns about the perils of video games that glorify violence and desensitize young people to both horror and beauty. As the trilogy makes clear, however, it is not only violent video games that desensitize people; it is also the neoliberal practices underlying twenty-first-century economics and politics (see, for example, Thorpe or Vials).

Crake's tastes eventually move from violent video games to a less gory but perhaps even more disturbing game that will interest him for the rest of his life: Extinctathon. Jimmy finds this game boring. Described as an "interactive biofreak masterlore game," Extinctathon provides a mysterious login screen: *"EXTINCTATHON, Monitored by MaddAddam, Adam named the living animals, MaddAddam names the dead ones. Do you want to play?"* (80, original formatting). On the surface, Extinctathon is a quiz game somewhat in the spirit of 20 questions whose topic is recently extinct animals. The gamification of the sixth extinction event in Earth's history might appear to highlight a callous, evolutionarily unwise approach to an existential threat. At the same time, the player chooses an extinct species as their token, suggesting the way that games, like fictional narratives, allow players or readers to inhabit the space of another, to develop empathy outside their lived experiences. By taking on the victim perspective in what can certainly be constructed as a crime against numerous endangered species, the Extinctathon player might gain new insights into the conundrums around environmental stewardship. In fact, the quiz-game portion of Extinctathon is just a front, since this product is actually an underground messaging site for the God's Gardeners and other subversive groups. It is also the game that gives titles to two of the three novels in Atwood's series, since Oryx, Crake, and MaddAddam are all user names in Extinctathon.

Why does Atwood make Extinctathon a central metaphor for her project of exploring from many angles the genocide of the human race? Given that John and Mary from "Happy Endings" both die at the end—the same way the human species will become extinct, just like every other species to ever live on the Earth and presumably on any other planet—this game in some sense signals the generative representational potential of starting at the end of a story and working back through the how and why. Each now-extinct species has its own story. The crake, for example, is a fairly common small bird—the type of species that will never be featured on environmental posters because it is not especially endangered or especially memorable. Crake's use of this unremarkable animal as his avatar suggests that destruction can come from unforeseen places. The oryx, on the other hand, has a storied past when it comes to environmental narratives. A large antelope whose horn can be a surprisingly deadly tool (the oryx is rumored to have killed lions), the oryx is a majestic creature whose extinction was prevented only by captive breeding programs. Indeed, the oryx is a success story of environmental intervention, since oryxes have been saved from extinction and even reintroduced into the wild. These stories, along with Jimmy's "Snowman" (Abominable Snowman) persona, provide a compelling counterpoint that accompanies each character's story arc within Atwood's apocalyptic exploration. As a word, *extinct-athon* evokes the long, arduous, journey of a marathon, decathlon, or danceathon, as well as the focus and energy needed to withstand the challenges. As a game, it gives a voice to the victims of the sixth extinction event while also providing a cyberspace for resistance.

Although Atwood relies largely on computer games in exploring the representational potential of games to figure various power dynamics, she also uses one real-world game that problematizes criminality in ways that are perhaps even more complex. Pre-apocalypse, the criminal justice system in Atwood's world uses Painball as a punishment for criminals. Here, criminals are divided into teams and fight to the death in a spectacle consumed by a jaded populace that seeks realism in its goriest entertainments. This is a clear nod to dystopian novels such as Stephen King's *The Long Walk* (1979, as Richard Bachman) and *The Running Man* (1982); it is an idea upon which Suzanne Collins capitalized in her *The Hunger Games* trilogy (2008–2010). On one hand, Painball serves as a shorthand to emphasize the dystopian nature of the society before Crake unleashes his bioterrorist attack and the apocalypse that follows. At the same time, Atwood deploys the Painball motif beyond the apocalypse, as two of the characters in *MaddAddam* are known only as "the Painballers." These are the two men who accompany Blanco (a more fully developed villain) and participated in kidnapping and raping women before they are captured by Toby only to be released by the kindly Crakers, who have no concept of self-protection. These Painballers serve as a type of moral compass that opens up ethical dilemmas for the various post-apocalyptic characters. Toby finds herself unable to kill these criminals even after she rescues their victims. Near the end of *MaddAddam*, the Painballers undergo a kind of trial at the God's Gardeners' settlement, and the group votes anonymously on whether or not to enact capital punishment, a practice most God's Gardeners would have firmly opposed prior to the cataclysm. The result of a single vote for leniency, visually embodied by a single white stone among the black stones, acts as a marker of a new post-apocalyptic ethics in which all the characters' hypothetical musings about criminality, justice, and morality—their game theory—are challenged by the reality of a nearly posthuman world.

Epistemology and Storytelling: An Exploration of the Dangerous and Delicious

For Todorov and other scholars of detective fiction, the detective's fundamental role is to uncover the story of the crime that has preceded the action of the narrative. In classical detective fiction, the detective not only uncovers the story but also tells it, generally in a reveal scene that gathers together the various suspects and exposes which one is to blame. Atwood, of course, eschews such an epistemologically simplistic reveal scene, with its clear-cut sense of truth and culpability. And yet, the MaddAddam trilogy borrows a great deal from these traditions as Jimmy/Snowman attempts to understand and recount the crime of genocide in *Oryx and Crake*, and as Toby and Ren attempt to articulate a number of related crimes, including rape and murder, in *The Year of the Flood* and *MaddAddam*. As Jimmy, Toby, and Ren ponder and understand the various snippets of narrative they had access to before the pandemic, their interweaving stories highlight the web of plots that lead up to and emanate from a moment of crime, demonstrating the simultaneous tenuousness and importance of story to the understanding of human lives and futures.

Characters across Atwood's oeuvre regularly reflect upon the power of storytelling, often with reference to the detective genre. For example, in her short story collection *Moral Disorder* (2006), a teenaged Nell imagines how high school teachers develop the English curriculum, articulating a deeply perceptive understanding of the power of all literature, using the detective genre as a metonym:

> They [the teachers] knew something we needed to know, but it was a complicated thing—not so much a thing as a pattern, like the clues in a detective story once you started connecting them together. These women—these teachers—had no direct method of conveying this thing to us, not in a way that would make us listen, because it was too tangled, it was too oblique. It was hidden within the stories.
>
> *(75)*

This idea that truth is too complicated to be reduced to mere facts but must be contained within stories is as central to ustopia as it is to detective fiction. Throughout the MaddAddam trilogy, characters regularly acknowledge the gaps in their own knowledge and perspectives, raising the need for accompanying narratives. In *Oryx and Crake*, when Jimmy thinks he is the only human left on the planet, he nonetheless understands—or at least allows readers to understand—the limits of his perspective. Earlier, for example, in musing about his construction of Oryx, Jimmy engages in deep self-reflection:

> How long had it taken him to piece her [Oryx] together from the slivers of her he'd gathered and hoarded so carefully? There was Crake's story about her, and Jimmy's story about her as well, a more romantic

version; and then there was her own story about herself ... There must once have been other versions of her: her mother's story, the story of the man who'd bought her, the story of the man who'd bought her after that, and the third man's story—

(114)

The potentially infinite regress of story both paralyzes and energizes Jimmy, who takes great pleasure in language play before the pandemic, but who is rendered nearly powerless by the Crakers, an audience whose experience he cannot fully control because they have so little human context.

Toby, in her role as a wise woman storyteller, is equally aware of both the power and perils of storytelling in her narration of *The Year of the Flood* and *MaddAddam*. Like Jimmy, she acknowledges the inherent multiplicity of stories in any situation: "There's the story, then there's the real story, then there's the story of how the story came to be told. Then there's what you leave out of the story. Which is part of the story too" (*Madd* 56). Unlike Jimmy, however, Toby is able to find her way through the insight that language always conveys reality only incompletely. Wearing the red hat of "Snowman the Jimmy" and referring to his watch in her storytelling to the Crakers, Toby does not get derailed by the Crakers questioning her mythology. Rather, she is very soon able to anticipate the questions and objections her interlocutors might raise. For example, Toby knows she can use the word "important," since the Crakers have located it as "somewhere between dangerous and delicious" (105). This charming definition of a word English teachers sometimes circle (perhaps with the comment "important *how*?") speaks to an optimism that recalls the intersections of Margaret Atwood and George Orwell. In writing about her project in *The Handmaid's Tale* (1985), Atwood notes that her novel, like Orwell's *Nineteen Eighty-Four* (1949), uses an Afterword to limit the scope of her dystopian vision to a carefully bounded time and place; Gilead, like Newspeak, is constructed as a nightmarish moment in someone's past, although perhaps in our future if we are not careful (*In Other Worlds* 146). In "Politics and the English Language" (1946), Orwell notes the blandness of an English language treated in a tired, utilitarian way. By contrasting Jimmy's and Toby's interactions with the Crakers, Atwood embodies a post-apocalyptic language alive with possibility, as emblematized in the delicious dangers of the important.

Throughout the trilogy, the Crakers reveal much about the power of storytelling. Crake believes he has developed a species that will be more resilient because of its lack of interest in stories or myths. The novel shows repeatedly that story is fundamental to even posthuman life. *Oryx and Crake* is largely the story of Jimmy telling the story of the apocalypse to the Crakers, not only from his own limited perspective as a storyteller, but also toward what he sees as their limitations in comprehension. In the latter two novels, however, the trilogy moves beyond oral traditions and gestures toward the importance of print in not only preserving but also making possible human achievement. Toby and Ren both keep journals while they experience long solitary stints in the aftermath of the apocalypse; these journals hold meaning despite the fact that their writers cannot imagine anyone else ever having access to their words. Blackbeard, a Craker child, becomes a vehicle for showcasing writing as a technology with nearly magical properties. As a child, he is delighted by the ability of scrawled words on a page to make Ren say aloud what Toby has told him she is writing down. As an adult, he becomes his community's record-keeper, showing that just as the humans merge with the Crakers through the creation of new babies that typically represent hope at the end of a ustopian narrative, so too does Blackbeard's work as a scribe and composer of stories presage a viable future for both the Earth and its now much transformed most dominant species. Atwood does not include a detective who clearly places blame and ushers in a return of the status quo; rather, she uses the conventions of crime and detective fiction to provide an incisive critique of contemporary society while also gesturing to a forward-looking possibility of hope.

Conclusion

In *The Great Derangement*, Amitav Ghosh calls for new literary fiction that addresses head-on the existential threats of climate change, noting that much of the literature on this topic has been relegated to genre fiction, where climate change becomes, in the popular imagination, a science fiction trope analogous to time travel or alien invasion (7). As one of Canada's preeminent writers, Atwood would seem to fit the bill for producing literary fiction engaging with what is surely the most important topic of the twenty-first century. And yet, Atwood's trilogy is perhaps not a straightforward literary exploration in the vein Ghosh was imagining. *MaddAddam* is replete with genetic engineering advances and corporate structures whose naming conventions evoke golden-age science fiction tropes. It also draws upon the tropes of crime and detective fiction, using a Todorovian doubled narrative structure as well as a preponderance of games in figuring epistemological and ethical questions. This melding of genre fiction conventions with a literary style speaks, I think, to a certain earnest hope within Atwood's vision that captures something of the Canadian spirit in an era marked by both an unprecedented (although highly inequitable) standard of living for humans around the planet as well as an unprecedented threat to that fragile prosperity.

14
INTERPRETIVE MYSTERIES AND IMPOSSIBLE CRIMES IN EMILY ST. JOHN MANDEL'S SPECULATIVE FICTION

On the surface, science fiction and crime fiction seem to be at opposite ends of the genre fiction spectrum given their contrasting interactions with reality and with temporality. In terms of reality, crime fiction (which includes detective fiction, noir, and true crime) appears to be grounded in the realities of crime—why it is committed as well as how its perpetrators are detected and punished. Speculative fiction (which includes science fiction, fantasy, utopia, and dystopia) would appear to be much further from reality, with its creation of worlds outside—spatially and temporally—the one we currently inhabit. In terms of temporality, detective fiction, as described by Tzvetan Todorov and many critics of the genre to follow, is constructed around a dual narrative; the reader follows the story of the detective, whose job is to uncover a previous narrative, the narrative of the crime that is revealed. According to this formulation, detective fiction is, then, concerned largely with understanding and processing the past. Science fiction, on the other hand, as Isaac Asimov and other writers of the genre have long observed, is akin to the thought experiment in physics, a way to consider a new advance in science or technology and to ponder, predict, and play with attendant consequences on humans, on societies, and on ethical questions. It is, seemingly, fundamentally concerned with the future.

Questions of temporality and reality increasingly invite generic hybridity. As speculative fiction writer Ursula Le Guin has observed,

> The purpose of a thought-experiment, as the term was used by Schrödinger and other physicists, is not to predict the future—indeed

DOI: 10.4324/9781003125242-17

> Schrödinger's most famous thought experiment [i.e. Schrödinger's Cat] goes to show that the 'future,' on the quantum level, cannot be predicted—but to describe reality, the present world.
>
> *(Left Hand ii)*

Similarly, although the detective story is generally structured around the uncovering of a past narrative and often of a larger, sociocultural past identity, its rhetorical dimension is, like that of science fiction, often very much concerned with the present and even the future. As we examine the hybrid potentials of speculative fiction and crime fiction, I want to keep in mind possible continuities and dissonances at sites of reality and temporality, and to think about how a hybrid speculative crime work might represent the question of hope. It is for this reason that I end our exploration of Canadian crime fiction by turning to the gorgeous, immersive, crime-inflected tapestry of speculative fiction produced by Emily St. John Mandel in *Station Eleven* (2014), *The Glass Hotel* (2020), and *Sea of Tranquility* (2022).

Structurally, each of these novels centers a pair of characters around which the other characters form a loose constellation. In *Station Eleven*, we have Arthur Leander, a Shakespearean actor who dies on page 1 and yet is central to the rest of the novel, and Kirsten Raymonde, who witnesses Arthur's death and is the protagonist, 20 years later, of the post-apocalyptic portions of the novel. In *The Glass Hotel*, we have Jonathan Alkaitis, the international financier at the center of a massive Ponzi scheme, and Vincent Smith, who pretends to be his wife and whose death after Alkaitis's imprisonment leads to an ethically complex investigation. In *Sea of Tranquility*, we have Gaspery-Jacques Roberts, a twenty-fifth-century time traveler attempting to solve an existential mystery and Olive Llewellyn, a twenty-second-century novelist on a book tour during a pandemic. No character appears in all three novels, but several appear in two.

Thematically, Mandel draws upon tropes from crime and speculative fiction to propose, critique, and ultimately gift to the reader generative metaphors for approaching twenty-first-century life and its attendant anxieties. In *Station Eleven,* she uses a pandemic apocalyptic and post-apocalyptic scenario as a setting to consider at least three mysteries: who was Arthur Leander, who dies in the opening scene, and what did his life mean (what has his life meant)? How are members of a traveling Shakespearean troupe in a post-apocalyptic world disappearing during their travels when they are on high alert? And, existentially, what does it mean to survive? How important is art to the survival of the individual and of the species? In *The Glass Hotel*, Mandel uses a mainstream literary fiction style that almost conceals both its speculative and detective roots as it explores the pre-math, present-math, after-math, and alternate-math of a massive financial crime. Again, the mysteries are wide-ranging. Who knew about the Ponzi scheme and when did they know it? How did Vincent Smith come to die alone in the night on a container ship in the middle of the ocean (as narrated in the opening chapter)? How do some characters from *Station Eleven* appear in *The Glass Hotel* in a perfectly ordinary hyper-capitalist twenty-first century apparently unaffected by the Georgia flu pandemic that decimated this very civilization in the earlier novel? And finally, *Sea of Tranquility* presents a time travel narrative, complete with a Time Institute, and a time traveler who visits 1912, 1990, 2008, 2020, and 2203 from his time in 2401 in order to ravel and unravel these and other mysteries and to get to big questions that engage twenty-first-century global citizens: why are we so attracted to apocalyptic and post-apocalyptic narratives? What if we are living in a simulation? And, if we are, does it matter? Mandel's novels do not answer all the questions they pose. As crime and detective fiction moves into a time increasingly wary of epistemological certainty, I believe we will increasingly see narratives that leave unanswered questions and instead revel in the productive hybridities between the crime fiction and speculative fiction that Mandel espouses.

Setting the Post-apocalyptic (and Postmodern) Stage in *Station Eleven*

Station Eleven is a very special novel. It distinguishes itself from even the best apocalyptic and post-apocalyptic novels that kill over 99% of the human population in several ways: it does not narrate the most stressful, difficult, and often gruesome time immediately after the mass death event; it focuses on artists and documentarians in the post-apocalypse instead of on the tradespeople, agricultural workers, and engineers that are often centered in such stories; and it eschews linear narratives and solo heroes, instead moving often between pre-apocalyptic and post-apocalyptic timelines and among a loose constellation of characters. The unusual narrative structure embodies some of the epistemological changes one might expect after the apocalypse, when concepts like borders, capitalism, and temporality are no longer structuring metanarratives. In my opinion, though, what really distinguishes Mandel's approach to the apocalypse is something more ephemeral, more difficult to articulate. Pieter Vermeulen reaches for lofty terms in his otherwise deeply theoretical reading of the novel: "The tone of *Station Eleven* is composed, tender, and melancholy, and it studiously avoids shock and dread" (11). Matthew Leggatt concludes his carefully argued article on Mandel's ability to divide those who reach for nostalgia from those who reach for hope with a remarkably accurate but perhaps somewhat evanescent statement:

> Indeed, while *Station Eleven* may not offer up a blueprint for a utopian society ... I would suggest that it offers up the *feeling* that it's there, somewhere in the distance: that if we keep exploring, not just in a physical sense but in a personal one too, then we might just be the ones boarding the ship sailing towards "another world just out of sight" [the final line of *Station Eleven*].
>
> *(20, original emphasis)*

Station Eleven undertakes many of the same projects as the postmodern or metaphysical detective novel in inviting readers to thoroughly engage in meaning-making that disrupts well-known tropes and even epistemological frameworks. As such, the novel is enormously generative, and we see a broad swath of critical approaches, all finding ample evidence to support even contradictory readings. Does *Station Eleven* elevate Shakespeare or interrogate the widespread elevation of Shakespeare? Carmen Méndez-García persuasively reads the novel as conservative "in its approach to the canonicity and conservancy of certain cultural products" (124) and specifically declares: "I find the use of Shakespeare not only clichéd, but also deeply problematic" (115). Charles Conaway also persuasively analyzes passages where the novel "attributes to Shakespeare a therapeutic value that helps its characters (and us) work through traumatic experiences" (6) before equally persuasively arguing that the narrative momentum lies in the action of the post-apocalyptic segments more than in the Shakespearean portions (11). Indeed, Méndez-García, Conaway, and others who have delved into Mandel's interactions with Shakespeare (including Jones, Leggatt, and Vermeulen) attenuate their arguments substantially in order to accurately analyze the novel's often contradictory impulses. We see this also with the question of whether or not *Station Eleven* embodies the utopian impulses we sometimes see in apocalyptic literature, with its emphasis on revelation, from the Greek *apo* + *kaluptein* (uncover or reveal). Here we have Vermeulen's analysis of Mandel's often ekphrastic use of beauty and hope alongside Leggatt's reading steeped in utopian scholarship suggesting that yes, *Station Eleven* is a utopian text. However, equally compellingly, Kirsten Bussière asserts that the novel can be read as a "degenerative utopia" in which "selective remembering is partnered with forgetting in order to create a mythology that idealizes the world of the past" (271) and thus creates a dangerous nostalgia that prevents actual problem-solving toward change.

I will avoid weighing in on these fruitful debates—which are, even as I write this, generating more scholarship at all levels—in order to highlight a few insights that emerge from reading *Station Eleven* through the lens of crime and detective fiction. First, the trope that David Lehman calls "the corpse on page one" (2) may be repurposed in order to investigate new temporalities within crime-inflected speculative fiction. Secondly, those who deal with crime, inside or outside a state apparatus, are always marked by those encounters and may be able to manage their trauma in part by choosing to mark their own bodies. And thirdly (though surely not exhaustively), the texts we read—and the ways we read them—matter in conflicts between order and disorder, a central tenet of postmodern detective fiction.

Station Eleven opens with a Corpse on Page One, as Arthur Leander, aging Canadian movie star, dies of natural causes on the stage of a Toronto theater as he performs the title role in an experimental staging of *King Lear* that plays with issues of temporality by portraying Lear's daughters as little girls instead of as grown women. Unlike the usual Corpse on Page One, Arthur's dead body does not invite reader investigation in the style of the classical murder mystery. Here there is no murder, and moreover, had Arthur survived the performance, he would presumably have died within days from the Georgia flu, like most humans on the planet. Rather, Arthur's dead body leads to an in-novel reader investigation of how all the characters we meet, pre- and post-apocalypse, relate back to Arthur. More broadly, Arthur's death scene sets the stage for readers to engage in analysis of various aesthetic objects and representations.

The opening line of *Station Eleven* refers to Arthur: "The king stood in a pool of blue light, unmoored" (3). This may be read as synecdochic foreshadowing. The king, standing for the population at large, is unmoored by the artificial snow that is part of this experimental staging and, perhaps, as we are later to learn, by the ravages of celebrity culture to which Arthur is subjected throughout his career. As he clutches his chest, signaling a fatal heart attack, Arthur delivers an incorrect line: "Down from the waist they are centaurs" (3). Although Arthur's death while playing Lear changes little for Arthur, who was fated to die very shortly in the pandemic, this utterance invites readers to think through its resonances. A centaur can indicate hybridity, blending human and animal features, which could be linked to pandemic origins. It might also be read as meditating on the long reach of Greek mythology and perhaps even of the power of story. Arthur's death allows Jeevan to put into practice for the first and last time pre-pandemic his recent paramedic training, which gives him the confidence to become a post-apocalyptic doctor figure. It also allows Jeevan and Kirsten to meet, setting the stage for both of them to become post-apocalyptic characters. These consequences of Arthur's death on stage are not crucial to the plot of *Station Eleven*, but the first aesthetic moment of drama alerts readers to the importance of thinking through the many other aesthetic objects that swirl through this novel, including the many plays and pieces of classical music performed by the Traveling Symphony as well as the eponymous *Station Eleven* comic books and Kirsten's tattoos.

Kirsten's tattoos serve as important markers of meaning and self-identity. One is a line of text from a *Star Trek* episode that is also emblazoned on the Traveling Symphony caravan: "Because survival is insufficient." The others speak to the issue of trauma that has arisen repeatedly throughout our exploration of Canadian crime fiction. Kirsten has two black knives on her right wrist. These are first introduced by Kirsten's refusal to speak about them to François Diallo, a librarian who interviews her for a post-apocalyptic newspaper project:

DIALLO: Okay. All right. I'm curious about your tattoo.
RAYMONDE: The text on my arm? "Survival is insufficient"?
DIALLO: No, no, the other one. The two black knives on your right wrist.
RAYMONDE: You know what tattoos like this mean.
DIALLO: But perhaps you could just tell me—
RAYMONDE: I won't talk about it, François, and you know better than to ask.

(132)

The knife tattoos, we eventually learn, signal the lives taken by any person. Kirsten's refusal to discuss them—and her indignation at Diallo's question—speaks to the unspeakable trauma contained within the symbol. Although the tattoos might be read as having pragmatic value, indicating to others that Kirsten is capable of self-defense, they are never described that way in the narrative. When Kirsten realizes that her friend August has killed for the first time, she thinks about how he will be altered: "She could have told him what she knew: It is possible to survive this but not unaltered, and you will carry these men with you through all the nights of your life" (296). The tattoos, then, act as a physical reminder—and a dangerous one to produce, given the lack of antibiotics 20 years after the pandemic—of the cost of survival, to the self as well as to others. They might also be seen as a way of choosing to mark and frequently be reminded of a trauma that is unspeakable but not unrepresentable.

The most traumatic moment narrated in the novel is also a moment of contradictory epistemological frames and, in an odd, ineffable way, of beauty. Throughout the novel, Kirsten treasures two graphic novels given to her by Arthur Leander: "*Dr. Eleven*, Vol. I, No. I: *Station Eleven* and

Dr. Eleven, Vol. I, No. 2: *The Pursuit*" (42). Although *Dr. Eleven* is a self-published venture that is never to move beyond its initial printing of ten copies, it has by novel's end acquired an outsized impact on the small world of the Traveling Symphony's territory. In a climactic scene, Kirsten faces a young man who calls himself "the prophet" and his teen acolyte. As the prophet prepares to execute Kirsten for allegedly having interfered with his plans to marry a 12-year-old who stowed away with the Symphony, he does not reach for lines from his dog-eared Bible, but instead quotes lines from *Station Eleven*. In this moment, Kirsten has a near-death experience typical to fictional detectives, who often face an antagonist without benefit of a weapon, expecting to die. This familiar scene is recast by Mandel through her apocalyptic (revelatory) focus on aesthetics:

> "This world," the prophet said, "is an ocean of darkness."
>
> She [Kirsten] was astonished to see that the boy with the handgun was crying, his face wet. If she could only speak to August. We traveled so far and your friendship meant everything. It was very difficult, but there were moments of beauty. Everything ends. I am not afraid.
>
> *(302)*

This is a familiar trope of detective fiction, wherein the detective faces the killer's gun and regrets the inability to communicate an important message—usually the killer's identity—to the outside world. For Kirsten, though, the message is one of acceptance steeped in aesthetic appreciation. She has fully assimilated and lived the idea that survival is insufficient, and her friendships and love of beauty have prepared her to face death unafraid.

In addition to providing her with a post-apocalyptic perspective on death, Kirsten's love of the *Station Eleven* graphic novels also gives her an unexpected practical tool for surviving her encounter with the prophet. Like a detective in such a situation, she tries to keep the conversation going. Recognizing the lines quoted by the prophet, Kirsten responds in kind, as if citing shared scripture: "We dream of sunlight, we dream of walking the Earth," she says, referring to the characters in the post-apocalyptic *Station Eleven* novels, who live in the Undersea, far from the Earth. "We have been lost for so long .... We long only for the world we were born into" (302). The boy with the gun, with tears on his cheeks, nods at Kirsten's recitation and acts decisively, shooting first the prophet and then, over Kirsten's desperate protests, himself. The prophet has taken from his reading (of the Bible and perhaps also of *Station Eleven*) the nostalgically facing message that he should consolidate power and rule the people of the area while taking on multiple child brides. Kirsten has taken the idea that longings for the past must be tempered by a recognition that the Earth of the past no longer exists, thus leaving an appreciation of history, but also of sunlight and of beauty in its myriad forms.

Kirsten and the other members of the Traveling Symphony are saved by the *Station Eleven*-mediated encounter with the comic-book quoting prophet, but the tragedy of this outcome is not ignored. When Kirsten and her group arrive at the Museum of Civilization (previously the Severn City Airport), Kirsten soon asks if there is a tattooist at the museum; she needs to mark her responsibility for the prophet's death on her body, since this third killing once again fundamentally changes who she is. At the Museum, which gathers artifacts from the pre-apocalyptic world, Kirsten makes a contribution that limns together pre- and post-apocalypse. She leaves one of the *Station Eleven* graphic novels at the museum with the expectation that she will pick it up next time the Traveling Symphony passes through. The graphic novel, written and self-published before the pandemic, has also had a climactic impact on the post-pandemic world, and thus exists as a sort of bridge between the two worlds. As a fictional text within a fictional text, it will also be recast by Mandel's next two novels as a possible bridge to even more than temporal worlds.

Alternate Realities in *The Glass Hotel*

Crime fiction has long centered murder, at least since W.H. Auden wrote in 1948,

> Murder is unique in that it abolishes the party it injures, so that society has to take the place of the victim and on his behalf demand restitution or grant forgiveness; it is the one crime in which society has a direct interest.
>
> *(557)*

The Glass Hotel, from its liminal position between crime and speculative fiction, examines an enormous crime other than murder: Jonathan Alkaitis's international Ponzi scheme, exposed on the day of the Christmas party of 2008, which will recall Bernie Madoff's $64.8 billion scheme, also revealed in December 2008. Like Atwood, Mandel is not concerned with solving the crime, but with understanding its impacts, not only on characters' lives but also on their views of reality.

The Ponzi scheme has devastating impacts on many characters. Alkaitis's daughter is left heartbroken. Alkaitis's employees experience the brutality of prison life, and the one who flees the country continues to fear arrest even years later. Some of Alkaitis's investors die by suicide, while others lose their homes and live or die in straightened circumstances. At the same time, the Ponzi scheme and its aftermath also highlights insights that would not otherwise be evident. A particularly innovative segment of the novel is the "Office Chorus," narrated by an unnamed character who is part of the Alkaitis team. This character sees value in a comment by their co-worker Oskar, who is derided by others:

> "It's possible to both know and not know something," he [Oskar] said later, under cross-examination, and the state tore him to pieces over this but he spoke for several of us, actually, several of us who'd been thinking a great deal about that doubleness, that knowing and not knowing, being honorable and not being honorable, knowing you're not a good person but trying to be a good person regardless around the margins of the bad.
> (168)

The double has long been used to figure the ethical nuances that often provide the narrative and philosophical momentum of detective fiction, as discussed at some length in earlier chapters (for example, Chapters 2 and 10). Here, Mandel explicitly evokes a sense of duality in the criminal rather than the detective, a move consonant with her interest in always exploring the less commonly considered side of an issue or convention, such as the aesthetic side of a post-apocalyptic world in *Station Eleven*. She shows here that the idea of doubleness in a character's epistemology—knowing and not knowing at once—is derided by logic, as represented by the legal apparatus of the state. And yet, it may nonetheless have substantial truth value, especially in a world in which assets are increasingly abstracted from objects with use value.

As Oskar later reflects upon the pleasures of working on Floor 17, where the Ponzi scheme was operationalized, he muses about "the edges of reality itself," asking, "was there any difference, actually, in the grand universal scheme of things, between a trade that had actually occurred and a trade that *appeared* to have occurred on Oskar's impeccably formatted account statements?" (194). This question is delightful from the perspective of postmodern slipperiness of meaning. Pragmatically, it is terrifying. What is a trade, really? It is a communication certainly not backed by any object of value in a Ponzi scheme, but arguably also not backed by an object of value since the United States, whose dollar serves as the world's reserve currency, left the gold standard in 1971. A Ponzi scheme has real victims, and Mandel shows us several of them. But a Ponzi scheme would not be possible in the world of *Station Eleven*, where characters' sense of reality is restored by their—often terrifying—nearness to their means of survival. *The Glass Hotel*, whose eponymous structure contains inhabitants of "the Country of Money" as well as a largely invisible staff, highlights the difficulty of twenty-first-century reality in a global, hyper-capitalist world.

The Glass Hotel is haunted by ghosts that abut and challenge the neoliberal epistemology of a world dominated by a Ponzi scheme. Oskar repeatedly places the language of science fiction alongside that of the gothic when he imagines alternate versions of his life. As he prepares for an FBI raid, Oskar imagines: "In the ghost version of his life, the parallel-universe version in which he'd gone to the FBI" (212) and "In a parallel version of events he might have run, and in his ghost life, his honorable life, his non-Ponzi life, he was never here at all" (215). The narrative also brings up the concept of the ghost metaphorically when the judge sentences Alkaitis to 170 years in prison:

> "This is academic," the judge had said, "but I'm required for technical reasons to impose a period of supervised release following your sentence." Idea for a ghost story: there once was a man who remained under supervised release for three years following the end of his 170-year prison term. Idea for a ghost story: there once was a woman who drifted unseen through the city of New York until she faded into the crowds and the heat.
>
> *(221)*

The ghostly woman drifting through New York refers to Vincent Smith, Alkaitis' life partner and the most common focalization for the reader. Both ideas—the speculative ghostly parolee and the ordinary ghostly woman—embody alternate realities that highlight the fragility of the concept of a single, impenetrable shared reality.

In a sense, *The Glass Hotel* itself can be read as a ghost version of *Station Eleven*. Indeed, *Station Eleven* invites such a reading when Kirsten and Auguste are separated from the Traveling Symphony and discuss alternate worlds through the frame of what Auguste calls "multiple universes" (199) or "parallel universes" (200–3) and what Kirsten calls "the other, shadow life" (201). Vincent, in *The Glass Hotel*, almost seems to pick up on that conversation from the earlier novel when she is in a boutique in New York:

> Imagining an alternate reality where there was no Iraq War, for example, or where the terrifying new swine flu in the Republic of Georgia hadn't been swiftly contained; an alternate world where the Georgia flu blossomed into an unstoppable pandemic and civilization collapsed.
>
> *(67)*

Vincent is thus signaling to readers a tenuous yet significant connection between novels, since her pandemic-free life shows that, absent the Georgia flu pandemic that creates the world of *Station Eleven*, life would continue along, with dinner parties and shopping trips and a devastating Ponzi scheme orchestrated by someone who appears to be living the American Dream. Vincent's "alternate reality" or "variation of reality" has its limits: "She could only play this game for so long before she was overcome by a kind of vertigo and had to make herself stop" (67). Vertigo—a feeling that brings together the cognitive and the physical—represents well the sensation that can accompany reading postmodern fiction. It also acts for Vincent as a signal that she should rein in her existential contemplations.

Within *The Glass Hotel*, however, with all its apparent realism, alternate realities cannot always be controlled. Vincent is able to easily extricate herself from Alkaitis after he is arrested for the Ponzi scheme; although they refer to each other as husband and wife, and even wear wedding rings, Alkaitis and the much younger Vincent have never married or shared finances. Against the backdrop of accusations that she must have known of her husband's criminal activity, at least at some level, Vincent recreates herself by leaving New York City to become a cook on a container ship, where she spends the second half of her twenties, apparently quite happy. In an odd twist, Vincent then moves to the center of an investigation, this time as the victim of an unexplained death at sea. This investigation involves two characters from *Station Eleven*. Miranda Carroll, author of the self-published *Dr. Eleven* comic books who died on a beach in Malaysia of the Georgia flu, is, in *The Glass Hotel*, a shipping executive concerned that one of the company's employees, Vincent Smith, will not get a full investigation into her death because it occurred in international waters. Leon Prevant, Miranda's boss in *Station Eleven* and presumably also a victim of the Georgia flu, is, in *The Glass Hotel*, a victim of the Alkaitis Ponzi scheme and thus delighted to get some freelance work as part of the Vincent Smith investigation. In the end, though, Leon sees the investigation as an exercise in corruption. At the end of the interviews of Vincent's friends and coworkers, Leon and his co-investigator learn, off the record, that Vincent's current boyfriend has a history of violence against women, making him a suspect in her death. The co-investigator insists they not include this detail in their report, arguing that the evidence is insufficient, the company will be hurt by the suspicions, and Leon is unlikely to get further work with such a report. Reluctantly, Leon agrees to the co-instigator's justification that Vincent's death was just as likely accidental given her predilection for taking videos of the ocean, even during stormy weather. Leon is left with the impression of having participated in a corrupt investigation.

In a world of greed, corruption, alternate reality, and cover-up, Vincent's story—and specifically her death—ends up raising epistemological and ethical questions unavailable to the characters but presented to the reader. Vincent's death, which frames the novel, is not in fact a murder, despite the circumstantial evidence collected by Leon and the other investigator. Their plausible story to protect the corporation is in fact the truth. Vincent has died in pursuit of her art, while filming an especially dangerous and spectacular sea. At the same time, she also dies because one of the alternate realities that infuse the novel impacts her reality. Vincent loses focus on her perilous project when she sees the ghost of Olivia Collins, one of Alkaitis's victims:

> There's an impression of a hand on the railing, a silhouette, and then Olivia Collins is standing beside me [Vincent] at the bow, looking down at the water. She looks much younger than she did the last time I saw her, also less substantial. The rain falls through her. I'm still holding my camera over the railing. I can't breathe.
>
> *(297)*

Is Olivia's ghost real? Or as "real" as a ghost in a book of fiction can be? Within the framework of the novel, does a specter appear to Vincent? Or is she a manifestation of Vincent's guilty conscience? To this point, the reader does not know that Vincent has anything to be guilty about. But as Vincent goes over the side of the ship, weightless, she "can move between memories like walking from one room to the next—" (4) as she tells us in the opening chapter, the only other first-person chapter in the novel. She moves to the memory of a scene we have seen before, where one of Alkaitis's friends and investors makes a sly reference to the Ponzi scheme under cover of discussing a musician who does not recognize opportunity. The investor smirks, but now we see from Vincent's first-person dying memory: "He knew, but of course, I knew too, if not the details of the scheme then the fact that there *was* a scheme" (300).

Vincent, like Oskar, who both knew and didn't know, has access to and even ownership of knowledge that she chose not to interrogate too closely. As the reader has followed her closely throughout this journey, perhaps we too have such knowledge—of genocides on the other side of the world, of the impending climate crisis, etc. The apparent interruption of reality by ghosts—of conscience or supernatural—while explaining an accidental death and not a murder, creates a duality of uncertainty at the sites of knowledge, morality, and complicity. Delightfully, and perhaps dreadfully, this duality is to be revisited and even intensified in the simultaneously more and less realistic novel, *Sea of Tranquility*, which might encourage us to recall the king who stood, unmoored, at the opening of *Station Eleven*.

Impossible Crimes in *Sea of Tranquility*

There is a moment early in *Sea of Tranquility* when two characters from *The Glass Hotel* appear: Vincent Smith and Mirella Kessler. The first time I read *Sea*, I felt a shock of pleasure at this. I would get to spend more time with a beloved character whose death was narrated—multiple times—in a previous novel. With this came a postmodern frisson of recognition. No fictional character can ever die because they were never alive and because a reader can always go back to them and encounter them in print. And yet, the appearance of Vincent and Mirella in a future novel feels more satisfying to me than would this appearance if I were rereading a previous novel. In an odd way, it feels more real, even though the explanation of how Vincent can reappear lies within an epistemology not of science but of science fiction: through time travel and/or the simulation hypothesis. Indeed, *Sea of Tranquility* centers on two characters separated by time and space: Olive Llewellyn, a twenty-second-century novelist from the second moon colony (Colony Two) who travels to Earth for a book tour, and Gaspery-Jacques Roberts, a twenty-fifth-century time traveler who grew up on the same street as Olive's childhood home, and who is now investigating an anomaly in an attempt to gather data for or against the simulation hypothesis.

The simulation hypothesis, based on skepticism of the very foundation of reality, provides yet another epistemological frame that invites readers to reconsider what they think they know—of past novels and perhaps even of the world. Within the novel, it is Gaspery's sister Zoey, a physicist, who explains, in 2401:

> Think of how holograms and virtual reality have evolved, even just in the past few years. If we can run fairly convincing simulations of reality now, think of what those simulations will be like in a century or two. The idea with the simulation hypothesis is, we can't rule out the possibility that all of reality is a simulation.
>
> *(111)*

Zoey does not mention Nick Bostrom's work on the simulation hypothesis from 2003 (sensible, since it's 400 years later!), but her futuristic approach to the question has not changed much. Bostrom makes the argument that the odds are quite high that humans experiencing the world in 2003 are actually living in a computer simulation devised by a more advanced civilization of the future. Bostrom, much like the fictional Zoey, notes rapid recent advances in computing when he asserts:

> One thing that later generations might do with their super-powerful computers is run detailed simulations of their forebears or of people like their forebears. Because their computers would be so powerful, they could run a great many such simulations.
>
> *(243)*

Furthermore, Bostrom asks us to "Suppose that these simulated people are conscious (as they would be if the simulations were sufficiently finegrained and if a certain quite widely accepted position in the philosophy of mind is correct)," suggesting that the odds are higher we are among these simulated beings rather than being original humans (243). This idea brings increased intellectual vertigo for readers. Without *Sea of Tranquility*, the fictional characters in two different novels can be victims of both a pandemic (*Station Eleven*) and of a massive Ponzi scheme (*The Glass Hotel*). By introducing the Simulation Hypothesis in *Sea of Tranquility*, though, Mandel is opening up the possibility that the novels are different versions of the simulation (as are, perhaps, the various alternate versions imagined by characters), again providing a postmodern frisson that might invite readers to wonder if other versions of themselves are reading other versions of Mandel novels in other simulations.

Like the reader, Gaspery struggles to process the idea of the Simulation Hypothesis. When he learns that his sister has tracked an inexplicable glitch in some historical videos and suspects it might be evidence of the simulation hypothesis, his musings may be relatable to any reader who has ever questioned the nature of reality:

> How do you investigate reality? My hunger is a simulation, I told myself, but I wanted a cheeseburger. Cheeseburgers are a simulation. Beef is a simulation. (Actually, that was literally true. Killing an animal for food would get you arrested both on Earth and in the Colonies).
>
> *(130)*

In a futuristic world in which meat is a pre-climate-crisis luxury, the "real" is an increasingly slippery concept, regardless of whether the characters are actually living in a simulation. This echoes the musings of Oskar in *The Glass Hotel* when he reflects that there may not be much difference between "a trade that had actually occurred and a trade that *appeared* to have occurred" (194) given that both exist in a kind of virtuality that interrogates the nature of money vis-à-vis "the real."

The three novels increasingly lean into postmodern skepticism about the nature of reality and perhaps especially the idea that the nature of reality can be known and understood. This is accomplished with a postmodern playfulness that revels in metafictional slippages when *Sea of Tranquility* moves, in Part 5 of 8, to "Last Book Tour on Earth, 2203," which features as its main character the female author of a pandemic novel written before a real-world pandemic, and thus in exactly the position of Emily St. John Mandel, another female author of a pandemic novel (*Station Eleven*) now writing *Sea of Tranquility* in advance of publication in 2022. Here again, Mandel centers questions of reality in a way relatable to her readers, especially in or just after the covid pandemic of 2020–2023. In a frisson-inducing segment about the details of home life during a pandemic-induced lockdown, Olive and her husband Dion both work from home, staggering their shifts so they can supervise virtual schooling and attempt responsible parenting for their young daughter. They both spend hours a day in holospace, "where one could transport oneself into a strange silvery-black digital room and converse there with flickering simulations of one's colleagues" (181). Olive and Dion have a conversation familiar to many of us who were lucky enough to experience extensive lockdown instead of the health ravages of the covid pandemic:

> "I don't know why it's so tiring," he said. "So much more tiring than normal meetings, I mean."
> "I think it's because it isn't real." It was very late, and they were standing by the living room windows together, looking down at the deserted street.
> "Maybe you're right. Turns out reality is more important than we thought," Dion said.
>
> *(181–2)*

Dion's statement is both flip and profound, as evidenced by Gaspery's continued investigations as well as, quite possibly, the reader's own experiences. The importance of reality—and specifically of "in-real-life" human interactions has been an ongoing question in workplaces around the world as we grapple with the impacts of not only the covid pandemic but also the shift to virtual work. What does it mean to move from the real world to the virtual workplace? The new modality is initially more exhausting, as Dion notes, but does it make the work—and the worker—less real? And, given the Simulation Hypothesis, does it perhaps flirt a little too closely with the very concept of the "real"?

As Olive moves through the book tour and the virus of 2203 becomes more concerning, her experiences join with Mandel's. Olive's novel,

Marionbad, includes a character named Gaspery-Jacques with a meaningful line of text tattooed on his left arm: "We knew it was coming." This recalls Kirsten's tattoo, "Survival is insufficient," which one of my former students had tattooed on his arm after we read *Station Eleven* in class. Olive meets readers who show her their tattoos and she is emotionally—and perhaps epistemologically—overcome:

> You write a book with a fictional tattoo and then the tattoo becomes real in the world and after that almost anything seems possible. She'd seen five of those tattoos, but that didn't make it less extraordinary, seeing the way fiction can bleed into the world and leave a mark on someone's skin. *(91)*

This is another musing on the nature of reality. For Mandel—as for many twenty-first-century producers and consumers of art—fiction is more than entertainment. It is a way of knowing, an epistemological frame that delivers truth if not facts (to use William Faulkner's famous formulation). "Survival is insufficient" is a truth. It is a reference to *Star Trek*, a pop culture product so committed to utopian ideals that some writers found it difficult to write for (Dyson 87). "We knew it was coming" cannot be so neatly referenced. It is a truth about many things, including Ponzi schemes and the climate crisis. It is also, subtly, a condemnation of the human ability to know and not know something at the same time, again extending an insight about reader complicity from *The Glass Hotel*.

The existential darkness of simultaneously knowing and not knowing is juxtaposed to an oddly hopeful exploration of future crime. In the twenty-fifth century, Gaspery commits a crime that does not exist within today's legal code because it is not part of our present understanding of the world. Gaspery saves life during time travel. In *Sea of Tranquility*, as in most time-travel novels, this is a horrifying crime because it threatens the timelines and therefore the reality of the characters in the future. It is also a very tempting crime, and Zoey worries from the start that her brother may be unable to prevent himself from doing it. Gaspery is punished for his crime by imprisonment—not in the twenty-fifth century but in the twenty-first—a neat trick organized by the Time Institute that effectively prevents bad time travelers (by nature good people) from doing further damage. In a review of *Sea of Tranquility* that praises Mandel's prose and insight, Constance Grady criticizes the facile nature of the time travel plot, arguing that the

> [Time travel] mystery's resolution, which forms the emotional fulcrum of this novel, is so pat and cliched that if I were to describe even

just the setup in this review, you would know immediately how it all worked out.

I would not disagree that Mandel relies upon familiar tropes of time travel paradoxes. At the same time, I see this as a strength rather than a weakness. Temporality, like the nature of reality, is a metanarrative under pressure in the twenty-first century, especially in the very same popular literature that treats questions about possible apocalyptic scenarios. Using a familiar trope to examine a crime born of kindness is an important part of Mandel's project.

In the end, *Sea of Tranquility* grounds the reader in an ethics of hope. After Gaspery is rescued from prison by his sister and is secreted in a time and place unsuspected by the Time Institute, he finds himself happy—a farmer who loves his wife and his violin. He reflects:

> This is what the Time Institute never understood: if definitive proof emerges that we're living in a simulation, the correct response to that news will be *So what*. A life lived in a simulation is still a life.
>
> *(246)*

In the end, Gaspery realizes that his return to the past where he has now lived most of his life—rather than in the timeline of his birth—gives him the important perspective that closes the novel:

> In those streets everyone moved faster than me, but what they didn't know was that I had already moved too fast, too far, and wished to travel no farther. I've been thinking a great deal about time and motion lately, about being a still point in the ceaseless rush.
>
> *(255)*

Conclusion

In *Sea of Tranquility*, Olive has many conversations that speak to the absurdity and beauty of life and art, a theme that weaves through the three novels. My favorite occurs in Cincinnati, when she and the local library director are discussing the new pandemic with rising anxiety until the director abruptly changes the subject:

> "Let me tell you something magnificent about this place," she said.
> "Oh, please do," Olive said. "It's been a while since anyone's told me anything magnificent."

> "So we don't own the building," the director said, "but we hold a ten-thousand-year lease on the space."
> "You're right. That's magnificent."
> "Nineteenth-century hubris. Imagine thinking civilization still exists in ten thousand years. But there's more." She leaned forward, pausing for effect. "The lease is renewable."
>
> *(82–3)*

The Cincinnati library lease recalls the 170-year-long sentence (with arrangements for parole) from *The Glass Hotel*. It also speaks to the human mind's difficulty of conceptualizing scope, as well as to how rapid technological advancements in the twentieth and twenty-first centuries have raised a cultural sense of anxiety or even dread about the future. What the librarian characterizes as nineteenth-century hubris could just as easily be described as optimism—an optimism evident in the utopian writings of European and North American thinkers, but no longer available to twenty-first-century readers let alone twenty-third-century characters.

In Mandel's innovative blending of speculative fiction tropes including apocalypse, alternate reality, ghosts, time travel, and even the simulation hypothesis, we find a powerful new hybridity that centers representational and existential mysteries, a seldom narrated financial crime, and a crime that will be impossible until we have time travel. By placing the epistemological and ethical questions central to the detective genre (how do we understand the various forces associated with a crime? How do we assign guilt? How do we move forward—personally and culturally—after a disturbance to law and order?) in conversation with the different and related questions addressed by speculative fiction (including the central interrogation: what does it mean to be human?), Mandel expands crime fiction in powerful ways. She showcases the potential of speculative and crime fiction to engage deeply with contemporary cultural anxieties, and also represents the possibility of writing new histories and futures. It is with optimism that I posit the idea that Mandel's swirling, tentative, sometimes contradictory approach to storytelling represents an exciting, frightening, activist, and absolutely generative direction for the future of Canadian crime fiction.

GLOSSARY OF PEOPLE AND TERMS

People

Margaret Atwood (b. 1939). Canadian writer from Ontario known for fiction (*Handmaid's Tale, Oryx and Crake*), nonfiction, and poetry. Atwood has won numerous national and international awards including two Booker Prizes, the Governor General's Award, and the PEN Center USA Lifetime Achievement Award. She showcases her activism through fiction, and uses detective and speculative tropes in much of her literary fiction.

Paul Auster (b. 1947). American writer of literary fiction whose *New York Trilogy* (1987) stands as a prototypical postmodern detective novel.

Linwood Barclay (b. 1955). American-born Canadian writer of thrillers who sets most of his novels in the US. Originally a journalist and humor columnist in Ontario, Barclay is concerned with the decline in traditional media and the rise of social media that can lead to mis- and disinformation.

Anthony Bidulka (b. 1962). Canadian writer from Saskatchewan who won a Lambda Literary Award (for LGBTQ+ excellence) for a novel featuring Russell Quant, a Saskatchewan private investigator. His novels often feature travel and bring a cozy sensibility to the hardboiled.

Giles Blunt (b. 1952). Canadian writer from Ontario who has lived in and written about the Near North. Best-known for his award-winning John Cardinal series, Blunt has also written screenplays including episodes for *Law & Order* as well as his own *Cardinal* series (four seasons).

Gail Bowen (b. 1942). Canadian writer born in Ontario but most associated with Saskatchewan, where she has lived her adult life and sets her Joanne Kilbourn novels. Bowen was an English professor at the First Nations University of Canada in Regina, Saskatchewan. In addition to writing over twenty novels, six of which have been adapted for TV, she has also written a number of plays.

Pamela Callow. Canadian writer from Halifax who is a non-practicing member of the Nova Scotia bar and has written a series of legal thrillers featuring Kate Lange, a fictional female lawyer who survives many traumas as she undertakes informal detective work as part of her legal work.

Raymond Chandler (1888–1959). American writer of hardboiled detective fiction whose detective character, Philip Marlowe, was central in establishing the conventions of the hardboiled genre. Chandler's essay, "The Simple Art of Murder" (1944) remains a central critical statement on the hardboiled detective figure as well as the genre.

Leonard Cohen (1934–2016). Canadian singer-songwriter, poet, and novelist. Born in Quebec, he has received national accolades such as induction into the Canadian Music Hall of Fame and the Canadian Songwriter Hall of Fame, as well as international recognition through induction in the Rock & Roll Hall of Fame. His song "Anthem" (1992) provides a metaphor—"there is a crack in everything, it's how the light gets in"—that I see as key to understanding Canadian crime fiction.

Arthur Conan Doyle (1859–1930). British writer who created Sherlock Holmes and cemented many of the conventions of detective fiction in the public imagination, including the neurodivergent detective, the use of forensics in detection, the fraught relationship between police and private detectives, and the detective sidekick.

C. Auguste Dupin (nineteenth century). Fictional detective who appears in Edgar Allan Poe's three detective short stories, generally considered the first of the genre. A Parisian aristocrat in reduced circumstances, Dupin uses "ratiocination" (reasoning) to get into the mind of the criminal. He introduces several conventions of detective fiction, including the gothic in detective fiction, the object hiding in plain sight, the detective sidekick, and the dark double.

Timothy Findley (1930–2002). Canadian writer from Ontario whose literary fiction has garnered many awards, including a Governor General's Award, the Canadian Authors' Association Award, and the Ontario Trillium Award. His single foray into detective fiction, *The*

Telling of Lies (1986) won an Edgar Award and stands as an exemplar of Canadian postmodern detective fiction.

Dashiell Hammett (1894–1961). American hardboiled detective fiction writer whose most famous detective characters—Sam Spade and the Continental Op—helped to establish many of the conventions of the hardboiled genre that are still deployed by writers of private eye detective fiction from around the world.

Sherlock Holmes (nineteenth century and beyond). Created by Arthur Conan Doyle in 1887, Holmes remains the prototypical fictional detective. Characterized by his extraordinary skills of observation and deduction, Holmes has been continually reshaped and re-represented across various times, places, and media.

Ausma Zehanat Khan. British-born American-Canadian writer of detective fiction and speculative fiction. A lawyer and law professor, Khan was also editor-in-chief of *Muslim Girl* magazine. Her Esa Khattak and Rachel Getty police procedural series has received much acclaim for its representation of diversity and multiculturalism, and the first novel in the series, *The Unquiet Dead* (2015), has been honored with the Arthur Ellis Award and the Barry Award.

Thomas King (b. 1943). American-Canadian writer, professor, and activist whose literary and critical work on First Nations has garnered many awards, including membership in the Order of Canada, the Governor General's Award, and the Stephen Leacock Memorial Medal for Humor. King's Thumps DreadfulWater detective series combines humor and trauma to showcase the importance of community to the telling of thoughtful and compelling stories.

Ross Macdonald (1915–1983). Pseudonym used by Kenneth Millar, the American-Canadian writer of hardboiled fiction whose detective novels featuring Lew Archer helped to establish many of the conventions of the hardboiled, especially the inclusion of the psychological dimension.

Hugh MacLennan (1907–1990). Canadian writer and professor who was born in Nova Scotia and is often associated with Quebec, where he taught at McGill University. MacLennan's novel *Two Solitudes* (1945) provided a model of English and French Canada as two highly separate entities that was highly influential in the twentieth century. He won many prestigious awards, including five Governor General's Awards.

Emily St. John Mandel (b. 1979). Canadian novelist and magazine writer from British Columbia who now lives in New York City. Her speculative fiction includes innovative detective elements and has garnered awards, including the Arthur C. Clarke Award, the Toronto Book Award, and the Prix des Librairies du Québec.

Ed McBain (1926–2005). Pseudonym used by Evan Hunter, born Salvatore Lombino, the American writer of the 87th Precinct novel series that set many of the conventions of the police procedural, including simultaneous ongoing investigations, the use of the detective team, and the focus on police bureaucracy and politics.

John McFetridge (b. 1959). Canadian writer born in Quebec who has set detective series in Montreal, Quebec and Toronto, Ontario. A TV and novel writer, McFetridge brings a fictional approach to thinking through compelling moments of Canadian history.

Robert B. Parker (1932–2010). American hardboiled writer who built upon the conventions developed by Raymond Chandler, Dashiell Hammett, and Ross MacDonald in the early and mid-twentieth century to bring the hardboiled to the East Coast (Boston) in the late twentieth century.

Louise Penny (b. 1958). Canadian writer born in Ontario who was a radio host and journalist with the Canadian Broadcasting Corporation (CBC) before becoming a full-time writer. A member of the Order of Canada and the Order of Quebec, Penny sets her Three Pines detective series in a utopian village in southern Quebec. She has also co-written a political thriller, *State of Terror* (2021) with former US Secretary of State Hillary Clinton.

Edgar Allan Poe (1809–1849). American writer known for his contributions to horror, science fiction, and detective fiction. Poe's three Dupin stories—"The Murders in the Rue Morgue" (1841), "The Mystery of Marie Rogêt" (1842), and "The Purloined Letter" (1844)—are widely considered the first modern detective stories.

Peter Robinson (1950–2022). British-born Canadian writer and professor who lived much of his adult life in Ontario. Robinson's most famous detective series, featuring Inspector Alan Banks, is set in Yorkshire, England and has won numerous awards, including multiple Arthur Ellis Awards, Edgar Awards, Martin Beck Awards, and Macavity Awards. Robinson received the Grand Master Award from Crime Writers of Canada, and several of his novels were adapted in the *DCI Banks* series (2010–2016).

Carol Shields (1935–2003). American-born Canadian writer and professor who lived in Ontario, Manitoba, and British Columbia at various times. Shields won numerous awards for her literary fiction, including the Governor General's Award, the National Book Critics Circle Award, and the Pulitzer Prize. Her postmodern detective novel, *Swann* (1987), presents a team of academics as detectives and leaves many questions unanswered.

Terms

Anthropocene Our current geological age, the period characterized by humans influencing the environment enough to constitute a distinct geological separation from the Holocene. Twenty-first-century writers in all genres must contend with the epistemological and ethical questions raised by debates around whether or not to recognize the Anthropocene.

Armchair Detective Likely originating from Sherlock Holmes' description of his brother Mycroft in the short story "The Adventure of the Greek Interpreter" (1893), this term refers to a detective who solves the case by working through the clues as reported and without leaving their chair.

Bloc Québécois A federal political party founded in 1991 that advocates for Quebec to separate from Canada. Often but not always a major political party, the Bloc campaigns only in Quebec. It is informally allied to the Parti Québécois, a provincial party.

Cozy A subgenre of detective fiction, typically featuring a female amateur detective living in a small town with a strong network of friends and/or family. There is no graphic violence, but there may be incisive analysis of social issues. This subgenre has only recently begun to receive substantial critical attention.

Crime Fiction An umbrella term that once referred to fiction from the criminal's point of view, most prominently *noir* fiction. More recently, it is used to incorporate detective fiction, *noir*, the thriller, and even true crime. This move in naming conventions acknowledges increasing hybridity in popular genres.

Cultural Mosaic A metaphor used to describe Canada's commitment to multiculturalism, where new immigrants to the country keep their cultural practices, forming a mosaic of different beliefs and traditions. This is in contrast to the idea of American assimilation or the "melting pot," a contrast that has been interrogated.

Detective Fiction A type of fiction that presents a mystery (usually containing the crime of murder) and a detective figure who follows clues and almost certainly provides the solution to the mystery by story's end.

Dime Novel A kind of cheap fiction published in the US between 1860 and 1917. Detective narratives flourished within this publishing medium in the US (and within *feuilletons* in France and **penny dreadfuls** in the UK).

Doppelgänger The German word for *double-walker*, this term is often used in cultural studies to refer simply to a "double," or a person who very closely resembles another. Within crime fiction, doubling often occurs between the detective and criminal, sometimes mundanely with the detective doubling the criminal's actions in trying to identify them, but sometimes more complexly with a close doubling that raises questions about the detective's morality.

Dystopia A genre that has the same rhetorical goals as utopia (critiquing one's current society while also imagining a better future) but reaches them by focusing on a negative, often fascist governmental structure. Crime fiction sometimes focuses on dystopian elements of society, and hybrid dystopian detective stories may use speculative elements to enhance the critique achieved by the elements of crime fiction.

Epistemology The branch of philosophy that studies knowledge and considers questions such as: What do we know? How do we know? What can/cannot be known? How do ideas about knowledge change over time and across places?

Ethics The branch of philosophy that studies morality and considers questions such as: How should we act? What constitutes a good life? What constitutes a good person? How do ideas about morality change over time and across places?

Feuilleton A kind of cheap fiction published in France in the nineteenth century. Detective narratives flourished within this publishing medium in France (and within **dime novels** in the US and **penny dreadfuls** in the UK).

Game Theory A mathematical approach to modeling the strategic choices available to rational actors. Informally used to understand the competitive relationship between writer and reader in classical detective fiction where the reader is given all the clues and is competing with the detective/writer to see who solves the mystery first.

Genre A concept in literary analysis that has been approached in two ways: formulaically and rhetorically. A formula-based approach to genre classifies works based on their recurring patterns and features, while a rhetorical approach to genre analyzes what a text is trying to persuade its readers of.

Genre Fiction A term used to delineate popular fictions in the standard genres (detective fiction, fantasy, romance, science fiction, western, etc.). Often used in contrast to literary fiction, where each text is seen by some (but not all) literary critics as being more unique.

Golden Age Detective Fiction The Golden Age of detective fiction is generally considered to be 1920–1939, between the two World Wars. This period saw the development of the puzzle mystery, complete with sets of rules and regulations for writers. More recent detective fiction, including most Canadian detective fiction, pushes back on those rules in some way.

Hardboiled   The hardboiled refers to a mode of crime fiction that rose to prominence in the 1930s in the US. It typically features a private investigator "tough guy" who is equally comfortable with physical and intellectual confrontation. This anti-establishment genre has developed in a variety of ways in recent years.

Hegemony   Popularized by Marxist philosopher Antonio Gramsci, hegemony is a cultural studies term used to refer to the dominance of one group over another. In the study of popular culture, American cultural hegemony can be seen worldwide, and is certainly an important element of how Canadians think about their own contributions to popular forms.

Heterogeneous   A broad term that means containing diverse characteristics. Cultural heterogeneity specifically refers to differences in cultural identity through markers of race, class, religion, language, etc. Canada's metropolitan areas tend to be more heterogenous than its rural areas.

Homogenous   A broad term that describes a group in which most individuals are similar or comparable. A homogenous culture has a clear dominant way of thinking and acting. Canada's rural areas tend to be more homogenous than its metropolitan areas.

Intertextuality   A feature especially valued in postmodern writing as well as classical detective fiction, intertextuality refers to an author's sustained use of a different text. Where an allusion simply mentions another text, intertextuality invites the reader to use a different text in depth in understanding the current one. See especially McFetridge and Penny for use of this feature.

Liminality   An anthropology term used to designate a sense of in-betweenness within a ritual (i.e., graduation, marriage) when a person is neither pre-ritual nor post-ritual. Within cultural studies, the term is not ritual-specific, but refers to a person's state as part-insider and part-outsider. Many detective figures work in the spaces between communities, at once associated with the police and with the community being policed.

Melting Pot   A metaphor used by Canadians to describe the assimilationist immigration policies of the US in contrast to the "tossed salad" or "cultural mosaic" approach to promoting multiculturalism in Canada.

Metafiction   In the simplest terms, metafiction is fiction about fiction, just as metacognition is learning about learning. A standard move in postmodern writing, metafiction describes a text that articulates an awareness of its own fictionality, a move sometimes characterized as "breaking the fourth wall."

Metanarrative In the simplest terms, metanarrative is a narrative about narrative. In cultural studies, it is also used to identify dominant narratives that shape our cultural understanding. For example, the metanarrative of the American Dream shapes American—and Canadian—understandings of the potential of democracy.

Mountie An affectionate term for a member of the Royal Canadian Mounted Police (RCMP), Canada's national police service. Traditionally represented in red serge with tall hats and horses, the Mounties were founded in 1873 and speak to Canada's generally positive view of its police force. The RCMP has lately made commitments to increased diversity and inclusion.

October Crisis Between October and December of 1970, tensions ran very high in Quebec on the issue of a possible separation from Canada. The situation rose to crisis level when the Front de liberation du Québec (FLQ) kidnapped a Canadian cabinet member and a British diplomat, leading Prime Minister Pierre Trudeau to invoke the War Measures Act during a time of peace for the only time in Canada's history.

Oka Crisis A months-long stand-off in 1990 between the Kanienkehaka (Mohawk) people and the Canadian government over control of **The Pines**, an Indigenous territory allocated for a golf course expansion. Media coverage of the crisis led Canadian news June–September 1990.

Parti Québécois Provincial political party in Quebec that advocates for the separation of Quebec from Canada. Founded in 1968, the Parti won its first provincial majority in 1976. It has informal ties to the Bloc Québécois, a federal party.

Penny Dreadful A kind of cheap fiction published in the United Kingdom in the nineteenth century. Detective narratives flourished within this publishing medium in the UK (and within **dime novels** in the US and *feuilletons* in France).

The Pines The name of the territory contested in the **Oka Crisis**.

Police Procedural By far the most common kind of detective novel in Canada, which follows a police detective and their team. This genre treats crime and its detection through a realist perspective and generally results in serial fiction, whether in novels or television productions.

Postmodernism Although named as an aesthetic and philosophical period following modernism (after World War II), postmodernism can best be seen as an intellectual movement that questions the possibility of epistemological certainty. Postmodern writing typically features metafictionality, **intertextuality**, unreliable narrators, and parody.

Postmodern detective fiction is a small but powerful subgenre that clearly delineates the conventions of detective fiction.

Quebec Independence Referenda Quebec has had two referenda where voters of the province voted on whether or not to separate from the rest of Canada. The referenda were called by the Parti Québécois government and advocated for negotiations on Quebec sovereignty. The referendum of 1980 received a "yes" vote of 40.4%, while the referendum of 1995 received a "yes" vote of 49.42%.

Quiet Revolution The significant economic and social changes that occurred in Quebec during the 1960s and 1970s, when the government became more secular and sovereigntist ideas became more prominent.

Serial Fiction A series of three or more novels. Much of crime and detective fiction is serial, which allows readers to really connect with the characters.

Serial Killer A person who murders three or more persons. The serial killer figure appears regularly in thrillers and occasionally in most contemporary varieties of detective fiction.

Sûreté du Québec Sometimes called the Quebec Provincial Police (making it parallel to the Ontario Provincial Police), the Sûreté is Quebec's provincial police force.

Thriller A fast-paced type of crime fiction that focuses on keeping the reader on the edge of their seat. Subgenres include the legal thriller, medical thriller, psychological thriller, and technological thriller.

Trauma Theory A cultural studies approach that applies insights from the psychological study of trauma to the understanding of literary texts. Key early theorists include Elaine Scarry and Cathy Caruth.

Truth and Reconciliation Commission A group charged in 2008 with documenting the history and legacy of the Canadian Indian residential school system. Their report, published in 2015, proposes 94 calls to action aimed at beginning reconciliation between Canadians and Indigenous Peoples.

Two Solitudes Based on Hugh MacLennan's 1945 novel, *Two Solitudes*, this phrase is used to refer to the idea that Canada's two founding groups—the French and the English—exist and think very separately from one another. This idea has been much interrogated in the late twentieth and twenty-first centuries.

Ustopia A term coined by Margaret Atwood to clearly indicate that utopias often or even always contain dystopian elements.

Utopia Named after Thomas More's book, *Utopia* (1516), this genre contains within it the paradox that a utopia is both a perfect place (from the Greek *u-topos*) and no place (from the Greek *eu-topos*). Novels or tracts about perfect places were very popular in nineteenth-century

European and American writings. Elements of the genre are still seen today.

Whodunit A popular term for a detective story that includes the features of Classical or Golden Age detective fiction, especially the ability for the reader to compete with the detective in trying to solve the crime, which is never graphically described.

FURTHER READING ON CRIME FICTION

Anderson, Jean, Carolina Miranda, and Barbara Pezzotti. *Serial Crime Fiction: Dying for More*. London: Palgrave Macmillan, 2015. An essay collection delving into why so much crime and detective fiction is serial. Scholars take a number of approaches in considering this question using different examples, all leading to the conclusion that seriality allows authors to engage in a sustained exploration of topical sociocultural issues.

Anderson, Patrick. *The Triumph of the Thriller: How Cops, Crooks, and Cannibals Captured Popular Fiction*. New York: Random House, 2007. A highly accessible study of how detective fiction gave way to the thriller, arguing that the roots of the modern thriller can be found in Poe and Doyle. Anderson argues that the thriller both raises the anxiety that we live in a dark, meaningless world and provides a happy ending to assuage that fear.

Ascari, Maurizio. *A Counter-History of Crime Fiction: Supernatural, Gothic, Sensational*. London: Palgrave Macmillan, 2007. A scholarly monograph arguing that crime fiction includes such diverse subgenres as the cozy and the hardboiled, yet ignores the gothic and the supernatural. Ascari includes philosophical and historical investigations into how questions of rationality and divinity have been explored in American and European crime, detective, and sensational fiction.

Breu, Christopher. *Hard-Boiled Masculinities*. Minneapolis, MN: U of Minnesota P, 2005. Using psychoanalytic and Marxist theory, Breu provides compelling readings of key American hardboiled classics from popular fiction (Dashiell Hammett and various dime novels) as well as from literary fiction (Ernest Hemingway and William Faulkner). Insightful analyses of gender, sexuality, and politics.

Brownson, Charles. *The Figure of the Detective: A Literary History and Analysis.* Jefferson, NC: McFarland, 2014.   This monograph centers the figure of the detective as knowledge agent while it provides an excellent history of the detective genre. Brownson's use of "cool" and "warm" knowledge invites readers to consider the visceral side of epistemology.

Cassuto, Leonard. *Hard-Boiled Sentimentality: The Secret History of American Crime Stories.* New York: Columbia UP, 2009.   In this insightful monograph, Cassuto makes the provocative argument that sentimental fiction (long seen as feminine) and hardboiled fiction (long seen as masculine) draw upon the same domestic ideologies of gender. Using popular and canonical texts (Theodore Dreiser, Dashiell Hammett, James M. Cain, and John D. Macdonald), Cassuto provides influential readings of the hardboiled detective and the femme fatale.

Dechêne, Antoine. *Detective Fiction and the Problem of Knowledge.* New York: Palgrave, 2018.   In this monograph, Dechêne traces the origins of the postmodern or metaphysical detective story back to Poe (using more than the three Dupin stories typically considered the first of the detective genre), arguing for the importance of the sublime and the grotesque in understanding what he calls the "metacognitive detective story."

Dove, George N. *The Reader and the Detective Story.* Bowling Green, OH: Bowling Green State University Popular Press, 1997.   This well-researched monograph explores the appeal of detective fiction through games and play, arguing that the conservative repetition of generic conventions provides readers comfort while the genre's hermeneutic investments provide intellectual stimulation.

Forshaw, Barry. *Death in a Cold Climate: A Guide to Scandinavian Crime Fiction.* New York: Palgrave Macmillan, 2012.   Using lots of quotations from interviews with writers, Forshaw provides an overview of major writers and themes in Nordic Noir crime fiction, focusing on the political and cultural critique enacted by the genre. Especially relevant for Giles Blunt readers.

Gregoriou, Christiana. *Crime Fiction Migration: Crossing Languages, Cultures and Media.* New York: Bloomsbury Academic, 2017.   This monograph uses an advanced linguistic approach to studying crime fiction that has moved across languages and across media. It speaks compellingly to the prevalence and flexibility of the crime fiction genre in our interconnected global world.

Haliburton, Rachel. *The Ethical Detective: Moral Philosophy and Detective Fiction*. Lanham, MD: Lexington Books, 2018. This monograph argues that detective fiction is absolutely invested in questions of ethics, and can in fact be more effective than textbooks in engaging students to think deeply about ethical questions. As a professor of Philosophy, Haliburton is able to clearly explain philosophical concepts and how they are addressed by detective fiction. Her literary examples range beyond the classics of the genre and include several Canadian writers, including Giles Blunt, Gail Bowen, and Louise Penny.

Hoppenstand, Gary, ed. *The American Thriller*. Ipswich, MA: Salem Press, 2014. This essay collection includes essays by several different scholars. It provides one essay for each of the major thriller types—crime, legal, techno, and psychological—as well as one essay for several leading (male) authors in the genre: Robert Bloch, Michael Crichton, Lee Child, Robin Cook, John Grisham, Thomas Harris, and James Patterson.

Howe, Alexander N. *It Didn't Mean Anything: A Psychoanalytic Reading of American Detective Fiction*. Jefferson, NC: McFarland, 2008. This monograph provides accessible and compelling psychoanalytic readings of classical detective texts (Doyle, Poe, Hammett, and Chandler) before moving into less travelled territory, namely Philip K. Dick's antidetective fiction and Marcia Muller's feminist hardboiled fiction.

Lehman, David. *The Perfect Murder: A Study in Detection*. Ann Arbor, MI: U of Michigan P, 2000. This monograph examines the appeal of the detective genre, arguing that its privileged status within popular genres can be explained in part by the fact that literary criticism shares many similarities with detective work. Lehman provides an engaging history of the genre covering the major detective writers from Poe through the postmodern detective.

Malmgren, Carl D. *Anatomy of Murder: Mystery, Detective and Crime Fiction*. Bowling Green, OH: Bowling Green State University Popular Press, 2001. Now a bit dated in its distinction between mystery, detective fiction, and crime fiction, Malmgren is a fine example of critics who see the genre as mostly conservative. He locates the pleasure of mystery fiction in the reader's complicity with the detective in "murdering" ambiguity and clearly linking sign and signifier by restoring a rational world and removing all trace of unintelligibility that has erupted as a result of a crime.

Plain, Gill. *Twentieth-Century Crime Fiction: Gender, Sexuality and the Body*. Chicago: Fitzroy Dearborn, 2001. In this monograph, Plain carefully lays out the arguments in favor of detective fiction's conservative and subversive potentials, arguing that since the genre is based on understanding death and the body, issues of gender and sexuality—played out conservatively and subversively by different practitioners—are central.

Rushing, Robert A. *Resisting Arrest: Detective Fiction and Popular Culture.* New York: Other Press, 2007. Using a psychoanalytic approach to detective fiction, Rushing argues that the genre taps into our psychological needs much more than our intellectual or puzzle-solving ones. He provides compelling readings of a number of disparate detective texts, grouping them around different psychological concepts like jouissance, irritation, and repetition.

Rzepka, Charles J. *Detective Fiction.* Malden, MA: Polity Press, 2005. A clear, accessible history of detective fiction and its appeal with new readings of several classic texts. The new reading of Poe's "Murders on the Rue Morgue" is especially influential.

Skene-Melvin, David. *Canadian Crime Fiction.* Shelburne, ON: The Battered Silicon Dispatch Box, 1996. This bibliography of Canadian crime fiction from 1817 to 1996 is wide-ranging and comprehensive. It includes entries on novels written by Canadians, novels written by non-Canadians but set in Canada, and novels that have any sort of "Canadian connexions." It also includes lists of short stories and plays under the same rubrics. A short introduction to the genre describes the subgenres and argues that Canadian crime fiction is more psychologically rooted and "caring" than its American counterpart.

Walton, Priscilla L., and Manina Jones. *Detective Agency: Women Rewriting the Hard-Boiled Tradition.* Berkeley: U of California P, 1999. This co-written study of women writers placing female detectives in hardboiled situations and rewriting the conventions of the hardboiled genre has been enormously influential to feminist approaches to popular literature in general and to our understanding of readers' potentially active roles in constructing meaning in and through detective fiction.

Wilson, Christopher P. *Cop Knowledge: Police Power and Cultural Narrative in Twentieth-Century America.* Chicago: The U of Chicago P, 2000. This well-researched monograph provides historical and cultural analysis for the development of the representation of police within American crime fiction. Canadian crime fiction draws upon many of the generic conventions developed within US police procedurals.

Winston, Robert P., and Nancy C. Mellerski. *The Public Eye: Ideology and the Police Procedural.* New York: St. Martin's Press, 1992. This classic take on the police procedural uses Marxist analysis to argue that this genre influences the public's perceptions of real-world police.

Zunshine, Lisa. *Why We Read Fiction: Theory of Mind and the Novel.* **Columbus, OH: The Ohio State UP, 2006.** Drawing upon work from cognitive science, Zunshine argues that humans find pleasure in reading fiction in part because it allows us to stretch our cognitive abilities. Her chapter on reading detective fiction contributes to her overall argument and allows scholars and readers of detective fiction to understand their own enjoyment of the genre in an intellectual way.

WORKS CITED

Adams, James Truslow. *The Epic of America*. New York: Little, Brown, and Company, 1931.
Anderson, Jean, Carolina Miranda, and Barbara Pezzotti. *Serial Crime Fiction: Dying for More*. New York: Palgrave Macmillan, 2015.
Anderson, Patrick. *The Triumph of the Thriller: How Cops, Crooks, and Cannibals Captured Popular Fiction*. New York: Random House, 2007.
Andrews, Jennifer, and Priscilla L. Walton. "Revisioning the Dick: Reading Thomas King's Thumps DreadfulWater Mysteries." *Detecting Canada: Essays on Canadian Detective Fiction, Television, and Film*, edited by Jeannette Sloniowski and Marilyn Rose, Waterloo, ON: Wilfrid Laurier UP, 2014, pp. 101–22.
Atwood, Margaret. *Bodily Harm*. Toronto: McClelland & Stewart, 1981.
———. *Madd Addam*. New York: Doubleday, 2013.
———. *Moral Disorder*. Toronto: McClelland & Stewart, 2006.
———. *Murder in the Dark*. Toronto: McClelland & Stewart, 1983.
———. *Oryx and Crake*. Toronto: McClelland & Stewart, 2003.
———. *In Other Worlds: SF and the Human Imagination*. New York: Doubleday, 2011.
———. *Surfacing*. Toronto: McClelland & Stewart, 1972.
———. *The Year of the Flood*. New York: Doubleday, 2009.
Auden, Wystan Hugh. *The Complete Works of Auden: Prose, vol. 4, 1956–1962*. Princeton: Princeton UP, 2010.
Ayoob, Mohammed. "Fiction in the Time of Islamophobia." *The Hindu*, 23 Jan. 2019, www.thehindu.com/opinion/op-ed/fiction-in-the-time-of-islamophobia/article26062547.ece
Bailey, Anne Geddes. "Misrepresentations of Vanessa Van Horne: Intertextual Clues in Timothy Findley's *The Telling of Lies*." *Essays on Canadian Writing*, vol. 55, 1995, pp. 191–213.

Balogh, Peter. "Queer Eye for the Private Eye: Homonationalism and the Regulation of Queer Difference in Anthony Bidulka's Russell Quant Mystery Series." *Detecting Canada: Essays on Canadian Detective Fiction, Television, and Film*, edited by Jeannette Sloniowski and Marilyn Rose, Waterloo, ON: Wilfrid Laurier UP, 2014, pp. 179–204.
Barclay, Linwood. Goodreads Author Comment. www.goodreads.com/questions/486114-why-do-you-set-your-novels-in-the-usa-when
Barclay, Linwood. *Broken Promise*. New York: Signet, 2016.
———. *Far From True*. New York: Signet, 2016.
———. *Parting Shot*. New York: Signet, 2017.
———. *The Twenty-Three*. New York: Signet, 2016.
Bedore, Pamela. "The Aesthetics of Utopian Imaginings in Louise Penny's *A Trick of the Light*." *Canadian Literature*, vol. 247, 2022, pp. 14–33.
———. "A Colder Kind of Gender Politics: Intersections of Feminism and Detection in Gail Bowen's Joanne Kilbourn Series." *Detecting Canada: Essays on Canadian Detective Fiction, Television, and Film*, edited by Jeannette Sloniowski and Marilyn Rose, Waterloo, ON: Wilfrid Laurier UP, 2014, pp. 151–77.
———. *Dime Novels and the Roots of American Detective Fiction*. New York: Palgrave Macmillan, 2013.
Bethune, Brian. "The Interview: Ausma Zehanat Khan's Unique Lens on Islam." *Maclean's*, 2 Feb. 2016, www.macleans.ca/culture/books/the-interview-crime-author-ausma-zechanat-khans-unique-lens-on-islam/
Betz, Phyllis M. *Lesbian Detective Fiction: Woman as Author, Subject and Reader*. Jefferson, NC: McFarland, 2006.
Bidulka, Anthony. *Amuse Bouche*. Toronto: Insomniac Press, 2003.
———. *Date with a Sheesha*. Toronto: Insomniac Press, 2010.
———. *Dos Equis*. Toronto: Insomnia Press, 2012.
———. *Flight of Aquavit*. Toronto: Insomniac Press, 2004.
———. *Stain of the Berry*. Toronto: Insomniac Press, 2006.
———. *Tapas on the Ramblas*. Toronto: Insomnia Press, 2005.
Bjornerud, Marcia. *Timefulness: How Thinking Like a Geologist Can Help Save the World*. Princeton: Princeton UP, 2018.
Blunt, Giles. *The Delicate Storm*. London: HarperCollins, 2003.
———. *Forty Words for Sorrow*. New York: Berkley Books, 2001.
———. *Until the Night*. Toronto: Vintage Canada, 2012.
Bon Cop, Bad Cop. Directed by Érik Canuel, Alliance Atlantis Vivafilm, 2006.
Bostrom, Nick. "Are You Living in a Computer Simulation?" *Philosophical Quarterly*, vol. 53, no. 211, 2003, pp. 243–55.
Bousson, J. Brooks. "'It's Game Over Forever': Atwood's Satiric Vision of a Bioengineered Posthuman Future in *Oryx and Crake*." *The Journal of Commonwealth Literature*, vol. 39, no. 3, 2004, pp. 139–56.
Bouthillier, Guy, and Édouard Cloutier, editors. *Trudeau's Darkest Hour: War Measures in Time of Peace, October 1970*. Montreal: Baraka Books, 2010.
Bowen, Gail. *Burying Ariel*. Toronto: McClelland & Stewart, 2000.
———. *Deadly Appearances*. Toronto: McClelland & Stewart, 1990.
———. *The Endless Knot*. Toronto: McClelland & Stewart, 2006.

---. *The Gifted*. Toronto: McClelland & Stewart, 2013.
---. *The Glass Coffin*. Toronto: McClelland & Stewart, 2002.
---. *Kaleidoscope*. Toronto: McClelland & Stewart, 2012.
---. *A Killing Spring*. Toronto: McClelland & Stewart, 1996.
---. *The Last Good Day*. Toronto: McClelland & Stewart, 2004.
---. *Murder at the Mendel*. Toronto: McClelland & Stewart, 1991.
---. *Verdict in Blood*. Toronto: McClelland & Stewart, 1998.
---. *The Wandering Soul Murders*. Toronto: McClelland & Stewart, 1992.
---. "We May Be Dealing with COVID Fatigue, but History Shows us There's a Way Through: Author Gail Bowen." *CBC Opinion Column*, 24 Jan. 2022, www.cbc.ca/news/canada/saskatchewan/opinion-gail-bowen-history-covid-fatigue-1.6321766
---. *What's Left Behind*. Toronto: McClelland & Stewart, 2016.
Bryden, Diana. "Canada and Postcolonialism: Questions, Inventories, and Futures." *Is Canada Postcolonial? Unsettling Canadian Literature*, edited by Laura Moss. Waterloo, ON: Wilfrid Laurier UP, 2003, pp. 49–77.
Burrowes, Colin. "Twenty Years Later Walkerton Inquiry Members Discuss Impact of Recommendations with WCWC Staff," 1 Sep. 2021, https://midwesternnewspapers.com/20-years-later-walkerton-inquiry-members-discuss-impact-of-recommendations-with-wcwc-staff/
Bussière, Kirsten. "Survival is Insufficient: Degenerate Utopian Nostalgia in Popular Culture Post-Apocalyptic Fiction." *The Australasian Journal of Popular Culture*, vol. 9, no. 2, 2020, pp. 261–75.
"The Canadian census: A rich portrait of the country's religious and ethnocultural diversity." *Statistics Canada*, 26 Oct. 2022, www150.statcan.gc.ca/n1/en/daily-quotidien/221026b-eng.pdf?st+nz8SNlut
Callow, Pamela. *Damaged*. Halifax, NS: Pamela Callow, 2010.
---. *Indefensible*. Halifax, NS: Pamela Callow, 2011.
---. Personal Interview, Phone, 3 Nov. 2021.
---. *Tattooed*. Halifax, NS: Pamela Callow, 2012.
Caruth, Cathy. *Unclaimed Experience: Trauma, Narrative, and History*. Baltimore: The Johns Hopkins UP, 1996.
Cassuto, Leonard. *Hard-Boiled Sentimentality: The Secret History of American Crime Stories*. New York: Columbia UP, 2009.
Cawelti, John G. *Adventure, Mystery, and Romance: Formula Stories as Art and Popular Culture*. Chicago: U of Chicago P, 1977.
Chandler, Raymond. "The Simple Art of Murder," *The Atlantic Monthly*, vol. 174, 1944, pp. 52–9.
Cliff, Brian. "At Home in Irish Crime Fiction." *Clues: A Journal of Detection*, vol. 39, no. 1, 2021, pp. 13–23.
---. *Irish Crime Fiction*. New York: Palgrave Macmillan, 2018.
Conaway, Charles. "'All the World's a [Post-Apocalyptic] Stage': The Future of Shakespeare in Emily St. John Mandel's *Station Eleven*." *Critical Survey*, vol. 33, no. 2, 2021, pp. 1–16.
Corak, Miles. "If there is such a thing as the Canadian Dream, It Would Look Very Much Like What Americans Say is the American Dream." 15 Apr. 2019, https://milescorak.com/2019/04/15/if-there-is-such-a-thing-as-the-canadian-dream-it-would-look-very-much-like-what-americans-say-is-the-american-dream/

Corrigan, Maureen. "A Muslim Detective Takes on Hate Crime and Other Evils." *The Washington Post*, 19 Feb. 2018. www.washingtonpost.com/entertainment/books/a-muslim-detective-takes-on-hate-crimes-and-other-evils/2018/02/18/8990ec88-1012-11e8-8ea1-c1d91fcec3fe_story.html

Cranny-Francis, Anne. *Feminist Fiction: Feminist Uses of Generic Fiction*. New York: St. Martin's Press, 1990.

Cuder-Domínguez, Pilar. "Embodied Borders: Countering Islamophobia in Ausma Zehanat Khan's Crime Fiction." *Clues*, vol. 41, no.1, 2023, pp. 52–61.

Cross, William and Lisa Young, "Are Canadian Political Parties Empty Vessels? Membership, Engagement and Policy Capacity." *Choices*, vol. 12, no. 4, 2006, p. 16, www.irpp.org/choices/archive/vol12no4.pdf

D'Haen, Theo. "Timothy Findley: Magical Realism and the Canadian Postmodern." *Multiple Voices: Recent Canadian Fiction*, edited by Jeanne Delbaere. Sydney: Dangaroo Press, 1989, pp. 217–33.

Darroch, Heidi Tiedemann, and Manina Jones. "A Mystery Milestone: Gail Bowen and Canadian Crime Writing." *Canadian Literature*, 2022. https://canlit.ca/article/a-mystery-milestone-gail-bowen-and-canadian-crime-writing/

Daxell, Joanna. "The Native Detective a la King." *Beyond Comparison/Au-dela des comparaisons*, edited by Roxanne Rimstead. Baldwin Mills: Topeda Hill, 2005, pp. 51–9.

Deveau, Danielle J. "What's So Funny about Canadian Expats? The Comedian as Celebrity Export." *Celebrity Cultures in Canada*, edited by Katja Lee and Lorraine York. Waterloo, ON: Wilfrid Laurier UP, 2016, pp. 167–84.

Donaldson, Emily. "Linwood Barclay Emerges from the Pandemic to Talk about the Latest Genetic Mystery He's Penned." *Globe and Mail*, 22 June 2021. www.theglobeandmail.com/arts/books/article-linwood-barclay-emerges-from-the-pandemic-to-talk-about-the-latest/

Dove, George. *The Boys from Grover Avenue*. Bowling Green, OH: Popular Press, 1985.

Dyson, Stephen Benedict. *Otherwordly Politics: The International Relations of Star Trek, Game of Thrones, and Battlestar Galactica*. Baltimore: Johns Hopkins UP, 2015.

Findley, Timothy. *The Telling of Lies*. New York: Penguin, 1987.

Fisher, Max. *The Chaos Machine: The Inside Story of How Social Media Rewired Our Minds and Our World*. New York: Little, Brown, and Company, 2022.

Flaherty, David H., and Frank E. Manning. *The Beaver Bites Back? American Popular Culture in Canada*. Montreal: McGill-Queen's UP, 1993.

Forshaw, Barry. *Death in a Cold Climate: A Guide to Scandinavian Crime Fiction*. New York: Palgrave Macmillan, 2012.

Francis, Daniel. *National Dreams: Myth, Memory, and Canadian History*. Vancouver: Arsenal Pulp Press, 1997.

Frye, Northrop. *Anatomy of Criticism*. Princeton: Princeton UP, 1957.

Ghosh, Amitav. *The Great Derangement: Climate Change and the Unthinkable*. Chicago: Chicago UP, 2016.

Gilbert, Reid. "Mounties, Muggings, and Moose: Canadian Icons in a Landscape of American Violence." *The Beaver Bites Back? American Popular Culture in*

Works Cited

Canada, edited by David H. Flaherty and Frank E. Manning. Montreal: McGill-Queen's UP, 1993, pp. 178–96.

Gillies, Mary Ann. "Trauma and Contemporary Crime Fiction." *Clues: A Journal of Detection*, vol. 37, no. 1, 2019, pp. 40–50.

Gilmore, Rachel. "'I'm Not Comfortable Living Here': More Americans Did Actually Try to Move to Canada Since Trump's 2016 Election." *CTV News*, 12 Sept. 2020, www.ctvnews.ca/world/america-votes/i-m-not-comfortable-living-here-more-americans-did-actually-try-to-move-to-canada-since-trump-s-2016-election-1.5064819

Gilmore, Scott. "The North and the Great Canadian Lie." *Macleans*, 11 Sep. 2016, www.macleans.ca/politics/the-north-and-the-great-canadian-lie/

Grace, Sherrill. *Tiff: A Life of Timothy Findley*. Waterloo, ON: Wilfred Laurier UP, 2020.

Grady, Constance. "The Author of *Station Eleven* Wrote a New Pandemic Novel." *Vox*. 26 Aug. 2022, www.vox.com/culture/23032674/sea-of-tranquility-review-emily-st-john-mandel

Green, Hannah. "Finding the 'I' in Irony: Thomas King as Trickster, Narrator, and Creator." *The Quint: An Interdisciplinary Quarterly from the North*, vol. 8, no. 4, 2016, pp. 8–36.

Grella, George. "Murder and Manners: The Formal Detective Novel." *Novel: A Forum on Fiction*, vol. 4, no. 1, 1970, pp. 30–48.

Haliburton, Rachel. *The Ethical Detective: Moral Philosophy and Detective Fiction*. Lanham, MD: Lexington Books, 2018.

———. "The Expressive-Collaborative Construction of Morality in Canadian Detective Fiction." *Clues: A Journal of Detection*, vol. 37, no. 1, 2019, pp. 70–80.

Hall, Katharina, editor. *Crime Fiction in German: Der Krimi*. U of Wales P, distrib. U of Chicago P, 2016.

Heilbrun, Carolyn. "Gender and Detective Fiction." *The Sleuth and the Scholar: Origins, Evolution, and Current Trends in Detective Fiction*, edited by Barbara A. Rader and Howard G. Zettler. Westport, CT: Greenwood, 1988, pp. 1–8.

Hemingway, Ernest. *Death in the Afternoon*, New York: Scribner Classics, 1932.

"Highest Court Asked to Rule on old Lone Ranger Term." *CBC News*, 22 Dec. 2004, www.cbc.ca/news/canada/highest-court-asked-to-rule-on-old-lone-ranger-term-1.491423

Holquist, Michael. "Whodunit and Other Questions: Metaphysical Detective Stories in Post-War Fiction." *New Literary History*, vol. 3, no. 1, 1971, pp. 135–56.

Hoppenstand, Gary, editor. *The American Thriller*. Ipswich, MA: Salem Press, 2014.

Horn-Miller, Kahente. "IO STER IS (It's funny): Humor as Medicine in Kanienkahaka Society." *The Quint: An Interdisciplinary Quarterly from the North*, vol. 7, no. 3, 2015, pp. 21–49.

Hutcheon, Linda. *The Politics of Postmodernism*. London: Routledge, 2002.

Hunter, Catherine. "Hiding the Unhidden: The Telling of Stories and *The Telling of Lies*." *West Coast Line*, vol. 24, no. 2, 1990, pp. 99–108.

Jiwani, Yasmin. "Framing Culture, Talking Race: Race, Gender, and Violence in the News Media." *Canadian Cultural Poesis: Essays on Canadian Culture*, edited by Garry Sherbert, Annie Gérin, and Sheila Petty. Waterloo, ON: Wilfred Laurier UP, 2006, pp. 99–114.

Jones, Keith. "Almost Shakespeare—But Not Quite." *Critical Survey*, vol. 33, no. 2, 2021, pp. 43–50.

Jones, Manina. "Canadian Noir: Consumer Culture, Colonial Nationalism and the *Cardinal* Series." *Forum for Modern Language Studies*, vol. 56, no. 3, 2020, pp. 280–94.

———. "Northern Procedures: Policing the Nation in Giles Blunt's *The Delicate Storm*." *Detecting Canada: Essays on Canadian Detective Fiction, Television, and Film*, edited by Jeannette Sloniowski and Marilyn Rose, Waterloo, ON: Wilfrid Laurier UP, 2014, pp. 83–100.

Kaplan, E. Ann. *Climate Trauma: Foreseeing the Future in Dystopian Film and Fiction*. New Brunswick: Rutgers UP, 2015.

Khan, Ausma Zehanat. *Among the Ruins*. New York: Minotaur, 2017.

———. *A Dangerous Crossing*. New York: Minotaur, 2018.

———. *A Deadly Divide*. New York: Minotaur, 2019.

———. *The Language of Secrets*. New York: Minotaur, 2017.

———. *The Unquiet Dead*. New York: Minotaur, 2015.

King, Thomas. *Cold Skies*. Toronto: HarperCollins, 2018.

———. *Deep House*. Toronto: HarperCollins, 2022.

———. *DreadfulWater Shows Up*. Toronto: HarperCollins, 2002.

———. "Godzilla vs. Post-Colonial." *World Literature Written in English*, vol. 30, no. 2, 1990, pp. 10–16.

———. *A Matter of Malice*. Toronto: HarperCollins, 2019.

———. *Obsidian*. Toronto: HarperCollins, 2020.

———. *The Red Power Murders*. Toronto: HarperCollins, 2006.

———. *The Truth About Stories*. Minneapolis: U of Minnesota P, 2008.

Klein, Kathleen Gregory. *Diversity and Detective Fiction*. Bowling Green, OH: Popular Press, 1999.

Knepper, Marty S. "Contemporary Cozy Mysteries: Agatha Christie and the 1990s." *Reading the Cozy Mystery: Critical Essays on an Underappreciated Subgenre*, edited by Phyllis M. Betz. Jefferson, NC: McFarland, 2021, pp. 17–48.

Knight, Stephen. *Australian Crime Fiction: A 200-Year History*. Jefferson, NC: McFarland, 2018.

Knox, Ronald. "Detective Story Decalogue." 1924. *The Art of the Mystery Story*, edited by Howard Haycraft. New York: Carroll & Graf, 1946, pp. 194–96.

Koren, Manina. "Telling the Story of the Stanford Rape Case." *The Atlantic*, 6 June 2016. www.theatlantic.com/news/archive/2016/06/stanford-sexual-assault-letters-485837/

Langer, Beryl. "Coca-Colonials Write Back: Localizing the Global in Canadian Crime Fiction." *Detecting Canada: Essays on Canadian Detective Fiction, Television, and Film*, edited by Jeannette Sloniowski and Marilyn Rose. Waterloo, ON: Wilfrid Laurier UP, 2014, pp. 3–17.

Lecker, Robert. "'A Quest for the Peaceable Kingdom': The Narrative in Northrop Frye's Conclusion to the Literary History of Canada." *PMLA*, vol. 108, no. 2, 1993, pp. 283–93.

Leggatt, Matthew. "'Another World Just Out of Sight': Remembering or Imaging Utopia in Emily St. John Mandel's *Station Eleven*." *Open Library of Humanities*, vol. 4, no. 2, 2019, pp. 8, 1–23.

Le Guin, Ursula K. *The Left Hand of Darkness*. New York: Ace Books, 1969.

———. *The Wind's Twelve Quarters*. New York: HarperCollins, 1975.

Lehman, David. *The Perfect Murder: A Study in Detection*. Ann Arbor: U of Michigan P, 2000.

Lesser, Wendy. *Scandinavian Noir: In Pursuit of a Mystery*. 2020.

Lévesque, René. *Option Québec*. Toronto: McClelland & Stewart, 1968.

Lynz-Qualey, Marcia. "An Attempt to De-criminalize Muslims: The Detective Novels of Ausma Zehanat Khan." *Muslim World*, vol. 111, no. 2, 2021, pp. 191–203.

MacLaine, Brent. "Sleuths in the Darkroom: Photography-Detectives and Postmodern Narrative." *The Journal of Popular Culture*, vol. 33, no. 3, 1999, pp. 79–94.

MacLennan, Hugh. *Two Solitudes*. Toronto: Macmillan, 1945.

MacShane, Frank. *Selected Letters of Raymond Chandler*. New York: Columbia UP, 1981.

Mandel, Emily St. John. *The Glass Hotel*. New York: Knopf, 2020.

———. *Sea of Tranquility*. New York: Knopf, 2022.

———. *Station Eleven*. New York: Knopf, 2014.

Manning, Frank E. "Reversible Resistance: Canadian Popular Culture and the American Other." *The Beaver Bites Back? American Popular Culture in Canada*, edited by David H. Flaherty and Frank E. Manning. Montreal: McGill-Queen's UP, 1993, pp. 3–28.

Marshall, George. *Don't Even Think About It: Why Our Brains are Wired to Ignore Climate Change*. New York: Bloomsbury, 2014.

Mason, David. *Investigating Turkey: Detective Fiction and Turkish Nationalism, 1928–1945*. Academic Studies Press, 2017.

McFetridge, John. *Black Rock*. Toronto: ECW Press, 2014.

———. *A Little More Free*. Toronto: ECW Press, 2015.

———. *One or the Other*. Toronto: ECW Press, 2016.

Méndez-García, Carmen M. "Postapocalyptic Curating: Cultural Crises and the Permanence of Art in Emily St. John Mandel's *Station Eleven*." *Studies in the Literary Imagination*, vol. 50, no. 1, 2017, pp. 111–30.

Merivale, Patricia and Susan Elizabeth Sweeney. *Detecting Texts: The Metaphysical Detective Story from Poe to Postmodernism*. Philadelphia: U of Pennsylvania P, 1999.

Miller, Carolyn. "Genre as Social Action." *The Quarterly Journal of Speech*, vol. 70, no. 2, 1984, pp. 151–67.

Moss, Laura, editor. *Is Canada Postcolonial? Unsettling Canadian Literature*. Waterloo, ON: Wilfrid Laurier UP, 2003.

Nickerson, Catherine Ross. "Murder as Social Criticism." *American Literary History*, vol. 9, no. 4, 1997, pp. 744–57.

Noor, Poppy. "'How to Move to Canada': Americans Rush to Google After Unwatchable Debate." *The Guardian*, 30 Sep. 2020, www.theguardian.com/us-news/2020/sep/30/how-to-move-to-canada-google-searches-trump-us-debate

Ostry, Bernard. "American Culture in a Changing World." *The Beaver Bites Back? American Popular Culture in Canada*, edited by David H. Flaherty and Frank E. Manning. Montreal: McGill-Queen's UP, 1993, pp. 33–41.

Pablo, Carlito. "Women in Canadian Police Services Continue to Increase, Now Represent 22% of Sworn Officers." *The Georgia Straight*, 10 Dec. 2020. www.straight.com/news/women-in-canadian-police-services-continue-to-increase-now-represent-22-percent-of-sworn

Patrick, Ryan B. "How Ausma Zehanat Khan Crafted a Mystery Based on Canadian and International Real-World Events." *CBC*, 2 May 2017. www.cbc.ca/books/how-ausma-zehanat-khan-crafted-a-mystery-based-on-canadian-and-international-real-world-events-1.4533394

Louise Penny. *The Beautiful Mystery*. New York: Minotaur, 2012.

———. *The Brutal Telling*. New York: Minotaur, 2009.

———. *Bury Your Dead*. New York: Minotaur, 2010.

———. *A Fatal Grace*. New York: Minotaur, 2006.

———. *Glass Houses*. New York: Minotaur, 2017.

Penzler, Otto. "Linwood Barclay On Reading Voraciously, Making a Career in Writing and Meeting Ross Macdonald." https://crimereads.com/linwood-barclay-on-reading-voraciously-making-a-career-in-writing-and-meeting-ross-macdonald/

Pepper, Andrew. *The Contemporary American Crime Novel: Race, Ethnicity, Gender, Class*. Chicago: Fitzroy Dearborn Publishers, 2000.

Perkowska-Gawlik, Elżbieta. "Victimization in Academic Mystery Fiction." *The Campus Novel: Regional or Global?*, edited by Dieter Fuchs and Wojciech Klepuszewski, Rodopi, 2019, pp. 111–21.

Pezzotti, Barbara. *Politics and Society in Italian Crime Fiction: An Historical Overview*. Jefferson, NC: McFarland, 2014.

Pierce, J. Kingston. "McFetridge Sows Crime Among His Roots." *Rap Sheet*, 20 Aug. 2016. http://therapsheet.blogspot.com/2016/08/mcfetridge-sows-crime-among-his-roots.html

Plain, Gill. *Twentieth-Century Crime Fiction: Gender, Sexuality and the Body*. Chicago: Fitzroy Dearborn Publishers, 2001.

Propp, Vladimir. *Morphology of the Tale* (1928). Trans. Laurence Scott. Austin: U of Texas P, 1968.

Ramon, Alex. *Liminal Spaces: The Double Art of Carol Shields*. Newcastle Upon Tyne: Cambridge Scholars Publishing, 2008.

Ricks, Christopher. *Dylan's Visions of Sin*, 1st American ed., New York: Ecco, 2004.

Robinson, Peter. *In a Dry Season*. Toronto: Viking, 1999.

———. *Gallows View*. Toronto: Viking, 1987.

———. *Not Dark Yet*. New York: HarperCollins, 2021.

Rushing, Robert A. *Resisting Arrest: Detective Fiction and Popular Culture*. New York: Other Press, 2007.

Rzepka, Charles J. *Detective Fiction*. Malden, MA: Polity Press, 2005.

Saito, Saturo. *Detective Fiction and the Rise of the Japanese Novel, 1880–1930*. Harvard University Asia Center, 2012.

Samuels, Alexandra. "Father of Student Convicted of Rape: Steep Price for '20 Minutes of Action.'" *USA Today*, 6 June 2016. www.usatoday.com/story/news/nation-now/2016/06/06/father-student-convicted-rape-steep-price-20-minutes-action/85492660/

Sargisson, Lucy. *Utopian Bodies and the Politics of Transgression*. London: Taylor & Francis, 2002.

Scarry, Elaine. *The Body in Pain: The Making and Unmaking of the World*. New York: Oxford UP, 1985.

Schneller, Johanna. "How Tracey Deer Faced the Trauma of Living Through the Oka Crisis to Bring her Film *Beans* To Life." *CBC Arts*, 13 May 2021. www.cbc.ca/arts/how-tracey-deer-faced-the-trauma-of-living-through-the-oka-crisis-to-bring-her-film-beans-to-life-1.6024710

Sedgwick, Eve Kosofsky. *Between Men: English Literature and Male Homosocial Desire*. New York: Columbia UP, 1985.

Shead, Jackie. *Margaret Atwood: Crime Fiction Writer. The Reworking of a Popular Genre*. Burlington, VT: Ashgate, 2015.

Sherbert, Garry. "Introduction: A Poetics of Canadian Culture." *Canadian Cultural Poesis: Essays on Canadian Culture*, edited by Garry Sherbert, Annie Gérin, and Sheila Petty. Waterloo, ON: Wilfrid Laurier UP, 2006.

Shields, Carol. *Swann*. New York: Penguin, 1987.

Skene-Melvin, David. *Canadian Crime Fiction*. Shelburne, ON: The Battered Silicon Dispatch Box, 1996.

Slemon, Stephen. "Afterword." *Is Canada Postcolonial? Unsettling Canadian Literature*, edited by Laura Moss. Waterloo, ON: Wilfrid Laurier UP, 2003, pp. 318–24.

Sloniowski, Jeannette. "Generic Play and Gender Trouble in Peter Robinson's *In a Dry Season*." *Detecting Canada: Essays on Canadian Detective Fiction, Television, and Film*, edited by Jeannette Sloniowski and Marilyn Rose. Waterloo, ON: Wilfrid Laurier UP, 2014, pp. 123–50.

Sloniowski, Jeannette, and Marilyn Rose, editors. *Detecting Canada: Essays on Canadian Detective Fiction, Television, and Film*. Waterloo, ON: Wilfrid Laurier UP, 2014.

Smolkin, Sheryl. "Author Gail Bowen: A Saskatchewan Success Story." 5 Mar. 2015, www.savewithspp.com/2015/03/05/author-gail-bowen-a-saskatchewan-success-story/

St-Amand, Isabelle. *Stories of Oka: Land, Film, and Literature*. Winnipeg: U of Manitoba P, 2018.

Statistics Canada. "Number, rate and percentage changes in rates of homicide victims." *Statistics Canada*, 2 Aug. 2022, https://doi.org/10.25318/3510006801-eng

Stougaard-Nielsen, Jakob. *Scandinavian Crime Fiction*. Bloomsbury, 2017.

Tisdale, Jennifer. "Women Are Using Social Media to Warn Each Other of the Whereabouts of Brock Turner." *Distractify*, 23 Aug. 2022, www.distractify.com/p/brock-turner-today

Thomas, Clara. "'A Slight Parodic Edge': *Swann: A Mystery*." *Multiple Voices: Recent Canadian Fiction*, edited by Jeanne Delbaere. Sydney: Dangaroo Press, 1990, pp. 104–15.

Thorpe, Charles. "Postmodern Neo-Romanticism and the End of History in Margaret Atwood's MaddAddam Trilogy." *Soundings: An Interdisciplinary Journal*, vol. 103, no. 2, 2020, pp. 216–42.

Todorov, Tzvetan. *The Poetics of Prose*. 1971. Trans. Richard Howard. Ithaca, NY: Cornell UP, 1984.

Traub, Courtney. "From the Grotesque to Nuclear-Age Precedents: The Modes and Meanings of Cli-Fi Humor." *Studies in the Novel*, vol. 50, no. 1, 2018, pp. 86–107.

Tumarkin, Maria. *Traumascapes: The Power and Fate of Places Transformed by Tragedy*. Melbourne: Melbourne UP, 2005.

———. "Twenty Years of Thinking about Traumascapes." *Fabrications*, vol. 29, no. 1, 2019, pp. 4–20.

Vacante, Jeffrey. "The Decline of Hugh MacLennan." *University of Toronto Quarterly*, vol. 85, no. 1, 2016, pp. 43–68.

Van Dine, S.S. "Twenty Rules for Writing Detective Stories." 1928. *The Art of the Mystery Story*, edited by Howard Haycraft. New York: Carroll & Graf, 1946, 189–93.

Vermeulen, Pieter. "Beauty That Must Die: *Station Eleven*, Climate Change Fiction, and the Life of Form." *Studies in the Novel*, vol. 50, no. 1, 2018, pp. 9–25.

Vials, Chris. "Margaret Atwood's Dystopic Fiction and the Contradictions of Neoliberal Freedom." *Textual Practice*, vol. 29, no. 2, 2015, pp. 235–54.

Walton, Priscilla L. "Interrogating Judicial Bodies: Women and the Legal Thriller." *South Central Review*, vol. 18, no. 3/4, 2001, pp. 21–37.

Walton, Priscilla L., and Manina Jones. *Detective Agency: Women Rewriting the Hardboiled Tradition*. Oakland: U of California P, 1999.

Watson, Kate, and Rebekah Humphreys. "The Killing Floor and Crime Narratives: Making Women and Nonhuman Animals." *Tattoos in Crime and Detective Narratives: Marking and Remarking*, by Kate Watson, Katherine Cox, and Maurizio Ascari, Manchester, England: Manchester UP, 2019, pp. 113–29.

Wernick, Andrew. "American Popular Culture in Canada: Trends and Reflections." *The Beaver Bites Back? American Popular Culture in Canada*, edited by David H. Flaherty and Frank E. Manning. Montreal: McGill-Queen's UP, 1993, pp. 293–302.

Wilgar, W.P. "Poetry and the Divided Mind in Canada." *Dalhousie Review*, vol. 24, no. 3, 1944, pp. 266–71.

Wilson, Christopher P. *Cop Knowledge: Police Power and Cultural Narrative in Twentieth-Century America*. Chicago: The U of Chicago P, 2000.

Wilson, Edmund. "Who Cares Who Killed Roger Ackroyd." *The Art of the Mystery Story: A Collection of Critical Essays*, edited by Howard Haycraft. New York: Simon & Schuster, 1944/1947, pp. 390–97.

Winston, Robert P., and Nancy C. Mellerski. *The Public Eye: Ideology and the Police Procedural*. New York: St. Martin's Press, 1992.

Wright, Richard. "How Bigger Was Born," 1940. *Native Son*. New York: HarperCollins, 1991, pp. 433–62.

Zunshine, Lisa. *Why We Read Fiction: Theory of Mind and the Novel*. Columbus: The Ohio State UP, 2006.

INDEX

American hegemony 3, 33, 46, 89; *see also* hegemony
anthropocene 196, 205, 212–13, 249
armchair detective 145, 147, 249
Arthurson, Wayne 4
Atwood, Margaret 2, 15, 22, 93, 214–23, 226, 245; *see also* dystopia; genre fiction; postmodern detective fiction; ustopia
Auster, Paul 12, 61, 175, 216, 245; *see also* postmodern detective fiction

Barclay, Linwood 16–21, 81, 93–6, 99–107, 245; *see also* dystopia; serial killer; thriller
Bidulka, Anthony 16–20, 22, 143–5, 147–54, 245; *see also* cozy detective fiction; gender; genre fiction; hardboiled; LGBTQ+; liminality; postmodern detective fiction; serial killer
bilingual detectives: Dougherty, Eddie 28, 31, 36, 81; Gamache, Armand 199; Getty, Rachel 81
Bjornerud, Marcia 196
Bloc Québécois 7, 249
Blunt, Giles 4, 16–21, 44–8, 50–1, 53–7, 78, 81, 88, 157, 201, 245; *see also* First Nations peoples; gender; North, the; police procedural; serial killer

Bon Cop, Bad Cop 1
border *see* liminality
Bowen, Gail 4, 16–20, 22–3, 78, 129–32, 135–6, 141–2, 246; *see also* Canadian national identity; First Nations peoples; gender; LGBTQ+; postmodern detective fiction
buddy cop 1–2

Callow, Pamela 16–20, 22, 159–63, 165–7, 170, 172–3, 246; *see also* liminality; serial killer; thriller
Canadian Confederation 4–5, 15, 92
Canadian national identity 1, 4, 15, 21, 28–9, 42–4, 78, 92, 112; and Bowen, Gail 130–1, 138; and King, Thomas 60
Cawelti, John 217
censorship 130
Chandler, Raymond 3, 10, 67, 93, 144–7, 153, 220, 246; *see also* hardboiled
classical/Golden Age detective fiction 9–10, 12, 54, 105, 182, 188, 197, 215–6, 250, 254; *see also* whodunit
climate change 43, 93, 182, 197, 205, 211, 226
climate fiction (cli-fi) 205–6
Cohen, Leonard x–xi
cozy detective fiction 13, 54, 69, 77, 212, 249; and Bidulka, Anthony 22,

145, 148, 150, 152, 245; and Penny, Louise 195, 212
cultural mosaic 78, 249; *see also* multiculturalism

detective subgenres *see* classical/Golden Age detective fiction; cozy detective fiction; hardboiled; police procedural; postmodern detective fiction; thriller
dime novel 8–9, 15, 16, 46, 54, 249–50, 252
domestic noir 14
doubling 40, 156, 173, 219, 235, 250; dark double 170, 172–3; doppelgänger 39, 249–50; doubled narrative structure 226
Doyle, Arthur Conan 3, 36, 215, 246–7; *see also* Holmes, Sherlock
dystopia 92–3, 250; and Atwood, Margaret 216–17, 221, 223, 225; and Barclay, Linwood 21, 94–8, 102, 107; and Findley, Timothy 179; and speculative fiction 47, 227

epistemology 177, 224, 235–6, 239, 250, 256
ethics 140, 223, 243, 250
ethnicity 36, 68, 79, 189

female detective 13–14, 18, 23, 122, 127, 132, 160; female hardboiled 144–5; *see also* female protagonist; gender; male-female detective duo
female killer 19–20, 154, 173–4
female protagonist 13, 130; *see also* female detective
female victim 12, 18–19, 48, 97, 115, 119, 136, 152, 162
feminism 13, 136, 145, 151–2; *see also* gender
feuilletons 8, 249–50, 252
Findley, Timothy 15–20, 22, 175–84, 191, 246; *see also* dystopia; genre fiction; postmodern detective fiction
First Nations peoples 4, 6, 16, 34, 43–4, 46–7, 92; and Blunt, Giles 51–4, 56; and Bowen, Gail 130–1, 137–8; and King, Thomas 61, 64–5, 70, 81; and Penny, Louise 206, 211–12

Francis, Daniel 14, 29–30, 42, 112, 211
French Canada 2, 29, 45–6, 54, 57
French language 1–2, 4, 6, 8, 27, 30, 32
Frye, Northrup 5, 8

game theory 219, 223, 250
gender 8, 13, 16, 18–20, 23, 160; and Bidulka, Anthony 22, 150, 152; and Bowen, Gail 136; and Blunt, Giles 47; and King, Thomas 61, 67; and McFetridge, John 40; and Robinson, Peter 112–14, 119, 121–3, 128; and Shields, Carol 188–9; *see also* female detective; feminism; LGBTQ+; male-female detective duo
genocide 77, 86, 217, 221–2, 224, 238
genre fiction 8, 13, 22, 60, 175, 227, 250; and Atwood, Margaret 226; and Bidulka, Anthony 144; and Findley, Timothy 176; and Shields, Carol 177
Gillies, Mary Ann 164–5, 196
Grella, George 10, 80, 217

Haliburton, Rachel 4, 9, 196, 257
Hammett, Dashiell 3, 10, 67, 147, 247–8, 256–7; *see also* hardboiled
hardboiled 3, 10–13, 132, 144–5, 251; and Bidulka, Anthony 22, 144–9, 151–3, 245; and Chandler, Raymond 3, 93, 144–6, 246; and Hammett, Dashiell 3, 10, 147, 247; and King, Thomas 66–7, 69; and Macdonald, Ross 3, 93, 247; and Parker, Robert 248; *see also* female detective
hegemony 9, 153, 251; *see also* American hegemony
heterogenous 251
Holmes, Sherlock 3, 32, 36, 246–7, 249; *see also* Doyle, Arthur Conan
homogenous 115, 251

intertextuality 12, 66, 176, 178, 181, 216, 251–2
Inuit language 44

Jones, Manina 21, 46, 56, 141, 160

Khan, Ausma Zehanat 15–21, 23, 75–90, 247; *see also* liminality; multiculturalism; police procedural

King, Stephen 223
King, Thomas 15–21, 23, 58–74, 78, 81, 247; *see also* Canadian national identity; First Nations peoples; gender; hardboiled; police procedural; serial killer
Klein, Kathleen Gregory 3, 145

liminality 2, 177, 251; and Bidulka, Anthony 150; and Callow, Pamela 173; and Khan, Ausma Zehanat 83, 85; and McFetridge, John 28, 36, 41; and Penny, Louise 203
Le Guin, Ursula K. 214–15, 227–8
LGBTQ+: and Bidulka, Anthony 22, 145, 147, 150, 153–5; and Bowen, Gail 130; *see also* gender; transgender

Macdonald, Ross 3, 10, 67, 93, 247–8; *see also* hardboiled
MacLennan, Hugh 2, 28, 31–2, 247, 253
male-female detective duo 18, 20, 79, 81, 90; *see also* gender
Mandel, Emily St. John 22, 228–44; *see also* postmodern detective fiction
McBain, Ed 3, 11, 112, 248; *see also* police procedural
McFetridge, John 16, 18–19, 21, 27–41, 46, 81, 88, 200–1, 248, 251; *see also* gender; liminality; police procedural; serial killer
melting pot 78, 249, 251; *see also* multiculturalism
metafiction 12, 148, 176, 178, 190, 214–16, 241, 251–2
metanarrative 176, 229, 243, 252
Miller, Carolyn 8–9
Mountie 14, 55, 92, 112, 144, 211, 252
multiculturalism 5, 21, 80; and Khan, Ausma Zehanat 77–9, 81–2, 86, 89–90, 247; *see also* cultural mosaic; melting pot

Nickerson, Catherine Ross 4
Nordic Noir 3, 21, 46, 51, 55–6
North, the 6, 42–3, 47–50, 56–7; *see also* Blunt, Giles

October Crisis 30, 35, 41, 46, 200, 252

Oka Crisis 44–5, 51, 252
Orwell, George 179, 225

Parker, Robert B. 66–7, 248; *see also* hardboiled
Parti Québécois 30, 34, 37, 249, 252–3
penny dreadful 8, 249–50, 252
Penny, Louise 16–20, 22, 29, 107, 195–7, 199–200, 202, 204–13, 248; *see also* cozy detective fiction; First Nations peoples; liminality; police procedural; postmodern detective fiction; thriller
Poe, Edgar Allen 3, 36, 181, 219–20, 246, 248, 256–8
Pines, the 45, 252
Pinkerton, Allan 36
police procedural 3, 9–11, 14, 111–13, 144, 163, 252, 258–9; and Blunt, Giles 46, 54, 56; and Khan, Ausma Zehanat 247; and King, Thomas 21, 59; and McBain, Ed 3, 11, 248; and McFetridge, John 21, 28, 36, 41, 46; and Penny, Louise 17, 22, 195–6, 206, 212; and Robinson, Peter 22, 113–14, 123, 128
postcolonial theory 58–9, 80, 153
postmodern detective fiction 9, 12–13, 15–16, 176–7, 181–4, 191; and Atwood, Margaret 215–20; and Auster, Paul 12, 61, 216; and Bidulka, Anthony 145, 148; and Bowen, Gail 131; and Findley, Timothy 175–9, 181–3; and King, Thomas 60–1, 68–9; and Mandel, Emily St. John 22, 230–1, 235, 237, 239–41; and Penny, Louise 207; and Robinson, Peter 112; and Shields, Carol 18, 175–7, 184–6, 189–91
postmodernism 92, 175–7, 179, 191, 252

Quebec Independence Referenda 27, 253
queer theory *see* LGBTQ+
Quiet Revolution 29–30, 41, 253

race 16, 20–1, 36, 54, 67, 81; racialization 6, 20–1, 78, 145, 151
religion 77, 82, 90, 159
Robinson, Peter 16–20, 29, 22, 94, 111–16, 121, 124–5, 127–8, 248;

see also gender; police procedural; postmodern detective fiction
Rose, Marilyn and Jeannette Sloniowski, *Detecting Canada* 3, 14, 93, 112, 114

serial fiction 15–16, 59, 150, 247–8, 252–3
serial killer 11, 17, 253; and Barclay, Linwood 96–7; and Bidulka, Anthony 150, 152; and Blunt, Giles 48–9; and Callow, Pamela 162–3, 167–9; and King, Thomas 62; and McFetridge, John 33
sex crimes 22, 112, 114–19, 121, 128
Shields, Carol 15–20, 22, 176–7, 184–91, 248; *see also* gender; police procedural; postmodern detective fiction
speculative fiction 46, 227–9, 231, 234, 244; *see also* dystopia
suicide 72, 77, 95, 123, 139, 160, 185, 234

Sûreté du Québec 44, 201–2, 211, 253

thriller 11–12, 14, 253; and Barclay, Linwood 93; and Callow, Pamela 18, 22, 158–61, 163, 167, 170, 172–3, 246; and Penny, Louise 195, 206–7, 212, 248
Todorov, Tzvetan 9, 11, 28, 60, 196, 215, 223, 226–7
transgender 19–20, 22, 134, 152–3; *see also* LGBTQ+
Trauma Theory 22, 158, 164, 171, 253
Truth and Reconciliation Commission of 2015 20, 253

ustopia 93, 216–18, 224, 226, 253; *see also* Atwood, Margaret
utopia 47, 92–3, 214, 217, 227, 230, 250, 253

whodunit 9–13, 215, 254; *see also* classical/Golden Age detective fiction

Printed in the United States
by Baker & Taylor Publisher Services